Availab
from
Spec

Daddy on Demand
by Helen R Myers
&
Déjà You
by Lynda Sandoval

A Father for Danny
by Janice Carter
&
Baby Be Mine
by Eve Gaddy

The Mummy Makeover
by Kristi Gold
&
Mummy for Hire
by Cathy Gillen Thacker

The Pregnant Bride Wore White
by Susan Crosby

Sophie's Secret
by Tara Taylor Quinn

Her So-Called Fiancé
by Abby Gaines

Diagnosis: Daddy
by Gina Wilkins

DADDY ON DEMAND

He couldn't bear the raw, naked emotion of need.

Despite weeks of iron will and brutal lectures to keep his hands to himself, he crushed her to him and hid his face in the fragrance and silkiness of her hair.

Collin swallowed painfully. "Thank you for being here…for doing this. I couldn't – "

He kissed her as he had in a dream, with tenderness and care, and sighed with relief when she opened to him. When his tongue touched hers, she murmured softly and let herself lean against him.

"Brina…I gotta go potty."

It was Sabrina who eased back and called down the hall, "I'll be right there." Then she looked at Collin and asked softly, "Are you OK?"

He could only offer a barely perceptible nod, and then she was off.

"I don't know if I'll ever be OK again," he finally replied to the empty room.

DÉJÀ YOU

"Just lie here with me?"

Surprise riddled through him.

Erin's complexion blazed red. "I know it seems weird, but…"

Don't be an idiot, Nate's brain warned. *Do not get in bed with this woman.* "If you're sure."

"I'm not sure of anything. Except that I don't feel like being alone right now." Fumbling and formal, they moved side by side on the bed, her beneath the covers, him on top. For a few agonising moments, they remained that way.

Erin cleared her throat. "May I…may I put my head on your shoulder? Oh, God. Never mind. This was an idiotic idea."

"Shh." Nate slid his arm beneath her and urged her head onto his shoulder. "It's OK. Friends, right?"

"Right."

He felt her nod, closed his eyes. They might be strangers, and their meeting unconventional, but damned if she didn't feel absolutely perfect in his arms.

First published in Great Britain 2010
Harlequin Mills & Boon Limited,
Eton House, 18-24 Paradise Road, Richmond, Surrey TW9 1SR

Daddy on Demand © Helen R Myers 2009
Déjà You © Lynda Sandoval 2007

ISBN: 978 0 263 87987 2

23-0810

Harlequin Mills & Boon policy is to use papers that are natural, renewable
and recyclable products and made from wood grown in sustainable forests.
The logging and manufacturing processes conform to the legal environmental
regulations of the country of origin.

Printed and bound in Spain
by Litografia Rosés S.A., Barcelona

DADDY ON DEMAND

BY
HELEN R MYERS

DÉJÀ YOU

BY
LYNDA SANDOVAL

MILLS & BOON

DADDY ON
DEMAND

BY
HELEN R MYERS

Helen R Myers lives deep in the Piney Woods of East Texas. She cites cello music and bonsai gardening as favourite relaxation pastimes, and still edits in her sleep – an accident, learned while writing her first book. A bestselling author of diverse themes and focus, she is a three-time RITA® Award nominee, winning in 1993.

To dear friend and former neighbour
Donna Danley
of
Backwoods Farm
Thank you from the bottom of my heart.
You know all of the reasons why.

Chapter One

"Are you alone?"

The tender yet suggestive question posed by the female calling on his cell phone would have put a wicked grin on Collin Masters's face if he didn't immediately recognize that it was his sister. Watching elevator floor numbers light up as he descended from his high-rise condo, he replied, "Not for long if there's any justice in this world. I'm in the elevator on my way to meet someone who has legs more fabulous than her red hair and an appetite for champagne and yours truly."

"Cancel," Cassidy Masters replied, all semblance of gentleness vanishing from her voice. "I'm on my way over there."

Collin adored his kid sister and only sibling, but he didn't appreciate her ordering him as though he was a member of her USAF chopper crew. "Not remotely funny, Captain Masters. You stay in San Antonio at—" He never could remember which of the Texas bases she was currently stationed at.

"I'm within ten minutes of your building. I borrowed one of the club planes and flew into Addison Airport."

Although it gave him pause that she was only a few miles north of his location in Dallas, Collin opted for humor. "For your information, this is the first date I've been on in weeks. Catch my drift? Lonely boy needs some TLC."

"Keep Lonely Boy zipped away for another hour or two. This is important."

"But—"

"Darn your hide—don't make me say this over the phone!" Cassidy sighed. "I'm being deployed, Collin."

The news hit him with such a jolt, he thought the elevator had abruptly jerked to a halt between floors. When instead it settled calmly on the ground level and the doors opened, his stomach eased back in place with the rest of his anatomy, but not without aftershocklike jitters.

"Crap. Sis, I'm sorry."

"It comes with the wings…and it's not like we didn't know this could happen."

A million and one questions flooded Collin's mind. He allowed only one to be voiced. "When do you leave?"

"Six weeks. Eight tops. Just long enough to get through the training classes I'm not current on, update my shots and get my personal business in order."

Uh-oh, Collin thought, beginning to feel a new queasiness in his belly. Yes, they had covered this subject before, but that was conveniently tucked away in the part of his brain labeled Denial.

"I take it by your silence that you're putting two and two together," Cassidy drawled. "Make the call or calls you need to and I'll see you at 1850 give or take some traffic."

She disconnected, successfully avoiding his complaint about not understanding military counting any better than he remembered base names. No, he amended, she was just guaranteeing that he wouldn't have a chance to back out of their deal. He loved her with all of his heart—save what portion wasn't owned by her precocious daughters, his nieces—but how could he do what she was about to ask of him?

A movement across the lobby caught his attention and he realized that he was standing in the open elevator probably looking like he'd free-fallen down the shaft. Across the lobby, a sweet-faced giant named Sonny—the lobby security guard—watched him with perplexed amusement.

Offering back a sickly smile and weak wave, Collin shut his phone and hit the button that would return him to his floor.

It was closer to twenty minutes before Sonny announced Cassidy's arrival. By then Collin had called Nicole, canceled their dinner reservations and downed a chilled shot of Grey Goose. Scotch would have been the shock absorber of choice, but he knew it would take more than one to see him through this meeting, and then there was the breath test concern. Cass had the olfactory senses of a bloodhound and he didn't want her thinking she was leaving her precious three-year-olds in the hands of an irresponsible drunk.

"Oh, who are you kidding?" he muttered catching sight of himself in the hallway mirror with his hair and tie already askew from anxious yanking and raking.

Deployed…his kid sister was heading off to war. This is what he deserved for assuring her that, "You can be anything you want to be," some four years ago upon learning that she was pregnant. The lowlife *sperm donor* that she'd called boyfriend at the time had been urging her to have an abortion because the would-be rock star thought kids would be a turnoff to fans. It sure hadn't hurt legends like Mick, Ozzie and McCartney, but afraid to test that theory, Dave from Denton had fled to parts unknown.

By big belly time, Cassie had finished her master's degree, graduating with honors. By the time the twins were two, she was on her way to flying Pave Hawk helicopters for the U.S. Air Force. To Collin, who could barely bring himself to fly commercial without one hand on the barf bag, his kid sister was amazing. But sitting in any cockpit in a war zone was an idea he'd been refusing to contemplate. Yes, there were many female pilots these days, but as far as he was concerned, the war was supposed to be over before it was Cassie's turn to serve her country on the front lines.

The knock at the door and cheery call, "There's no use hiding, I know you're in there," put an end to his lozenge-size history recap. There was nothing to do but let her in. He did so knowing his slumped shoulders and bowed head was not what she needed to see, but that was the best he could do for the moment.

The sight of his twinkling-eyed sister with her animated mouth wryly curved in a half "this sucks" twist had him opening his arms. Six years older than her thirty-two, he was big brother on every level but in intelligence and bravery. The other difference was that they looked nothing alike. Each resembled one of their parents. She was the original golden girl complete with willowy figure and natural corkscrew curls that she preferred to hide under a hat or helmet, her eyes blue enough to keep the attention of anyone with a pulse. Tall, thin, and cursed with unruly ash-brown hair, his chief attribute was sad, lost-in-the-fog gray eyes. Back in his school days, they'd saved him from far more punishment than he deserved. When a modicum of maturity stuck to him, he concluded his second asset was his wicked imagination, which he suspected ESP'd women of particularly loose morals and no great need for commitment. The gift for smooth talking—buffered by his lingering British accent—once had their maternal grandmother, who'd finished raising him and Cassie, recommending that he become a minister. "I'd be willing to bet five dollars that before you reach thirty, you'd own your own TV network," she'd declared. "That is if some jealous husband doesn't shoot you first." These days he knew there was no mistaking that Cassie had inherited her spunk and frankness from her.

"Crap," he muttered again into his sister's ear as he hugged her tightly.

"Not the four letter word I used when I got the news, but close enough," she replied.

He pushed her to arm's length to study her youthful, but somber face. "Are you scared?"

"Eventually, I'm sure I will be. Probably during the flight over, but hopefully I'll be so tired from the prep stuff that I pass out ten minutes after we take off.

Considering that the government uses charter services whose planes have about the wear and tear of dinosaur bones, sleep may prove a double blessing."

That did little to help Collin's growing dread. "Don't they realize that you aren't just a single parent, you have twins?"

"A contract is a contract. Besides, since I was attending Squadron Officer School, I didn't get to deploy with the rest of my squadron, so it's only a four-month tour. That's nothing compared to the guys who are going for six months or a year." Hands on her hips, she shook her head. "Collin, surely you've paid attention to the news? Some of our guys are doing this for the third, fourth and fifth time."

Avoiding a politically correct reply or apology with an indistinguishable mutter, he massaged the growing stiffness at the back of his neck. "Let me make a call or two. I'm sure I can get you infected with hepatitis or something within hours."

Cassidy finally laughed and shut the door behind her. "I can see that I have my work cut out for me. I'm sorry, Favorite Brother, but I need you to drop the Hugh Grant or Tom Hanks reluctant-and-awkward-hero act and be *my* hero."

"If only that was possible. Unfortunately, I did everything but sell my soul to a man who makes ten times the ridiculous money I first did with my firm creating advertising campaigns designed to separate people from their hard-earned salaries. The best I can do is promise to have my secretary ship you tons of product samples, few of which you are likely to use in a third world country with severe plumbing problems and little or no electricity."

This time there was the hint of tears in her eyes as she again hugged him. "Maybe this whole crazy mess is going to be a gift after all. You've been pushing me to let go of fears and reach for my dreams for so long, I think you've lost sight of your own."

"My accountant would disagree with you in a heartbeat. Unlike you, he goes orgasmic when he sees reports of my seventy-hour workweeks."

"You know perfectly well that happiness isn't about how much money you make. Especially when it comes at the cost of denying yourself someone special to share your success with. Maybe having this time with the girls will finally take off those self-inflicted blinders you wear when it comes to having a real relationship."

"Pearls of wisdom coming from—" Collin's heart did another debilitating plunge and he stepped back against the entryway table pressing his right hand to his chest. "No. Oh, no. I know what I promised, but that was when you were delirious in labor—or I was delirious with fear? At any rate, I can't keep the girls while you're gone. You're looking at a man who has never remotely craved an opportunity to change diapers "

"Then you're in luck. Genie and Addie are well past the diaper stage. They're in fast-track preschool."

"Next stop MIT?" As she lasered him with the infamous Masters's matriarchal look, he held up both hands and rethought his defense. "What was I thinking with a military mom who names her daughters versions of *general* and *admiral?*" He had teased her from day one about Gena and Addison's names, which he'd turned into those nicknames. But he had little doubt that her three-year-olds were mavericks in the making, the next evolution of all that their gutsy mother was striving to be. That made what she was asking of *him* all the more insane.

"Look at you," he tried to explain with unabashed awe. "You're a *pilot*. You navigate thousands of pounds of metal through the air. You're a walking hero 365 days a year even if you never left the country." Dropping his hands at his sides, he looked at her helplessly. "What do I have to offer your babies, Cass? On weekends, when there is such a thing on my calendar as downtime, I've been known to sleep fourteen hours and wake up in the same position when I first crashed onto the bed."

"You'll adapt. Learn to do what I do. Juggle. Manage. The difference is you'll be doing it with a seven-figure income."

He bent at the waist and lifted his left knee as though she'd thrown him a sucker punch—or kick. "Ouch, girl."

Cassidy grimaced. "Sorry. Doesn't it help that even if you weren't the next in line to be the kids' legal guardian that you are the one and only man I adore and trust?"

"Give me your commanding officer's phone number." Collin snatched up his cell phone stationed on the kitchen bar. "There are issues about your judgment he needs to know about."

Unperturbed, Cass stood her ground. "If I didn't think you could rise to this occasion, I would take the offer of one of my fellow pilots' wives and leave the girls on base with them. I even asked the kids what they would prefer and do you know what they said?"

"Buy us a suite at Disneyland and sign our guardianship over to the Jonas Brothers?"

"They want 'Unca Colon.' Declared in unison might I add."

Collin almost choked. "Please tell me that you're talking to an orthodontist about that speech impediment?"

Secretly, however he dealt with a new guilt surge knowing how he'd dropped the ball as "Unca" last Christmas. Instead of spending it with them and Cassie, he'd flown to Tahiti with a redhead whose name he could no longer recall. "Tell them they'll hate it here. No presents and nothing but oatmeal and algebra. By a tutor who can barely speak English," he added seeing nothing but advantage in heaping on negatives.

Nonplussed, Cassie replied, "I was thinking more like this could be an opportunity to show them the museums and galleries in the areas. Take them to the botanical gardens over in Fort Worth plus the Dallas arboretum and zoo. Focus on something else besides the corporate bottom line for a change."

"Forgive my arrogance, but that bottom line is why you get to poke fun at my salary, kiddo."

"It's the detriment to you having a *life*. It's going to blow up in your face one day. I don't want you to vanish like our parents did when their balloon suddenly burst due to Dad's bad business deals."

Since he had a better memory of those shadow people that continued to haunt their past, Collin stiffened. The last thing he wanted to be accused of was emulating their parents in any variation.

"Give me a second…or a week," he replied. "I'm sure I can think of a better solution for you. One you'll end up thanking me for."

That had Cassidy sucking in her cheeks and enunciating her words with particular care. "There is no one else, Collin. And should worse come to worst, at least this way they would already be used to being around you 24/7."

Her innuendo had him dropping his head on his chest. "I beg you—do not go there." The prospect of losing her shook him to his core and he quickly tried to hide his fear in humor. "Let's focus again on my day job that— to paraphrase you—overpays me. What happens to the girls while I'm at the office? Do you realize I could quickly screw up that 'Road to MIT' plan of yours?"

Cassidy spread her arms wide. "You can't delegate even an iota or work from home? Then ask someone in this granite fortress who they would recommend as a nanny."

"There are—let me count." He did the math. "Four children in this building. 'Children' being a euphemism, since one is in college. In fact she confided to me in the elevator last week that she is taking pole dancing as a college elective."

"Oh, she was just flirting with you. The ninety-year-olds want to fatten you up and the little girls hear that voice and they want you to be their knight in shining armor."

He wasn't knight material, but it was a waste of time to argue with his sister. "The point being that the other three are products of split-custody agreements and only visit on odd weekends, and increasingly only on holidays."

"Ask at the office."

"You think I would hand over the care of your precious darlings to total strangers?"

Cassidy crossed her arms over her chest. "Faster than your brain registers eye candy. Look, I know you have to work, but surely somewhere in your vast circle of acquaintances and associates there's someone who can refer a person good with kids, who can keep them growing while they're away from their lessons and friends in San Antonio." Suddenly her eyes widened and she snapped her fingers. "I've got it! Your ex. I think she'd be perfect."

Ex? "I don't have an *ex,*" he grumbled. "You know I never date anyone long enough to call her 'girlfriend,' just to avoid the unpleasantness of said nomenclatures."

"I mean your ex-*employee.* The assistant you fired."

"Sabrina." Her name came off his tongue as quickly as her image flashed before his eyes, but his physical response to that was like getting a puncture wound in his lungs. The coughing fit that followed soon had Collin bending at the waist. "I did not fire her," he wheezed.

"Right, that would have been the compassionate thing to do. Or to tell her the truth—that you were hot for her. But, no, you exiled her to the basement of your building to be a secretary to—who is that fossil down there?"

"Norbit, the head of Reference and Research."

"Yeah, yeah, the glorified file clerk. Bet he cuts his own hair and wears thick glasses with black plastic frames and carries his meals to work in a construction-worker type lunch box."

It annoyed him to no end that she could deduce character types so well. "Star Trek, to be factually correct, and he can do the Spock finger greeting on command."

"Be still my heart."

"He's also phenomenal at Trivial Pursuit."

"Stop gushing or I'll have to change my daughters' names to something other than Masters."

Tempted to laugh, Collin instead muttered, "See if I

ever confide in you again. You're not supposed to use confidences against a person."

This entire conversation was the reason why he'd begun to put longer breaks between their phone calls and limited most of their communication to text messaging once a week. It was easier to hide from her probes into his personal life—in other words his happiness—even if it risked losing what was left of his family.

"I'm so worried," she drawled. "How much does she love her new job?"

He almost tried countering with "She who?" but knew it would make him look more foolish, so he simply confessed. "She quit."

"Smart woman." Shoving her dropped flight bag out of her way with her foot, Cassie strolled into the living room. "I grew fond of chatting with her when I would call your office and you were tied up with some so-called meeting or presentation."

Collin's gaze drilled into her back. "There's nothing *so-called* about my appointments."

"You just pray that Donald Trump hasn't gotten wind that she's on the market and goes groveling after her. I could cope better being overseas knowing she was watching my girls."

"Excuse me, a minute ago I was the hero. Now everything hinges on her?"

Cassie shot him an unrepentant grin. "Remember Gran's favorite quote? 'Don't ask a question that you don't want an answer to.'"

Sabrina Sinclair stood before the door of the apartment she shared with her latest roommate, Jeri Swanson, and frowned at the key that no longer fit in the dead bolt. She might be in dire need of getting off her feet after having completed a twelve-hour shift at work, but this was the door to Apartment 314 and the lock had worked fine when she left here at six this morning. Hoping that her airhead roomie hadn't already taken off with her latest boyfriend for another night of clubbing, she knocked on the door.

"Jeri? It's me. Are you in there?"

"No, she is not, and you might as well get going, too."

The voice calling up to her from the bottom of the stairwell had Sabrina backtracking to look over the shaky wooden railing, down at the elderly woman below. "Mrs. Finch? Is something wrong?"

"Don't play innocent with me. I told you that I wouldn't put up with any more tall tales regarding the rent."

Although three stories away from the frail but feisty woman's shaking and arthritis-bent finger, Sabrina reared back. "But Jeri paid it yesterday. I had to get to work early for inventory and she took my money to add to what she owes and paid you."

"Did she now? Maybe that's what she told you, but I haven't seen a cent of the $900 you two owe me, or the other $450 still due from last month. So today I changed the locks on the door right after she left—which you might be interested to know was barely an hour after you did."

A sickening feeling overcame Sabrina and she gripped the railing. Jeri wasn't by nature a morning person; that's why she preferred waiting tables at a dinner-only steak house—when she worked. In better circumstances, Sabrina would never have accepted her as a roommate to begin with, let alone trusted her to take care of the rent money, since Mrs. Finch hinted strongly that she preferred cash. Now it appeared that her trust had indeed been badly invested.

Her throat raw with the growing need to scream or cry, Sabrina asked, "Did she say where she was going? When she'll be back?"

"Don't know, don't care, and you're a dumber duckling than I first suspected if you wait for her, or waste another thought on that one. From the racket her and her man friend made, I don't think their problem was anything that a drying-out spell in the Dallas County Jail wouldn't fix."

"I see." And Sabrina did. Once again she had erred on the side of The Golden Rule and been burned. There was nothing to do but apologize again—this time profusely— and start over. She needed to get inside and get into a hot bathtub to ease her aching body, then get some sleep in order to plan how to repair the damage done to both her landlady and herself. "Mrs. Finch, if you'll let me in, I promise you that I will work extra overtime and have the rent paid up within two paychecks, and I assure you that Jeri won't be allowed in here again."

"Nope. Done with the lot of you. Tired of promises. Tired of the noise and the trouble. You get out of here now or I'll call the police on you."

"But my things are in there."

"No they aren't. Your friend took your personal stuff and I'm keeping the furnishings as part of the rent owed. I've been walked over for the last time."

As if things couldn't get worse, midway through that pronouncement, a handsome, well-dressed man with wavy, ash-brown hair stepped beside Mrs. Finch and tilted back his head to gaze up at her.

"Oh, Lord," Sabrina whispered.

Collin Masters? What on earth could compel him to come here—and why now for pity's sake? Hadn't he caused her enough humiliation and grief?

"May I be of some assistance?"

She didn't buy his wide-eyed innocence for a second, or that pretense of concern even if it did sound more sincere with his pedigreed accent. Hoping he hadn't heard everything, Sabrina started down the stairs at record speed ignoring the protests from her aching limbs. "No, you cannot. This is a private conversation."

Ignoring her, Collin turned his thousand-watt charm onto Mrs. Finch. "Am I to understand there's a matter of rent due?"

The diminutive woman's eyes lit with hope as she leaned toward him to conspiratorially share. "A total of $1,350."

"Wait a minute!" As Sabrina reached them, she skidded on the dirt-slick linoleum floor and had to brush her already untidy hair out of her eyes. "You said you're keeping my furniture," she told Mrs. Finch. "That should come off the debt."

"If I can sell any of the discount junk, I'll be lucky if it covers the expense of the locksmith and a cleaning woman to make the place presentable again."

The hurt heaped onto injury stole Sabrina's breath and she pressed her hand against her chest as she protested. "That's not true or fair!" No doubt Jeri had her grandmother's pearl earrings and her grandfather's pocket watch, but what of family photos that had no price as far as she was concerned? Her personal papers?

"Allow me." Collin reached into his suit jacket and pulled out his checkbook.

Keeping her gaze on Collin's moving pen, Mrs. Finch told Sabrina, "What's fair is being free of any more excuses from you and having to tolerate your partying friends. If they'd have spent less on liquor, you wouldn't be in this mess."

"I'll make the check out for $1,500," Collin said writing fast. "Does that sound fair to you, Mrs. Finch?"

The woman was part bloodhound; before Sabrina could open her mouth, she sighed and whimpered. "I suppose it will have to do. There's the lost sleep and, being a widow woman, the constant fear someone will murder me in my bed, but that comes with the situation, doesn't it?" Then beaming at Collin, she added, "You're such a dear man. Exactly who are you?"

"A friend."

"No, he's not!" Sabrina glared at Collin before realizing her protest fell on deaf ears. Redirecting her attention to her landlady, she appealed to her compassionate side as a grandmother and mother. "Mrs. Finch, we're talking about my birth certificate, my school records and tax receipts. You're certain that was all taken?"

Accepting the check, the woman nodded. "Looks like a first-class case of identity theft to me, sweetie. You sure are a lousy judge of character."

With a killing look toward Collin, Sabrina muttered, "Tell me about it."

Pocketing the checkbook and pen, Collin extended his hand to her. "Let me get you somewhere so you can think clearly."

Wanting badly to slap away his hand, she felt the cold

draft called *reality* still her. Mrs. Finch had accepted his money. Now she was indebted to a man she despised.

"This can't be happening," she whispered.

"I'm sorry." Placing a hand at the small of her back, he gestured to the front door. "My car is outside. I can follow you to wherever you would like to go or drive you and bring you back to your car after we eat and talk."

Her numbness made her slow to react, but she shook her head. "I can't."

"Well, you certainly can't stay here."

"No…but I don't have a car anymore."

"Excuse me?"

It should have bothered her that Mrs. Finch was standing by soaking all of this in, too, but what value did pride have under these circumstances? "The lease ran out and I turned it in." She looked at him with a last feeble surge of resentment. "Thanks to *you,* I couldn't afford it any longer."

"Now just a moment…I didn't make you quit your job. If you remember correctly, I didn't even lower your salary. You left all on your own."

"Stanley Norbit has foul breath and was stalking me daily through that dungeon. He's creepy."

While Collin couldn't see himself inviting old Norbit to his apartment for a dinner party, the eccentric man's work ethic and performance was second to no one. "He may be a bit socially stunted, but he's never let me down when I had an eleventh-hour request."

"Try wearing a bra and shave your legs and then talk to me."

"I respect my tailor too much to do that to him."

Not at all amused by his attempts to make light of her latest catastrophe, Sabrina began to storm out of the building, but stopped at the front door to make herself clearly understood. "I would apply as a mortician's apprentice before I would work for someone like him again. But first and foremost, you made me the laughingstock of the firm, and you never realized that. You don't go from working on the top floor for the executive vice-president and wind up in the basement for a joke of a department head, who until then, ran a one-man operation. Not without everyone speculating as to why and drawing their own obnoxious and humiliating conclusions."

Sabrina kept her chin raised, though fully aware that in dusty and tattered jeans, an oversize T-shirt recently used while painting her apartment and scruffy sneakers, she resembled a bag lady, not an executive's assistant. Seconds away from long-repressed tears, she summoned the last of her dignity and declared, "I promise you, Mr. Masters, I will pay you back every cent of what you gave Mrs. Finch, but now, *please* leave me alone."

Collin followed her out of the building. "At the risk of you slinging that cowhide version of a bowling ball at me, may I ask what you're going to do without a place to stay, clothes to change into and money? I'll wager you don't even have enough cash in that purse to buy yourself a hot dog."

Not even change to feed a parking meter—if she had a car.

Standing in the shadow of the ancient building, surrounded by the towering glass-and-steel high-rises that was today's Dallas, and its future, Sabrina didn't need a stronger sign that *her* future lay in his hands. It was an amber day full of glittering leaves and enough wind to finish pulling her hair out of her loose ponytail. She quickly rewound the elastic band around the honey-gold mass and tried to come up with a game plan. There was little she could do for the rest of the dust and grime after a day's work of supervising restocking shelves— and doing plenty of that labor herself—at Bargain Bo-nanza's main warehouse. Every morning as she dressed, ignoring aches and exhaustion, she had to remind herself that she was a "manager," and that would look good on her résumé. But with the economy what it was, she wondered when she would be able to risk hunting for a job that actually used her brains more than her questionable brawn.

Collin ventured closer and studied her face. "You've grown very quiet. Do I need to worry about catching you in a dead faint? When did you last eat?"

"I guess sometime around…" She remembered buying some vending-machine sandwich that she'd heated in the break room's microwave. Then she'd been called to some delivery paperwork problem in the warehouse. When she returned, a cashier trainee, who regularly snatched up any and all snacks or leftovers, was devouring her sandwich. One look at his grease-covered lips around her ham-and-cheese melt had killed Sabrina's appetite.

"There's a great bistro near where I live," Collin said, carefully directing her to his black Mercedes parked directly in front of the building. "It's open until people quit ordering, but should be relatively quiet at this hour." He added almost gently, "I'll bet they can make anything you could want."

Humiliated by the reflection that she saw in his car's window, Sabrina tried her best to make him leave by being her least gracious. Casting him a sidelong look, she countered, "And what do *you* want?"

Holding up an index finger to beg her patience, Collin got her seated inside, then trotted around the front of the glistening mechanical indulgence, and climbed in behind the camel brown steering wheel. "Right now a triple Scotch would be sheer bliss."

"No one asked you to write that check. What happened, did that Wynne, Wooster, what's his name that you hired after dumping me make a pass at you?"

"Geoffrey Wygant is an excellent assistant and you'll be happy to know is in a twenty-year relationship with his partner, Duke."

The last Duke she'd known was a rottweiler on a farm neighboring her parents' place in Wisconsin. Homesickness mixed with her shame and she shook her head with abject misery. "Excuse me. I shouldn't have said that. I was just—"

"Dealing with shock and low blood sugar." Collin spun the Mercedes into traffic and turned a sharp right at the next corner. "Geoff happened to be the first applicant since you who could spell as well as the kids on *Are You Smarter Than A Fifth Grader?* Most impressive is that he possesses an unbeatable knack for matching clients to restaurants."

So much for her favorite bathtub fantasy where Collin Masters admitted his mistake and came with flowers and the keys to a white Porsche to beg her to come back. No matter how many magazines she read or how much Internet surfing of dating Web sites she tried at her brothers' prodding, Sabrina could never compete with such experience and élan. She choked on a bitter laugh and ended up coughing.

"I'm serious."

"It's not that," she wheezed for the second time. "I think I've lost the ability to breathe and think at the same time. Congratulations," she added, hoping she sounded sincere. "Truly. I wish you a long and happy working relationship." But that meant that she was back to square one regarding the reason for his intrusion into her miserable life.

As though reading her mind, Collin said abruptly, "Okay, to keep you from jumping out into traffic, I'll answer your question about why I'm here. Cassidy is being deployed."

"Oh, no!"

And here she thought things couldn't get any worse. Not only did she like his sister, she had come to understand how close Collin was to his only sibling. This had to be his worst nightmare come true. At least she could work through her situation. What if...?

"I'm so sorry," she added quickly.

"Thanks."

Collin pulled into the restaurant's parking lot and handed the vehicle over to an eager valet. There wasn't time to talk again until they were seated in a quiet corner booth by the bar and they'd ordered drinks. "Everything is excellent here, but if you're really hungry—and you look like you could use four, even seven courses— the prime rib would turn an acorn-loving squirrel into a carnivore."

She was about to insist that he add the cost to her IOU, then recognized how petty that would appear, so she nodded. "Thank you. Then the prime rib it is." Her mouth watered just saying the words. Thank goodness the waitress had already brought a loaf of bread and whipped butter with herbs and promised to quickly bring Collin's salad choices for them. Then she saw the condition of her hands.

"If you don't mind, I'd like to go wash up a bit."

"Of course. Wait a minute—you aren't going to sneak out on me, are you?"

Did he really think she had suddenly thought of anywhere else to go, or could afford to turn down such a dinner? Struggling not to forgive him completely, she gestured to her condition. "I've been rummaging my way through a super warehouse since dawn. Even if you had managed to transpose my head onto someone in a *Girls Gone Wild* video and it got back to my family in Wisconsin, I don't think I would be upset enough to turn down this meal."

"I'll keep that I mind for the future should I need additional leverage."

Trying not to smile, Sabrina made a hasty retreat for the ladies' lounge. She sucked in her breath when she saw her appearance in the mirror behind the sink. The view under those lights was worse than she anticipated. Not one for the made-up look, the mascara and lip gloss she had put on first thing this morning had long worn off by sweat and nervous lip gnawing. As for her hair...all she could say for it was that it was relatively clean. She quickly grabbed a brush from her purse and gave her shoulder-length mop an energetic workout until the results were closer to a glossy if limp cape. Rinsing her face, she touched up her lashes and lips, but resisted anything else. It would seem too obvious to do more. Besides, she was trying to save him from losing his appetite, nothing else. Nothing at all.

"So how is Cassie taking this?" she asked slipping back into the booth.

Collin was already half through his Scotch. "Oh, she's the stiff-upper-lip sort. You know she's besotted about flying up in the skies with pigeons, ducks and whatnot. This is the downside of that."

"But the babies..."

"It's been a few months since you've seen pictures." He immediately reached for his billfold and flipped it open to a photo of the girls in miniature versions of Mommy's flight suit standing in the doorway of their mother's Pave Hawk surrounded by the grinning crew.

"Oh—how darling! They look more and more like her."

"Well, Gena adores inheriting the curls to where she screams if someone comes near her with scissors, so Cass is rethinking the blessing in that. On the other hand if Addie keeps demanding hers be cut off, Cass has threatened to have what's left of the mop mowed into a Mohawk."

Sabrina smiled and took a sip of her wine. "So who is Cassidy entrusting them to while she's gone? That has to be the world's hardest decision."

"It is." Collin spun his glass between his hands repeatedly. "I'm glad you feel the same way I do."

"Excuse me?" Something about his fixation on his drink and the fidgeting had Sabrina drawing a conclu-

sion that sent her stomach into doing new flip-flops.
"Oh, my—not you!"

"That was flattering. Who else would you expect?"

Granted they were all the other had relative-wise, but
there had to be other options. "Didn't you once say during
a phone call to some client that your idea of a perfect
Sunday was sleeping until noon and having girlfriends
wearing panties labeled Monday through Saturday?"

"I'm in advertising, Ms. Sinclair. I say things to make
clients feel better about themselves, their product and
their ideas. The better they feel, the more lucrative the
account, which—might I remind you—made it possible
to pay you handsomely until you quit."

"We're talking about your own flesh and blood."

Collin continued to work his glass like a worry stone.
"Some adjustments will have to be made, of course. In
fact, considering your passionate opinions, you'll undoubtedly approve of Cassidy's recommendations."

"I'm almost willing to bet my next paycheck that I
will."

Laughing mirthlessly, Collin replied, "It's you."

"Excuse me?"

"Cass demanded that I hire you to help me. To move
in with us."

If the wineglass had been between her fingers,
Sabrina would have snapped it into orbit. "She *didn't*."

"She's been a fan of yours from day one. Surely you
sensed that?"

"She was nice to me and I appreciated that. You'd be
surprised how many of your snooty callers aren't capable of being civil to anyone they deem lesser than themselves."

Frowning, Collin replied, "Why didn't you tell me?"

Frustration just made her all the hungrier and Sabrina beheaded the loaf of bread with one strong whack of the serrated knife. "Because I assumed by the way they acted that they were more valuable to you than I was. Tell Cassie thanks, but she's wrong. I'm not cut out for the job."

Clearing his throat, Collin continued. "She thinks of you as remarkably levelheaded and reliable. Hindsight being what it is, I can't argue there."

What had he objected to? That she was too sunny and glass-half-full for his cynical self? Considering the condition of the world these days, people like her were in short supply. But since he'd just performed a knight-in-shining-armor rescue, she bit back the impulse to tell him as much.

"Please thank Cassidy for me," Sabrina said spreading butter onto her bread. "Tell her that she'll be in my thoughts and prayers, but I couldn't possibly accept."

"You could, but you won't."

She leveled her gaze on him. "Can't." But seeing anxiety in his eyes, she immediately undermined herself by asking, "When does she leave?"

"Before Thanksgiving if not sooner. There's some training courses she's compelled to take. I don't suppose you'd at least be willing to go shopping with me after we eat and help me pick out bunk beds and girly things like sheets and towels and whatever will make the second guest room seem less of the white space than it currently is?"

"Me? I can't see that I'd be much help to you."

"Remember the phone call I asked you to make when Addison felt jilted after her mother was unavoidably scheduled for an overnight flight and was late getting home? You had Addie convinced that there'd been an FAA computer glitch shutting down the entire southern part of the U.S. Not even Santa could have gotten through had it been Christmas Eve. Frankly, I should have put you into the company's intern program then and there."

"So why didn't you? I was qualified. I have my degree."

"Because…I don't remember."

"Liar."

Collin reached for his glass, found it empty and sighed. "So I am. What if I promise to tell after Cass comes back?"

Sabrina took a sip of her wine, but decided she would leave it unfinished. If she was feeling halfway tempted by his offer, that was proof the drink was going straight to her head.

"What you just did for me back at Mrs. Finch's," she began, "that was kind and generous, but you can't just crush a person's dreams, then in the second you find yourself in a bind, expect me to forget the offense."

"Nor should you. This would be a good time to talk salary."

As he did, Sabrina grew increasingly conflicted. What he offered would not only guarantee that she could pay him back in a matter of weeks, but she could also save for a new place before his sister's return. She doubted many nannies saw that kind of income unless they worked for one of Hollywood's elite.

"What haven't I said that would explain why I'm not getting some positive response from you?" Collin asked when she remained silent.

Their attentive waitress brought Collin another drink and Sabrina waited for her to leave before summoning the courage to speak the rest of her mind. "All right," she began. "If I take this job, I'd like to know the truth about why I lost my position. Not later. Now."

Collin slumped against the high-backed booth. "I see utter and complete failure in my future—and a likely trip to the E.R."

"I've never committed bodily harm in my life."

"Trust me, there's a first time for everything."

So it was worse than she thought? What could she possibly have done?

Looking everywhere but at her, he continued, "Okay. I want a promise that you won't file legal action, or let what I say impair your decision."

"Have you lost your mind?"

"The girls really need you and, therefore, I promise to act the perfect gentleman throughout."

"Maybe being a full decade younger than you makes you think that I lack the ability to meet your standards in maturity—"

"Okay, so I'm laughable in that vein and should have stopped while I was ahead."

"But if I accept a job, professionalism is guaranteed," she said, folding her hands primly before her.

Collin had been slowly shaking his head since she began speaking and didn't stop when she did.

"What is your problem?" she snapped.

"The truth is...the only reason I did what I did was...I found you too tempting to be around."

Sabrina couldn't believe her ears. "You didn't just say that?"

"Speaking that once in one's lifetime should be sufficient punishment. Sort of like dousing charcoal with lighter fluid."

"But you made my life hell and ruined any chance I had for advancement by shoving me into a cellar where you knew I would have to quit."

"Guilty."

Instead of calling him the few choice names that flashed neon bright in her mind, Sabrina grabbed her purse and began to wriggle out of the booth.

"Wait! You promised."

"Oh, don't worry. I won't slug you with this bag. I just wish I had known sooner what a lowlife you can be."

"A coward when it comes to serious relationships and commitment, maybe, but I take exception to 'lowlife.' I once bent the entire frame on my car to avoid squashing a teensy squirrel. And remember how you cooed that I have current photos of my nieces in my billfold?" Collin urged her back into the booth. "Sabrina, does it matter at all that I have hated myself every day since?"

"No. You'd say anything to be rescued from having to care for those children on your own." But inside, Sabrina's heart was pounding. Like the most repressed lonely heart, her mind had locked in on one phrase: *"I found you too tempting to be around."*

What was wrong with her? She hadn't fallen for him or his so-called charisma, and knew exactly what an incorrigible flirt he was. Most of all she didn't need a man in her life to feel fulfilled.

Raising her chin, she looked him straight in the eye. "If you'd been direct and honest with me, we could have saved each other a great deal of humiliation and embarrassment. Under further consideration, I'll take the job—not only to help Cassidy with her babies, but also to make *my* point. As far as I'm concerned, you *are* entirely resistible."

Chapter Two

"They're too young for bunk beds."

Rushing ahead of Sabrina to hold open the door to the furniture store for her, Collin thought of several replies he could make. So far on the drive from the restaurant to here, she had criticized or rejected ninety percent of his ideas for changing the third bedroom in his condo. While willing to take the heat for the offense that put him at the top of the food chain in her opinion, he was about to send out a "systems overload!" alert.

"You don't know my sister's kids," he said with increased emphasis. "They're three going on graduate school."

"Three means their bones are still soft, and many a child that age sleeps restlessly or wakes in the middle of the night needing the bathroom, or in this case, missing her mommy. A fall from the top bunk could be dangerous, even fatal."

"Why didn't Cassie say anything about that? I'm sure I mentioned the idea to her. I think." Collin rubbed his forehead as doubt set in. The truth was it seemed like a month since his sister had sent his comfortable existence into chaos and panic, and no, he didn't remember anything they'd discussed regarding the kids other than the fact that she would be gone for four months.

"She must have a million and two things on her mind," Sabrina said stopping in the doorway. "As a woman and mother, she's used to multitasking, but she could have missed that one thing." Then looking beyond him into the store, her expression changed. "Oh, I am not dressed for this or prepared for them."

Glancing over his shoulder Collin spotted three eager salespeople standing beyond the store's foyer watching them. "You're fine. Besides, they don't care, they're just anxious to make a commission." Once she did enter, Collin came up behind her and whispered in her ear. "Anyway, exactly what experience in child care do you have, Ms. Expert on Bunk Beds? I suppose you babysat during high school. That's not exactly a degree in pediatrics or child psychology."

"I fell out of my plain, old, twin-size bed at four and almost lost my eye when I knocked my face on the edge of the night table." Sabrina indicated the scar below her right eye. "See?"

Collin peered down at her high-cheek-boned face and milkmaid complexion. "See what? Your skin is flawless."

"Oh, you wouldn't admit it now just to be disagreeable. I didn't even wear makeup today because I knew I'd get dusty and go crazy feeling my skin get all yucky."

Amused at her irritability, Collin opened the second door of the glass-encased entryway. "You're welcome."

Sighing, Sabrina passed him. "Thank you for the compliment—and the door."

This woman was more self-deprecating and modest than he had remembered, and Collin filed away that tidbit of new information. "You really fell out of bed? So this whirling dervish persona has been a lifelong thing?"

"I have three older brothers. I was always being left behind and hated it. I had to learn to speed up if I didn't want to be left out of things."

Brothers, thought Collin, all older and probably protective where baby sister was concerned. More reasons to keep his thoughts in check—and his hands to himself.

"Bet you didn't have to try too hard to be included. But back to the bed problem…don't they make those beds that can stand alone while the kids are young, yet can be stacked as they grow up?"

"I suspect you can ask her," Sabrina said of the woman who was approaching them. "Oh, I wish you'd have let me stay in the car."

"Darling, you look *fine*," Collin declared in a normal street voice. "Anyone with a clue as to what kind of day you've had with trying to prepare the condo and talking colors with painters and whatnot will commiserate completely. Ah, the cavalry," he added beaming at the saleswoman who was within hearing distance.

"Good evening. I'm Brenda. What can I do to help you?"

"We need a bedroom suite for twin girls."

As he hoped, the woman turned to Sabrina and dropped her gaze to her tummy. "Oh, how lovely for you. Congratulations!"

Sensing Sabrina was about to correct her, he quickly grabbed her hand and squeezed. "Thank you very much. Um…we're receiving a ton of baby things already and thought we'd skip the crib part and prepare for the toddler-to-teen stage. Do you by chance have white bunk beds we can keep separated until the girls are old enough to cope with the height thing?"

"Of course, sir. Let me show you—and how insightful of you to already be cognizant of child safety. You'd be surprised at how many first-time parents overlook that in their excitement to create the perfect room for their new family."

"Isn't he wonderful?" Sabrina slid him an adoring smile, all the while twisting his pinky until he was forced to release his grip on her hand.

"Remind me not to underestimate your strength again."

"Pardon?" the saleswoman asked.

Collin cleared his throat. "I was just telling Sabrina to be careful maneuvering around all of this furniture. She's refused to quit her warehouse managerial job yet and I fear doing way too much and staying on her feet too long."

The saleswoman nodded knowingly. "You do look amazingly small for carrying twins. If you don't mind my asking, how far along are you?"

"Oh, I wouldn't be showing at all if I hadn't indulged in dessert tonight," Sabrina replied through gritted teeth. "Stop exaggerating, Collin, *dear,* and let's get this done or I'll go wait in the car, hugging the barf bag."

Despite the woman's worried look, he laughed uncomfortably, "Don't frighten the poor woman with all of these beautiful furnishings, darling."

Sabrina grabbed his sleeve and held him back until he found himself gazing into her flushed face and blazing eyes. He'd never seen her closer to eruption—or more provocative.

"Call me 'darling' one more time and so help me, I *will* get sick," she whispered fiercely.

"Whatever you say…dear."

It was forty-five minutes later when they finally exited the store. By then Sabrina was certain she'd sweated through her clothes. Collin had taken some secret glee in making it seem that the furniture was for their children and she could have, should have taken one of several opportunities to correct the situation—and make him look the fool. Now she was the fool for not exposing him, she thought, shivering as they walked to his Mercedes.

It had been a lovely Indian Autumn day in Dallas, but the nights held the bite of fast-approaching winter. Also fatigue from her relentless schedule lately didn't help.

"Sorry, why don't you take my jacket?" Collin asked, starting to remove it.

But that would leave him in shirtsleeves. As annoyed as she was with him, she couldn't do that to him. "Thank you, but if you'll turn up the heater once we're in the car, that should be fine." Besides, the idea of being surrounded by his masculine scent the whole drive to his home was more than she wanted to bear.

"Consider it done, but we'll head to a mall next and get you some warmer clothes."

Groaning inwardly at the mere idea of another stop, Sabrina replied, "I appreciate the gesture, but if you'll give me an advance on my salary, I'll do it tomorrow after work."

"You can't return to that place. Besides, they're delivering the beds and dressers tomorrow. Plus you need to be on the phone warning your credit card companies, your bank and the DMV of potential identity theft."

Stopping midstep, Sabrina covered her face with her hands. The mess her life was in rushed back at her with the devastating results of a tornado. She should never have accepted his offer. Bothering her parents in Wisconsin was out of the question; they still worked their two-hundred-acre farm, but she should have called her oldest brother Sayer, who plucked up businesses and property in trouble like some people haunted garage sales. The problem was that he would have sent her a one-way ticket home and she would never be let off a leash for the rest of her unmarried life. Her brother Seger didn't need the burden any more than her parents did, what with a second child on the way and his construction business suffering due to the economy. As for Sam, well, he was Sam—sweet, devoted to their parents, and denying himself a life to keep the family farm intact. No, she'd done the right thing to handle this herself regardless of the headaches involved. Only how could she fulfill new commitments when she hadn't completed the old ones?

"What?" Collin asked hovering beside her. "I'm just trying to be helpful. You're usually the pragmatic one. How can the idea offend you? Consider it part of the package."

No longer the trusting ingenue she'd been when she first ventured beyond the safe haven of her family and college, she dropped her hands and surmounted a strong defense. "Why? So you can continue embarrassing me in front of salespeople? Did you hear that woman back there? She thought I looked pregnant."

"No she didn't, she said—"

"I was there, Collin, I *know* what she said!"

His lips twitching, he replied, "Well, your mood does make you act like you're...*with child.*"

Throwing back her head, Sabrina screamed into the night.

"Fine, fine." Glancing around with chagrin, Collin urged her to the car. "Home we go. I'm sure there's an unopened package of pajamas from a Christmas past that I can offer you. If not, will a Dallas Cowboys' jersey signed by all of the cheerleaders do?"

Sabrina yanked the car door out of his grasp and slammed it, almost knocking him off balance.

As Collin climbed into the driver's side, she said in a defeated tone, "Thank you for the offer. On second thought, it would be wiser to purchase a few items tonight. Because I really need to go into work in the morning and give notice."

"How can you do that? I told you—"

"I remember the furniture and the calls, okay? There's just the small technicality that this is still my employer."

"Who worked you like a slave because they were saving money by having you do management and the work of two others."

Sabrina almost regretted telling him as much as she had about conditions at the place during dinner. "That's beside the point. I owe them two weeks' notice if I'm going to ask for a referral down the road."

"I'll give you a referral—as my assistant. This way you don't need them."

"That's not ethical."

"Let me tell you something—if you were going to be fired, they wouldn't think twice about showing you to the door without notice. That's what the severance check is for. It clears their conscience."

He was probably right, but it just wasn't the way she was brought up, or the way she wanted to think the world was. She had asked her boss, the district manager, to allow her to hire one or two more people, but he'd point-blank told her it wasn't going to happen.

"I'll think about it," she told Collin.

It was close to an hour later when, empty-handed, she returned to the car. She gave him a look through the passenger window that warned him not to utter a word until she spoke. He leaned over and pushed open the door.

"Can you please come inside?" she asked, sounding even more defeated that she had earlier.

"What's happened now? Don't tell me that they wouldn't accept the credit card. There's no balance on the account. I rarely use it."

"Thanks. So that's why they think I stole it. Either you come in and assure them that I didn't, or I will sleep in an orange jumpsuit in a holding cell tonight."

It was when she motioned over her shoulder with her thumb that he saw the security guard that had accompanied her and was standing watching them.

"Good grief." Collin hurried out of the car and locked

it with his remote. "We definitely have to talk to your obstetrician about those hormones, darling."

Passing an openmouthed Sabrina, he went to assure the security guard.

At least this time it was only an additional fifteen minutes of humiliation for Sabrina to endure, but enough was enough. "Please can we just go somewhere that I can get to sleep?" she asked him.

Collin got them back to the high rise. Conversation was kept to a minimum because she didn't trust herself to speak without having a total meltdown. All she could think was what had she gotten herself into? What had she done to deserve all of this?

As he escorted her into the lobby, they were greeted by the night security guard.

"Evening, Mr. Masters." When he spotted Sabrina, his gaze darted back to Collin. "Sir? Everything okay?"

With formal politeness, Collin announced, "This is Nanny Sabrina. Ms. Sinclair. Sabrina, this is Sonny Birdsong, not only the best security guard in the city but, if you start your day in a bad mood, his whistling will make you think you're in an Audubon wildlife sanctuary."

Chest swelling from that praise, Sonny nodded. "Welcome, ma'am. If I can be of any assistance while you're toting the little ones, don't hesitate. I must admit, I'm looking forward to having a few more young faces around."

"You're very kind…Sonny. So you're updated about what's about to happen? Will I need to sign in with every going and coming? What are your regulations?"

"If I could take a copy of your driver's license, that would be perfect for now."

Immediately digging into her purse, Sabrina crossed over to the counter to make that available to him. Thanking him when he returned it to her, she added, "Are there city buses in this part of town or do residents rely on cabs? The reason I ask is that I was hoping to take the twins on short field trips appropriate to their ages."

Sonny eagerly reached for a flyer. "This is the DART bus schedule and I'll be happy to assist you if you need help with strollers or anything."

"That's so good of you. I think the girls are beyond strollers, but I will rely on your expertise regarding the parks and— Oh! Is the farmer's market still tourist-shopper friendly?"

"We have several residents who shop there daily, and one chef who resides here and is also a regular shopper there."

"Wonderful. I'll ask about where his establishment is located tomorrow. By the way we're expecting furniture deliveries tomorrow."

The dark-haired man with the dimple in his right cheek replied, "I'll direct them to the freight elevator and alert you as they head up."

"Bless you. You've already reassured me a great deal."

Sonny blushed and slid Collin a self-conscious look. "Any time, miss. Have a good evening. Good night, Mr. Masters."

Waving, Collin waited for the elevator doors to shut. Only then did he muse, "I wondered how long it would be before you made a pet out of him. You'll be having everyone in the building nosing around you like a litter of pups within a week."

"If it weren't for those two little girls and your sister,

I would tell you to take a flying leap into the Trinity River, Mr. Employer."

Collin looked taken aback. "What animosity! If you weren't smaller than my sister, I'd be worried. All I was pointing out was that you're a fixer and a caretaker, a natural mommy. Most women would be flattered by such a compliment."

"Maybe I didn't see what you said as a compliment. I may not have worked for you all that long, but you're a fairly easy read, *boss.*"

"All men are," Collin replied with a sigh. "We need medals and sports jerseys and tool belts before we're even remotely interesting to a woman, otherwise we're considered as shallow as most wallets. Sonny doesn't know how lucky he is. He's got the uniform *and* the gun. And before you let your head get turned, let me inform you that my cleaning lady, Graziella, has him in her sights for her eldest daughter Isabella."

Staring in disbelief, Sabrina replied, "Is everything fodder for your audience-of-one comedy routine?" Sabrina told herself she would not cry, but this day had pushed her last button and she had run out of thick skin. The tears started welling in her eyes before she could turn away to hide them.

"Wait a minute. There are No Crying Clauses in our contract."

Feeling and hearing shifting beside her, she looked over to see him fumbling in pockets.

"Please stop," he continued with increased unease. "I don't have a hanky or tissue. Would it help if I took back every compliment and tease? I can also say 'Sorry' in four languages."

Despite everything, Sabrina had to smile. "I'd for-gotten that you weren't just a little crazy, you're seri-ously crazy."

Collin shrugged, his expression suggesting he didn't see that as a problem. "I was only trying to keep up your spirits." More gently he asked, "Are you going to be all right?" He began to reach out to stroke her hair as it fell forward hiding her face from him, then quickly dropped his hand.

"For someone who came home from work and realized she'd lost her entire adult and independent life? Yeah. Or rather I will be. Don't forget, I come from stoic farmers."

"Yes, with three protective brothers," Collin added under his breath. "We will *not* forget that again."

They arrived at his floor, ending her chance to wonder about his last comment. What she had to focus on now was getting a quick tour and some desperately needed sleep. She was dead on her feet and that filling but won-derful meal was making it difficult for her not to yawn.

As she entered the spacious high-rise condominium, Collin locked up behind them. Joining her at the other end of the foyer, he gestured self-consciously. *"Mi casa, su casa."* Stepping forward he nodded toward the kitchen. "Graziella is pleased with the microwave, but I can't say whether the dishwasher or oven have ever been turned on. As for the refrigerator…well, there are mostly wines in there at the moment, since I tend to eat out rather than cook—or else bring home takeout."

"Is that going to continue?"

"My eating? I certainly hope so."

Sabrina slid him a sidelong look. It wasn't fair that

his English accent made everything seem deeply considered and intelligent even when intentionally ridiculous. "I mean shouldn't you consider spending dinnertime with the girls? You know, establish family time, a schedule?"

Collin's eyebrows lifted in genuine surprise. "Hadn't given that much thought to it. You see? You're already invaluable. Well, I suppose I could ask Graziella to make us something. Although, she has eight children, plus her parents now live with her and her husband."

"Then she has more than enough to do. I'll do the cooking."

"You can cook?"

"Yes, sir, you hired a bargain. I can also bake, crochet…and butcher a chicken or duck for you if you've a mind for fresh poultry or fowl."

Urging her into the living room, Collin pointed toward the French doors that led to the balcony. "Pigeons rest on that railing. Don't let me find them on the dinner table. Sometimes we talk."

"Why am I not surprised?"

"When you're brainstorming ideas for a demanding client, one uses the audience that's available."

He did a slow 360-degree turn. "Should be roomy enough for two active children. Large-screen TV and all the equipment for games and videos. Great view of the city."

Sabrina had begun biting her lips as she passed the chrome and glass coffee table murmuring, "Sharp corners and so much glass." The balcony concerned her the most, though. "There'll be no running, and the view will be mostly closed drapes unless there's a childproof lock put on those balcony doors."

"The barrier is shatterproof and steel—and the railing well over their heads. No way they can fall through. Are you just covering that you're afraid of heights?"

"Afraid, no. Mindful, yes. And you'll thank me when we return those children back to their mother without casts or stitches."

Upon arriving at the far side of the condo, she saw that her room would be right beside the children's, across the hall from the condo's second bathroom. There were no windows in the children's room or hers, and only a small one high up in the bathroom.

Collin's master suite was on the far side of the condo. She didn't ask for, nor did he offer a tour, but considering that this had to be at least a two-thousand-square-foot living space, the layout gave her considerable relief. Until the girls arrived, she would still feel awkward staying here alone with him, but the doors had locks and she didn't have to worry that every word could be overheard if she was on her cell phone.

She placed her purchases on the lush cream-colored carpet beside the queen-size sleigh bed and wondered who or what had inspired this much decorating when the third bedroom that would be the girls' was empty? A sleigh bed had always been a fantasy of hers, although this one was bare of linens or blankets. The bone-colored walls were also bare, but at least there was a large armoire for storage and a good-size closet.

"I've never gotten around to finishing things on this side," he told her. "The only reason that I got this far was from thinking maybe Cassie would visit. She and the babies could have all snuggled in the bed and still had room for a puppy." He shrugged. "Alas, no visit."

"And no puppy. Should we look for one after the girls arrive?" She meant that mostly to pay him back for all of his teasing her, but she also thought she'd sensed a flash of loneliness in him.

"Maybe the stuffed toy variety," he drawled, moving on. "I've plenty of linens in the main hallway closet by my room. I'll get you a set and a blanket. Keep that credit card I gave you and pick up whatever else you feel is right for here and for the girls' room."

"Thanks," Sabrina said to his back.

What about towels and supplies in the bathroom? she wondered.

While he was gone, she went to check, and sure enough there was an assortment of dark blues and greens as far as towels were concerned, and adequate toiletries, but things like no-tearing shampoos and a first-aid kit were definitely lacking. Sabrina concluded that a shopping list was a must-do in the morning.

Returning to the bed, she sank onto the mattress only to jump up, reminded of her day working in a grimy warehouse. But how she yearned to curl up on that pristine bed—covers or not. Today's ordeal was taking its toll; nevertheless, she couldn't deny that things could have ended much worse.

Inevitably, however, her mind returned to Collin's admission about being attracted to her. While he'd seemed genuinely chagrined at the admission, she could never let herself forget what an actor he could be. Regardless, as her gaze settled on her work- and cold-roughened hands with her chipped nails, she grimaced and thought herself a bigger fool than ever. Maybe she might have imagined herself a possible temptation when she'd worked as his assistant, but there was no possibility of that now.

Sabrina had begun taking the labels off her purchases and was neatly folding them for storage in the armoire when Collin returned. He'd shed his jacket and tie along the way. She saw his gaze drop to the lace-and-satin bits of fabric and he all but dropped the stack of linens and blankets onto the bed before backing toward the doorway as though recoiling from a pit viper.

"The sheets are Egyptian cotton. You know me, spare no expense in spoiling the most important person in your life."

"Your self-indulgence is my good fortune," she replied with a smile. "I'll sleep like a baby."

"Good." His gaze fell to her lingerie again, and then he shook his head. "Well, I'd better let you get to that then. Oh—" he drew something out of his shirt pocket "—your personal key to the front door."

Sabrina considered the shiny brass instrument on her palm. Seconds ago it had rested against his heart. "I want you to know I appreciate the trust this represents. I won't let you down."

"The only thing I was always sure of—am sure of—is that I have no cause for concern in that department." For an instant their gazes met and held, then he blinked and continued. "There's another key with security. That's Sonny, and Dempsey Freed, who is usually the night guard. Sonny is working extended hours to cover for Dempsey, who apparently couldn't resist stepping into an altercation on the street this morning and needed some emergency dental surgery."

"Poor man! Was he protecting one of the building's residents?"

"More like fighting off a junkie trying to remove the copper numbers on the front of the building to cash in. Dempsey was a welterweight boxer, an Olympian in his youth and he takes his responsibility here as seriously as Sonny does." Backing into the hallway, he pressed his hands together and tilted his head toward his side of the condo. "If you're all right, I'll leave you to it."

"I'm good. Thanks again."

"Sweet dreams," he murmured.

Chapter Three

The next morning, grateful that Collin slipped out early, Sabrina called her boss at the warehouse and gave him the news that she was quitting effective immediately. She still felt badly for terminating so quickly, but had to admit Collin was right; if things were the other way around, she would get no such window of time or courtesy to ease into the transition. What's more, she had been wondering how long she could keep up those strenuous hours that had never been in her job description in the first place, while the district manager kept telling her there was no budget for additional employees.

Not surprisingly, Mr. Burger was displeased to learn that she wasn't at the store. What made her realize that

Collin had done her yet another favor was when Burger finally asked, "How much is it going to cost me to keep you?"

Only now was he willing to negotiate?

Out of sheer curiosity, she told him a figure close to what Collin was paying her and the man laughed harshly. "Good luck, sweetie," he said, and hung up on her.

She sat there staring at her cell phone for several seconds before declaring with Collin's accent, "Then all's well that ends well, I suppose."

Sabrina made several more calls—all related to her compromised identity and credit situation—and then reached for the list of numbers that Collin had left for her on the kitchen counter. Pouring herself a second mug of coffee, she punched Cassidy's phone number into the wireless phone on the counter. She fully expected to be asked to leave a message and was unprepared to get Cassie herself.

"Oh! I didn't expect—this is—"

"Sabrina!" Collin's sister replied with delight. "I recognized your dismay instantly. How typical of people who spend any time at all around my brother."

Before this morning Sabrina might have giggled and agreed with her. But she was far more humbled and grateful to him now. "No, I'm fine, really."

"Well, I appreciate you getting in touch so soon. You've accepted the job?"

It was on the tip of Sabrina's tongue to admit that she didn't have much choice, but this was Cassidy Masters, who believed in choices and had made critical and smart ones for herself and her family. "Yes, I have. Only I'm not sure I'm qualified to fill your shoes, even part-time.

Are you certain that you want me for this? It's such a serious responsibility."

"That's exactly why I told Collin to find you. I knew that's how you'd see this. Didn't he tell you?"

Sabrina pressed her hand to her heart. "You're too kind."

"And you're going to be wonderful. My fear is if my kids will want to come back home with me when I return."

"*My* fear is how to keep them from crying because they're missing you beyond bearing."

Sighing, Cassie replied, "They're going to cry, Sabrina. And misbehave. And test your wits. But I know if anyone can work through that, you will. While I sensed from the first that you have a tender heart, I quickly came to understand that you're not a quitter."

Hoping she was right, Sabrina thanked her again and began asking questions. "You're going to need to tell me about the girls' routines, likes and dislikes, and definitely any medical information I need to know about. And will they be able to talk to you sometimes? I know from other people who have had family deployed that they'll be able to e-mail almost anytime. But the girls are so little yet and that will hardly be enough."

"Sure, e-mails and phones are both an option. This is not our fathers' and grandfathers' war," she added drolly. "But listen, I want you and Collin to come down here as soon as you can. That way we can cover all of the questions, and you can take some of their things they'll need back with you. Then you can take the rest when you come for them—or when I drop them off—the last day."

"The last day." Sabrina's throat locked on the words.

"None of that," Cassie ordered. "This will be a perfect opportunity for you to start getting to know them."

"Does Collin know this is how you want to do it?"

"He will as soon as I call him."

Cassidy's laugh was subtly irreverent and Sabrina was reminded how brother and sister had that in common. "I don't know how thrilled he's going to be to have to sit in a car with me for two five-hour trips."

"If he complains, he's lying through his teeth."

Had Collin admitted his attraction to his sister? Surely not—and she wasn't about to, either, for fear that it would trigger doubts about having her stay on as the nanny after all.

"Uh-oh. You've grown very quiet," Cass said. "Did he pretend to be insensitive and rude to you?"

"If anyone was rude, it was me. I was still angry with him for causing me to quit."

"So was I, believe me."

"Oh, dear," Sabrina replied. "He told you why he transferred me."

"He didn't have to. I have good instincts and can put two and two together. Thank goodness the man put you up on a pedestal and refused to drag you off, otherwise he would have had a fling with you, then felt the need to buy you a nice piece of jewelry and find you a position with a deeper pocket than his."

"Well, I wasn't interested in having an affair with him then, and I definitely am not now."

Cassidy sighed. "No, you're the kind of girl a man marries, and Collin is practically allergic to that union, thanks to our parents, bless their souls."

What did that mean? She had never broached the

subject with him—there had been no reason to, even when she was his assistant, although she did notice that his only contact information in case of emergency was Cassidy. She had assumed that they'd passed away.

"That's really none of my business, but I hope if he is involved with someone, that he doesn't bring her here—I mean for the girls' sake."

Cass chuckled. "By all means, for the girls' sake."

Flustered, Sabrina slid off the bar stool. "I'd better get off this phone. The furniture is being delivered and the security guard is supposed to ring to warn me that they're on their way upstairs."

"You're wonderfully efficient. I'll get back to you as soon as I have my schedule lined out."

"I'll be here," Sabrina murmured after the other woman disconnected.

It shouldn't have surprised Collin at how eager he was to get home that evening, but it did. Not good, he thought, yet it didn't stop him. He'd been invited to cocktails with associates across town; there was also some gala over by the new Dallas Cowboy football stadium in Arlington and another in the Dallas theater district. He felt no temptation whatsoever to choose any of them and, thirty minutes before the rest of the staff quit for the day, Collin told his assistant Geoff that he had an appointment and was leaving.

He arrived at the condo with a big sack of Chinese takeout. Sabrina was nowhere to be seen, so he set down the bag and pulled at his tie as he cautiously ventured through the hall. He would have called out to her, but if she was napping from all of her work and emotional upheaval, he wouldn't want to wake her. Instead he found Sabrina on a stepladder draping yards of orange, lavender, pink and sage chiffon off the ceiling fan and fastening them to the four corners of the room.

"Good grief, woman, this is supposed to be an upgraded nursery, not a harem."

With a yelp, Sabrina came off the ladder and would have tumbled back into one of the two dressers bookending either side of the doorway if Collin didn't catch her by her trim waist and help her back upright. She then slapped him with her ponytail as she whirled around to face him.

"Oh, no," she gasped. "Sorry. Sorry."

Ruefully rubbing his cheek, he quipped, "Was it something I said?"

"You're early." She checked her watch and frowned. "Very early. Didn't you tell me that you had some function this evening?"

"It's a good thing I changed my mind about attending or you'd have a concussion or worse."

"I wouldn't have fallen if you'd announced yourself."

"What, in my own house?" He wagged his right index finger at her pert nose. "I don't think I like the idea of you on a ladder with no one about, either. Where did you get it? I certainly don't own one."

"From the custodian, Mr. Salazar. Very nice man. He wanted to do this for me, but he had his hands full replacing bulbs in the lobby." Sabrina gestured to her handiwork. "Do you really hate it?

Collin saw that the beds and other furnishings had arrived, and that sometime thereafter, she'd been out and had purchased a happy orange twin bedspread, one in purple and throw rugs in lavender, and embroidered throw pillows with bangles and mirrors and beads. Posters of Disney heroines adorned the walls.

"Who said anything about hate? It's just—different. It's definitely bright." He looked from poster to poster. "I'm not sure how much use they'll have for stories about mermaids and princesses at MIT. You do realize they know their numbers to twenty and can identify their names when they see them? They're learning to write them now. I believe calculus is scheduled to start next week."

"They can go back to being overachievers when their mommy returns. For now we're immersing them in storytelling and the art of using your imagination."

Amused, Collin watched her stretch to reach for the pink light bulbs on one of the dressers and felt his blood heat several degrees as her periwinkle sweater pulled across the gentle mounds of her breasts. "I certainly get that."

"Don't worry, I cleared it with Cassidy." Sabrina stretched her arms this time to encompass the room. "And look, I'm making this as easy for you as I can. No pink walls to paint over after they return home, no cutesy wallpaper or painted murals."

As she started up the ladder again, Collin stayed her. "Have you eaten today?"

Her eyes lowered, she said, "Sure. I found some crackers in the pantry, and I admit I helped myself to the cheese you had in the refrigerator."

"All that?" He took the bulbs from her and put them back on the dresser. "Enough for today. I don't need you falling off the ladder again, this time from hunger." He took her by her elbow and directed her down the hall. "I'll buy you dinner."

"Two nights in a row? That's not necessary."

"Frugal little thing. For your information, I brought back takeout. There's a nice bottle of Shiraz in the red section of the cooler that should accompany it well."

Visibly touched, Sabrina said, "That was thoughtful of you."

"You are literally saving my sanity. The least I can do is keep you alive."

Sabrina's brief laugh ended in a groan. "There's no danger in that. My brothers will tell you that they had to fight for their share of food at our table when we were growing up."

"Being a brother myself, I can assure you that we can be thoughtless lugs, when we aren't outright pigs." Collin stopped at the dining-room table and pulled out a chair for her. "Now this is an order. Sit and I will serve tonight."

Sabrina balked. "I'm not in any condition to sit at this table. Couldn't we sit at the kitchen counter on the bar stools?"

"Grand idea." Inclining his head, he led the way, ditched his tie and suit jacket over one of the four bar stools, then drew out another for her. Once he had her seated, he collected two long-stemmed wineglasses from a cupboard and the wine. "Do you like Shiraz?"

"I had it once and honestly couldn't tell the difference between it and the other red. I don't remember what that was."

"Bet it was a Syrah. Sometimes even I can't tell the difference, but then Syrahs are sometimes marketed as Shiraz. It's a dark-skinned grape with a history that goes back to the BCs. Do you like Asian food?"

"Almost all. Particularly Thai."

"I will bring that next time. This time it's Chinese."

Collin enjoyed her politeness mixed with irrepressible honesty. She made him happy that he'd come home. She made him want to hug her with her youthful eagerness to please, seasoned with an instinct to stand her ground when the situation mattered. Refreshing, that was the word. She looked and was the genuine article. It didn't hurt that her eyes matched the color of her sweater, although it was too long and hid her cute bottom, particularly in those slim-fitting jeans. He made the right choice to come home instead of slumming about tonight with people who were more acquaintances than friends, and who relentlessly altered their opinions to gain favor.

He knew she watched with studentlike attentiveness as he used the latest in cork-removal technology to open the bottle. "This is a client's latest invention. I think our ads are three times better than the product."

"I remember you always made a point to test the quality and value of the item you were being asked to market. Not all of your people did that."

"Their success ratio exposes them sooner or later, and they move on. Jacobs left shortly after you did."

Sabrina gasped. "You knew?"

Pouring, Collin nodded. "I knew."

"I'm so glad. It had bothered me. I'd wake up at night wanting to write you an anonymous note to expose what a sloppy businessman he was."

"Not handwritten, I presume? You didn't believe me when I told you that you had the loveliest penmanship I'd seen in years." Noting her cheeks blooming even as he touched his glass to hers, he changed the subject. "So the delivery went smoothly? You're pleased with the furniture?"

"Yes and the men were happy to come to somewhere so elegant. Tony, the supervisor, said they'd never delivered bunk beds to anything higher than two floors."

Collin barely swallowed his first sip of wine before something struck him. "How did you tip them?"

Sabrina shrugged. "I used what I had on hand."

And would probably never ask to be reimbursed. "I'm so sorry." He immediately reached for his coat and drew out his billfold.

"It's not necessary."

He drew out everything in his wallet and set it on the counter. "Household money. Nothing comes out of your salary. Put it wherever is most convenient for you to access. We'll talk later about whether it's more comfortable for you to buy groceries with the credit card or with cash."

"Thank you. I'll bring you receipts."

"I don't need them."

"Well, I'll keep a ledger and it will be here in the kitchen for you to review whenever you want to."

With that Collin took another sip of wine and got up to bring out plates and silverware. He was aware of her watching him the whole time. "What?" he finally asked.

"I'm just not used to being waited on. Everything smells heavenly. It's making me realize I'm hungrier than I thought I was."

"How are you about sushi?"

She responded with a polite smile and no comment.

"I'm the same way. You'd be surprised how often clients request it, or else I'm attending a function where it's prominent. Ah!" He pulled out two sets of wrapped items. "Chopsticks instead of the silverware?"

"Oh, great!"

Collin couldn't explain it, but the food and wine tasted better with Sabrina to share it with. "It's not any of my business, but are you okay with the other employer?"

"It worked out fine."

"And you notified whomever you had to about your accounts and all?"

"Also talked to Cassidy."

"And your family."

"I'll get to that."

"Sabrina—"

"They have my cell number. If there's an emergency, they can get hold of me."

Collin decided to back off, for now. But he would feel better if her family—brothers included—knew she'd switched jobs. "What about Cassidy?"

She looked startled. "You didn't talk to her?"

"I ended up in meetings most of the day. We kept missing connections. What's the latest?"

"I should let her tell you."

Collin went to make the call shortly after Sabrina excused herself and turned in for the night. That it was only minutes before midnight was testament as to what a great time they'd shared this evening. Just as he retired to his room, his sister's number showed up on his cell phone's display.

"Practicing ESP or giving up sleep altogether?" he asked her as his gaze moved to the digital clock on the night table.

"We just came off the field. I'd feed the original Declaration of Independence into a paper shredder for an apple martini right now."

Instantly sympathetic, Collin asked, "That's disturbing considering how physically fit you are."

"Oh, that's not the problem. As sick as I am of being wet, cold and forbidden to use the legs I was born with, it's the animal life I'm expected to sample that makes this a torment."

"Then I'll skip mentioning that Sabrina doesn't like sushi any more than we do."

"Funny man. If you'd stayed in England, I'd have grown up to be an only child. Almost a princess—albeit a Plains Princess."

Chuckling, Collin replied, "Speaking of fairy tales…Sabrina has the kids' room looking outstanding. I can't wait for you to see it. Gena and Addie are about to be submerged into a fantasy world."

Cassie sighed, the sound of her boots hitting the floor discernable. "You'll have to send me a photo—first tell me what your calendar looks like. Can you and Sabrina come down this weekend?"

So that's why Sabrina had been reluctant to share what she and Cass had talked about. "That's rather short notice."

"I want both of you to come so the girls get used to the idea of being around you two as a unit, and so you can haul some of their stuff up there. I'll bring the rest when I drop them off."

This was happening way too fast for him and the combination of fatigue and stress in her voice worried him, as well, but he tried not to expose any of that. "All right," and added with as much cheer and irreverence as he could muster, "What can we bring you? Diapers for the long flight overseas?"

"Just your pretty face—and Sabrina."

"Love you, Captain."

"See you Saturday, English."

Chapter Four

Sabrina had seen photos of Cassidy Masters, and she'd enjoyed talking to her many times, but she found her even more striking in person.

"It's so good to finally be face-to-face," she said as Cass hugged her. She felt like a shrimp to Cassidy's five-eight, and her figure was willowy, her big blue eyes wide set and intelligent.

"You, too." Pushing her to arm's length, Cassie studied her with the eye of an unabashed analyst. "Oh, dear, you look far too tenderhearted for these two mighty mites. Ladies," she addressed her daughters with a more formal tone, "This is Miss Sabrina, whom I was telling you about." To Sabrina she added, "They're better at their numbers than enunciation, as you'll soon find out. Can you tolerate being called, 'Miss Brina'?"

"That's much better than *Unca Colon,*" Collin drawled standing behind Sabrina.

"Oh, let's just make it *Brina.*" She crouched down to be at eye level with the two little girls. "Let me see…" She remembered who loved her long tresses and who wasn't a fan of her curls. "You must be Gena," she said to the child with the enviable mane. "And Addison, that's a very colorful sweatshirt." It was bright orange and adorned with handprints in every other Day Glo color.

"I made it myself for Halloween. Do you twick-ow-tweat, or are you too old, like Mommy?"

Trying not to giggle that most of the child's *Rs* came out as *Ws,* she nodded. "Yes, too old. But it's fun to be the one to hand out treats and see everyone's costume. What are you going to be, Gena?"

"Either a princess or a bride."

"It depends on how much time we have to do her hair," Cassie piped in.

"But if there's no time, I still get to wear a tara."

"Tiara. That's right." Cassie rolled her eyes at Sabrina. "Come in and please ignore our mess. Between my training and packing for all of us, things are upside down."

That was hardly the case, Sabrina thought, glancing around the house. Military-base living was modest, but nothing like what her previous apartment was like. And except for the girls' open suitcases on the coffee table, and a few boxes stacked by the door, the place was clean and the walls bright with fresh paint—white in the living room, yellow in the kitchen, peach in the master bedroom and lavender in the girls' room.

"I hear you've done a fantastic job at Collin's place," Cassie said as they entered the girls' room. "Thank you for working so hard to make them feel special. I know they're going to love it."

"I hope so. It was fun to do."

Addison tugged at her jeans and asked, "Bwina, do you have little girls we can play with?"

"I'm afraid not, sweetie. But I'm looking forward to you teaching me games you like to play. And we're going to go to fun places like the park and zoo and do lots of surprise things for Mommy."

"Is Unca Colon gonna have fun with us?"

Sabrina lifted her eyebrows at Collin. She wanted him to handle that question.

"Well, I do have a job so I can pay for that fun, but I hope to join you ladies on weekends at the very least."

Whether it was for his formal address or the tickle on her belly, Addison laughed. "We not ladies, we little girls."

"Wash up time." Cass directed her daughters toward the bathroom. "We're going to have lunch in less than fifteen minutes."

"You needn't have gone to any trouble," Collin said as the two diminutive blondes sped out of the room. "I would have gladly taken you all out somewhere for a treat."

"Believe me, the treat is firing up the grill and not caring if you get mustard or ketchup on your face and hands," his sister replied. "Besides, I want to spend as much time picturing them as they are, and not having to be on their best behavior because they're in public."

"They're extremely well behaved," Sabrina assured her.

"Yeah, they're pretty good, but when they're over-tired, they can find an earsplitting octave that you'll want to restrict to once every full moon. Go flip those burgers and dogs, Unca Colon. I'm going to pass on more boring tidbits to Sabrina."

As soon as the door closed behind him, Cassie turned back to Sabrina, her expression relaxing to weariness and worry. "How was the drive down?"

"Better than expected. It can't help but get awkward every once in awhile considering our history."

"He likes to watch you when he thinks you won't notice."

"I suppose I am becoming like a second kid sister to him."

With a badly faked cough, Cassie replied, "Right. That's exactly the conclusion that I came to."

Feeling heat in her cheeks, Sabrina shook her head. "You don't have to worry that I would—or *he* would, for that matter—behave improperly in front of the girls."

"I'm so not worried. In fact, I wish you would drive the old fossil a little crazy."

"Oh, please don't start."

"I hereby quit. I'll just point out that a complete stranger would notice you're good for him."

"Thank you, but you know the chant better than I do. Your brother is 'not the marrying kind.' What about you?" Sabrina asked. "Do you ever have time for a life, let alone romance?"

Cassidy glanced over her shoulder to make sure the girls were still down the hall. "Believe me, I could have a different man every night if that was what appealed, and I have to admit one or two have been tempting, but as you can tell, right now it's the girls and the job that need to take priority."

"It must feel like a huge responsibility to fly something where everyone counts on you to get them home."

"It does, but I count on them just as much to do their jobs, so it's a team thing."

The girls returned and Cassie effortlessly changed the subject to who wanted to drink milk and who wanted to drink spring water.

"I try to keep soft drinks out of their diet as much as possible," she told Sabrina. "They can thank me for their healthier teeth and digestive systems later. Oh, and for afternoon snacks, I always keep carrot and celery sticks. Add a little peanut butter and they're good until dinner. They like apples with peanut butter, too. And bananas."

"I know Collin doesn't have any peanut butter in the house, but I'll get it. What about D-E-S-S-E-R-T-S? What is and isn't permitted?"

The spelling had Cassie smiling. "That won't work much longer. Not only can they now spell their names, not just recognize them in print, they can spell cat and dog. But back to your point—it's your call. I know the calendar is charging into the most sugar-intense time of the year on top of the kids craving comfort food for one reason or another."

"You're making it so easy for me. I thought since you're so slender, you might be concerned about them gaining too much weight."

"Those two take after me. I burn triple-digit calories just breathing. That's one thing you don't have to worry about. If they tell that you they're hungry, feed them." Cassie added, "I would love not to look like a boy going and coming. Please tell me yours aren't a boob job?"

Sabrina gasped. "Why, no!" She couldn't imagine

what her family's reaction would be if she did such a thing. "With a B-cup, I'm considered the flat-chested one in my family."

"You're from Wisconsin? Your family is Scandinavian?"

"On my mother's side. My father's people are English."

"Ever curious to see the old family haunts?"

"If it wasn't so cold. I hate being cold."

"I'm with you there. So where am I going? The mountains of Afghanistan—during the winter, no less."

"Make a snowman, Mommy, and send us the picture," Addison said returning to the kitchen.

"I will, my glass-half-full girl."

Sliding Sabrina a wry look, Cassie started pouring the children's drinks. "What will you have, Sabrina? I do have beer or wine if you'd prefer."

"Oh, no, thanks. That and the long drive back to Dallas will put me to sleep."

"I'll have a glass of that wine," Collin told his sister returning with the tray of grilled food.

"You're driving," Cassie sang, gently reminding him.

"Actually, we're staying the night at a hotel just down the road," he sang back.

Cassie glanced at Sabrina's startled face. "Would have been nice if you had told her that." Then she concentrated on getting the rest of the food onto the kitchen table.

As Collin poured himself the wine, Addison studied him with furrowed brow and pursed lips. "I don't get it," she began.

"Well, if *you* don't, love, I'm sure the experts at NASA haven't got a clue. Tell me what the problem is."

"What do we call you when we live by you, Unca Colon? You can't be Daddy Colon?"

Collin had taken a sip of the chardonnay and launched himself for the paper towels. Cassie and Sabrina covered their mouths and had to turn away.

Seeing no adult corrected her sister, serious Gena took over. "He can't be our Daddy, Gena. He's our *Uncle Daddy*."

It was dark by the time Sabrina and Collin left the base. After a picnic-style lunch, and a tour of the base, they went through photo albums and then snacked. Afterward, she helped Cassie give the girls their baths, learned how they liked their hair dried, listened to prayers and tucked them in. She was exhausted and told Collin that she didn't know how Cassie did all she did and fulfilled her military responsibility.

"I'm more impressed than ever with her," Sabrina said as Collin navigated the crowded Saturday-night streets of San Antonio as expertly as he drove in Dallas. "She wasn't kidding when she said she burns calories like a grand prix racing car did fuel."

"What pleased me is that you two got along famously," Collin said.

"Thanks, but who wouldn't? She's smart and funny, and radiates charisma." She almost added, "Like someone else I know," but she wasn't about to swell his head more than it already was. His nieces clearly adored him and had taken full advantage of his presence to ask for repeated piggyback rides and sleight-of-hand tricks with his pocket change that always became theirs. "How's your back?" she asked him instead.

"As soon as we check in, I plan to nurse it with a single malt. I did the math and I almost toted around the equivalent of a side of beef today."

Sabrina glanced at the next hotel they drove by. That made three quite nice, executive-type inns. "Where exactly are we going to stay?" she had to ask.

"The Hilton on the River Walk. I made reservations the evening after I spoke with Cassie about coming down. Please don't scold. Blame it on my need for creature comforts."

"Wouldn't think of it, but that's way over my budget," she told him. "Why don't you drop me at the place we just passed and pick me up in the morning?"

"Not on your life. I have your room reserved, as well. Business expense. Besides, I want you to join me for dinner. I need real food, not toddler munchies."

"Please don't ask me to do the bag-lady-at-the-steak-house act again."

Collin scoffed at her protest. "You look terrific. If you insist, we'll stop in the hotel lobby store and pick you up a glitzy pair of earrings."

"You're kind to think that's all it would take. Surely you know people in the city? You know half of Texas. Wouldn't you rather touch base with them?"

"You're just fishing to see if I have an old flame lurking in this area code."

"I am giving you an out if you were only being polite."

"Look, we are about to spend the next four months inundated with baby talk, kiddie videos and mushy cereal. I would consider it a gift and pleasure if you'd properly dine with me."

With her resistance to him melting faster than ice

cream in a microwave, Sabrina replied, "Well, I know I couldn't sleep yet if I tried…and I am somewhat hungry."

Collin nodded and murmured, "Thank you. Pick you up at 7:00."

In less than an hour, Collin escorted Sabrina to the blissfully dark hotel restaurant. He still wore the black T-shirt he'd had on earlier, but added a matching sports jacket that he'd brought along in his usual "expect the unexpected" way. With delight and even amusement, he discovered that Sabrina not only didn't need help from his plastic, but she'd been delightfully creative. Responding to his soft knock, she emerged from her room wearing the same tunic sweater, but now it was worn over sexy black leggings that she'd picked up in a shop in the lobby. She'd cinched her trim waist with a black leather belt and had slipped into sparkly slides, things also picked up there. There were no glittery earrings, just the delicate hoops that seemed to be a staple with her; however, the added mascara and lip gloss had her looking absolutely glamorous and sexier than ever.

"My, you'll spawn several thoughts among diners this evening, but none of them will have anything to do with bag ladies."

"Thank you…I think." She self-consciously ducked her head, and tucked her hair behind her right ear. "Isn't the decor nice? That hunter green on the walls is cool and soothing."

"I honestly hadn't noticed."

Sabrina continued noting the decor until they reached the restaurant where they were greeted warmly by the maître d'.

"We have your table ready, Mr. Masters."

As they approached it, a handsomely dark waiter eagerly pulled out a chair for Sabrina, who demurely thanked him. Collin was seated by the maître d'. He couldn't fault the younger man for his admiring study of Sabrina, but if it continued through dinner, it was going to get on his nerves.

"A cocktail before dinner, sir?" the maître d' asked. "Or may I show you the wine list?"

"Both, please," Collin replied. "A cosmopolitan for the lady, a double Chivas on the rocks for me. Perhaps you can recommend your most mellow Cabernet with dinner?"

"Excellent. I will see that our wine steward finds exactly what you desire. Thank you, sir."

As he and the waiter left them for the moment, Collin glanced up to see Sabrina's wide-eyed stare. "Yes?"

"You remembered."

Soon after he'd hired her, she'd mentioned having watched *Sex and the City* on reruns and listening to them go on about drinking cosmopolitans. She'd yet to taste one. "I hope it proves worth the wait," he said, pleased to surprise her.

Leaning closer she whispered, "But you're ordering wine, too?"

"I promise to get you to your room with dignity intact."

"What's the special occasion? Your birthday isn't until July and mine is in August."

"How about a salute to your own loss of freedom? Well, at least until nearly spring?"

"I'm getting paid. Your sister is taking all of the risks."

Collin could see he was not making himself clear. "After watching you with Cass and the girls today, I realized all that we're asking of you. You won't have much opportunity for a night life—or any form of personal life."

"In all honesty, I didn't have much of one anyway." Sabrina looked everywhere but at him. "I worked. That was it."

It was disconcerting to feel something akin to relief. What a rat to not want her to have someone special in her life when he knew perfectly well he could never have her. "What about your parents? Won't they and your brothers be disappointed if you don't come home for at least one holiday?"

"I wouldn't have been able to if I'd stayed at the warehouse job, either. From Thanksgiving to Christmas is the busiest time. No one gets time off. Oh!"

"What?"

She gave him a sickly smile. "I need to tell my parents that I moved and give them your number."

Collin could almost imagine their reaction. Seismic waves would probably be recorded as far south as Galveston. "Thanks for the warning. I should check in with my health-care provider and beef up my policy." Where were their drinks?

"I just turned twenty-eight, not eighteen."

"That still makes me thirty-eight and the single man you're living with."

Thankfully, the waiter arrived with their drinks, then took their order. Collin didn't wait for him to get more than a step away before taking a needful sip of Scotch. The burning down his throat was nothing compared to how his stomach would feel as he worried about the entire Sinclair clan appearing in the lobby.

"I am not living *with* you."

"They might buy that if I was seventy." As she opened her mouth to speak, he raised his hand entreating her to wait. "Please don't point out yet again how completely resistible I am."

Instead Sabrina took a second sip of her cosmo.

"Do you at least approve of it?" he grumbled.

A smile pulled at Sabrina's lips. "It's not on the level of a margarita, but it's interesting." When their waiter returned with their salads, she made eye contact with him and her smile was as flirty as his.

"He's not an hour over twenty-one," Collin said when they were again alone.

"Maybe I like them that way."

Collin narrowed his eyes. "You did that to get at me."

"Did it work?"

"No."

She threw back her head and laughed. "This is kind of fun."

"What other unpleasant characteristics don't I know about you besides your sadistic streak?"

"If you want to be rid of me, all you have to do is suggest to Cassie that I move into her place. This way the girls stay put in familiar surroundings and with their friends. Come to think of it, I might even get a social life with all of those soldiers around."

"Yes, but you wouldn't be making the salary that you are." He was not enjoying this conversation one bit. He should never have confessed his interest in her. He should have thought up some other story; he was in the business of lies, for pity's sake.

"You've got me there." Sighing, Sabrina picked up

her salad fork. "Okay, I'll quit teasing. I don't know how you do it, though. Being a flirt is work. Were you like that as a boy?"

He didn't want to talk about his childhood any more than he wanted her to torment him, but at least the past was the past. "Hardly. My parents didn't divorce pleasantly, didn't my sister tell you? Mother kept Cass here and my father took me back to England."

"That much I picked up from office gossip the first time I was your employee." Intercepting his dark look, she grinned, but said, "Sorry. Go on."

"There's not much to tell. It wasn't a month before he shipped me off to an academy—a fancy rendition of a boarding school. You see, he didn't have any use for me, he was merely getting back at my mother."

"That was small of him. I'm sorry."

"I'm hungry." Stabbing an olive in his Mediterranean salad, Collin thought the subject was done. He was wrong.

"So you eventually developed the 'I'm a catch' persona due to a need to prove your father wrong for pushing you away? Or your mother not fighting harder to keep you?"

"Neither. I was starving for attention and discovered people gave it to me if I flattered them enough. But it also helped to keep people from asking too many questions." He pointed his fork at her. "Until you."

"Hint taken. New subject." Sabrina nodded out the window at the tree-lit canal where a barge was passing full with tourists listening to a guitarist playing for them. "Can we walk off dinner down there?"

"I suppose. I'm certainly not going to leave you on your own."

"It's not like I can lose this hotel."

"I've only been there once before and enough time has lapsed to not bore me to tears."

"Thank you," she said demurely. "I promise not to keep you out too late."

Collin could only shake his head.

"I love doing the typical tourist things," Sabrina said.

It was now almost nine o'clock and the crowd had thinned out some. At least there were fewer children and older folks than when she'd first watched from the hotel restaurant. The temperatures weren't exactly chilly, but she was glad she had her jacket to tie around her shoulders. Collin had his hands shoved into his jeans' pockets and remained on the quiet side.

She worried that she had made a mistake and gone too far with him. She couldn't blame it on the liquor, either, since she'd said those things before she drank—and never did finish the cosmo and maybe had two sips of the wine. But she hadn't needed the alcohol; she was high on being with him and knowing he'd wanted her company.

When he didn't remark on her comment, she stopped and gazed up at a lit storefront on the second floor. She liked this open-air-mall type of shopping.

"Oh, look. Tattoos."

"No." Collin took hold of her arm just above the elbow and urged her forward.

"It's my skin."

"Then respect it more. I'm going to follow an old military custom. You work for me, therefore your skin is my property until we end this contract. You do not mar my property. Not even if you invite me to watch."

She knew better than to respond to that line. Instead she gazed up at the twinkling white lights in the trees and outlining the arching bridges over the canals. "This is like Christmas 365 days a year."

When she spotted a store with postcards, she asked Collin to wait and dashed inside to buy a handful to send to her niece, Trudy.

"Going to rebuild your scrapbook collection?" Collin asked when she emerged with her bag of choices.

"I don't do that, but my niece, Sayer's daughter, does. Like most people from out of state, she thinks Texas is still the Wild West."

"There's another gift shop. Want to get some T-shirts for the other nieces or nephews? There's an Alamo piggy bank."

"Okay, I can take a hint. I'm done." She glanced down at her feet. "Besides, these heels aren't the best idea on this sidewalk."

"What you women do for fashion."

"Be nice. I could have gone upstairs and changed into my sneakers, and then I'd be ready to walk the whole length of this place."

"I promise you that I would have slung you over my shoulder and carried you back to the hotel if you'd tried."

Seeing his crooked smile, she felt better. He was over being annoyed with her.

In the elevator, though, they were joined by a couple who were unabashedly enraptured with each other and had no interest in waiting until they were in their room to begin getting intimate. Cuddling in the opposite corner, the young woman was leaning back against her partner and the hip action while slow was flagrant. He had his arms around her and his fingers were diving inside her sweater to stroke the sides of her breasts. It was a relief to get out at their floor. The couple was heading several levels up.

Sabrina stopped once the elevator doors closed again and pressed her hand to her chest. "Do you think they'll make it there?"

"What I do know is that there'll be no need for them to rent an adult film."

Continuing down the long hallway, it was strange how they avoided looking at each other. Conversation dried up, too. She was relieved to reach her door.

"Well, thank you again. I did enjoy it." She concentrated very hard on getting her room key out of her purse. "Um…what time do you want to leave in the morning?"

"Is 7:00 too early for you?"

"Not at all. Good night then." She knew he was going to be a perfect gentleman, waiting until she was inside with the door safely shut and secured behind her, and that made her self-conscious and clumsy. She missed the slot completely the first time she tried. The second time she withdrew it too soon and the green light didn't come on. "This is humiliating," she told him. "Could you at least wait by your own door?"

Instead he took the card key from her and calmly unlocked her door for her. Holding it open with his left hand, he handed the card back with his right, then caressed her lower lip with his thumb. "You are an utter delight. Good night."

Shutting the door and turning the second bolt, she stood there and waited. Then she heard a brushing sound against the wood and footsteps as he walked to his room.

She waited for his door to open and close…and waited. Her heart began to pound anew.

Finally he did retreat into his room.

Sabrina touched her fingers where he'd stroked her and wondered if he would ever kiss her—and would that be enough?

Chapter Five

Shortly after the calendar flipped to November, Cassidy delivered Gena and Addison up to Dallas. Sabrina couldn't imagine what they were feeling and did her best to put on a bright smile, as did Collin, who had taken the afternoon off to be there, too.

Cass described how excited the girls had acted all the way up from San Antonio. Getting a new room would be like going on vacation. It hadn't really registered in their three-year-old minds that the cost of that meant not getting to see their mommy for months. As soon as everyone hugged, Genie and Addie ran down the hall to see their room. Squeals of delight quickly emanated from there.

"Sounds like a hit to me," Cassie drawled. Then she groaned as she lowered their suitcases to the floor and let her shoulder bag slide down her arm. "That stuff weighs more than the backpacks we hauled during training."

Shoving her purse out of her way, she came to Collin for a hug. "You look almost ashen. Everything okay? Too late to run scared now."

"It was too late as soon as you told me that you were being deployed," he said looking none too happy with that memory. He held out his hand. "You and Sabrina talk. Give me your keys and I'll go get the rest of their things from the car."

"I'll go, too. That's too much to carry in one trip."

Collin plucked the keys out of her grasp. "There must be a hundred last-minute instructions or girly things you'll want to pass on to Sabrina, and I'd only embarrass her and annoy you by asking what all that means."

He was out the door before his sister could say anything else. Cassidy looked from the closed door to Sabrina.

"What's wrong?"

"He's anxious for you, you must know that?"

Running her hands through her short, wind-swept curls, Cassie's lips curved with sardonic amusement. "That I get. It's the tension that wafted out of here the instant the door opened. And you were hanging back watching him, then refused to make eye contact when he looked over his shoulder at you. My brother doesn't doubt himself or get worried about women because he simply doesn't let himself care beyond mutual gratification. I'm getting the feeling that you're messing with his damaged mindset."

"He's been working a great deal of overtime so he can take some days to spend with the girls."

"And when he's not at the office?"

"He's sleeping."

"Alone?"

"Cass! There's nothing to tell. At least not what you're thinking." And that wasn't a lie in that what she was waiting for from Collin hadn't happened. Sabrina gestured down the hallway where the happy sounds continued. "Don't you want to come and see their room? I want to take your picture in there and then have it blown up into poster size so that the girls will feel you're not so far away."

Cass wrinkled her nose. "Darn it all—I wanted him to have at least kissed you by now. You must really have him conflicted."

Conditions were no easier for her. But what was saving Sabrina some wear on her nerves was the certainty that if she behaved like every other woman he'd known—like the proverbial moth to the flame—she was the one who would be reduced to ashes.

She picked up a pink suitcase with purple piping. "Come see what the fuss is all about. We added a few things since we got to visit with you."

An hour later Collin watched Cass say a difficult goodbye to the girls, rise from her knees to hug Sabrina as one would a sister and stride toward him where he waited by the elevator. He wrapped an arm around her shoulders and urged her to lean on him, even though that made his eyes burn worse and made the lump lodging in his throat all but strangle him.

Only when the elevator doors closed them in the car was he able to mutter, "Well, this sucks even more than I expected it to. You should have flown up. It's too many miles back to the base with no chatterboxes in the backseat to keep you alert."

"I've got an audiobook to play. It will be novel to indulge in adult fiction for a change instead of reading manuals and course studies, or kiddie books." But her expression looked anything but enthused about that. "I wish you'd have just given me a hug up there and let me be gone."

"I want to see you to your SUV."

"You're not going to make me cry."

Not only did Collin do that, but he also pressed his lips to her temple. "If you do something stupid and brave and get hurt, I will never forgive you."

"I'm shaking in my boots."

"You damn well should be."

Cassidy stepped back and studied his face. "I know you'll take care of my babies, but I hope you'll take care of this, too." She pressed her hand flat against his heart.

"I'm trying."

"Now see—it's comments like that which worry me. I love you, English."

"Me, you, Captain."

When he returned to the condo and locked the door, he experienced such a wave of weakness and loss that he had to lean back against it to stay standing. His heart had just dropped into one of the dark places in his soul.

"Collin?"

He didn't realize Sabrina had been in the kitchen and had heard him return. Seeing him frozen there against the door, she came to him, her eyes radiating her concern. And then she did exactly what Cass had done, placed her hand flat against his heart and he stiffened and sucked in a sharp breath. It literally hurt, as though she'd reached into his body and physically touched that organ.

He couldn't bear the raw, naked emotion of need. Despite weeks of iron will and brutal lectures to keep his hands to himself, he crushed her against him and hid his face in the fragrance and silkiness of her hair.

Sabrina gently eased her trapped arms free from between them and wrapped them around his waist. Slowly, she stroked his lean, too tense back. "She'll be all right," she whispered to him.

"You can't know that."

"But I feel it."

"How, when this is so wrong on every level?"

The more gravelly and bitter his voice grew, the softer and more tender hers became.

"There's just an inner peace."

"Peace." He exhaled shakily and stroked his cheek against her hair. "I don't know the meaning of the word anymore. I don't know that I ever did." He swallowed painfully. "Thank you for being here...for doing this. I couldn't—"

"Shh." She stroked his cheek and then brushed a kiss there. "You don't have to."

He gravitated to the source of that sweet caress until his lips were aligned with hers. "Oh, yes, I do," he rasped and feathered a kiss to her lower lip. "Yes, I do," he murmured again as he repeated the caress to the right corner of her mouth, then the left. Shifting his hold to frame her face between his hands, he looked deeply into her eyes, then focused on her lips again. "Yes."

He kissed her as he had in a dream, with tenderness and care, and sighed with relief when she opened to him.

She was his link to sanity and his soul and he cherished the gift of her. When his tongue touched hers, she murmured softly and let herself lean against him.

"Bwina...I gotta go potty."

It was Sabrina who eased back and called down the hall, "I'll be right there." Then she looked at Collin and asked softly, "Are you okay?"

He could only offer a barely perceptible nod, and then she was off to help Gena. What had just happened? he wondered. He felt as though he'd been in one of those out-of-body experiences.

"I don't know if I'll ever be okay again," he finally replied to the empty room.

By the time he felt in control of himself again, the giggle and chatter level was going strong in the girls' bedroom. Collin noted that Sabrina's voice came across as excited as his nieces' did. She was attempting—and succeeding—in getting their focus off of their mother's departure, at least temporarily.

At the doorway of their room, he saw that the grand unpacking had commenced. Dolls and stuffed animals were already strewn about. Clothing was being put away; however, some modeling appeared to be necessary.

"These are my favorite shoes," declared Gena hugging ultrashiny patent leathers to her pink-and-glitter sweatshirt.

Collin compressed his lips to hide the smile as "are" came out "aw" and "favorite" sounded suspiciously as "faborite."

"They're beautiful," Sabrina cooed. "They're so shiny. Who keeps them that clean for you?"

"Mommy. But she teaching me."

"Then you can teach me so we can make Mommy proud when she gets back and sees that they're still in good shape, okay?"

"I will. I teach Addie all the time."

"Which are your favorites, Addie?"

"My sneakers." But Addison was more interested in the giant polar bear that she had dragged from the far corner of the room and was attempting to sit in its lap. "Is this yours?"

"No, it's yours. Everything here is for you girls from your Uncle Collin. He's very happy to have you visiting with him for awhile."

"Addie," Gena explained, all solemnity, "'member? Mommy told us. He don't have little girls and borrowed us so he won' be lonesome while Mommy is gone."

Collin saw Sabrina touch her fingertips to her mouth and turn away. He was certain something had stabbed his heart, as well, especially as Gena said "bowwowed." He cleared his throat. "Is that okay with you, Addie?"

Both tots turned to him.

"I guess," Addie said, but didn't sound quite convincing. "If you promise to give us back."

"Oh, I most definitely do."

"When?"

"In time for Valentine's Day."

Gena and Addie exchanged looks.

"Is that before Santa?" Addie asked her sister.

"Only if the groundhog comes outside and sees his shadow. If the sun doesn't come up, then it's after."

Addison frowned and rested her cheek against Bear. "I hope the sun comes out."

Blinking back tears, Sabrina said brightly, "Know

what? We forgot New Year's! That's when we wear
happy, bright hats with feathers and sparkles, and throw
streamers and play with balloons to welcome a new
year and get ready for you girls turning four!"

"Can I sleep with Bear until Mommy comes gets
us?" Addie asked.

"He takes up a bunch of the bed, but if that's what
you want," Sabrina said sending Collin an anxious look.

"Which bed?" he asked the child.

"Orange. It's like the sun." She hoisted up Bear and
crawled onto the bed to gaze up at the shimmering
orange chiffon.

"What about you, Gena?" Collin asked.

"I'm older. I don' need to sleep with toys. And I get
purple." But she didn't get onto her bed. Instead she
stood beside the stuffed giraffe that was twice her height
and slowly stroked its neck and back.

Collin pushed away from the doorjamb and crouched
beside Sabrina where he gave the back of her neck a
secret squeeze. "It's okay to have an animal friend to
nap with even if you are a few minutes older, Gena. Just
don't forget to brush your giraffe and put a blanket on
him so he doesn't get cold at night."

"Okay. What do I feed him?"

Crap, Collin thought. "You want to handle this one?"
he said under his breath to Sabrina.

"I do, because your mom told me that she'd arranged
for the sandman to come by after you go to bed. He'll
take care of that for you."

"Who feeds Bear?" Addie demanded. "He don' like
sand or grass, he likes fishes. I seen that on TV."

Sabrina nodded several times, which indicated to

Collin that she was thinking as desperately as he was. Unfortunately, for him, being close to her like this and picking up the luscious scent of her made him think about her taste and the temptation of her body against his.

"Now I remember what your mom told me!" she burst out. "Do you know how the postman carries different kinds of stamps with him for people who need to mail something but forgot to go to the post office? That's what sandman does. He brings the things that are needed."

"Does he know the Easter bunny?" Addie asked.

"I hear they are excellent friends," Sabrina assured her.

"Girls, play for a minute while I check on something with Brina, okay?" With that he crooked his finger and motioned her to follow him, whereupon he led her farther down the hall. Hands on his hips, he asked in a hushed voice, "And how are you going to explain a lack of food crumbs or grass when they wake in the mornings? Do not think that you're going out to the park across the street at night with scissors to clip grass, and I'd better not hear about some sacrificed goldfish found dead on that carpet."

"Of course not. Giraffe and Bear will be here looking well fed and cared for because that's the magic of stories. What's happened to your imagination, Ad Man?"

Although the question was posed with a tender smile, Collin took a step toward her, which had her smile waning and she took a step back, which immediately put her against the wall. "You know perfectly well what's happened to it," he said close enough to drown in the alluring depths of her eyes.

He'd touched her. Now all he thought about was doing it until he knew every inch of her better than he knew himself, knew what gave her the most pleasure and heard her cry out for him.

"Collin, I need to get back to the girls," she whispered.

Muttering that he had to call the office, he bid a hasty retreat before he made a bigger fool of himself than he already had. As much as he wanted to keep his word to his sister that he would use this opportunity to bond more with the little ones, he couldn't do it and not fall for Sabrina.

Who are you kidding? You're halfway there already.

That left him with only one solution.

Chapter Six

"**G**ood morning, Sonny!" Sabrina said to the beaming security guard, who met them as the elevator doors opened to the building's lobby. She had called to let him know they were on their way. "Girls, this is Mr. Birdsong. He watches over everyone who lives in the building. This is Gena and this is Addison."

"Mr. Masters's nieces. It's a pleasure, ladies."

"Why do they call you a bird's song?" Addie asked, her head tilted as she gazed up at the friendly giant.

Grinning, Sonny began whistling and it did, indeed, sound like they'd just stepped into the park.

"Do you know what that is? A robin. This is a cardinal…and a bluebird."

The girls were enthralled as he duplicated each feathered creature's song.

"Can you do my friend Tassie's parakeet?" Addie asked.

"He never seen it, Addie," Gena replied before Sonny could reply.

"Besides, we can't take all of Mr. Birdsong's time," Sabrina added.

"Birdsong is too much of a name for such little ones to deal with," he told Sabrina as they crossed the lobby. "If you don't mind, let them call me Sonny like every-one does." At the front door, he bent over and rested his hands on his knees to address the girls again. His teeth were as white as his starched shirt and his security badge had a shine no less than his twinkling eyes. "You all look pretty and set for a day on the town. Where are you headed?"

It was Gena and Addie's third day at the condo and since the weather was obliging, they needed fresh air—definitely more than they were getting stepping out onto the balcony waving at pigeons. After a healthy start of oatmeal and bananas, Sabrina decided to test her mettle with the two energetic prodigies. They were dressed for a sunny day, but with temperatures not rising over sixty degrees Fahrenheit, hats and scarves were currently a necessary addition to their light jackets.

"We're going to the Dallas Farmers Market and then to that wonder-world grocery store, Central Market at Greenville and Lovers," she told Sonny. "Mr. Masters doesn't want us taking a bus so could you get us a cab?"

"I can do you one better. There's a van bringing back one of our elderly residents from a doctor's appointment at any moment. The driver's name is Gus Genovese. He's older himself, but far healthier. He'll drive you through the stalls and you can keep your purchases in the car while you shop. Gus has been taking care of people in this building for almost six years now."

"That's wonderful. He doesn't have other appointments today?"

"Nothing on the log. It's early in the season. Once the cold sets in and flu season, and church holiday and party events, you have to book further in advance. But I think for you three, he'll always make the time. Gus is a widower, a self-made man."

"He sounds like an answer to a prayer for me," Sabrina replied. "What a relief that I won't have to try to call for a ride back. Let me quickly get their car seats."

Gus turned out to be a young sixty-eight. A New Jersey transplant, he'd sold his truck refrigeration conversion business after the death of his wife Emily. With no children and too much free time on his hands, he found his independent shuttling service perfect for this stage in his life.

"You can only sit at home and watch so much TV," he explained after they got the girls settled in the second row of van seats. "My wife had the green thumb. Me, I can't grow weeds. I don't like clubs and social organizations. Seemed like whenever I walked through the front door of a place, I was being sized up by the hungry widows, or asked to attend a funeral. Don't get me wrong, I like the ladies, but it would be hard to match my Emmy, and I'm not interested in spending the rest of my life in a funeral home or cemetery. You get to a certain age, you start giving yourself permission to be particular with whom you spend your time."

"That makes sense to me." Sabrina glanced back at

Gena and Addie. "I do appreciate your help with their forward-facing car seats—and your patience."

"They're adorable kids, and very well mannered. I can see you're doing a good job with them, Mrs. Masters."

"It's Sabrina. Sabrina Sinclair. I'm the nanny."

"So, Mr. and Mrs. Masters both work in demanding fields?"

"Captain Masters, the girls' mother, just left for Afghanistan. She's a helicopter pilot."

"What is this world coming to? Bless her."

"Her brother offered to take in the girls and hired me."

"Well, you're still doing a great job. I have an eye for these things," he said touching his right index finger to his temple. "Now tell me…what are we looking for at the Farmers Market?"

Sabrina showed him her list, which included gourds and small pumpkins, and Indian corn to make a centerpiece, then vegetables for soup, some spinach and plants for a mini kitchen herb garden.

Gus was taken aback. "You're more than a nanny."

"I grew up on a Wisconsin farm. I'm handy."

"You have that fresh, wholesome look. It's very good to see. These days I run in to professional people—people who you can have an intelligent conversation with—who have no idea how to boil an egg, and can't tell you what their grandparents' names are, what they did and where they came from."

"I left the farm hoping to become a professional," Sabrina quipped.

"Nothing wrong with that," Gus said with a shake of his head. "Just don't make it all you are."

As they parked in the first barn, the girls thought the

pigeons walking between the cars had followed them from the condo. Gus patiently told them that they were "cousins." Thereafter, every bird was greeted with, "Hi, cousin! Bye, cousin!" The girls also thought that the mounted police should offer them a free ride on their "ponies," but they weren't able to charm their way into making that happen. Overall they were well behaved and enjoyed the outing.

By the time they reached the gourmet grocery store, Gus had become a friend and accompanied them inside. He pushed one basket so an exhausted Gena and Addie could ride, while Sabrina pushed another cart and did the shopping.

"You're making pasta from scratch?" Gus had noticed how she inspected different flours.

"Back in Wisconsin, we grew up eating a good deal of egg noodles," she told him. "My mom is a great cook. If you like, I'll fix you a plate and you can have it Friday if you're planning on being near the building."

"Fridays is one of the busier days, but even if it wasn't, for home cooked, I'd think up a reason. Thank you so much."

It was humbling to Sabrina that Gus wouldn't let her even tip him when they returned to the building, yet he assisted her with getting everything upstairs. And she all but teared up when he presented her with his pot of yellow chrysanthemums.

"I thought you bought them to cheer up your place, or for a friend," she told him.

"It is for a friend—three new ones who allowed me to be part of their day. I had such a *real* time, as the kids say. Here's my card and my cell-phone number is on the back. I don't give that out as a rule, but you have your hands full and I don't like the idea of you getting stranded somewhere without support. Call me anytime."

Sabrina had to kiss his cheek. "I can't tell you what that means to me. I'll tell you my story about the opposite of your kindness next trip. Safe drive home!"

"Bye, Gus!" the girls called as he headed back for the elevator.

They were yawning even as Sabrina peeled them out of their jackets. Sabrina knew they were past due for a nap, but that would give her time to unpack, get dinner and create that autumn centerpiece for the dining-room table. Collin would call if he got tied up. At least that's what she kept telling herself. But he had begun to keep his distance from her, though he was being warm and attentive to Gena and Addie.

"Will Mommy call when we wake up?" Gena asked as Sabrina finished taking off their sneakers and covering each with a blanket.

This was a question they were asking more and more. She didn't know how much longer they would accept variations of "be patient." "I can't promise, sweetheart. I know she will soon, though. Mommy had to fly far— across two oceans. She doesn't have phone service like we do until she gets to her destination."

"When Unca Colon gets home, will he read to us? He promised to finish last night's book."

"If he promised, I'd count on it."

"Hi, lover," a sultry voice cooed. "How have you been?"

Swinging his feet off his desk, Collin signaled to

Geoffrey that he needed a moment. His assistant touched his pen to his forehead and discreetly took himself and his legal pad out of the office, closing the door behind him.

"Demi...how are things in Austin?"

"They look excellent in my rearview mirror. I'll be passing through Dallas on my way to Paris—France, not North Texas—and thought I'd see how my favorite kisser was."

Although flattered, Collin knew better than to let his head get too swollen. "Alas, still second-best to Senator Barry Barrows."

"No more, you aren't. I've filed for a divorce. Enough of that pretense and heaven knows I'm fed up with backroom, front-room and bedroom lying. Are you free this evening? I'd love to have a drink and talk about old times. It's been a dry three years and I'm so thirsty for good company."

Who wouldn't jump at the chance to see Demi Taylor Barrows, the woman who dropped him for a rocket launch up the social register? There were no hard feelings; they both knew that "future" had never been in their pillow-talk vocabulary. If she wanted a night of discreet fun before she started scouting for husband number three, he was her man. Anything but clingy, she was a bachelor's dream.

Without guilt, he scratched through the charity event penciled in on his calendar and replied, "When and where?"

For maybe fifteen seconds after he hung up, he felt the old juices rising. Then Sabrina and the kids consumed his attention like a flock of birds on takeoff. He had been good since the girls' arrival. Who would it hurt if he spent a few hours with Demi instead of going to the event? Sabrina knew in her heart that he had to pull back. She had to remember that he was the wrong man to pin any hopes on. If she didn't yet, this would be a perfect nail in the coffin of their non-romance.

Feeling his independence intact, he buzzed Geoff to announce he was heading out for the day.

"You're not enjoying yourself." The raven-haired temptress stroked his thigh as she sipped her third martini, her gaze—under expensive lash implants—never wavering from his face.

If he finished his drink, he would be under the table. Getting home late was one thing. Not getting there at all—he was no longer certain he could live with himself after that.

"Too much on my mind, I'm afraid." Collin patted the hand on his leg before redirecting it her glass.

"That was my soon-to-be ex's excuse. Don't turn into that old, wet sock."

As her fingers returned to flirting with his leg and tightening subtly, Collin knew they were fast approaching the point of no return.

Demi turned his face toward hers and kissed him. She was a lethal kisser. She knew exactly how to invite and when to control. But for reasons he didn't need to voice, her ministrations were leaving him cold tonight.

With a sigh of disappointment, she leaned back. "Well, this isn't flattering at all."

"I apologize. I really shouldn't be here."

"But do you want to be?"

"The old Collin Masters would."

"You said you weren't involved." The slight edge in her voice warned that she would not take it kindly to be played for a fool.

"I'm not. It's just…complicated. A family thing."

She studied his face, looked determined for a few seconds, then sunk back against the leather seat. "I believe you, and so I'll call again…if the opportunity rises."

As soon as she slid from the booth and headed for the elevators, Collin paid the tab and strode toward the valet parking area.

It was fast approaching midnight when he eased the door shut on his condo. The usual night-light was on in the kitchen, but now that the girls were here, there was one in the hallway, too. That was why he easily spotted Sabrina sleeping on the couch.

She looked like a kid herself in her white fluffy robe, her face scrubbed and her features relaxed. Her blond hair created almost a halo of light around her head. It was soothing to just stand there and take in the peaceful scene and her gentle beauty.

"You okay?"

He didn't realize that her eyes had opened. Caught in the act, he combed back his mussed hair and belatedly wiped his mouth, concerned that Demi had left traces of her lipstick on him. "Yes. Yes, of course. Just beat. Unexpected meetings. People flying in and out in a mad dash. You have to be accommodating and drop everything."

"Then you missed the charity event?"

"Yes. As it turned out—"

"You don't owe me an explanation." Sabrina rose and

at the same time tightened the belt of her robe. "I prepared a plate if you didn't get a chance to eat. Lobster bisque soup from the market's gourmet deli, and some shrimp rolls. Just stick it all in the microwave on Reheat for—"

"I did eat. Thanks for thinking of me, though. It sounds delicious. Perhaps tomorrow." Her thoughtfulness made him feel like an even bigger rat. "How did it go with the girls?"

"They loved the outing and made a new friend. They also enjoyed Sonny's birdcalls. He's very dear. He's the one who introduced us to Gus."

"Who's Gus?"

Smoothing back her hair, she stifled a yawn. "Excuse me. The new friend we made today. Another good man, who drove us all over and helped me enormously with the girls. Anyway, despite a short nap, they were exhausted by bedtime, so they didn't fuss too much about missing you reading to them."

"I told you that I had the event."

"That you said would still be an early night."

"But then the meeting changed all that." Feeling increasingly the louse, he added, "When I saw you on the couch, I wondered if something was wrong or if one of them was ill."

"No, I wanted to be closer to the phone in case you called."

"I should have. I'm sorry."

"Like I said, no real damage done. Good night." She didn't look at him as she passed him, but at the beginning of the hallway, she stopped and glanced back. "Lovely perfume your client wears. It's good that sometimes late hours aren't all torture."

Collin opened his mouth to ask for an opportunity to explain. But to what end? So she would grasp that he'd intended to hurt her? That message had already been deeply embedded. There was no discount on hurt for an eleventh hour change of heart.

He watched her turn into her room and close her door, then sighed and started for his room. That's when he saw the dining-room table, the pumpkin, gourds, corn, flowers and candles artfully arranged to create a seasonal image of harvest and bounty. Once again Sabrina had made things beautiful and welcoming for the girls. No, he realized, for all of them.

Ripping at his tie, he headed for his bedroom. He wanted his bed and the oblivion of his sleep, but if he got what he deserved, he'd be staring at the ceiling until dawn.

"One, two, tree, four, five...now you stir, Addie. My arm hurts."

As Gena shoved the bowl of eggs toward Addie, Sabrina stood behind them ready for a quick save should anything go sliding off the kitchen counter.

"Six, seven, nine...eight, nine, ten." Addison stopped and wiped at her face. "Where's Unca Colon? I think we need help."

Sabrina used a clean towel to brush flour from the child's forehead. "We'll be fine. Besides, he's still at the office."

"He said he would be here."

Not wanting to rebuke them for creating the perfect family scenario to ease their growing separation anxiety from their mother, Sabrina took over the beating of the eggs and attempted to keep things casual. "When was that?"

"Last night," Gena said. "After he read us the story. He isn't going to be gone again tonight, is he? Is he mad because Mommy hasn't called?"

"Oh, sweetheart, not at all." Sabrina immediately hugged both girls and kissed the top of each small head. "And we've talked about this, haven't we? It's the hardest time as your mom travels to her new base because there are mountains and oceans and there's no cell-phone reception. She told us it could take a week, even two weeks."

"Dead zone," Gena said ominously. "We heard it on TV."

"I don't like dead," Addie whimpered. "I want Mommy."

Sabrina was starting to feel like crying herself. This pendulum swing had been going on all day despite her attempts to keep the girls entertained and busy. She was beginning to feel like an abject failure—and furious with Collin for promising to be here a second time and then not showing up.

"You know what?" she began brightly. "We need to sing like the seven dwarfs did when they worked. I'm going to get one of your CDs and put it in the stereo. Won't that be fun?"

They were in the chorus of the third song when the front door opened.

"Hello? I'm home!"

As the twins squealed with delight and ran to greet their uncle, Sabrina reached for the remote and turned down the volume on the stereo. She wasn't even upset with herself for getting flour on the thing; wiping it off and washing her hands gave her a chance to get her heart calmed down.

He was really here. It wasn't even 4:00 p.m. and he was here.

By the time she was drying off her hands, he was in the kitchen trying to dodge the girls' flour-covered fingers.

"Now, girls—ladies… Oh, fudge, this is going to be an expensive dry-cleaning bill." Then with a resigned sigh, he let them wrap their arms around his legs for a hug and bent to kiss each forehead. "Kiss for General, kiss for the Admiral," he droned.

They giggled and he glanced up more cautiously at Sabrina. "You needn't have used the towel. I have a little more space that's clean on my jacket sleeve." He tugged it around to show her.

"I only just learned we were expecting you."

"Is that all right?"

She exhaled shakily and pressed a hand to her diaphragm. "Oh, yes. It's been a day. You're a welcome cavalry." Behind the twins' backs, she pantomimed "phone" holding her hand to her ear with thumb and pinkie extended, and then shaking her head no and shrugging to indicate Cassidy hadn't called yet. Then she pointed to the girls and made a sad face, her fingers drawing tears down her cheeks.

"Ah." Crouching down to the little ones, he looked each in the eye. "What if I told you that I had a brief call from your mommy and she said she was going to call you just before your bedtime to hear your prayers?"

They gasped and then screamed in joy and started hopping and dancing, and clapping their hands.

Rising, Collin saw Sabrina's concerned expression. "Really," he said quietly. When he saw tears flood her eyes just before she spun away and pretended to hunt something in the far cabinets, he slipped off his jacket and stripped off his tie, and asked the girls to bring them to his room and place them on the bed. As they took off chanting, "Mommy's calling! Mommy's calling!" Collin went to stand behind Sabrina and gently took hold of her upper arms.

"I'm sorry that this has been harder than either of us anticipated. I'm sorry for everything."

Although she had stiffened at his touch, she didn't push him away. "I thought that you were going to let them down again."

"And you," he said, adding what she wouldn't. "But you see, I couldn't do that."

She turned then, brushing against him and making them so close they were almost sharing the same breath. She smiled into his eyes. He dropped his gaze to her mouth.

"Unca Colon, we almost made 'sketty without you!"

As the girls came dancing back into the kitchen, Collin closed his eyes and groaned softly in agony. Then he smiled regretfully at Sabrina, who uttered a breathless laugh.

"It's not 'sketty," Gena lectured her sister. "It's noodles. Are you really gonna wear a apron like us and help?"

Unbuttoning his shirt cuffs, he rolled up his sleeves and with sheer bravado declared, "Are you kidding? Look at this equipment. We guys love gadgets and gizmos." To Sabrina he shrugged as though saying, "What the heck is this stuff?"

"I hope you don't mind that I invested in a pasta machine."

"Certainly not. If it irons ties, I may use it myself."

The girls giggled.

"Do you have a spare towel that I can use as an apron?"

Sabrina pointed to a drawer and he helped himself, tucking the terry cloth into the waistband of his slacks. Then he rubbed his hands together. "Where do we start?"

"Well, we have one batch ready to be fed into the press, and I was going to make a second batch for Gus," she said.

"I have heard that name before."

"He gave Bwina flowers," Gena offered in a sing-song voice.

"The flowers in that beautiful centerpiece on the dining-room table?" He slid a mischievous glance at Sabrina, but said to the girls, "I don't like them anymore."

Despite her smile and the girls' giggles, Sabrina said, "Don't. He's sixty-eight and a sweet man. He's a widower."

"Old," Gena said nodding.

"Yes, but I happen to know she once liked an older guy," Collin commented.

Gena looked concerned while Addison thought that was hilarious. To Collin's relief, Sabrina took it all with good humor.

"What can I say? I just don't have any sense."

"Is Gus older than you?" Gena asked him.

This time Sabrina burst out laughing, which had both girls going again. Collin grabbed one under each arm and spun them around and around. "Stop laughing at me or I'll go faster and faster until we fly out of this building!"

They screamed, "Do it! Do it!"

"So much for intimidation," he said to Sabrina. "They're definitely a pilot's daughters."

Their comfortable atmosphere extended through dinner. Sabrina earned high praise in the form of clean plates and requests for seconds of the beef medallions and baby carrots she used to round out the meal. Afterward, Collin suggested he clean up the kitchen while she gave the girls their baths.

The girls were tucked into bed ready to listen to him read to them when the phone rang. He'd brought one of the remotes from the living room so they could catch the call right away.

Sabrina watched from the doorway and whether it was exhaustion or the relief and joy that the girls were getting this contact with the person they loved and needed most in the world, she unashamedly let the tears course down her cheeks. She saw that even Collin had to blink several times when toward the end of their conversation, they scrambled from under the covers to recite their prayers. Sabrina couldn't take anymore and went to get tissues and then get out of earshot.

Several minutes later, Collin joined her.

"Would you like a glass of wine or brandy?" he asked.

"Nothing for me, thanks. I don't think I'll have any trouble sleeping after I turn in."

"The kids are already asleep," he said. "As soon as they blew kisses to Cassie, and I disconnected, they were out."

Sabrina sighed her relief, but added, "She timed this perfectly. I was at my wit's end trying to reassure and entertain them."

"Cass sends her love and thanks you again."

"You didn't tell her that I was upset and anxious, did you?"

"Absolutely not. It wouldn't be fair to either of you." He sat down on the opposite side of the couch. "She's had a tough time of it, too. There's been rough weather—snow already—and she had no heat in her quarters until just awhile ago."

"Awful."

"She said she should have her e-mail account set up by tomorrow and should be able to call twice a week and e-mail every day. I'll put the laptop I use here in the kitchen on the bar, so you can download whenever you want and the girls can sit with you and participate."

Shifting to sit sideways and tucking her feet beside her, Sabrina hugged a pillow to her. "Thank you. That will be fun. I've never done chat-room type stuff, but I can see where it would be helpful for all of us. Don't you know letting the girls have a go at the keyboard and sending that on as a message to her would be hysterical?"

Collin smiled. "Knowing Gena, she can type better than she can speak."

More softly she continued, "Thank you for coming home early tonight, too."

"I'm glad I could. I'll do it every day that I'm able."

"That's not necessary. That's why I'm here."

"Originally. But things change."

Sabrina had come through the dinner preparations cleaner than any of them and her white tunic top and slim jeans and socks looked just as fresh as when she'd put them on this morning. The only change was that she'd released her ponytail and brushed her hair to fall in a glossy cape around her shoulders—and that she was visibly tired. Beautiful, but worn out.

As she rocked her head side to side as though fighting a kink, he reached out his hand. "Would you do me one great favor? Turn around and sit here so I can rub your shoulders?"

"You've got to be tired, too."

"Nothing like you. Come on."

After only a slight hesitation, she made the shift.

Collin swept her hair over her right shoulder enjoying the softness of it against his skin. He then began massaging either side of her neck, while his thumbs gently worked her spine. Slowly, he worked his hands toward her shoulders, then back again. "You're almost a rock of tension."

"That's what everyone always says when they work on you so you feel obligated to tell them they did a good job."

"I'm not?"

"I'm going to fall off this couch like a wet rag when you stop."

Smiling, Collin worked up her neck. "Cassie asked me a question that had me thinking."

"What did she ask?"

"She wanted to know what we were doing for Thanksgiving. Did you make plans already?"

"It's still two weeks away."

"Well, you cook so much already, wouldn't you like a day to be pampered like everyone else?" She stiffened despite his ministrations. "What?"

"You're not thinking of sending me home for the holiday after all?"

He would rather jump off a diving board into six

inches of water. "I thought the four of us could go somewhere. They're quite well behaved—when they're not insulting their *old* uncle—and I've heard chatter at the office that there are some nice hotel buffets in the Metroplex and virtually all of them welcome children. Marvelous feasts with entertainment and elaborate spreads."

"I know exactly what you're talking about. Shortly after—"

"Don't turn around," Collin ordered as her animated personality kicked into gear. "Let me work."

"I was just going to say that shortly after I moved here, I salivated over the ads in the Dallas newspaper listing the menus and descriptions of ice and chocolate sculptures, and the photos of man-size flower arrangements, and inside gardens. I believe that was for Easter. You're willing to indulge the girls like that?"

"If you think they'd enjoy it? Not be bored and squirm and refuse to eat?"

Sabrina chuckled. "You saw their appetite at dinner. That is generous and thoughtful. The girls will be over-the-moon happy. Should I look into making reservations?"

"If you don't mind, I'd like to handle that. This way you get a surprise, too."

"Since I've never been, that would be plenty of a surprise."

"You'll have your hands full making sure the girls have new outfits for the occasion." This time instead of kneading or massaging, he stroked his hands up and down her arms. "I'd like you to choose something for yourself, as well. You know the drawer in my desk where I leave my card."

She went very still, but didn't try to face him. "You pay me well, Collin. I can buy my own dress."

The words came quietly and without resentment costing him a moment to realize what she was thinking. Sighing, he said, "Why is it that everywhere you go when someone performs a service, they expect some gratuity, even where salaries are decent? But you won't let me do anything nice for you and you work as hard, maybe harder than most."

There was no stopping her from turning then to face him, and while he was relieved he didn't see anger or resentment in her expression, he didn't see acceptance of his argument, either.

"That's because it would make me feel like—"

"A mistress? I wish you were my mistress," he muttered, a little annoyed at getting trapped between his good intentions and his history. "I'd enjoy playing dress up with you as much as Gena and Addie do their dolls. But you're my employee and fast becoming my best friend, and I guess I'm not allowed to make your life a little more pleasant for fear of offending the 'politically correct' police."

Her startled expression quickly evolved into a blooming of happiness, and she murmured, "Oh."

Oh? "I'm more brutally honest than I've ever been with anyone before and you say, 'Oh?' Come here, you little brain freeze." He swept her across his lap as easily as he would a pillow and rested her in the cradle of his crossed legs and the crook of his arm. "Now what do you have to say, Ms. Understatement?"

"Only that you have an unusual perspective on relationships."

"It's your fault."

"If you're going to be an eccentric, at least wear the mantle with pride and own up to it."

"I'd rather you finish driving me crazy."

Lifting her to him, he surrendered his sanity and sought her mouth for a homecoming where he was reconnected with the missing parts of himself. It was still foreign to him and so he could not trust it completely, this completion that she brought, yet he ached for it more than he'd lusted after anything. That again told him how much he trusted Sabrina, and trusting made the rest better.

When she slid her arms around his neck, he tightened his and breathed her in. Touching her was a panacea, as he'd already proven while trying to ease the kinks out from a day of hauling kids around and picking up after them. But he restrained himself from going too far. The drapes weren't pulled and one of the twins could wander out here at any moment. Still, he couldn't quite let her go before he brushed the backs of his fingers across her breast.

Her soft gasp into his mouth was his reward and he pressed his lips against the side of her neck and let her lead his hand back to do what she needed.

"That's not much of a bra for a responsive woman," he murmured feeling her become a hard pebble ready for his mouth. "I think you may need more shirts with double pockets."

"This isn't generally a problem unless I'm around you."

Groaning he kissed her a little harder and then put her back on the other side of the couch. "Who said confession is good for the soul?" Grimacing as he sat forward and leaned his elbows on his knees, he asked, "As soon as I'm able to get up without aching, I'm going to bed. Are we okay?"

"Yes."

"I'll make the reservations tomorrow."

"It would probably be more fun to keep it as a surprise for the kids."

"I agree." He caressed her with his eyes. "Are you going to be going out anywhere?"

"My best friend wants holiday clothes for his nieces."

"Would you like to go out solo after I get home and search for your own outfit?"

"You're offering to sit with the girls?"

"That's what friends are for."

Chapter Seven

On Thanksgiving, Sabrina and the twins learned that Collin had arranged for them to go to the Gaylord Texan Resort on Lake Grapevine just north of DFW Airport. November in Texas could bring a pendulum swing of weather—from thunder snow to rose-blooming conditions. Today it was partly cloudy with just enough of a chill in the air to feel seasonal, and neither Sabrina, nor her "party of four" was disappointed.

The resort was a sprawling series of structures that featured a giant atrium in the hotel that routinely was turned into a nature walk for adults and a child's wonderland, the decorations depending on the holiday. Interspersed between the several restaurants scattered along a man-made creek made to resemble the San Antonio River Walk, there were walking paths to enjoy a splendid view of all the offerings. For this holiday the atrium was surrounded by thousands of autumn flowers from chrysanthemums to pansies to begonias. A giant train set was hooked up to run beneath shrubs and around trees, under walkways, and through candy-decorated mountains. Everywhere else there were ducks and ducklings, ponds and fountains, flowers and statuary both romantic and comic, plus music. Music tweaked ambiance at almost every corner.

The girls were openmouthed with wonder upon entering, and were soon pointing and scampering not to miss a thing. Sabrina thought they looked adorable in their velvet dresses with starched lace collars. Gena had chosen a red one for herself. Addison requested and found a deep blue. Sabrina had picked up a little black number for herself during the evening shopping sprint Collin offered; very simple and demure since it was long sleeved and ran to the knee. But it delineated every asset, something that had Collin staying ultra close.

The girls wanted to tour more of the gardens, but their reservations were for noon, which was only ten minutes away. Sabrina took Addie by the hand and Collin escorted Gena. The girls' complaints soon petered out at the opportunity of going up escalators and the assurance that today they would be tasting their first Shirley Temple.

The hostess who signed them in asked if they needed booster seats.

"No, thank you," Gena announced. "We older than we look."

"And we learned manners," Addison stated, leveling

a look at the young woman as though challenging a contradiction.

Collin leaned over to Sabrina and murmured, "Imagine the attitude when they think they can order their first cosmo." To the laughing hostess, he confided, "They're actually forty-year-old laboratory escapees we picked up hitchhiking their way to the 2024 Olympics.

Sabrina wasn't sure whether that or his name won them a nicely placed table close to the dessert display, but the twins were ecstatic.

"Doesn't she realize that by the time we leave, the kids will require chocolate detoxification?" Collin whispered to her.

It wasn't quite that bad. The chocolate fountain had the girls begging to skip turkey and head for it right away. But with some assurances that there would be plenty for everyone, they did eat a balanced meal.

"I can't get over the ice sculptures," Sabrina told him as they sat back with the last of their champagne and waited on the girls to finish their desserts. She'd counted no less than ten, everything from turkeys and Indian heads, to baskets with handles filled with fresh fruit to swans to penguins. "This was such a treat, thank you."

"You're having as much fun as Gena and Addie."

She had to ask. "Aren't you?"

"I'm enjoying being with three of my four best girls."

He looked so handsome in his gray suit that brought out some of the silver in his gray eyes. She'd never seen it on him before and concluded that he, too, had seen this as an occasion to add to his wardrobe. "Speaking of Cassie, do you think one of the waiters would take a few pictures of us so we can e-mail them to her? She'd love seeing the girls in their outfits."

An attendant quickly recognized what she wanted and came to assist. He had just finished a third photo when a distinguished man with black hair and silver sideburns stopped beside the photographer.

"Masters. It is you."

Sabrina could see that Collin looked practically stricken for a moment, but to his credit he recovered quickly.

Indicating to the photographer that they were done with the picture taking, he rose and circled the table to shake hands with the equally tall and trim man. "Lloyd. Happy Thanksgiving. Are you here with your family?"

"A fair portion." He indicated a large table with at least a dozen people seated around it. "I didn't realize— You *have* a family?"

Clearing his throat, Collin began, "May I introduce Sabrina Sinclair, and these are my two nieces, Gena and Addison. They're staying with me while their mother, my sister, is serving in Afghanistan. Ladies, this is a longtime client, Mr. Lloyd Royston."

"Happy Thanksgiving, Mr. Royston," Sabrina said.

"Curious," Royston said as he studied her. "Have we met?"

She was about to remind him when and where, until she noticed Collin's barely perceptible frown and negative shake. "No," she said dropping her voice an octave, and cooling her smile to where it didn't reach her eyes—very unlike the sunny assistant to Collin Masters. "I don't believe I've had the pleasure."

Before Collin's client could say anything else, Addie yelped and clapped her hand to her mouth. For a few seconds her eyes were wide and bright with anguish. Then she looked at her bloody hand and gasped. "Let's go! I need a Sleeping Beauty Band-Aid!"

They couldn't have dreamed up a better distraction. Sabrina quickly dug out a tissue from her bag and wet it in the glass of drinking water and dabbed at the bit of bleeding on the child's lip and gum. "Collin, we should probably get her home before she bleeds on her dress."

"Right." He shook hands again with Lloyd and, murmuring a quick "Sorry," scooped up an anxious Addie, then ushered Sabrina and Gena out of the ballroom.

"Call me!" Lloyd Royston directed behind them.

"Are you okay?" Sabrina asked Collin once they were at the bottom of the escalator on the lobby level.

Collin kissed Addison between her eyes and put her back on her feet. "I am now. Thank you for catching on so quickly." Taking Addie's hand, he started urging them toward the valet area.

"You're welcome, but do I get to know why that was important?"

Addison braked to stare aghast at the marble floor. "My shoe fell off!"

"His divorced daughter," Collin said patting his pockets. "Whom you were blessed never to meet. He thinks she needs a husband." Handing Sabrina a neatly folded handkerchief, he crouched to help Addie slide back into her shoe.

Sabrina quickly dabbed a bit of blood from the child's lip. "Sweetie, just hold this handkerchief there." Then to Collin, she continued, "Doesn't she?"

"Not when her ex is in *the business*," he all but whispered.

"What business?" she whispered back.

"*The* business. And to add to her appeal as a prospective bride, *she* wanted the divorce, he didn't. Yet Lloyd thinks I'm the answer to his problem—and if he succeeds, he feels he would deserve a discount on his ad campaigns with the firm."

Pursing her lips, Sabrina nodded. "He spends a great deal of money with you."

Collin looked like he'd just heard bad health news. "It would hurt to lose him...almost as much as becoming shark bait."

"So you have your solution."

"I do. I do?"

Sabrina shrugged. "Give him the discount. Find someone else for the daughter."

"What kind of intern thinking was that?" Collin chided as they continued into the atrium. "You may recall that it's Lloyd's account that pays for my new Mercedes every year. The discount is almost equal to the car lease."

"All right...picture next year's model...and your daily dread whenever you get behind the wheel and key the ignition."

As Collin gulped, Sabrina paused as Addie stopped to coo into a dovecote. She beamed over at him. "They're going to remember this for the rest of their lives."

By the time the resort was in his rearview mirror, Collin had regained his sense of humor. "This went so well, we should talk about Christmas."

Sabrina chuckled. "Sorry for teasing you so horribly."

He reached across to squeeze her hand. "That was

actually quite an astute business decision. How are you doing back there, Addie?"

"I want to tell Mommy about the blood."

"Oh, yes. That's the first thing she wants to hear. Since you've already talked to her today, we can e-mail her a picture of us at lunch and inform her that the bleeding has stopped."

"What are we gonna do now?" Gena asked.

"Go home and watch the Cowboy game while you and your sister nap. Your uncle has a commercial or two running during the show."

"Can we watch? I'm not sleepy," Gena replied.

"I am," Addie countered. "I want my money."

When she faked a big yawn, Collin laughed. "You little mercenary. You didn't lose a tooth. You bit the inside of your mouth. Besides, the sandman doesn't visit until it's dark. Sunshine hurts his eyes."

"It's getting cloudier, Addie," Gena told her sister, patting her hand. "Don't worry."

Shaking his head, Collin glanced at Sabrina again. "Cloudy or not, you still look radiant today."

Mischief lit her eyes. "A man even remotely contemplating an engagement of convenience should not be flirting—even with his best friend."

"We'll stay away from buffets for Christmas. Less of a chance of running into Machiavellian clients."

"I'm going to ask Gus to go with us to see a matinee of *The Nutcracker.* It's a shorter performance for little ones their ages who can't sit through the whole production."

Despite her protests and disclaimers, Collin thought he was hearing far too much of Gus lately. "What's wrong with me?"

"*The Nutcracker,* Collin. Droves of screaming, chattering children and starving mothers on the edge of low blood sugar. That's hardly something you'd enjoy."

"And Gus would?"

"He'd be pleased to help me with the girls and pretend for awhile that he has grandchildren."

"If he wants grandkids, I can introduce him to Lloyd's daughter." At Sabrina's gasp and disapproval he reasoned, "They're my nieces. I'll take you to the play."

Once upstairs in the condo, Collin went to change and Sabrina put the girls in sleepers. Afterward, he helped her bring blankets and a few board games to the living room. He already had the TV on to the pregame show, although he kept the sound down to where he could follow what was going on when he wanted to.

"You all choose a game," Sabrina told the girls, "and I'll be right back after I change."

"Must you?" Collin said looking up at her beseechingly as he stroked her calf. He could envision her seated beside him with her skirt slipping higher on her thighs.

"Behave," she murmured. "And keep an eye on Addie in case the wound reopens."

She was back in less than five minutes wearing a scoop-necked peasant shirt over the black leggings he remembered so fondly from their trip to San Antonio. The only downside to the situation was that she settled in between the girls.

"I'm taking that as an act of aggression," he told her.

"Don't bother with the sad puppy eyes," she replied. "This way you can help Gena and I'll help Addie."

"This is Parcheesi," Addie declared, although pronouncing it "Paw-cheesy. "I know my numbers that high."

"You're still going down, young lady," Collin promised.

Collin had two of his men safe when the football game started. He wasn't an avid fan of football or any sport, but he kept up with all of them because he never knew where his clientele were coming from or what their interests were. Today's game was relatively interesting, but not enough to keep his gaze from drifting to Sabrina as she split her time between both girls. He admired how she could go from sophisticated young woman at the resort to fellow playmate for the girls. She was far more well-balanced than he was, mature, but in touch with her inner child. Too often he'd let his inner child control the adult—especially when reality bit.

"Bwina, are we gonna make Christmas cookies like we made pasta?" Gena asked. They'd all stopped to watch the commercial featuring gifts that add to the holidays' traditions.

"Not with the same machine, but absolutely we will. All kinds of cookies."

"Can we send some to Mommy? I don't think she is having Christmas this year."

"What a wonderful idea. We'd better get started tomorrow so that she gets them in time."

Addie frowned. "If we do everything early, we won't have anything fun left to do by Christmas."

Sabrina winked at Collin and replied, "Oh, you'd be surprised how much there is to do. There are plays and photographs to take with Santa, and going for drives at night to look at Christmas lights…."

"Can we go to the Norf Pole? We never seen snow before."

"Yes, we did," the ever worldly Gena replied.

"Uh-uh."

Gena rolled her eyes. "How do you think Mommy could buy you that snow cone?"

Addie's face lit up and she gushed to Sabrina, "My tongue turned blue!"

"Mine was pink."

Before the end of the fourth quarter, the girls ran out of fuel and curled up in their blankets and fell asleep. Turning down the sound on the TV a bit, Collin suggested they get them to their beds.

"You handle turning down the covers and getting the night-lights," he said, easing Gena into his arms. "I'll come back for Addie."

Once they returned to the living room, Collin went to the computer, while Sabrina closed the draperies and folded the blankets, which she returned to the closet on his side of the condo. As she cleaned up the last board game they'd been playing, she heard the printer running. By the time she returned from the children's bedroom, Collin was waiting for her on the couch.

Between two glasses of wine that he'd poured them was a sheet of paper. The set up looked almost celebratory, except for his somber expression.

"What's wrong?"

"Cassidy answered the e-mail we'd sent earlier telling her about Addie. She went on her first rescue mission today."

No wonder he looked so troubled. "Is she all right?"

"Yeah. They got their guys, but they took small arms fire."

"Oh, no!"

As he reached for his glass and took a long sip, Sabrina sat down beside him and laid her hand on his knee. "You're sure she's not hiding something from you?"

He nodded to the e-mail. "Read it."

Not sure she was ready for this, she took up the sheet of paper.

Hey Bro,
Sending this separate of Addie's news. Please keep the kids from reading it. Had our first mission this afternoon. First things first—all is well. A convoy came under attack. A couple of Apaches settled the matter, then we were sent in to pick up the survivors. That's when someone in the bad guys' wreckage took a couple of shots at us. My baby has extra air-conditioning, but she can still fly with the best of 'em.
Sorry if I still sound a little too pumped. The adrenaline hasn't worn off.
XO for the pix. I can't stop looking at the girls. They've already grown! Tell Sabrina she looks hot and that I hope that drives you nuts.
Miss you, English!
Love,
Me

Sabrina put down the paper and exhaled shakily. "It's like in a movie. I can't believe she sounds as collected as she does." Sabrina stroked Collin's back. "No wonder you're so pale."

"Her first time out." Collin turned to her, but his stare was inward. "If this is what happens the first time out—how could I have been so stupid as to let her go?"

"It wasn't your decision to make," she reminded him. "She's her own person and she's well trained and strong. She's proven that to you yet again. Frankly, I think it's wonderful how close you are and that she's willing to share even this much with you."

"I don't want to hear it," he ground out. "And I don't want to hear the glass-half-full crap, either."

He didn't mean to hurt her, Sabrina knew that. Still the sting was there. "You want to be alone. I understand."

"No!" As she rose, he reached for her and buried his face in her womb. "I'm sorry. That was fear and anger talking. She's the only good thing to come from my family and she has no right to do this to me, or her girls."

Sabrina stroked his hair and tried to understand his perspective. It was a fair one, but it wasn't the only legitimate one. "Some people feel a higher calling," she said simply. "Don't you grasp that she would never have left if she didn't think you were at least as good parent material as she is?"

Uttering an indecipherable oath, he said, "More misguided faith. Her last mistake was her friend the sperm donor."

"Thickheaded man." Sabrina shoved him against the couch and moved the wine and e-mail aside to sit down on the coffee table so that they were face-to-face. "I want you to tell me what your parents did aside from being self-absorbed narcissists who could only manage to love each other—and didn't succeed *there* with grace—to make you unwilling to meet the world on any other terms except 'Life's a joke and then you die'?"

"I think this evening has been fun enough without dredging up them."

"I deserve to know."

"How so?"

"Your conduct." She pointed to herself with her thumb. "You made me part of this neo-Greek drama. You didn't invite me in via seduction, you bamboozled me, and then you started to seduce me. Ever since, you've made it a challenge to live up to my own standards."

"I thought I was the one being seduced. Wait a minute." Collin shook his head. "Who says *bamboozled?*"

"It's a legitimate word." She clutched her head. "You make my world feel like I've been thrust into a boxing ring. There I was thrust against one rope, then you bounce me to another, then I'm in a clench…what's next? I'm flat on my back and out for the count?"

His expression said that he'd lost her back with "bamboozled." "Somehow the name Sabrina and boxing don't gel. "You like boxing?"

"I hate boxing. But growing up it was on our TV all the time. Besides that, men outnumbered women two-to-one in our household, and that many men under one roof creates its own dramas. Certain images become the metaphors of our lives."

"Maybe we should be discussing your childhood."

"You're the subject at hand," she said into her goblet.

Disgruntled, he dismissed her argument. "Well, what you're claiming isn't accurate. Granted I needed your help, and your misfortune created the opportunity for me to—"

"Take advantage."

He leaned forward. "I tried to protect you. But like Cass, you're too brave for your own good." His gaze grew caressing. "And you've stayed."

Laughing throatily, Sabrina reached for her wine. After a needful sip, she pointed at him with the glass. "You are a piece of work, you know that? I get it now. You're walking no-fault insurance."

He looked taken aback. "No. I'm live-and-let-live."

"If that's true, don't be afraid to let Cassidy do what she does. She's good at it."

Collin slumped back against the leather couch and looked away. After a few seconds, he slid her a sideways glance. "Did we just have a fight?"

"There were no raised voices."

Collin put down his wine and took her glass, as well. Reaching for her hands, he said, "Good. Because that's not how I want to spend the rest of our Thanksgiving." Touching his lips to each of her palms, he drew her closer to straddle his lap.

Although she didn't resist, Sabrina slid a concerned glance toward the hallway. "Even clothed, this is inappropriate."

He directed her hands to his chest. "How do you do that? Go from caretaker, to vulnerable child, to temptress, to woman warrior in the span of a few sentences?"

"My opponent is no slouch."

"Best friend," he amended.

"Slightly warped friend, but worthy of my flexibility."

With his hand at her nape, he drew her in for the kiss that had been building all day. "Heal me."

Chapter Eight

The countdown to Christmas soon felt more like time trials at the Indy 500, but Sabrina loved every minute. She hoped that time was being equally kind to Cassidy.

As promised, she and the girls started baking the day after Thanksgiving and by the following Monday, when Collin's cleaning lady, Graziella, arrived for her usual duties, she brought along an offering from her kitchen.

Sabrina had been worried about how she would be viewed by the older woman. All of the clichés and stereotypes regarding females in the workplace lay heavy on her mind the first day of their meeting. But except for one finger-in-the-face directive that "Mr. C must always be happy," Graziella soon embraced her…and she adored the girls.

Nevertheless, Sabrina was no ingenue and was wise

to the long-held perspective elders often had that they always knew better. So when Graziella arrived with daughter Isabella in tow and announced that Isabella would take the children to the park, Sabrina knew she had a challenge on her hands.

"We already have our day scheduled," Sabrina explained.

"But first I explain and you write down the story and recipes of these cookies for Miss Cassie's Christmas box," Graziella directed.

"Oh, boy," Sabrina replied with an uncomfortable little laugh. "Graziella, first of all, if we take the time to do that, Cassie's box will arrive a month after she's already back in San Antonio. Second—nothing personal, Isabella—I'm not letting those children out of my sight."

"But Mr. C know my Isabella," the diminutive woman said as she removed her coat and placed it and her purse on the nearest kitchen bar stool. "Is okay."

"Is not okay. Is sounding okay to you maybe, but Collin did not tell me anything about this, so with all due respect, it's not happening. Add to that, as soon as we get your cookies in this box, I'm out of here. I have just enough time to get to the post office before the girls' appointments for haircuts. That's per their mother's orders. See? I have my orders. Then it's on to pictures with Santa. Understand? Full day."

Graziella said something to Isabella in Spanish that had the quietly pretty girl gasping then covering her mouth in a giggle. It took all of Sabrina's restraint not to give Mama Mia an earful of what she thought when people spoke about someone in a foreign language—

unless you were sitting in a police station. Ready to dial Collin at the office, Graziella opened her plump arms wide and laughingly declared, "You pass!"

Pass what? Sabrina wondered.

After a bosom-to-bosom hug by the little mama bear, Graziella explained. "I have to be sure."

"About your cookies? Cross my heart as a former FFA student. I will get your cookies packed with the utmost care and Cassidy will relish them—and share with her squadron."

"No." The cleaning lady touched her palm. "I have to be sure everything is as Mr. C say. I see you very good here with the babies, but I don't can see you outside. Now I no have to worry for Mr. C to not get hurt."

Tempted to call Collin so he could inform his cleaning lady that it was not in Graziella's job description to review *or* police her, Sabrina checked herself. Yes, the woman was an unabashed meddler, but her intentions were good.

"I'm glad we're on the same page," she told her. "You know what? I am running behind now. Why don't you put the cookies you want in the box, and I'll go get the twins' jackets on."

When they left the condo, relieved of her duty, Isabella accompanied them for the ride down the elevator. She was the same height as Sabrina with gorgeous wavy hair the color of licorice. Her equally dark eyes were kind and her smile was shy as she peeked at Sabrina from under her dark lashes.

"Please, Miss Sabrina, excuse Mama. She was half grown before she moved to this country and her ways are old-fashioned."

"I understand people set in their ways," Sabrina replied with a wry laugh. "Are you going to visit with Sonny while your mother works?"

Startled, Isabella then appeared embarrassed. "No. I would get in trouble."

"Why? I thought your mother approved of Sonny."

"She does. But first Sonny has to present himself to my family and ask permission from my father."

"Permission to marry? I didn't realize things had gotten that far."

"Permission to date."

"How old are you?"

"Twenty-one."

Sabrina banged her head lightly against the elevator car wall. How could it be that the more things changed, others almost regressed? With her irrepressible independent spirit stirred, Sabrina said casually, "Sonny is great, isn't he, girls?"

"Yeah!" they cheered in unison.

"He gives us piggyback rides up the elevator," Addie said.

"He can whistle anything in the universe," Gena added. "Even real bird music."

Isabella's smile radiated young love. "He sang a lullaby in church. It was so beautiful, I cried."

"You belong to the same church? Then what's stopping him from speaking to your father?"

"Sonny respects tradition, but he wants to know I will be a strong woman of this century. He believes in asking for a girl's hand in marriage, but the decision to date should be our own."

As the elevator doors opened, Sonny was there to

greet them. His eyes widened with surprise and pleasure as he spotted Isabella with them.

"We're running late, Sonny, so I see Gus out there and Isabella needed to talk to you. Go ahead and take care of her and we'll be on our way. Have a good morning!"

Once they were outside, Gus greeted the girls with hugs and got them into the seats that he now kept in his van. "Something wrong with Sonny?" he asked Sabrina.

"I told him that we were fine and he should talk to Graziella's daughter Isabella."

"Ah. I know a bit about that story."

"It's a shame that they're wasting time."

"Knowing you, you've just helped things move along."

On Wednesday, Collin accompanied Sabrina and the twins to the matinee of *The Nutcracker.* He didn't doubt it would be as torturous as waxing was for women, but he really wanted the twins to know he was more than an evening uncle, and to convince Sabrina that he'd heard what she'd said on Thanksgiving and was trying to take it to heart.

The audience was everything she had warned it would be when she tried to give him an out—a mix of kids in need of their ADD medication to little wannabe actors and dancers with just enough training to have an attitude. As for the adults, he saw that he was, indeed, one of the few males not on Social Security. More disconcerting was how many of the women looked like second-string Stepford Wives, or the eternal cheerleader. One or two gave him such a thorough going-over that it prompted him to slouch in his seat, which had Sabrina struggling not to lose herself in giggles. Fortunately, they were among the last to get to their seats and the theater lights soon dimmed.

"I've never been so grateful for darkness in my life," he whispered as the curtain rose.

A little over an hour later it was over and they were caught up in the mass exodus of people searching for their cars. Enraptured by what they'd witnessed, Gena and Addie danced, pranced and twirled all the way.

"Look at that. Isn't that sweet?" Sabrina indicated as they walked behind them.

"Yes, dresses and tights instead of jammies makes all of the difference."

"Grump." But Sabrina still linked her arm through his. "Thank you for taking the time. Now they'll always say, 'My uncle Collin introduced me to the ballet,'" she said, using his British accent.

"Kind of you to enunciate. There may be three or four people left in the vicinity who haven't heard them mispronounce my name." Despite the sarcasm, he covered her hand with his to keep her close. He liked the feel of her there, liked that her breast pushed against his arm, covered as it was by a red Chanel-style suit and matching shawl. "I'm speechless and proud at how well behaved they were. Does Cassie know she has two untapped fortunes there—if etiquette and manners ever come back in style?"

"Stop. With that many children, you have to expect a little misbehavior." As Gena almost managed a respectable arabesque, Sabrina cheered. "I was four times that age when I saw my first production of this ballet…and I acted just as spellbound."

"I'd bet a thousand dollars that your father didn't accompany your mother."

"Easy win. Mother didn't go, either. A teacher took four of us who showed a glimmer of interest in the performing arts. Small town, small school, small talent."

Her wistful tone drew his attention. "That's not self-deprecating humor, that's masochism."

"It's the truth. I followed orders and got the business degree, so I could always 'pay the rent.' Oops. Kinda messed up there, didn't I?" She burst into laughter.

Collin didn't like the undercurrent of shame that he heard in her voice. Did that still bother her? What happened wasn't her fault—except for having placed her trust unwisely. Was it pressure back home that made her so hard on herself? She didn't call Wisconsin. Not that he could see by his phone bill. If she had called on her cell phone, it wasn't when he was there.

Not wanting her to lose the joy he'd seen on her face during the ballet, he had a brainstorm. Once they had the girls secure in back, he said, "I'm starving. Is anyone else hungry?"

"Me!" the girls screamed in unison.

He looked over at Sabrina. "Let's go to the Cheesecake Factory and splurge."

The girls squealed in delight.

"You don't need to do that," Sabrina told him. "I'm taking them ice skating with Gus the day after tomorrow. That's quite a bit of treats for a week. If we return them spoiled to Cassie—"

"She'll reconsider continuing her military career so I never get to have them again?" When Sabrina's only response was to look out the passenger window, he dropped the droll humor. "Going with Gus again, huh?"

"You won't be available Friday."

So she did remember when the firm's office party was held. He hadn't asked her to come, and of course he couldn't. Okay, wouldn't, although sometimes a spouse or significant other did attend if the couple were heading somewhere right afterward. The thing was that no one knew she was helping with the children except Geoff, and Collin preferred it to stay that way. Speculation about his personal life was bad enough without providing the bait for a feeding frenzy, especially if it got out that she was actually living under his roof. Besides, who would watch the girls?

Still something nagged at him. At a traffic light, Collin turned to her. "You're not angry, are you?"

"Nope."

"Hurt?"

"I'm not an employee of the firm," she said matter-of-factly. "And not having to see old what's-his-name again is a gift."

"Hurt that I didn't bring up the party myself. I was hoping you'd forget the date and therefore not worry."

"I'm not worried, Collin. I know exactly what I am and where I stand in all this."

Thankfully the light turned green forcing him to concentrate on the road. But part of his mind replayed that conversation all over again, and after he did, he still didn't understand what the heck he'd missed.

A pallor fell over the intended mini-party at the restaurant. The girls didn't know it because he and Sabrina made a point to be cheerful and keep them entertained, but Sabrina did everything but strike up a conversation with the people dining on either side of them to avoid speaking to him. And she refused to meet his gaze. Heaven knows he tried.

By the time they returned home, his neck ached from the strain of not reaching for her and shaking her until she explained what he'd done wrong. He didn't need her to forgive him—well, not yet, he amended—he just needed the pressure relief of knowing.

Determined to get to the bottom of things, he paced and waited, removed his jacket and tie, and waited. He waited long enough for Sabrina to get the girls out of their velvet holiday dresses and changed into their play clothes before appearing at the doorway of their room.

"Is that what you want to play with, Gena?" Sabrina asked as the child took a doll out of the closet. "Your Ballerina Barbie? What about you, Addie?"

"I want to draw the dancers to send to Mommy."

"Oh, she will love seeing that. Okay then, and I'm going to change now and do a few chores."

"But first Uncle Collin needs to talk to Brina," Collin said stepping into the room to take her wrist before she could sneak by him. "Play nice. We'll be back in a few minutes."

"Okay," they chimed, already engrossed in their fantasy world.

Sabrina resisted his hold, but didn't say a word until they were in the living room and clearly heading for his bedroom. In her high heels, she had to take three steps to every one of his to keep up.

"Let me go!" she finally whispered, furious. "I am not going in there with you."

But she did because he knew she didn't want a scene in front of the children. Collin had bet on that. He also knew he'd pay a price for it, and the cost was her fury when he shut the door behind them.

Although she didn't raise her voice, it and her hand shook as she demanded, "Let me out of here."

Leaning back against the door, Collin crossed his arms. "As soon as we clear this up. Now what's wrong? Don't say 'nothing' because I may be male and hopeless, but I know that in Womanese 'nothing' always means something. You said you understood about the party and my reason for not telling you. Granted, I copped out by trying to get through the day by omission. I know your memory is too good for that to have worked."

Standing in the middle of the room, her own arms crossed, Sabrina shook her head. "You aren't from Mars. I doubt you belong in this solar system."

He might have laughed if she'd looked slightly amused. Rueful would have been a consolation prize. However, the knowledge that he was way off course had his heart getting splinters as it fell past his knees.

All at once her annoyance seeped from her expression, her entire body. She stood there ready to drop. "When I worried about the girls getting spoiled, I said 'we.' If 'we' return them spoiled. And when you replied, you said 'I' will never get them again." She swallowed but kept her chin up. "I want you to know, Collin, that I give wholeheartedly to those little girls, too. Every day. All day. I thought you felt that, too. You certainly pretend to when you want to try and coax me into your bed. I believed that we had actually become a unit that was seamless and functioning as—"

Pushing himself away from the door, he had her in his arms before she could say "one." With one hand around her waist to keep her standing and the other at the back of her head to encourage her to lean on his shoulder, he pressed a kiss to her hair. "What can I tell you? I didn't hear it. I've functioned like this for so long that the words are—they're like intuition, they're just there before I know it."

He kissed her again near her ear and whispered, "It is 'we.' I can't look at the girls anymore without seeing your imprint on them. Haven't you noticed how Gena watches you at dinner, and puts down her fork or spoon before speaking? Do you know that when I'm reading to them in the evening, Addie said that she thought she needed hand cream, too, because you never go to bed without using some and you have beautiful skin? Oh, and Gena now sits in bed and brushes her hair until I finish reading. They've seen you sit on the side of the tub and do that, haven't they?"

"Why haven't I noticed that?"

"Because by then, you're worn out and it's my time to catch up with them. And I'm happy to do it because I adore seeing what's going to show up next."

Sabrina hung her head. "I'm sorry. It just stung so."

"It would have gutted me." He lifted her chin to touch a soft kiss to her lips. When she kissed him back, he had to have more, and then they were holding each other with the desperation born from having faced the risk of losing something still too new and rare to define.

Collin eased back to use the door to steady himself, and so he could use both hands to lift her against him. He wanted her fitting him the way they would in bed. Shuddering at the rush of pleasure, he sought the ultimate kiss at the same time cupping her bottom, while rocking himself against her to the rhythm of their tongues.

His breathing grew strained. "I want so badly to lie you down over there and spend the rest of the day and night making love to you," he whispered.

"We've already been in here too long."

"I know. Just one more." But instead of seeking her mouth, Collin deftly released the top two buttons of her jacket, parted it and saw the lacy shell of a bra in glistening white that he'd seen on her bed that first night. Brushing his thumb over the delicate peak already outlined by the satin, he tasted the warm flawless skin between her cleavage. Then he covered her with his mouth and stroked her with his tongue.

"Collin."

"I know, love." Regretfully, he fastened the buttons depriving himself of that exquisite view.

Finally touching his forehead to hers, he gazed deeply into her eyes. "It's going to happen."

"I hope so."

Chapter Nine

"Mommy, we are going to ice skate today," Addison declared to her mother on the phone. Although excited to talk to her, she enunciated each word carefully as Sabrina had taught her to do.

Stroking her hair to let the child know she'd done well, Sabrina pressed her ear closer to hear Cassie.

"That's great, sweetie. Draw me a picture and tell Gena to, too."

"When you coming home? Santa won't know where to put you presents."

"Well, I guess he'll keep them for me until I get there. Put Sabrina on, okay? Another hug and kiss to you and Gena!"

As Sabrina took the cordless from her, she whispered "Follow Gena and finish putting up your morning

toys, and get out your jackets. We'll be going soon."
Then as the child ran to her sister, who had already
spoken to her mother, Sabrina asked Cassie, "How are
you holding up?"

"The nation's second greatest national product after
poppy seeds is mold and it's taking over my quarters. I
swear I haven't stopped coughing since I got here."

"That sounds grim—and scary. I hate that for you.
All of you."

"Yeah, and I'm in one of the plush quarters. The
poor kids are in tents. Enough from the vacation resort
flyer. Talk, girl, talk to me. I'm in serious withdrawal."

Sabrina had been tied up with projects the last two
times Cassidy had called and had thought it more important for her to talk to her children and brother. She
was delighted to be needed, though.

"What do you want to know? Addie's mortified that
she splatters a bit when she talks, she's working hard on
her elocution. Did you notice? It wouldn't surprise me if
she ended up with Collin's accent before she's through."

Cassie laughed. "That would be kind of cool. Would
you do me a favor and find out what Collin was hinting
about with Gena wanting her ears pierced?"

"She does? He didn't say anything about it."

"Well, for some reason she told him and he asked if
it was all right."

Sabrina touched the gold loop in her left ear. Oh, my,
she thought. He was right about the watching-learning-
patterning thing. "How do you feel about that?" she
asked. "I mean, I'll do whatever you want, but she's so
young and her hair…she could have a ripped lobe before
she was five and brood over the scar for years."

"That's what I think."

"I didn't get my ears pierced until I was twenty-one. At that point I understood about the threat of infection and everything."

"The voice of reason. I won't worry now. I wouldn't want her to wear anything but high-quality gold anyway, and that brings up the concern that kids who grow up receiving lavish gifts can't find their ceiling as adults," Cass said.

"Well put. All I can say is that I'm doing the best that I can."

"Oh, I know you are, and I appreciate you beyond words. You've got an ice-skating date to get to and I have to hit the sack. I'll be waiting for a full recap. Love ya, Brina."

"Love you, Cass."

Downstairs Gus met them with open arms and a smile. Dressed in a ski sweater and jeans that made his silver hair and dark eyes all the more handsome, he acted as excited as the girls did.

"Do they know where they're going?" he asked Sabrina as they settled them in the van.

"Go ahead and ask them," she replied with a wink.

"Where to, ladies?"

"Skating!"

"This is a treat for me," he said once he was behind the wheel and heading up Central Expressway to cut west on LBJ Freeway toward the Galleria. "When I was a kid in New Jersey, my sisters and I skated through the winter on the pond near the house. We all did. One of the gang actually made the United States skating championships."

"That's terrific. I'm glued to the TV whenever any of the skating comes on. Did your friend do well?"

"He finished sixteenth. Still a big deal, but too costly to keep trying to inch up. So he went into the family appliance business. From then on all of their TV commercials featured Micah on a rink surrounded with the latest in washers, dryers and refrigerators. He became a bigger deal than some of those who finished silver and bronze in the Olympics. Remember, back then they didn't have the exposure opportunities you have today. I like to think Micah was the pioneer of all that."

"Micah is an unusual name for a boy in the north, isn't it?"

"His mama loved the Western show—*The Rifleman*."

"Sure, I've seen it on satellite. It was one of my father's favorites. What a fascinating story."

Sabrina was tickled that she could witness Gus experiencing a "moment" again. She was also glad to have him here. He helped get Gena into her skates while she prepared Addie.

The beginners' trainer was a tiny blonde, only a few inches and pounds over most of her students. But she was clever with kids and made the introduction to ice entertaining and soon the kids—down to the shiest—shuffled and fell for the first time.

Sabrina studied the parents lining the rink and knew some of them saw national stars in their little ones. All she wanted for the girls was to have one more expanding experience to share with Cassie.

After the initial instruction, the students were told to pair up. Addie started to reach out to a little girl she'd been talking to, but Gena quickly grasped her hand.

"Isn't that interesting?" Gus observed with a nod.

"I'm not surprised at all," Sabrina told him. "Gena always comes off as the confident leader, but Addie is the one willing to go outside her comfort zone." She made a mental note to share that experience with Cassie.

"How are they at home?"

"Like this. Addie didn't complain, did she? They play well together. They discuss and work through issues. Compromise. The only squabble I've witnessed wasn't even that. Addie can be a prankster and during a bubble bath that included considerable splashing, all Gena had to say was, 'That's enough now.' And it was."

Gus chuckled. "Don't you want to see them in twenty years to find out how they evolved?"

"I'm sorry that you don't have grandchildren."

He made the universal "What can you do?" flick with his hand. "It wasn't in the cards."

Sabrina hoped they now knew each other well enough to venture toward more personal questions. "Adoption wasn't an option?"

"We talked about it, but that's all we did. Em's plants became her children. I loved her, so that was that."

Sabrina understood evasion between couples. She'd watched it in her parents for years.

Gus patted her hand. "Don't let me get you depressed."

"You're not."

"Good. Because I'm not."

"You made me remember something about my parents that I never understood until you spoke. You can love someone and still shut them down in your own way."

"Yes. Yes, love is a two-edged sword. You're wise for such a little girl."

Touching her shoulder with his, she teased, "It's the twenty-first century. It's politically incorrect to say *girl* to anyone over twenty-one."

"The world's gone mad when women don't want to be complimented anymore." But he said it with a smile.

Sabrina glanced from his wistful face to the ice. "Would you like to rent skates with me and have a turn or two around the rink after the class? We're in no hurry to get back. Collin's office Christmas party is today and the less I have to think about that, the better."

His face brightened, then fell. "You're not worried, are you?"

Gus knew she cared about him, and it was easier being honest. "I don't believe I need to be. But Collin's childhood wasn't a happy one and he hasn't dealt with all of those issues."

"If the man has any sense in him, he won't let you get away. As for me—" he grinned "—I'm probably no match for a *girl* from Wisconsin, but I think I could stay on my feet. Full disclosure, for years, I would go to a roller rink over by the house while Em was communing with nature. She said it was my need to show off."

"I'd like to see a little of that."

Sabrina didn't stop grinning all the way home. The girls had a marvelous time, but she'd had the opportunity to skate with a man who was Fred Astaire on ice.

"This has been an unforgettable day," she told him as he pulled into the high-rise's driveway.

"I'm the one who's grateful. Perhaps we could go again before the girls return home? My treat this time."

"And after the Christmas madness. Oh, that would be

lovely. As it is, I don't know how I'm going to get the S-H-O-P-P-I-N-G done." She glanced over her shoulder and to her relief saw the girls had about dozed off. "It would be better to have Collin with me, but we both can't be gone at the same time."

Gus shifted into Park and turned to her. "Most of my nights are free. Maybe I could sit with the girls. If you don't mind me bringing an audiobook and my crocheting—"

"You crochet, too?"

His expression turned sheepish. "I don't often mention it, but it keeps my hands busy and the audiobooks save my eyes for driving. I donate my creations to the church and nursing homes."

"What a caring thing to do. Collin has an excellent stereo system. I'm sure he would be happy to let you use it. Let me talk to him and synchronize dates, all right?"

"Anytime."

"We meet at last," Collin said shaking Gus Genovese's hand.

"Mr. Masters, good evening."

"Collin, please. Let me take your jacket."

It was the following Monday and after some further checking into Gus's past—without informing Sabrina about that—Collin had agreed to let him sit for the girls, while they did some whirlwind shopping.

"Sabrina is saying good-night to the girls," he said, hanging the handsome leather piece into the coat closet. "You undoubtedly know you can do no wrong in her eyes."

"The feeling is mutual. She's a special person."

"That she is." Collin let him past the kitchen into the living room. "You know with all of the 'Gus this,' 'Gus that,' I hear from all three girls, you give a man's ego a workout."

"At my age, that's a compliment."

"And you're too modest. Go ahead and set your things on the couch or anywhere, and I'll show you the entertainment system. You're probably familiar with them."

Putting down his large canvas bag beside the couch, Gus raised his gaze to the far wall. "I don't have anything quite so professional, but after my wife passed, there didn't seem to be any reason not to enjoy a few creature comforts."

"I'm sorry for your loss."

Gus closed his eyes briefly and nodded. "Thank you. It's an adjustment, but if you're lucky, you meet a person here and there to remind you that life is still a gift. Sabrina and your wonderful nieces for example. Did you like the photos of them ice skating?"

"Very much." Collin grinned. "Born hams, both of them. They get it from their mother. By the way, Cassidy thanks you for everything you're doing, as well."

"Please tell her that I thank her for her service. I hope she gets home to her loved ones soon. Sabrina showed me a photo of her with her girls and it's a heart grabber."

"It's a copy of the one Cassie sent me. Sabrina and my sister have grown close from this and I wanted her to have her own copy." Clearing his throat, Collin picked up the master remote and gave the older man a cursory rundown of things. A minute later Sabrina emerged sliding on her red wool coat with the Christmas tree pin on the left shoulder.

"Gus," she said, immediately hugging him. "How are you?"

"Always better after seeing you, my dear. Don't you look festive, but your pin has competition from your sparkling eyes."

"You know how I love this season."

Gus held up a finger. "I see you're not wearing a scarf and it's already down into the thirties out there." He went to his canvas bag and reached deep bringing out a red-and-green crocheted scarf that he unfolded for her. "If you'll permit me…"

"Gus! I love it! I knew your work would be wonderful. Oh, I'll treasure this." She hugged him again and this time kissed his cheek.

More than ready to leave, Collin slipped on his leather sports jacket. "You already know Dempsey downstairs."

"Talked to him for a moment on my way up."

"Now, Gus," Sabrina directed, "help yourself to anything you'd like. Did you have dinner? I made New England clam chowder today."

"And here I was trying to count calories for the holidays," Gus replied patting the subtle swell of his belly beneath the green corduroy shirt.

"You're in great shape. I told Collin how well you skate." She stopped at the bag. "May I see what you're working on?"

"Of course. It's not too large yet," he explained, "but I think you can get an idea of what I'm doing."

Sabrina gasped at the gorgeous rich autumn colors of the afghan. "This is beautiful!"

He smiled and shrugged. "I'm pleased you think so. You have a good eye for color. I make notes of what you're wearing sometimes and try to find the yarn to match. Do you recognize these? It's like the sweater, slacks and scarf you wore just before Thanksgiving. The chiffon scarf had an unusual pattern that I've been trying to carry through here."

She blushed and shook her head. "I'm flattered."

"We'd better be going," Collin said urging her to the door.

"Have a good time!" Gus called.

After Collin shut the heavy front door, he took Sabrina's hand in his and murmured, "He makes notes of what you wear? Does he draw pictures, too?"

"I told you he's a Renaissance man," she replied stroking her scarf and playing with the fringes.

"He's hustling you."

"I think he sees me as the daughter he never had, and if you're going to act half your age," she said as they reached the elevator, "you can take care of this list on your own." She tapped his sleeve with the index card covered with small print.

As soon as they stepped inside the car, Collin took hold of the lapels of her jacket and brought her up on her toes for a kiss. "That's what I think about your threat."

Dreamy-eyed, she murmured, "That wasn't a threat, that was a scold, Testosterone Boy."

His chest was tight as he hugged her. The idea of them being alone for a few gifted hours had him feeling like he'd swallowed a shot of Scotch on an empty stomach. She went straight to his head. "You know what we should do instead? Sit in the Mercedes and neck for a couple of hours."

"And for Christmas wrap up what for the kids?"

"Where's your sense of romance?"

HELEN R. MYERS 151

"Where's your sense of magic? What happens in cars—whether a Mercedes or a VW—is not about romance, it's about lust. Good evening, Dempsey," Sabrina added as the elevator doors opened and the small but muscular security guard waited to greet them. "How's the expectant daddy tonight?"

Dempsey Freed grinned, which exposed his two missing front teeth, formerly two broken off teeth, the result of his altercation a few weeks ago. He was waiting for his partial to come in and being an excellent sport about it.

"Great, Miss Brina. Looks like a Valentine's baby now. Susie thanks you for the box of Christmas cookies and the gift certificate you sent. We used it to get the car seat you looked up on the Internet for us. Evening, Mr. Masters. I'll have things covered here for you tonight. Enjoy your evening."

Collin tucked Sabrina's arm through his and led her to the parking garage. "I hope you realize half this building will go into a state of depression when you leave." He'd had no idea she'd been so generous. Again.

"If you can't be good to each other at Christmas, the world is in sad shape."

"You're supposed to be saving your salary, not giving it away to every person who hits a bump in the road."

"Yes, sir, Mr. Scrooge. I'll remember that, sir."

While Collin drove, Sabrina perused her list again with the help of the tiny flashlight on her key chain. "Cassie said one large gift and maybe two or three small ones are more than sufficient. Where's the nearest Toys R Us?"

"Los Angeles. I have no idea. What's wrong with one

of the malls down LBJ Freeway? Doesn't every department store have a toy department?"

"No. Let's see…I'd like to look at the PlayStations, too, and see what's available for the twins' age group. But I guess you're heading in the right direction. The Galleria will have the American Girl dolls store."

"As long as you don't ask for a puppy or kitty, I'm fine with whatever you choose for them. Personally, I think we should skip the toys and shoot straight to the jewelry counter. Time flies. College is just around the corner. They could have a nice little inventory of gold and fine gems by then."

Sabrina did an about face. "Thank you for bringing that up. What's this about encouraging Gena to ask to get her ears pierced?"

"I was just listening."

"She's *three*. There's plenty of time for that when she understands the gun hurts regardless of what anyone tells you. There are hygiene issues, regardless of whether you're using 14K gold or not. And there's the 'lost' factor. Do you think Cass is going to thank you every time she has to get the plumber's wrench and take apart the bathroom sink because an earring might be down the drain?

"I'm willing to find some children's play jewelry, but that's it," Sabrina continued. "Right now, the kids want hands-on and huggy things. By the way, we need at least one stuffed animal apiece."

Collin lifted his eyebrows. "To put where? The bedroom is a zoo already."

"Okay. What about one of those animated kinds like in the Hallmark commercials?"

Groaning, Collin replied, "What do you want for Christmas?"

"That's easy—for Cassie and all of our service people to get home safely...and then maybe a good job."

Shaking his head, Collin reached for her hand and squeezed it gently. "Very sweet. I meant what would I be allowed to give you?"

"You've already given me memories I'll cherish. You won't take the money back that I owe you for the apartment and the clothes."

"Incidentals in the great scheme of things. It makes me happy to see you speechless, then exasperated." Collin smiled remembering the last "payday" when he refused to take anything back. "How about diamond studs?"

To his surprise, she shivered. "No, thank you," she said softly.

"What's wrong? Uh-uh—and don't say 'nothing.' We made a deal, remember?"

Taking a deep breath, she replied, "That's what you do when an affair is over. Even Cassie knows it, so this is ingrained with you. I can't take jewelry from you."

"When did you and Cassie talk about that?"

"The first time? You had me pick up the diamond toe ring at your jewelers and I'd just returned to the office and Cassie called. I was breathless from running to grab the phone and she asked where I'd been."

Swearing under his breath, Collin all but strangled the wheel. "All I can say is that was then, that was *them,* this is you."

But Sabrina was adamant about the jewelry. So he decided he was on his own regarding the gift hunt...and she would have to just deal with the consequences. As an idea formed in his mind, he began to feel good enough to smile again.

His satisfaction ended as soon as he saw how crammed the mall parking lots were.

"Do you know anything about holiday traffic?" she asked, as he muttered and fussed.

"As you've already pointed out, I rarely do my own shopping, and during the holidays, I tend to leave the country or metropolitan areas, so to answer your question, no."

After hunting a parking space for ten minutes, they ended up walking from the far end of an aisle. Inside the mall it sounded like someone had released a thousand beehives.

"Good grief. What do you expect to accomplish here?" What he was really thinking was, thank heavens he didn't let her do this alone. Before they walked the length of one corridor, he spotted two people who were either undercover cops or pickpockets.

Sabrina hooked her arm through his. "Come on. There's an American Girl store over by where the ice-skating rink is. Gena and Addie were easily tricked by Gus into letting me know which dolls they would love to have. They both want blond Bitty Baby Doll Twins."

Now those Collin had heard of—and had coveted the account when they'd first launched. Even he hadn't believed the fad would grow into such a phenomenon.

They tried the next larger department store and came across sweet faux-fur jackets in the children's department. "Oh, Collin, how about these for the horse-drawn carriage through Turtle Creek? Look, they come with matching muffs."

He was confused. "This is acceptable? This will probably make them grow up to want the real thing."

"Or adult-size faux. I would wear a faux fur."

He wouldn't tell her, but he could watch her going soft and tender all night over imagining the children dressed up.

"They'll look like Lara in *Doctor Zhivago* on the troika."

Collin wanted to see *her* on a carriage with her lover—him.

"Get them."

They were burdened with packages before the mall closed, and returned to the condo just as Gus was removing his CD from the stereo. He rushed to catch a slipping stuffed plastic bag from under Sabrina's arm and one hand's worth of shopping bags.

"The trip looks as though it was a success." He glanced around. "Where do you want these?"

"Right here by the kitchen bar. Are the girls asleep?"

"Gena called for you wanting a drink of water. I think waking up, she had forgot you'd gone out, so I spoke to her before going into their room, waited for her to return from the bathroom and read her a short story before she went back to sleep. I hope you don't mind."

"Not at all. As you saw, she's the leader, but there's vulnerability going on in her." Sabrina gestured to the living room. "Did you enjoy the audio?"

"Very much, and your glorious tree… I'm having a better holiday season than I expected by far. But I'm sure you must be exhausted and children rise early. I'll just get my things."

While Gus returned to the living room, Collin began reaching for his billfold. Sabrina motioned him to put it away and quickly searched for a bag. When he returned, she held out a flat wrapped package to him.

"I know you said no fee for tonight, but we wanted you to know we're so grateful for making this possible."

"Oh, my. Christmas early."

Gus opened it quickly and Collin's gaze was torn between Sabrina standing with her clasped hands to her lips and Gus's gasp of delight as he saw the audiobook by his favorite thriller writer. "It's his newest! I wasn't allowing myself to think about it until I finished what I had at home. This is—this is grand. Thank you, dear."

Sabrina hugged him and walked him to the door. "I wanted to ask you about Christmas Eve. Do you have plans?"

"Only to attend the candle service at my church."

"Well, we would like to make the evening special for the girls, invite the people who've made their time here easier. It will be a casual, festive supper and carols. We'd love to have you."

"I'd be honored."

Chapter Ten

"What's our horse's name?"

"Toffee." The dapper carriage driver smiled over his shoulder at Addie. "Because of her sweet, rich color. You'll see she walks just like she's on an elliptical machine once she's harnessed to her carriage. She's a proud girl and always working to keep her figure. There's talk her mama must've been a Tennessee walker and her papa a mustang."

As the girls listened with rapt attention, Sabrina met Collin's gaze and he winked at her. He had decided she should sit between the twins where they could get the first and best view of all of the decorations. He sat with his back to the driver, taking pictures and video, and running interference; as when a blanket slipped, or a sip of hot cocoa was required. At the moment, though, truth in advertising was Addie's concern.

"Horses have figgers?" Addie asked, scrunching her nose.

Gena had been tense from the moment they'd climbed into the carriage. She'd grown increasingly so once they merged with the sea of cars, limousines, tour buses and pedestrians for the evening tour through the Dallas subdivision of Highland Park, along Turtle Creek. Leaning forward to glare across Sabrina at her sister, she snapped. "Addie—don't' talk! You'll crash the horse."

Encouraging her to sit back, Sabrina smoothed the faux-fur blanket around her. "Are you warm enough? It was a good idea to bring these on such a nippy night. You know, Toffee's driver has known her for a good while. If he feels she is a strong and fit horse, this traffic probably doesn't bother her one bit."

The driver must have heard her. He said over his shoulder, "She's been in Manhattan traffic. Now that's a packed house." He pointed for Gena. "Watch her ears. The ears tell you plenty—how she's feeling about things around her, what she's hearing and what kind of job I'm doing."

"There are too many lights."

Sabrina heard the tears of anxiety rising in the child's voice and asked her, "Do you want to sit beside Uncle Collin? You don't have to see the oncoming lights then, especially at intersections."

"I want to go home."

"We'll go home as soon as the ride is over. We've barely begun and the best decorations are ahead of us."

"I want to go home to Mommy!"

It all came together for Sabrina. Now she understood

what had been building in the child, the oldest and self-appointed responsible one. What a trick nature sometimes played on fragile souls. Gena felt fear was a flaw for her, and Sabrina suspected it wasn't due to anything Cassie or anyone else had ever said or done, except to say, "…minutes older." Yet she was far too young to deal with her mother's absence and at this of all times of the year.

Sensing Collin was watching her for a hint of what to do, Sabrina said, "Hold her in your lap. Remind her that she's a little girl."

Collin immediately swept aside his throw and reached for Gena. Cradling her across his lap, he covered them both.

"Is Gena sick?" Addie asked.

"No, sweetie. She just needs a minute to rest her eyes. There were a bunch of lights at the intersection, weren't there?"

"Look at that snowman!"

Yes, Sabrina thought torn between a laugh and sigh, it was all about perception. Addie's view of the world was only minutes different, but she was immune from what troubled her twin.

"And look at the giant, lit snowflakes on that tree," she replied putting her arm back around the little girl. "Oh, and there's a family of penguins ready to ski."

She couldn't hear but an occasional word of what Collin said to Gena, but body language told her enough. He was giving her what she needed, the right to be a child without worry.

Although traffic was heavier than what she'd remembered from her brief tour in her car last year, everyone remained fairly well mannered, as cooperation was essential what with so many means of travel. The coach buses and the stretch limousines had the hardest time of it. Most of this venerated community's streets were narrow having been built in the years when Dallas was a fraction of its current size. Turns wouldn't be easy on a day with no traffic. Add horse-drawn carriages and thousands of family vehicles out to partake of the wondrous lights, and the people walking often appeared to be making the best progress. Yet most of the time they kept moving and the spirit of the season often had people waving from car to car, pedestrian to carriage riders.

"I think they know me," Addie said as a couple walking with their arms around each other's waist waved at her.

Smiling, Sabrina said, "Maybe they think you're a celebrity." At Addie's blank look, she explained, "That's someone who is in the news so much, everybody knows their name, but you don't sometimes remember why."

"Like a movie star?"

"It can be…or a TV star."

Addie liked the sound of that and sat taller so she could be seen better by her admirers. "Everybody looks at me because nobody else has a coat or— What is this called, Brina?"

"A muff, sweetie. You know, like earmuffs? We talked about that before when we first took your things out of the bags."

"Right. Nobody else has a muff or coat like me."

"And me!"

Whatever Collin had been telling Gena for the last fifteen or twenty minutes must have eased Gena's fears because Addison's image of herself had ignited Gena's competitive spirit again.

Wriggling to sit up, Gena pointed and said, "I want to sit there now, please."

Wanting to help, Sabrina said, "It's definitely getting colder. Let's all snuggle on this side."

Addie shifted closer to her, Gena took the next spot, allowing Collin to switch over to the other end of the bench. They soon had the throws spread nicely again, and Gena quickly gasped and waved her muff to a group waving on the sidewalk. "Addie, I'm famous, too!"

As she and Addie waved and waved, Sabrina met Collin's wry smile.

"Dr. Masters may have overdid it a bit on the ego building."

Suddenly Addie gasped. "My nose!"

Sabrina quickly leaned over to see. "What? I just see—a snowflake." Her expression soon matched Addison's wonder, as more and more flakes began drifting down from the darkness. "It's snowing!"

"Santa's coming!" the girls sang.

Getting the exhausted little ones into the condo was no small feat. Collin carried Gena with relative ease, but with Addison's limp weight, Sabrina had to lean against the railing in the elevator as the car thumped and started rising to their floor. She was grateful that they'd decided to leave their fur throws and the thermoses in his Mercedes.

"I'm so glad I didn't wear my pretty high-heeled boots that I just bought," she told him in a hushed voice as they watched the floor lights blink. "Even in these Uggs, my feet are killing me. Poor Cassie is going to return and find out the days of toting around these little cherubs are over."

Collin looked sympathetic, but also pleased. "Maybe I'll get to give you that foot rub yet."

"I'm sure a soak in the tub would be the wiser solution."

"That tub? Not enough room to stretch out. My tub has the Jacuzzi jets."

The car settled at their floor and the elevator doors slid open. Collin lengthened his strides as they progressed down the hall and had the door unlocked and opened by the time Sabrina reached him.

"I could kiss you," she said, breathing shallowly.

Thankfully, they left lights on in the condo so that she didn't lose an elbow or cost Addie a knee or foot clipping a corner. The night-light was on in their room, too, and she softly groaned with relief when she eased the little girl onto her bed. Collin was right behind her with Gena.

"If you could get her down to her underwear, my back would really appreciate it," she told him, as he started working on the child's coat buttons.

Pausing, Collin came behind her and said, "Take off this heavy jacket first. That'll make it easier for you to move." Once he put it on the edge of the bed, he removed his own. Then he went back to work on Gena. "I'll put her pj's over her underwear. It can't matter for one night and makes less work for you."

Sabrina decided that was a good idea and they had the girls under the blankets almost simultaneously. The twins never opened their eyes. Addie stayed in the position she'd been placed, already deep in the land of sugarplums, and Gena sighed, then curled into a fetal position the way she usually slept.

Picking up her coat and the scarf from Gus, she followed Collin out of the room and closed the door to a crack. In the dimly lit hallway, Collin leaned against the wall across from her bedroom, his jacket slung over his shoulder.

"Don't retreat behind your convent walls yet, Sabrina Fair," he murmured.

Still feeling colder inside than out, she wrapped her arms around herself. "It's nearly eleven again. You have to go to the office tomorrow. Graziella is coming here."

"What if the revised forecast we heard on the radio is right and it keeps snowing all night? None of us will be going anywhere. We can sleep in." When she merely gave him a tolerant look, he came to her side and leaned closer. "I want some alone time with you." He reached over to stroke her cheek. "The Jacuzzi offer is still open."

"You know I can't do that," she whispered.

Ignoring her, he continued, "I could pour us a brandy and you could soak, your modesty intact due to all of the bubbles. Still, gentleman that I am, I could sit on the carpet with my back against the marble. It is BYOBB, of course."

She frowned slightly, then nodded slowly. "Bring Your Own Bubble Bath. Because, of course, there would be no reason for you to have any in there."

"I am in touch with my inner child, but he's not as young as he used to be."

She chuckled silently. "There you go getting irresistible again."

With a wicked smile he added, "Think of this as being a best-friend confessional."

"Because we're gluttons for punishment?"

His eyes grew serious. "Because even the chaste, honor-bound time I'm suggesting to have with you is better than no time at all."

He was being altogether too romantic and tempting. The fact was she planned on getting in a tub regardless. She had been chilled to the bone and she couldn't afford to get ill, not with two little girls to care for, the Christmas Eve party only three days away and her shopping still not completed.

"Will you tell me what you said to Gena to make her relax and have fun again?"

"That might take a brandy-and-a-half, but yes."

They held each other's gazes until Sabrina started unbuttoning her sweater. "I'll get into my robe."

Ten minutes later with the bottle of bubble bath in one hand and a bath towel in the other, she entered his room where only the lamp on the far night table was on and the king-size bed was still made up. Steam wafted from the half-shut door and she heard the low drone of churning water. She knocked softly.

"All's clear. I'm just putting our drinks down before I make my temporary, but respectful exit."

Entering the roomy bath, Sabrina saw he was doing exactly as he said, and although the two lit candles on the corner of the tub were highly romantic, she preferred them to the starker illumination of the overhead or vanity lights. The candlelight also encouraged quiet dialogues and honesty.

"Anything else I can get you while you get comfortable? Caviar? Chocolate? The *New York Times* Crossword Puzzle?"

"Just enough time to get the bubbles adequate to the

situation, and to get in there without giving myself a second-degree burn."

Clicking his heels together, he gave her a royal bow. "Done."

In full gentleman mode, he actually pulled the door shut for her. Sabrina took a slow calming breath hoping that she wasn't being a fool for doing this. The garden tub did look too inviting to resist.

She put down the towel on the corner of the marble tub, and poured a slow, long stream of the golden liquid into the churning and frothing water. Immediately, bubbles started rising and a heady fragrance permeated the room. It didn't take as much of the liquid as she thought it might. Testing the water, she found the temperature perfect and, with a glance back toward the door, she dropped her robe and stepped in.

A little over two minutes later, he knocked discreetly.

"It's okay."

"Just okay?" he said sounding slightly offended as he entered the softly lit room. He had shed his shoes and socks, and his shirt was unbuttoned to midchest, his sleeves rolled halfway to his elbow. "I draw the lady a bath worthy of a five-star hotel complete with my VSOP cognac and she tells me it's 'just okay.'" Stopping a few feet away, he raised his nose and sniffed. "Lord, that's almost a narcotic. Is it honeysuckle? You temptress, you."

Resuming his approach on the last step, he smoothly crossed his ankles and descended into a sitting position, at the same time turning until he was perfectly backed against the marble. "Is it good for you? It's damn hard on the spine for me. Hold on a second." He reached for her towel and used it as a pillow. "Better." He breathed in the scent again. "And all this time, I thought you used a honeysuckle shampoo or cologne. When I was dragged kicking and screaming to England, where I all but froze my butt off that first winter, it was this scent I wanted again. My soul ached for this spring smell."

"It is heavenly." Sabrina was also grateful for his reaction to her favorite scent. It already resolved a great number of mysteries, like how he would often hover over her when she worked for him, only to abruptly, almost rudely give her an order and vanish, sometimes for over an hour. Or how, after leaving his office having reviewed some phone messages or taking dictation, she watched through the window as he would get up and pace where she'd been standing. Once when he was out, she had needed his signature stamp and when she had opened his drawer, she had found a glove she had thought she'd dropped and lost. He must have been keeping it until the fragrance wore off. "Thank you for this," she murmured studying his profile.

"I live to serve," he quipped. "Hand me my glass, will you? I don't want you to think I'm cheating and copping a peek."

"You can turn around. The bubbles are more than adequate."

"Bless you." He did shift sideways, so he could rest his elbow on the tub and his head on his hand. He picked up his snifter in his left hand and smiled gently as he considered her. "I knew you'd look like a confection in there. Are those chopsticks really meant to hold up your hair or did you put them there to stab me if I lied and got fresh, or don't answer something that you wanted to know?"

Sabrina touched the red and black enameled wood

crisscrossing the casual bun on top of her head. "They're not chopsticks, they're geisha hair sticks. In high school we had an exchange student, Aiko, which means little loved one, who became a dear friend. When she returned to Japan, she gave them to me because I'd always admired how they looked in her hair."

"I shouldn't have teased, but if I told you that they made you look a little exotic and sexy as hell, that might have made you uncomfortable."

"Not put that way."

Inclining his head, he touched his glass to hers. "Then may I also add that you were born to wear white and all things strapless. Your neck and shoulders are lyrical."

"You can stop there."

"I must unless you stand up for me."

"Did you start imbibing in the short time before I got here?"

"Actually, I did. But the truth is still the truth. Tell me, did boys follow you like drooling puppies when you were growing up?"

"No, it was pretty cool up there so most of the time my assets were covered, and back then I carried about ten pounds of what you're likely to graciously call baby fat, but I call Mother's buttermilk and biscuits."

"Buttermilk…your skin looks like you bathe in the stuff." Collin rested his chin on his fist. "They don't call you, do they? Your family, I mean."

"No," Sabrina replied. She would rather not extinguish the magic of the moment by talking about that, but if she wanted him to share himself with her, she had to be as open, as well. "I need to call them."

"Why?"

"Because I'm living with a man and not married to him."

"If you tell me now that you're still a virgin, I'm going to have to leave to keep from stripping off my clothes and ravishing you this instant."

"They want to believe I am."

"Poor darling," he murmured. "That's harsh…and archaic as hell."

"Also hypocritical." Sabrina took another sip of her cognac. At Collin's raised eyebrows, she said, "My father had an affair…with the town librarian. He liked to read and my mother didn't, so he started talking to Ms. Alcott about books. I think given different circumstances, he would have been something else besides a farmer, but his father had had a bad heart and needed him—and that was that.

"I don't think the affair lasted long, but I remember the evening I came home from school choir practice and I had barely opened the back door when Mother slammed something down on the kitchen table and demanded, 'End it.' There was nothing else said, but suddenly it was clear to me what she meant. He did end it, and life went on." Sabrina looked up from the amber contents of her glass. "But she never let him touch her again. I didn't realize that until Gus said something about his marriage."

Grimacing, Collin muttered, "I could have gone the rest of the evening without hearing that name."

"Don't." She touched his hand. "I like him."

"That's the problem." When she withdrew her fingers, he kept staring at where they'd rested. "When this is over, will you go back to see your people?"

"I don't know. They're my family, but…they're very strong and willful. They can seep away your independence before you know it. I don't belong there anymore. I'm not resentful or anything, but their ways aren't mine."

"See? That's one of the things I admire about you—you reject their kind of rigidity yet you hold fast to your personal standards like a little nun does her chastity." Casting her a fleeting glance, he murmured, "You certainly don't kiss like one, though."

"Maybe this is where you can tell me about what you said to Gena."

"Not nearly as interesting a subject."

Sabrina didn't give up. "I've never been more proud of you. You held her as though she was spun glass and you kept her looking into your eyes as you spoke. That's hard to do with an upset child. I think you saved her from getting trapped in a place that could have debilitated her for years."

"You give me too much credit."

"You did."

"I just made her see that she wasn't alone, nor was she responsible for what was going on, and that because she was the firstborn, that didn't make her weak or bad if she felt fear."

Collin finished off the remnants of the cognac and poured himself another.

Silence grew like a third presence between them and Sabrina cupped the hot water over her shoulders to ward away the chill that was triggered. "You were talking from experience."

"The perceptions of a lost boy allowed to believe he'd done something wrong to destroy the fabric of his family. Then when we were suddenly reunited again and my mother showered me with affection and attention, I started to come out of that dark place I'd been lost in. But my father's streak of recklessness came back to bite him again and instead of facing it, he took her away on one of the last assets he hadn't yet lost."

"How could she leave you or Cassidy? Even with your grandmother, who apparently was a wonderful woman, but she knew what he was. He'd stolen her child for years. How could she trust him to do something like take on a world of oceans?"

He laughed mirthlessly. "Maybe when you figure that out, I'll stop being such an unreliable piece of crap."

Sabrina ached for him and the devastated little boy, who'd grown up to be a lost man with little faith. "So everything you'd said to Gena was just lip service?"

"I meant every word—for her. Her mother left out of duty. My mother left her own flesh and blood for a—"

He couldn't even bring himself to say the word, it was so vile. Seeing that and realizing why, despite being a virile man strongly attracted to the opposite sex, he really didn't trust women. Sabrina put down her glass. "I'm sorry. That's inadequate, I know."

"Sincerity is always appreciated, especially when it comes from you."

He began to lift his glass to his lips again when she stayed him. "Please don't."

"There's an angry snake striking at the walls of my insides, Sabrina Fair. I need relief from the pain tonight." His gaze swept over her again. "Unless you have another antidote?"

Bringing her knees to her chest, she hugged them and

rested her cheek there. "Don't cheapen this, or me. You know you wouldn't do it."

He exhaled on a brief, bitter laugh. "Darlin', I'd hate myself in the morning, but for a few hours of heaven tonight, it would be worth it."

Sabrina wouldn't believe him. That was not the man he'd been showing her that he could be.

"Would it? Knowing that I would be terribly disappointed—and if you hurt me again, end up hating you?"

He closed his eyes. She watched muscles along his cheeks flex, his pulse beat at his temples. When he looked at her again, the demon tormenting him had quieted and he rose, reached for her robe and held it up for her.

Was this some sort of test? She had her sense of modesty like most women, but she wouldn't hide herself from the man she wanted to love.

Holding his gaze, she rose from the water and bubbles and stepped out, turning to slide her arms into the robe. As he folded the soft white terry cloth around her, he held her tightly against him for a moment and pressed his lips to the side of her neck.

"I can survive in one place with you living in another," he said in all graveness. "But, no, I couldn't live at all knowing that I'd hurt you again."

And then he was gone. Seconds later Sabrina heard the front door quietly open and shut. Trembling from too many emotions packed into too few minutes, she collected the rest of her things and hurried to the sanctuary of her own room.

Chapter Eleven

"Merry Christmas, Sabrina, dear."

"Merry Christmas, Gus. I'm so glad you decided to come. And how distinguished you look."

"And you look like you just floated down from the top of that tree." Gus kissed her on both cheeks in the European fashion of his ancestors and stepped back to admire her gold-thread tunic with a neckline that hugged her just off the shoulders and gold lamé lounging pajama pants.

"You look like a judge in that black suit," she said, impressed with the tailoring. "Love the red-and-green tie. Just enough festivity. Oh, my," she added as he held out a small box to her. "What have you done? We all agreed the most anyone could bring was something edible from their Christmases past to share for dinner."

"And here it is," he confirmed as he also passed her a bottle of wine. "This is… Well, maybe you'll understand when you open it."

Placing the wine on the entryway side table, Sabrina slipped off the ribbon and opened the box to see a pair of diamond-and-ruby earrings. The delicate floral design left her too stunned to say anything except, "Gus."

"They were Em's. Her birthstone. I know they're not yours, but there's a quote in Proverbs 31:10 that says, 'Who can find a virtuous woman? For her price is far above rubies.' I never thought I'd know someone again who that fits so well."

"I don't know what to say. This is more than too much, it's such a responsibility and an honor."

"That's how I thought you would feel and why I know I leave them in such caring hands."

"May I wear them now?"

"I'd be honored."

Sabrina took out her gold hoops and slipped them into the pocket of her slacks. One by one she fastened the pierced earrings. With her hair up in an elegant French twist, she knew they would be shown off to perfection. "Now I feel as though I'm floating." She hugged him again and slid her arm through his. "Come say hello to the others. The girls particularly want so badly to open the presents you brought up yesterday. They walk around and around the big boxes discussing what could be inside."

"I hope you're not upset with me about my choices. There may be a few too many parts to step on and get lost."

Sabrina chuckled. "I'll pass that on to Cassidy someday when it all gets delivered to her place."

At the corner of the kitchen and living room, they came face-to-face with Collin carrying two glasses to where the bar was set up. "Gus. Merry Christmas."

"Merry Christmas, Collin."

It didn't take Collin seconds to spot Gus's gift on Sabrina. While his expression didn't change, the only thing he had to say was, "Excuse me for a moment, will you? I have to get these refills before I forget what they were."

As soon as he disappeared into the kitchen, Gus covered Sabrina's hand with his. "The blood has drained from your face. I shouldn't have come."

"Of course you should. You're my friend. The girls' friend. He just has had a trying few days. Gena, Addie," she called, "look who's arrived."

Sonny and Isabella were already there, along with Isabella's mother, Graziella, and father, Hector. The Nuñezes, as Sonny had described the experience with comical flair, had granted official permission for him to date Isabella. Would that have happened—at least at this point—without Graziella and her husband being invited here as guests? Who knew, but so far Graziella hadn't let her future son-in-law out of her sight.

A substitute for security had been approved, so Dempsey Freed and his beloved Susie, a sweet but visibly uncomfortable girl were also there. Susie, in her last trimester, came wearing a caftan and apologized at the front door. "I know I might as well have worn my bathrobe," she told Sabrina. "I can't even fit into Demps's sweats."

The party was for Addie and Gena, to surround them with the people they'd grown close to. But after three days of Collin coming and going like a shell of himself, Sabrina had hoped it would bring back the man they were all used to—the gregarious jokester and tender uncle. She'd wanted Susie to meet the charmer who would have made her feel attractive despite being in the awkward last stages of pregnancy. And she'd wanted to see him listen to Sonny and Dempsey converse as though their work was on par with that of the Secret Service. This polite, but preoccupied stranger she didn't know, and her inability to get through to him frightened her.

As Gus went to say hello to the girls, she retrieved his bottle of wine and brought it to the kitchen, placing it where Collin was making the drinks. He barely glanced at the label, which told her that he already knew its value.

"Nice."

"I'll tell him you're pleased."

"Also relieved that I didn't talk you into those diamond studs, after all. You'd have made yourself miserable trying to please both of us."

Spoken another way, the words could have cut deep, instead they just left her incredibly sad. Her throat aching, she rasped, "I think I'd like a glass of chardonnay, please."

He immediately stopped preparing the other drinks and served her. Holding out the glass, he looked into her eyes. "I'm wrong. Gold suits you as much as white. You take my breath away. As for what he said, it's true. It was right to give them to you."

Sabrina couldn't take the wine for fear of spilling it all over him. "What's happened to you?" she whispered. "Where's my friend? I miss him."

"I wish I could tell you." Putting down her wine,

Collin leaned over and kissed her right shoulder. "Honeysuckle girl," he murmured. He returned to the living room to deliver the other two drinks.

At least the twins had no problem letting anyone know what was going on in their minds. Dressed in new red elf pajamas with caps that had tiny bells on the ends, they asked for "bird songs" from Sonny and piggyback rides from Dempsey. Gus taught them how to stand on his shoes and danced with them when the stereo played "White Christmas." But the one they kept returning to was Susie. Sabrina had to warn them repeatedly to be very careful when touching her belly.

"It's fine," Susie told her when they began leaning down to place their ears against her. "They really are cute kids. But I'm sure glad I'm starting off with one."

"When we were in Mommy," Addison told her, "we didn't have as much room as him. Gena was here," she said stroking Susie's right side, "and I was on this side."

"Mommy has the pictures," Gena told them. "She sucked her thumb."

"But I don't do that anymore." Addie stroked Susie's belly again. "What's his name?"

Susie looked at Dempsey. "Her name. We're having a little girl and the truth is, we can't decide."

"That's because he's a little boy," Gena said matter-of-factly.

With Susie's mouth hanging open, Graziella announced it was time to eat.

If she'd had her way, Graziella would have sequestered the girls in the kitchen, but Isabella and Susie somehow managed to outmaneuver her and the girls sat between them taking bites from each plate. In between mouthfuls, they listened to the baby.

Susie told Sabrina, "I wouldn't mind hearing her myself. She's been just right there the last few days. I might as well have swallowed one of Demps's barbells. Though I have to say, that on the way here, I felt something funny. I figured it was the coconut shrimp Demps brought me for a snack."

That had the girls giggling. Concerned that they were getting overtired after their hectic week, Sabrina said, "Girls, if you won't settle down, Uncle Collin or I will have to put you to bed. It's not polite not to explain. Now what's going on?"

Addie looked at Gena, who nodded shyly. "Christmas baby," Addie told her.

"Oh, sweet." Susie, a tawny-haired blonde with a short pageboy and dark circles under her eyes from the strain of her pregnancy said, "But she's coming for Valentine's."

Addison shrugged.

"Our little mathematicians," Sabrina said, urging the girls to start heading for the bedroom. Signaling Collin she said, "I think it's time they lay down."

"I'll take care of it."

The girls were in the midst of saying good-night when Susie squirmed and announced she needed to find the restroom. Isabella took her plate and Dempsey helped her to her feet.

Sabrina led the way down the hall, but just as Sabrina began shutting the door for her, she heard Susie yelp.

"Susie?" She went back in and saw the face of a woman in panic.

"My water broke!"

Pandemonium broke out. It was Sonny who rushed downstairs to get the wheelchair. Collin called for an ambulance. Graziella got the children into their room and when they were told the ambulances were tied up due to emergencies elsewhere, Gus offered his van.

Within ten minutes the condo was empty, except for Sabrina, Collin and the girls. The senior Nuñezes followed daughter Isabella and Sonny to the hospital.

Sabrina went to see how things were in the girls' room and found them finishing their prayers for Collin and climbing into bed.

"Are we in trouble?" Gena asked her.

"No, baby girl," she said easing past him to give her a good-night kiss. "Life is a mystery and it doesn't matter what doctors say. Babies come when they come." She kissed Addison, too, then had to ask. "You heard the baby?"

"Uh-huh."

"Words?"

With typical Addison aplomb, she put up her hands in the universal who-knows shrug. "Just baby."

Collin said, "Why don't I read them *The Night Before Christmas?*"

"I can if you want." Sabrina hadn't seen anything to suggest he wouldn't be okay with the girls—they seemed to respond as usual with him, except there was maybe a little less laughter in the house until tonight.

He looked from Gena to Addie. "Is this the one?" he asked holding up the book.

"Yeah," they replied, grinning.

"Okay," Sabrina said, retreating, "I'll start cleaning up."

As she wound her way through the living room, she

turned the stereo low on instrumental Christmas music. Saying a prayer in her heart for Susie, she blew out the candles and turned out all lights except the tree. She had the trash collected and compacted, the leftovers put up, and the dishes stacked, ready to be rinsed and put into the dishwasher.

She felt the air move behind her. When Collin took hold of her bare shoulders, her breath caught.

"I can finish," he said quietly. "You have to be dead on your feet. Go ahead and turn in."

She gave a little shake of her head. "I need to stay busy. Someone's going to call to let us know." And yet she'd grown up on a farm and she knew this night could be the longest night for Susie and Dempsey. "Oh, Collin. This would be an awful time to los—"

He turned her around and took her into his arms. "Don't."

Standing there in the dim light, the panic receded as quickly and simply as his single entreaty. Grateful that he was here, loving the feel of being in his arms, she let him give what he could of himself.

"Did the kids stay awake for the whole story?" she asked.

"No, they were out by the time the big guy destroyed the chimney. Big surprise. They've only heard it nine times since Thanksgiving."

It felt good for a smile to come naturally. It felt even better that he'd tried to make a joke. "It'll be time to switch back to Dr. Seuss in a few days."

"February can't get here soon enough."

Sabrina knew he meant that in the best way, but the increasing uncertainty of the future had her unable to agree. Easing away to resume the last of her chores, she said, "I shouldn't have asked you for this party."

"It went brilliantly. Everyone understood your intentions and were proud to be asked."

"I promise after tomorrow's grand unwrapping, I'll keep things low-key," she continued as if he hadn't spoken. "Don't worry if you need or want to make plans for New Year's. I'll be busy taking down the tree and—"

Collin came up behind her, cupped the side of her face and turned her head to receive his kiss. It was slow and aching and it pulled a whimper of yearning from her when he finally pulled away.

"Stop thinking I'm angry with you. I'm just trying to get us through this."

"That's what I'm trying to do."

"No, you're trying to fix what's broken."

Something had been bothering her since the night in his tub when he told her about his parents. If she was ever going to get it said, it might as well be now.

"Collin, please. Maybe it's not as bad as you were led to believe. What you said about your parents the other night…"

He shook his head.

"No, wait. What if she didn't go willingly? What if your mother tried to break it off and he threatened to take you again, this time for keeps?"

Collin raked his hands through his hair. "Because it didn't happen that way. She was happy he was back. She acted all alive and girlish again. I watched it with disbelief and disgust. She barely saw Cassie or me. It was all him. He could have robbed banks or been a serial rapist, don't you get it? She was obsessed with him and I hope they got what they deserved. I hope—"

"Collin!"

Not only did she have to warn him that he was raising his voice, he was about to say something he could never take back. As it was, he began to walk away, unable to look at her.

"Please—"

He paused, but didn't turn around.

"Please don't go out like you did the other night. Close yourself in your room if you have to, but please don't make me worry about you out on the streets or behind the wheel."

"All right."

Aware that sleep wouldn't come until she'd heard about Susie, Sabrina took her time with the dishes. It was midnight when she left the kitchen, turned out the tree lights and headed for her room. Officially Christmas and no word from the hospital. Tempted to call, but unwilling to intrude, she changed into her black velour pajamas, thinking she would settle down on the couch and wrap herself in a throw to wait. As she returned to the living room barely lit by the hall night-light, she realized that she hadn't yet taken the presents out of Collin's walk-in closet to put around the tree. She hated having to disturb him, but it would be risky to wait until just before sunrise. The girls might hear her and come running.

She paused at his door, which remained open and saw him lying with his back to her. He had changed out of his suit and just wore jeans. Grateful that he was getting some rest at last, she padded barefoot to the closet, belatedly remembering the light automatically came on when you opened the door.

Collin rolled over.

"Sorry. Go back to sleep," she told him. "It's the gifts. I need to put them under the tree."

He pushed himself off the bed. "I wasn't asleep."

"Oh."

"I was waiting for you to go to bed and I would have done it."

They worked in silence after that. When they were down to the last two packages, she said, "If you'll finish this, I'll just get their stockings filled and turn in." It would be a relief not to keep seeing his bare chest and the dusting of hair that ran down his flat abs and beyond the unbuttoned waistband on his jeans.

"I haven't heard the phone ring."

"There's been no word."

"That's not good, is it?"

No, not since her water broke hours ago. But she tried to remain positive. "First babies can take their time."

He stood on the other side of the coffee table from her but said nothing and so she murmured, "Good night."

It took several more minutes to do the stockings. When she returned to the living room, she didn't know where to set them because they had no mantle, so she put the girls' standing up in one high-backed chair and hers and Collin's in another.

Just as she started for bed the phone rang. She quickly grabbed it before the rest of the household was wakened.

"Hello?"

"Sabrina, I'm sorry to call so late."

"Dempsey," she whispered. "It's all right. How are you? How's Susie?"

"Fine. Fine now. There were some complications, but he's out of the woods. Little Sam is going to be all right."

"Sam?"

"Sabrina—I have a son."

They talked for only another minute. Dempsey had just left Susie to get some sleep, and he was beyond exhausted himself. Thanking him for letting them know, Sabrina added, "Merry Christmas!" and disconnected. Overwhelmed she had to sit down and ended up on the edge of the coffee table.

The girls had been right all along. She couldn't understand how they'd known. She'd heard or read several times that we were all born with psychic ability and other special senses, and that as we matured and started reasoning, those abilities receded. If this wasn't a prime example of that, then it was nothing short of a miracle.

She looked down at the darkened manger with wonder. A son. Soft laughter bubbled up inside her. But the laughter turned to tears as relief and gratitude had to yield to exhaustion.

"Sabrina?" Collin was crouching by her before she knew it. "What is it? I heard the phone."

"It *is* a boy."

His expression reflected the shock she'd felt. "How can that be?"

"I don't know. I guess we can ask the girls in the morning."

He smiled crookedly and gently wiped at her tears with his thumbs. "That's good. Dempsey had tried not to be disappointed, but he wanted a son."

"They've named him Sam. I didn't get to ask his size or weight. After he said there'd been some complications, it was enough to know Susie and Sam were okay." She exhaled shakily. "This is crazy. I'm so tired I can't get up."

Without a word, Collin scooped her up in his arms. He didn't take her to her room, though; he took her to his.

"I know the exhaustion you're feeling," he finally said as they entered his bedroom. "I feel it, too, but I can't sleep." He sat her on the edge of the bed, turned down the covers and top sheet, and put her in. Then he came around to the other side and climbed in under just the bedspread. Shifting behind her, he drew her against him and kept his arm wrapped around her waist.

The last thought Sabrina had was how perfect it felt to be with him.

Sabrina was gone when he opened his eyes. He didn't expect her to still be there, but he was surprised he didn't wake when she'd left. Lying with her in his arms had been the most peaceful feeling he'd ever known.

Glancing at the clock, he saw it was just six and he had a thing or two to take care of himself before everyone rose.

A quick check into the living room told him the coast was clear. He could faintly hear her in the shower down the hall. Satisfied, he went to work.

Afterward, he had his shower and by the time he'd dressed in a black V-necked sweater and jeans, Sabrina was in the kitchen pouring coffee. She was wearing a white poet's shirt and jeans. Her hair, shiny clean and fragrant was swept over one shoulder. As the scent of honeysuckle seduced, he leaned over to kiss her behind her ear. "Merry Christmas," he murmured.

"Merry Christmas."

"Sleep well?"

"Lovely." Turning she handed him his coffee. "Did you get any rest?"

"The best I've had in almost a week." He let his gaze take in every inch of her face. "Did I miss a call while I was showering?"

"Not that I know of. That would definitely have roused the girls."

His gaze shifted to her earrings. "You thought I was upset about those last night. I meant what I said. He did a good thing. They'd go well with your chopsticks, too."

Putting down her coffee, she leaned forward to touch her lips in the vee of his sweater. "Kiss me. I heard a giggle down the hall."

He did slowly and deeply as though they had all the time in the world, yet knowing it would have to last him all day…and, as experience had taught him, a day can change everything. When she trailed her fingers from his collar down to the waistband of his jeans, she drew his hips to hers. Arousal had already stirred from the languid kiss; she made him press her back against the cabinets to show her how great his desire was.

"I'll think about that every time I look at you today."

She smiled. "I'd be content with you just looking at me."

"You'll get that wish, too."

The stampede of little feet drew a sigh from him and

with a rueful smile he stepped back and suavely gestured for her to lead the way. Grabbing her mug, she did.

"Merry Christmas, Gena. Merry Christmas, Addison," she sang as she turned the corner to find them dancing up and down at the vision of the lit tree and all of the bounty beneath it.

"Brina, look at everything Santa brought us! Unca Colon, look!"

"Yeah, it looks like we'll need to bring in a crane to lift you out of all the paper in a few minutes."

He sat down in the corner of the couch and lifted an eyebrow when Sabrina settled in the opposite corner. Patting the cushion beside him, she shifted over until they were touching shoulders. With the girls wholly preoccupied with their presents, he took her free hand and placed it on his thigh.

"Well, what happened?" he drawled to the wide-eyed little blondes. "Did you forget how to read your names on packages?" As the girls squealed and started tearing at paper, Collin reached behind and beneath Sabrina's hair to caress her nape. "We didn't take into consideration having to haul all of this to San Antonio."

Gus's gift of a play kitchen, which they opened and delighted over last night, was temporarily forgotten as the new windfall was exposed. The Bitty Babies were hugged and compared and the play stations threatened to cost Collin his hearing, but they, too, were a great success. There were videos, games, Hannah Montana T-shirts and new books to read.

"That'll teach you to complain about Dr. Seuss," Sabrina said under her breath as his eyebrows rose at the number of titles.

When half of their gifts were hidden by paper trash, Gena came upon a long gift with a name she couldn't read.

"Work it out," Sabrina told her. "You know your letters."

"That's a *C*," she declared.

"Whose name starts with a *C* here?"

She thought and said, "Sabrina!"

"We're narrowing down the field," drawled Collin turning to narrow his eyes at Sabrina. "And what have you done?" he asked under his breath.

"Unca Colon!"

He put down his almost empty mug and pretended to reach out greedily. With his best pirate voice, he growled, "Hand it over, me pretty!"

"It's heavy!"

"I'll help, Gena," Addie said, assisting her in tugging the long box to him.

"You didn't get Dempsey to recommend body building equipment, I hope?" he asked Sabrina.

She just shrugged and smiled a Mona Lisa smile.

Settling the thing on his lap, he tore it open with unabashed zeal, then threw back his head and laughed with delight.

"What is it?" Addie said looking upside down at the picture. "How did they get a piano in there?"

"It's a keyboard," Gena replied.

Collin looked over at Sabrina. "You remembered?"

At the first and last Christmas party she'd attended with the firm, he'd played a song or two on a keyboard that someone had brought in for entertainment.

"Until then I didn't know you could play or were musical. You were good. How could I forget? What I don't understand is why you gave up pursuing music when you have such natural talent?"

"I was concerned it would upset Cassie."

With a disbelieving glance, Sabrina said, "She'll box your ears for that. She hasn't stopped listening to music, has she? That stereo was going strong a few times while we were there."

His heart swelled at how supportive and encouraging she was, even after all he'd put her through. "Thank you," he murmured.

"Where's Santa's present to you, Brina?" Addie said, swatting at paper to see the floor.

"My gift is getting to have this wonderful time with you girls," she replied. "I think you should check out your stockings now."

"There's that *C* again," Gena said picking up the first stocking. "For you," she said, bringing it to Collin.

"Thank you," he replied. "How about a kiss for good elf work?"

She giggled and complied.

"I know this one," Addie said with relief. "See Brina, Santa didn' leave you out."

"Aw…well, I told you he hadn't," Sabrina assured her. "Thank you, sweetie."

As the girls attacked their stockings, Collin looked with bemusement at his. There was just one item, a small square jeweler's box. He all but held his breath hoping she hadn't spent much more of her money on him. He discovered he was wrong.

"Sabrina." The 18K gold-initialed cuff links left him speechless.

"I thought you'd complain a little less about formal

engagements if you had something you liked to wear," she said softly.

"I'll treasure them." Taking hold of her hand, he brushed a kiss across her fingers. Then he nodded to her stocking. "Let's see."

"Oh—" she shrugged "—restocking on the honey-suckle toiletries."

"Bless you, Santa. Let me see."

She shook her head and started to dig out what she'd slid in there last night, only to freeze. Her gaze locked with his, she drew out a pair of rhinestone hair sticks. The sticks were painted in black enamel and the stones were fastened in gold filigree. Sabrina whispered, "They're exquisite. How did you ever—?"

"A client works in and out of Japan. A friend flies for FedEx. Miracles do happen."

Sabrina fingered the beautiful detail work. "I'm so touched, I'm afraid I'm going to cry."

"I just hope I get to see you wearing them." His throat raw at her overwhelmed reaction to them, Collin nodded back to her stocking. "Let me see the rest."

"I told you—" She began turning the stocking upside down in her lap. Two skinny bottles of honeysuckle lotion and cologne dropped into her lap…along with a key chain…and key. "Oh, my God."

Collin's chest shook as she looked at the emblem on the key chain and back at him. "If you look out the balcony," he told her, "you might be able to spot it."

Glancing toward the children, Sabrina whispered urgently to him, "You can't do this!"

"I not only can, I did."

"It's too much."

"It will never be enough."

Rising, Sabrina went to him and framed his face with her hands and kissed him softly.

Giggles erupted behind her. "Brina kissed Unca Colon," Addie sang.

"That's because I got the best present, Miss Smarty Party. Want to see?"

They only spent a minute on the balcony because although sunny, it was a cold morning. As soon as they all looked down at the circular drive in the front of the building, they saw the ivory Lexus with the big white bow on the roof.

"I told you that you should always wear white," Collin said. "Merry Christmas, my Honeysuckle Girl."

Chapter Twelve

"Are we *there* yet?"

"Are we *there* yet?"

The question posed by the twins every few miles was a growing torment to Collin and from Sabrina's body language, he assumed she wasn't coping much better. He understood their excitement and impatience to see their mother again, and he was relieved beyond words that with only days before Valentine's Day, Cassie was back and safe. At the same time, the life that they had grown so accustomed to was about to end. They had become a family unit and that arrangement was almost over. If there was one thing Collin didn't handle well, it was endings, which led to the crux of his character flaws. If one wanted to avoid endings, it stood to reason that you avoided beginnings, any form of real bonding.

The superficial had its value. Those lessons were being driven home, minute after minute, mile after mile.

As they navigated through Bexar County traffic, Sabrina leaned toward him to ask softly, "You okay?"

He knew she was attuned to him and his inner turmoil. She'd been that way from the day she'd come to interview for the job at the agency. When people started living under the same roof, those intuitive qualities compounded. Collin suspected she could smell his dread and angst like a movie vampire scenting its next victim. Nevertheless, he had no intention of making her worry more than she needed to.

"Fine," he replied. "Just trying to keep those eighteen-wheelers from driving over us."

"Uh-huh. I was just wondering because…you missed the exit."

Collin couldn't believe it, but in the rearview mirror, he saw that the girls were openmouthed and about to come out of their seats. It figured that even at three they could remember their exit to home better than he did.

"This is a test," he announced in a caricature of an official's voice. "This is only a test. You failed. You should have been yelling, 'There it is!' way before I got there. Punishment is a mandatory stop at the dentist!"

"No way!" Gena declared.

"We missed Mommy. Is she gonna be able to find us?" Addie whimpered looking over her shoulder trying to see out the back window.

"Don't torment them, Collin," Sabrina said. "There's the next exit, Addie. He's getting out right here, aren't you, *Unca Colon?* He's going over the overpass and right back to where the base entrance is, okay?"

"Okay," Addie said sounding not quite trusting.

Fifteen minutes later they had their passes and were easing down the boulevard to the on-base living area.

"Not our house…not our house…not our house," the girls droned craning to see over the front seats. Then one of them gasped. The slim blonde who skyrocketed out of the brick one-story duplex was a dead giveaway as to why.

"Mommy!"

Collin figured it was a miracle someone didn't get hurt. He'd never seen Cassie so anxious to get her hands on her kids, and they exhibited a new dexterity in attempting to free themselves from their seats.

"Just time for a quick hug, kids," he quipped, "then you're heading back to Dallas."

He was roundly ignored and for the next few minutes he and Sabrina were mere onlookers as Cassie yanked open their door, finished freeing the girls and grabbed them into her arms. Collin's insides did bad things even with happy tears, but he had to watch plenty of them fall. He hadn't expected the little ones to fall apart as they did—but then he'd been trying not to remember his own childhood.

Finally Cassie forced herself to put down the girls long enough to hug Sabrina. "Great to see you and thank you again, so, so much."

"You know I hated that you had to go, but it was a total pleasure. Well, except that they got sick right at New Year's."

"Believe me, they'll get sick again and again. It's the season and this crazy weather. Do me a favor and take them inside so I can have a minute with that homely lug behind you? We'll bring in the girls' things."

Sabrina cheerfully urged the girls to show her where they would put all of their new things. Before the front door shut behind them, Cassidy stopped before Collin.

Hands on her slim hips, she demanded, "You going to be anal about this?"

"You know reunions are about as fun to me as good-byes. Sue me. It's still good to have you back."

"Thanks. Feels pretty good. Sorry for the excessive displays of affection."

He shrugged, narrowing his eyes as hers twinkled more and more with each taunt. "To each their own."

"You want to shake my hand or can you risk a hug?"

Feeling his throat beginning to ache, he sighed with dramatic weariness and extended his arms. As she snickered and wrapped her arms around him, he muttered, "You look lousy. Haven't unpacked your brush yet? Donate your makeup to your replacement in Kabul?"

"I look better than you. What happened, did Sabrina already find herself a new apartment?"

Despite all of the verbal abuse, they hugged each other tight enough to injure ribs. Collin wanted to tell her that he was beyond proud of her. No choppers were lost while she was there, but one pilot was critically injured during a mortar attack at their base as he'd emerged from his quarters. It could have happened to any of them and because Cass had played poker with him many a time, he'd asked her to call his widowed father and reassure him. She had served above and beyond her nation's call to duty.

"I need to get inside and assure my kids that I'm not a figment or vanishing in the next twenty-four hours," she told him. "Besides that, some of the people on this street still have spouses over there and these reunions are as tough on them as it is on us. Coming in?"

"Beats standing out here and being fantasized over by your lonely military wives."

Cassie threw back her head and howled with laughter. "Who would want your skinny self? These guys could pose for a Chippendale calendar."

Usually Collin enjoyed these verbal jousts with his younger sibling, but he'd reached his limit today. "Lead the way before Sabrina starts redecorating your girls' room."

"She's got my blessing. When are you going to tell that pretty woman that you're nuts about her?"

"Mind your own business."

Cass uttered a sound of disgust. "You all but devour her with your eyes, and in the two minutes you stood here beside her you couldn't keep your hands to yourself. Did you not use this time to your best advantage?"

"I repeat, it's not any of your business...but you might like to know the girls were not exposed to *Unca Colon* behavior, but rather *Uncle Daddy* conduct. Besides that, Sabrina deserved the respect, too."

"I'm sure she's thrilled with your noble restraint and every bit as frustrated as I am."

"Cass, damn it, do you mind?"

"Yes, I do. That is simply ridiculous. Last I looked there are doors and locks in your condo."

Yes, but had he and Sabrina gone further than they did, Collin doubted the well-built walls and solid doors could have contained the sounds of their pleasure. "Oh, move it," he muttered giving his sister a gentle shove the rest of the way up the sidewalk.

* * *

It was almost two hours later when they emerged
from the house to begin their goodbyes. Actually, Collin
had done his inside crouching down to hold Gena and
Addie for so long, they patted his face asking if he'd
gone to sleep. He slapped on his sunglasses when he
enfolded Cassidy in his arms.

"I'm sorry for being hard on you," she whispered in
his ear. "But it's just because I love you, English."

Sabrina began openly weeping and grabbing for
tissues as they pulled away, so Collin ran in to return
their passes by himself.

"Sorry," Sabrina said when he returned. "This is like
being inside a deflating balloon. Everything is so qu-
quiet, and empty, and there's no…air." She looked over
her shoulder.

"What?"

"Just checking to make sure we didn't forget something."

"If we did, we're mailing it."

His testiness had her staring at his profile, but he pretended he didn't notice. They had agreed that considering the early hour, they would drive on back to Dallas;
the weather was decent, the traffic okay. So why was he
now wishing they were driving into a blizzard—or the
opposite direction?

"Are you hungry?" he asked. Cassie had offered to
feed them lunch, but they knew that she needed one-on-
one time with her kids. "Before we get onto the interstate, you should tell me if you're hungry."

"I'm not."

He got onto the interstate. By the time they reached

Austin, he got out for gas. "I'm starving. Would you mind if we grab a bite? This way we wouldn't have to cook when we get home. I mean back. Not that I would expect you to cook." That's how conversation had been so far—when they said anything—fragmented sentences and lots of editing.

"I don't mind. I'll make myself a salad."

"You should have salmon with grilled vegetables. You've been taking care of everyone but yourself. Even Cass told me that she felt badly that the kids wore you down to the size of a twig."

"That's an exaggeration. It's just the bug I caught after the girls. I'll be back to my usual weight in a week or so."

Collin didn't want to remember how ill and frail she'd been, and still struggling to care for the kids so he could get back to work.

After filling his vehicle, he drove over to a steak house he'd spotted. Timewise it was the lull before the evening traffic began, so they were encouraged to take their time. Collin ordered the salmon and made Sabrina take a few bites off of his fork. Sabrina skipped the salad and ordered cheesecake with strawberries, and made Collin beg for a bite. Slowly they relaxed and the provocative teasing that was so prevalent in their relationship returned.

He'd finished his Scotch and she her wine a good while earlier, but they were enjoying not having to edit themselves for the girls, so Collin beckoned their waiter and ordered a bottle of wine and nachos, suddenly craving "munchies."

They were both stunned when they next looked up and saw a line had formed in the entryway of the restaurant. Their understanding waiter came to their table and said, "I can bring you another bottle, but you'd have to show me a hotel key."

Not only was the restaurant all but packed, the sun had set. Collin asked for the bill instead and including a two-hundred-percent tip, assuring him, "We're heading to the hotel now. Thank you for the concern."

Sabrina only questioned that once they were outside. Shivering as the cold encroached, she pulled up the collar of her red jacket and said, "We can't stay. We're staying?"

"It's the only responsible thing to do."

"Good luck finding two rooms at this hour, let alone two rooms close to each other."

He sensed her nerves as clearly as he felt his own and tried to purge them by using logic. "We've just spent four months sharing a home and sometimes a bed—and you're as pure as the day you claim I 'bamboozled' you." Collin at least earned a little smile from her for that. "If it comes down to it, is a night in the same hotel room with me a problem for you?" He had no business putting her on the spot, and yet he was all but praying there would only be one room left.

They actually had three, but the shower was broken in one and the freshly shampooed rugs were still wet in the other. By the time he shoved the card key into the door of the third room, he was done pretending that he hadn't meant for this to happen all along.

On the other hand, Sabrina was a different story. "Maybe if we just nap, we'll be fine in a few hours," she suggested as they stepped inside and looked around at the clean surroundings with the earthy tones and Santa

Fe decor. She particularly stared at the king-size bed. "We didn't even bring a change of clothes."

The only thing Collin cared about was whether she would be willing to take hers off again for him. Seeing her rise out of that bath like a vision had gotten him through every day and tormented his nights. "Tell me that this isn't what we both want?" he demanded. "We've been walking and talking around this since we left Dallas."

"Since before Christmas."

"Since I brought you to the condo that first night and you caught me looking at the lingerie you'd just bought."

Sabrina closed her eyes. "I just don't want you to be sorry in the morning—"

"I only need to know if you want me as much as your eyes tell me you do."

She placed her purse on the chair by the TV, slipped off her ponytail band and started unbuttoning her jacket. "I've wanted you since the first time I walked into your office and you looked up from something you were signing and did a double take."

Barely more than a year ago now, yet the months apart felt like an eternity. "What a bloody waste of time," he murmured. In two steps, he was framing her face with his hands and kissing her. That released a flood of pent-up emotion in both of them, and the kisses became devouring, urgent and needful.

With restless hands, Collin finished removing her jacket and his, tossing them in the direction of the chair. In the single shaft of light streaming out of the bathroom, they undressed each other, eagerly exploring and caressing each inch of skin exposed.

"I'm cold," she whispered.

It was anticipation, he knew, for her skin was on fire, particularly her breasts, which like an addict he returned to repeatedly for their responsiveness. She was adorable and alluring and Collin wanted this to be wonderful for her, so he quickly peeled back the bedspread and backed her onto the bed and covered her with his body and the sheet.

Gazing down at her, he stroked her hair, letting her get used to his weight and arousal. Already, he had to wrestle with his body's timeless urge for completion and slowed their kisses to once again build her need to match his own.

When he probed her soft core, her nails grazed his back and she slid her legs against his instinctively making it easier for him. She shook her head to the building force within her and, twining his fingers through hers, he rose over her.

"Look at me," he whispered.

When she did, he slowly entered her. His heart swelled to bursting just as he filled her. They watched each other experience the wondrous moment that proved they'd only been existing until now.

"My Honeysuckle Girl," he whispered against her lips. "My very own."

The only sounds after that were of two lovers reaching where they could only go together.

Chapter Thirteen

The next morning, the drive back to Dallas took exactly three hours and fifty-one minutes. Sabrina could determine that because there was little else to do except say "thank you," or "no thank you," depending on what Collin asked her—and to watch the clock on the radio console. She didn't even rebuke him for speeding. If he felt a need to get back faster—a crisis at the agency, he'd claimed first thing—then that's what she wanted, too.

As they wove through the city's streets, he finally said, "It's Lloyd Royston. He's pulling his account as I feared he would. Someone must've mentioned seeing us together somewhere else. Damn. What timing, since Lloyd just referred someone else to me and he's likely to pull out, too. I'm sorry I can only drop you off at the condo."

Stung that he would regret being seen with her, she replied with equal lack of consideration, "Whatever."

She could feel him glance at her profile, but she wouldn't be the one to point out what a clod he was being. Last night they'd made love three times—the last time leaving them so exhausted, they fell asleep with him still inside her. This morning had been like waking to a totally different person. Granted his mobile phone had begun buzzing seconds before eight, but he could have indicated with something more than a kiss on the forehead that she existed. He'd obviously forgotten or never cared how important last night had been for her. She felt as though her heart had ruptured and was rapidly dripping away her life's blood into her stomach.

But it wasn't like he hadn't warned her about himself. Wasn't there a saying about that? When people tell you who they are—believe them. She was a big girl. She could handle this. It would take no time to pack and find herself a nice hotel. She could give herself that much, then maybe go home after all, before she got serious about a job again. Then again, maybe not. Her hard-won independence was vulnerable right now and she didn't need her parents or brothers to undermine that, regardless of their good intentions.

Pulling before his building, Collin asked whomever he was talking to on his earpiece to hold on. Then he asked her, "Are you really okay? I wish I could tell you how long I'll be, but…"

"Fine. Take your time. I completely understand."

Before she could slam the door he yelled, "Wait!"

She opened the door and waited.

"I forgot to give you this."

The folded check just about finished her off. For services rendered, she thought, taking it with shaking fingers. She slammed the door and didn't look back. She doubted Collin noticed. He was racing out of the driveway before the biting February wind could rip the high-rise's door out of her hands.

"Miss Brina!" Sonny called from across the lobby. He had taken on the girls' shortened version of her name. "Everything okay down in San Antonio?"

In no frame of mind to do small talk, but terribly fond of Sonny, she fought to sound enthusiastic. "Yes. It was bittersweet, though. But great to have Cassidy back."

"I'm going to miss those two little rascals."

"Me, too. Um…would you by chance know if Gus is anywhere in the area?"

"He should be back around noon. He's on a run right now. Knee patient is at therapy. Something wrong with your new car?"

"No, it's perfect. I just wanted to catch up on a few things with him."

"Okay. I'll tell him to wait for you."

Just that little conversation had Sabrina feeling nauseous again as the elevator doors closed behind her. It wasn't Sonny's fault. It was a result of her resolve in knowing what she had to do.

Collin was later in getting back than he could have imagined. It left him with a bad taste in his mouth and a bad feeling in his gut. The bad taste was a result of having to cut short his time with Sabrina after everything went to hell at the office this morning. He'd intended for them to spend the rest of the day together, to talk, make love, plan. He would never have believed the world could look a hundred percent different after making love—but that was just it. They'd really been making love.

The bad feeling in his gut was from how Sabrina reacted. There was nothing he could put his finger on—there really hadn't been time to analyze it—but the feeling only compounded when he finally called her to let her know he was on his way home and only got his answering machine.

As he strode through the lobby of his building, he waved at Dempsey who'd just come on duty. "How're Susie and Sam?"

"Great! Tell Sabrina I have new pictures for her to look at."

"Will do."

In the elevator he impatiently watched the floor numbers flash on the wall panel, but then he began smiling because he was coming home and that word finally meant something again. Entering the condo, he was surprised to find it dark and everything still shut up like they'd left it yesterday morning. Poor darling, perhaps she'd suffered a relapse of the bug she'd caught from the kids a few weeks ago. That would be his fault. He'd been the one with the relentless appetite to see her perfect body, then love her into a fever's pitch.

"Hello?"

His gaze dropped to the foyer entry table where he saw her key chain and the condo key. Well, that told him she was home, at least.

But she wasn't in his room, or the kitchen.

"Sabrina?"

The dark living room and hall left him with a sickening feeling. When he entered her room, he knew why. She'd left it like she'd found it—empty and immaculate. Every trace of her was gone. The only hint that she'd ever been there was the lingering scent of honeysuckle.

Nevermore.

He sank to the bed shattered.

Sabrina considered taking off on Valentine's Day. Newly committed to being single the rest of her life, the holiday held no appeal to her—unless she could find chocolate at fifty percent off. But she liked her new job at Dogwood Grove Retirement Center where Gus was considering moving. He had suggested it to her during their long talk after she got into his van the day she left Collin and burst into tears.

A job in the health-care industry certainly seemed reliable work, what with the troubling economy and the aging population of the country. What's more, the people at Dogwood Grove were dear and some were without anyone to pay them any mind, let alone show love. Their loneliness pulled at her heartstrings.

By the time she got to the recreation center, she was glad she'd made herself get out of bed. Some of the staff had already put out pink carnations and another had brought in red heart balloons. Cookies in the shape of hearts were part of the morning snack offerings. The stereo was playing love songs, although most of the residents were still watching *Good Morning America*.

"Sabrina, it's about time," Mrs. Carlock called from the other side of the room. "We were about to send Arlene to call you. You have company."

She saw that the instant she turned around. Collin rose from his seat beside the elderly lady the moment she spoke. He looked his usual well-dressed self in his crisp gray suit and red tie—only his face was pale and there were dark circles under his eyes. It annoyed her that her heart did another plunge after the first shock of seeing him. He didn't deserve her compassion, let alone her concern.

As he came to her, she used the time to settle her tummy and threaten herself if she weakened one iota. So what if he'd made a gesture? How many times did she need to be humiliated before she got the message?

When she saw the bouquet of sunflowers mixed with every spring flower imaginable, she finally met his steady gaze. "What are you doing?"

"Trying to make you talk to me. Roses are easy on Valentine's Day. Try getting the spring flowers of Wisconsin when they aren't blooming yet. Would you mind looking over your shoulder at Gus and letting him know you're okay with this? I have the distinct feeling that he may pull out a gun if you continue to clench your fists as you do. He only agreed to direct me here with the understanding that if you got upset, I had to leave."

Shaking her head, she retraced her steps to where Gus stood sheepishly. "Thanks a lot, friend."

"I'm sorry, dear. It was a judgment call. If you're still not willing to listen to what he has to say, I'll see that security escorts him out."

"And what? Create a bigger scene?"

"He looks like a man who went through a great deal to find his way back to you."

Not wanting to prolong this, she returned to Collin

and signaled that he should follow her to a quieter and darker corner. "You shouldn't have pressured him to find out where I was. And why bother? You think explaining to me why you got cold feet for the—how many times have you dumped women, Collin?—clears the slate for you? I got exactly what I wanted from you, Collin—an education in the selfishness and stupidity of men. So go away with your clear conscience."

"I didn't dump you."

"And what was that check?"

"Your final salary for taking care of Gena and Addie."

She smiled bitterly. "Plus a little something for being so accommodating in bed?"

Twin spots of color appeared on his gaunt cheeks. "Never. Don't talk about us that way. I wrote you a larger check for the same reason. I wanted you to have the car."

Something happened to his voice and he looked away.

Yes, he wanted her body and she didn't sell herself cheaply. But he got it wrong; she wouldn't sell herself at all. She gave him her love.

"Why did you run away?" he rasped. "Of all the ways you could have struck out at me…"

"I did not run," she replied. "I left. You put out all the signals to indicate you had gotten what you wanted and I may be a fool for caring too much, but I am not stupid."

He nodded. "I hoped it was that."

"Excuse me?"

He took a long stabilizing breath. "I realize what I did wrong. The morning after we made love, I went into my old mode—I put job concerns first when it should have been you. You were all that mattered. When I saw the condo empty, I knew. I knew, Sabrina."

DADDY ON DEMAND

"Take the flowers already," someone called from the group of onlookers standing on the far side of the room. "This is no time to be stubborn. We can use all the cheer we can get around here."

Sabrina was determined she was not going to have her personal life played out in the middle of these people even if they would appreciate the entertainment. Taking the flowers with a curt, "Thank you," she brought them to Ms. Jimmie, the lady who had chastised her. Returning to Collin, she muttered, "Follow me."

Outside in the breezeway connecting one of the two living quarters, she stopped. The February wind was gusting, and she wrapped her arms around herself to keep from shivering. Her ivory pantsuit was designed for far more spring-like conditions.

"You're beautiful…but you're going to make yourself sick out here."

"I'm fine, but you need to go."

"I'm not leaving."

He said that with an almost serene smile. That, more than anything, had her starting to worry. "This isn't a contest to win, Collin, or a battle of wills. I give up trying to prove myself to you or anyone. I don't want to show you in a thousand different ways that I'm not like your mother. You described yourself best—more trouble than I deserve. You should remain a bachelor. In fact I applaud you for making that clear to me."

He slipped his hand into his pocket and came out with a small satin box.

Sabrina exhaled shakily. "Put that away. That's not fair."

"Now who's being stubborn?" Collin drew her out

of the wind and away from the front windows by tucking her into a small enclave sitting area beside the left wing. "I returned from the office that night with this, Sabrina. I wanted to surprise you. I was nervous and still scared, yes, but I knew you would never believe that I meant the words if I didn't come to you with a ring."

"I've been gone for ten days. What took you so long?"

"It took me that long to get Sonny and Gus to give me any help. They didn't want any part of me, any more than you did, until they believed I honestly loved you."

"They're good friends. They—what?"

"Sabrina, I love you. I knew it that night in Austin. Before. I won't deny that it scared me and I fought it. You know I've fought you from the moment I first hired you at the office. But I couldn't come to you until I knew that this—" he opened the box "—would make you see my heart."

The moment she saw the ring, Sabrina knew she had no resistance. Collin had been around her long enough to understand that she would never be bowled over with the ostentatious and the concept that more is more. The ring was an impeccable three stone diamond set in gold to compliment her coloring. Large enough to notice the stones were exceptional, but not to where she would be afraid to wear it daily.

When she raised her gaze to his, she could only ask, "Love happens, but you can kill it, crush it. Neglect it. What makes you think you can make the long haul?"

"My heart and soul."

What could she do? She held out her left hand. And when she wore his promise to her, she went into his arms and whispered, "I missed you so."

After more kisses and plans, they started back to the recreation center to make their announcement. "So twins run in your family?" she asked as he looped her arm through his.

"We're going to find out."

DÉJÀ YOU

BY
LYNDA SANDOVAL

Lynda Sandoval is a former police officer who exchanged the excitement of that career for blissfully isolated days, creating stories she hopes readers will love. Though she's also been a youth mental-health worker and runaway crisis counsellor, a television extra, a trade-show art salesperson, a European tour guide and a bookkeeper for an exotic bird and reptile company – among other weird jobs – Lynda's favourite career, by far, is writing books. In addition to romance, Lynda writes women's fiction and young adult novels and in her spare time she loves to travel, quilt, bid on eBay, hike, read and spend time with her dog. Lynda also works part-time as an emergency fire/medical dispatcher for the fire department. Readers are invited to visit Lynda on the web at www.LyndaSandoval.com, or to send mail with an SAE for reply to PO Box 1018, Conifer, CO 80433-1018, USA.

To Barbie,
Supplier of all things chocolate and caffeinated, and
a damn fine fire captain (and person) to boot.
<SWAK>

Chapter One

The fire raged.

Hot, thick, black smoke billowed and rolled around them inside the four-unit, two up, two down apartment building that was quickly losing its battle with the whipping flames.

Damn unattended candles.

Damn balloon construction on these cheap-ass buildings.

Damn them all if they didn't get control of this thing, and fast.

The fire had ripped through both levels of the apartments almost before the first due units arrived on scene. Numerous engine companies had responded to the first alarm. Engineer Erin DeLuca, her immediate supervisor, Captain C. J. Gooding, and Firefighter Ryan Drake—the crew on Engine Eight—had been assigned to investigate the bottom-floor, north-side apartment. They'd rescued everyone they could find from the entire building; now all the companies concentrated on tackling the fire, determined to knock it down against all odds. The wall of heat stifled her, and she knew it would get worse before it got better. Once they hit the flames with water, the resulting steam would be a hundred times hotter than the fire itself.

Through her helmet's crappy headset, Erin could hear the sounds of breathing, her own and that of every other firefighter trying to extinguish the virulent blaze. Beyond the Darth Vader breathing chorus came the crash of breaking glass; firefighters bumping into walls and furniture in the zero visibility; the *clomp-clomp* of crews moving about in the apartments above; garbled, back-and-forth radio communications as rooms were cleared; and, of course, the snap and hiss of the monster itself. With the cacophony, radio communications were nearly unintelligible inside her mask and helmet. Thankfully, they were all well aware of and accustomed to the limitations.

Her muscles strained as she and her crew carried in the charged one-and-a-half inch hose line that would hopefully black down the fire in this apartment, at least.

"Hillside Command, from Control."

"Go ahead." Erin heard the battalion chief respond to dispatch, from his strategizing position as incident commander outside the fire.

"You're thirty minutes into the incident, sir."

"Copy, thirty minutes. Thanks."

From her spot in the communications center, dispatch supervisor and Erin's friend, Lexy, gave the time. Erin couldn't help the niggling sense of alarm in her chest. Thirty minutes in, the fire was hot enough to melt steel, and it didn't seem as though they were any closer to controlling it than when they'd first arrived. She checked the LED readout for her air tank. Half-full, which meant some of the bigger guys on the scene were likely near empty.

Erin squinted to see through the blackness, but it was no use. She closed her eyes and let her hearing and sense of touch take over instead. She moved to the left, toward the snapping bursts of fire. Without warning, an ominous splitting sound came from above them. Everyone ducked back as the ceiling above them collapsed, raining down furniture and flame, wood and water and the two-firefighter crew that had been in that particular room upstairs. The ash and sparks settled, then everyone moved at once.

Erin immediately dropped to the ground and felt her way to the firefighter closest to her. When she reached him, she leaned down close to his helmet and mask, now jarred away from his face. Bad news.

Fumbling with her stiff gloves, she resituated his safety gear, but not before she recognized him. Her gut clenched. "I've got you, Sully," she yelled, knowing he probably couldn't hear her any better than she could hear anyone else through all the gear. "Can you talk?"

He groaned.

She peered up into the gaping hole just as flames engulfed what was left of the entire apartment overhead.

Her stomach dropped.

"Portable Eight-A to Command, Sullivan's down!" she said into her radio. "Second floor is fully involved. I've got Sullivan and I'm coming out."

"Eight-B to Command, we've got Arroyo," came the voice of Drake, amped to the max. "He's unconscious. Unknown extent of injuries."

"Command, from Engine Eight," came Captain Gooding's calm but urgent voice, "we have a collapse and a fully engulfed second floor. Repeat, we have a ceiling collapse from the second floor to the bottom level with two firefighters down."

From outside, the battalion chief's tone came across with a heightened sense of alarm. "Engine Eight's got a collapse. All units, abandon structure. Repeat, abandon structure."

Three sharp alert blasts rang out over the radio, then Lexy's calm, collected voice. "All units on the Hillside Fire, abandon, abandon, abandon. Repeat, abandon, abandon, abandon structure."

Erin heard the battalion chief calling for a PAR—personnel accountability report—from all the crews working the fire, to make sure no other firefighters were injured or unaccounted for. She hitched her elbows under Sullivan's arms and dragged him first to the wall, and then following the hose line, out toward the front door she couldn't see. Beneath the smoke, she could barely make out Drake and the captain carrying Arroyo the same way.

When she burst into the late-afternoon air, her bunker gear sooty and steaming from the temperature drop, her vision cleared. She glanced up at the apartments, sucking the last vestiges of air from her tank and feeling sick. They probably wouldn't be able to save much of the structure, if any. A total failure.

She hated that.

A Troublesome Gulch paramedic crew ran up to assist her with Sullivan. Erin glanced over, glad to see Brody Austin there, a damned excellent paramedic, not to mention one of her closest friends.

He laid his hand against the reflective letters that spelled out DeLuca on the back of her bunker coat and leaned closer, concern wrinkling his brow. "You okay?" he yelled.

She nodded. Her biceps shook and twitched from the exertion of dragging burly Jeff Sullivan out, and her breaths came in heaving succession, but she'd be fine.

Seemingly satisfied, Brody joined the other medics who had already started administering aid to Sullivan, while Erin ran back to the door to help the rest of her three-person crew deliver Arroyo to them, as well.

She, Drake and Captain Gooding watched until they were sure Sullivan and Arroyo would be okay, then backed off and headed to the designated rehab area. Fans blew cool air around them. Erin sat on the wide back bumper of the ambulance, unscrewed her air pressure regulator from her mask, pulled off her helmet, then yanked her Nomex hood down to dangle around her neck. Finally, she removed her mask.

Relieved to be free of it, she sucked in her first gulp of cool, fresh air. Sweat rolled down her skin beneath her bunker gear, and if her face looked anything like the others', whipped dogs had nothing on the three of them. She stuck one glove under her arm, extracting her hand and inverting the inside liner, then repeated it with the other glove. After she'd removed her air tank and bunker coat, she held out her shaky arm for one of the rehab EMTs to take her blood pressure.

Drake and the captain did the same.

The trio, breathing as though they'd just gone three rounds with the heavyweight champion of the world, watched from afar as fresh teams battled the fire from outside the unstable structure. Once an Abandon order had been given, their only option was to fight the fire defensively.

The head paramedic in the rehab area handed them each a cold bottle of water. Erin downed the entire thing in one extended swallow, and it didn't touch her thirst.

She glanced over at her captain. "We're going to lose this one, aren't we?" she asked, before wiping the back of her hand across her mouth.

Captain Gooding nodded, running fingers through her sweaty hair. "Damn it."

"Will they reassign us, Cap?"

"Probably not. BC called a second alarm. There are enough fresh crews here to take over. Take your time in rehab." She stared somberly at the fire for a moment, then stood and headed over to the other ambulance, where Sullivan and Arroyo were being loaded.

At least they'd gotten everyone out before the fire took the upper hand, Erin thought. Just then, someone yanked her arm from the side. Instinctively, she jerked away, whipping around to come face-to-face with a soot-covered woman who looked to be at least eight months pregnant. Her maternity dress hung in blackened tatters against her body.

"What's wrong?"

"Please," the woman sobbed, barely able to inhale, "help me."

Erin grabbed both of the woman's upper arms, bracing her. "Talk to me! Are you hurt?"

The woman, so hysterical she couldn't form sentences, gestured vaguely toward the building. "M-my husband…"

"What about him?" Erin demanded, giving the woman a small shake. She didn't want to be harsh, but time was of the essence. "Take a deep breath, then tell me."

"H-he went b-back in. F-for the cat." She shook her head and clutched at it as tears streamed down her face. "I haven't seen him s-since. Please!"

Alarm and dread rose inside Erin's throat, threatening to breach her panic dam. She hooked a hand around the woman's arm. "Come on," she said in a kind but firm voice, as she led her toward her immediate supervisor. "Hey, Cap!"

The older woman she respected so much spun to face them, then trotted over and met them halfway. "What's going on?" she asked, her voice hoarse.

Erin glanced down at the frenzied pregnant woman, who looked to be no more than twenty or so. "Her husband went back into the building to look for their cat. He hasn't come out."

Erin's and Captain Gooding's gazes locked, as the captain pressed her lips into a thin line. After a moment, she turned her back, immediately got on her radio and spoke with the battalion chief. They conferred, then Captain Gooding took the woman's other arm gently, supporting her. "Come on, honey. What's your name?"

"Suzette," the young soon-to-be-mother wailed. "We've only been married eight months! Please!"

"Okay, Suzette, okay," the captain soothed.

Between them, Suzette hung her head and gave in to the racking sobs.

"Where are we going?" Erin asked her superior, in a soft voice so as not to be overheard by Suzette.

"Victims assistance," Captain Gooding responded in kind.

Erin gulped. She knew the answer, but hope made her ask anyway. "Are we…going back in for him?"

The Cap met her gaze over Suzette's head, remorse and resignation in her expression. "No."

At the victims assistance staging area, a counselor, and a police officer—Erin's friend, Cagney—sat Suzette down and tried to explain the gravity of the situation. Erin stood back and watched as the confusion and horror moved into Suzette's expression. She knew the exact moment when Suzette realized the truth: her husband was never coming out.

All of a sudden, dizziness assailed Erin. Flashes, images, horrors filled her brain. She couldn't handle this. She started to back away from the cops, counselors and huddled *victims,* hating that word with a passion. She spun, eyes down, trying to block everything from her brain, but her ears buzzed and her hands shook. Part of her boiled with the insane urge to dash into the blazing apartments and search for Suzette's husband, although the chances of him still being alive were zero at this point. Not to mention, her disobedience of the Abandon order would get her ass fired, if not killed.

With no warning, the sky blazed orange as the bottom apartments flashed over, blowing out all the remaining intact windows. Like a freakin' Hollywood movie set. The entire structure succumbed to flames, and thick black smoke blasted out at the fire crews like an angry demon declaring victory.

"Nooooo!"

Erin heard Suzette's keening wail behind her.

Fixated on the fire, Erin struggled to breathe, her knees buckling slightly.

God. She knew.

She knew the pain Suzette was feeling right at that moment. Felt it, all the way down to her soul's core.

For so many years, so many fires, she'd been able to block out the memories of the accident that had destroyed her life, but the unexpected blow of young, pregnant, distraught Suzette had cracked her veneer, and inside lay a mirror. She saw herself in the young woman's eyes as the nightmare of her past rushed in through the cracks.

Prom night. Kevin, the love of her life. Alcohol for all of them except her, because of the secret inside her womb, the baby she and Kevin had accidentally created but had not yet revealed to the world. They were getting married two months later anyway, so what did it matter?

The evening started with laughter and loud music, the rustle of satin and taffeta, bottles passing, sexy Lexy, the prom queen, climbing over the stick shift to kiss and tease Randy.

Then, without warning, screeching tires, a crushing jolt, the disorientation of rolling, tumbling, smashing down the cliff and then fire. So much twisted metal, broken glass and fire.

Screaming, her dress in flames and melting to her skin, Erin saw Kevin crushed and silent. Her best girlfriend, Mick, broken and still. Lexy's boyfriend, Randy, crumpled and twisted inside the smashed cab of the Range Rover, with Lexy trapped and screaming beside him. Brody, holding one of Mick's shoes and walking dazedly around the scene, slipping, falling, getting back up, falling again.

Where were Cagney and her last-minute fill-in date? What was his name again? Erin had thought, as she finally sank to the ground and rolled to extinguish the flames engulfing her dress.

This isn't my life, she remembered thinking. *This is a newspaper article from somewhere else.*

"Kevin!" she'd screamed, clutching her hands to her searing abdomen, as she slowly lost consciousness, remembering, in her last lucid moment, their baby. "Kevin…!"

Erin's knees buckled again, and Brody appeared from nowhere, propping her up by her elbows. "Kevin," she gasped at him.

The lines around his eyes deepened. "Erin, honey. It's Brody. Can you hear me?"

She looked up, disoriented, then remembered where she was and why. She saw an expression of agonized understanding on Brody's face, and sagged against him. "Yes," she wheezed.

"You need oxygen."

"Yes." She needed a hell of a lot more than that, but the oxygen would do for now.

He guided her back to the rehab area, settling her next to Drake and slipping the clear mask over her face.

"You okay, DeLuca?" Drake asked, his eyes wide.

"She's fine," Brody assured the young firefighter, with a confident smile, despite the anguish that showed in his eyes. "A little smoke inhalation. Nothing to worry about." He leaned in, putting his hands on Erin's shoulders. "You listen to me. It'll be okay," he said, in a low voice. "I promise."

"How?"

He looked away, a muscle in his jaw pulsing. "I don't know. But, if I did it, you can find a way."

She shook her head. "We lost someone," she said, her words muffled, breath fogging the oxygen mask.

"I know," he said, his tone somber. "We're transporting the wife. She's gone into preterm labor."

Erin squeezed her eyes shut, absolutely refusing to cry on a fire scene. She'd *never* cried at work. Never.

Brody shook her. "Look at me."

She did.

"We'll help you. Faith and I. It *will* be okay," he enunciated slowly.

She nodded, totally numb, agreeing with him when she didn't agree at all, feeling that nothing in her life would ever be okay again....

Chapter Two

Despite a long shower and half a bottle of shampoo, the smell of smoke still hung in Erin's hair, an acrid reminder of the afternoon's horror. The chief had released the entire battalion after the fire—common practice after such a physically draining event. He'd called in the off-duty shift to cover the rest of their twenty-four hour tour.

Erin didn't feel released, however. She felt as though she'd been holding in a scream for hours, as though she was going to explode if she didn't do something. Finn, her Irish wolfhound, trailed her through the house, whining, toenails clicking on the hardwood. Knowing.

She ignored the ringing phone and listened dully to two concerned messages—one from her mother and the second from her closest friend, Faith—as she dressed in her most comfortable jeans, a well-washed Barenaked Ladies concert T-shirt and some simple clogs.

Clearly, the fire had hit the news.

As much as she loved her mother and her friends, at the moment, she couldn't deal. Brody would fill Faith in, and Mom could wait. Erin couldn't bear to recount the fire over and over and over again. Not now. Not with Kevin's death—not to mention Suzette's husband's—weighing so heavily on her soul.

She'd been in denial for so long, which had worked well enough. Now, this. She couldn't even think about her and Kevin's unborn baby. Sheer panic bubbled up inside her throat.

Go. Just go.

Finn's doggy door was open, his bowls were full and he was used to spending long hours alone, thanks to their twenty-four-hour shifts. Luckily, his abandonment issues had improved greatly. He hadn't eaten a couch cushion or torn up the trash in months. Still, she felt a pang of guilt about leaving him by himself, but she had to. He'd understand. That's what dogs did, what made them so special.

With shaking hands, she swiped her keys and small purse off the countertop and headed blindly for the door, not knowing or caring where she was going.

Her breath came in gasps. Sweat beaded on her forehead and upper lip. God help her, she needed to get out of Troublesome Gulch before her emotions roared even further out of control. Until all those raw, dangerous memories had been corralled back into their neat little mental stalls, gates locked, out of sight and mind where they'd lived for nearly twelve years. She couldn't bear it.

Escape.

Escape.

She whipped wet strands of her choppy-cut hair out of her face, but still it took three tries to get her key into the ignition of her Subaru Outback. By the time she cranked the engine to life, she was so amped that she accidentally kept the key engaged until the pistons squealed in protest. Jamming the stick into Reverse, she spun gravel pulling out of her driveway.

She didn't know she was heading toward I-70. She didn't realize she was crying until she hit the eastbound lanes, and by that time, she couldn't stop. She sobbed until her throat ached and her nose clogged, until her whole face felt swollen with grief. She only remembered to wipe her eyes because she didn't want to risk causing an accident that would force some innocent person to suffer the agony she'd been living through.

Poor Suzette.

She flinched, white-knuckling the steering wheel.

Sure, she had enough of a grip on reality to know she hadn't caused Suzette's husband's death, but she hadn't been able to prevent it, either. Or to help—not even a little bit. She'd lost her damned precious control. Where did that leave her?

It'll be okay, Brody had told her.

Right.

She couldn't be happier for Brody and Faith, or more impressed that Brody had been able to face his demons from that horrible prom night tragedy and come away with the love of the perfect woman. But, some people got lucky in this life, and the rest just muddled through.

Her tears dried up as miles of concrete spun beneath the wheels of her tires, and her face and brain grew numb. By the time the night had darkened to indigo and the pink-and-gold skyline of Denver glittered before her, Erin had resigned herself to a life as one of the muddlers. At least, that's the story she would cling to that night. Anything to keep her mind off…the rest.

She'd survived so far not confronting her issues. Why start now?

She drove until the city swallowed her car, until neon bar signs from a nondescript, yet crowded tavern drew her gaze. Without forethought, she pulled into the parking lot and stopped. Muffled music thumped out from the club's interior. Her vision blurred as she stared at the place, looking without seeing, caring not at all. She jumped and gasped when the tavern doors banged open, and a laughing couple emerged and headed toward a bright yellow convertible.

Talk about adrenaline overload.

After the couple roared off into the darkness, Erin pulled her keys from the ignition and shoved them into her purse. Hands in her pockets, she entered the bar. She made eye contact with no one, because she wasn't there to socialize. The loud music enveloped her into the kind of anonymity she craved. She spied an open bar stool on the far end of the bar near the restrooms sign and headed for it.

No sooner had she sat than the bartender sidled up and lifted his chin. "What's your poison, miss?"

Guilt, she thought. *Horror.* As if she cared. She cleared her throat, but her voice still came out hoarse from the sobbing. "Tequila."

"Shot?"

"Whatever," she said, not meeting his gaze.

Unfazed by her attitude—no doubt the man had

seen it all—he poured her a shot, set it on a napkin
with sliced lime and a salt shaker. "Start you a tab?"

She shook her head.

"Seven-fifty."

She dug a ten-dollar bill out of her purse and
slid it across the bar. "Keep the change."

The cash register keys blipped, and then the
drawer opened. "You need anything, lemme
know," the barrel-shaped man said as he pocketed
the change, then slammed the drawer shut, its
coins jangling like her nerves.

Then, thankfully, she was alone.

With a shaky hand, she reached out for the shot
glass. She lifted it tentatively toward her face, but
then the smell assaulted her nostrils, and she knew
she couldn't drink it. She hadn't been much of a
drinker since…and never when she was driving.
Certainly not a shot drinker. Tonight, stuffed full
with horrible memories, was not the night to
violate that particular personal code.

With a sigh, she set the glass back down and
rested her forehead in her palms. She couldn't
shake the pent-up tension, the racing energy.
Something had to give.

"Wanna dance?" came a voice close to her left
ear. Wholeheartedly unenthusiastic, she angled her
head and eyed the guy standing there. Well, it
might at least burn off some steam.

After an apathetic shrug, she slid listlessly from the bar stool and headed toward the crowded dance floor, assuming he'd follow her. She was right.

He caught up and tossed her a grin. "I'm Bill."

She nodded, hooking the long strap of her purse over her shoulder so it rested on the opposite hip.

They started dancing, and the feel of her body moving seemed to mask some of her pent-up emotions. Or at least keep her one step ahead of them. A bandage—not a cure—but she'd take what she could get.

"So…what was your name?"

She regarded Bill, then squeezed her eyes shut for a moment. "No offense, but we both know it doesn't matter. Let's just dance."

Bill shrugged and seemed to accept it.

The more she danced, the more the memories flooded back, no matter how vehemently she tried to fend them off. She needed to find a way back to survival mode. So she danced harder. After Bill, there were other dance partners, but she didn't see any of them, didn't let their names or faces linger in her brain. Who cared? They weren't Kevin, never would *be* Kevin, so none of them mattered.

Her ability to love—to feel, really—had burned to acrid gray ashes long ago. Wasn't that why she lived the way she did, and had, for so long? Alone?

Putting up a façade? Laughing when she wanted to cry? All of it pretty much a lie? What would Kevin think of her now?

The geyser of her emotions continued to erupt, so she danced faster, the multicolored bar lights smearing in her vision. All she knew was, she couldn't stop now, or she'd lose it. Completely.

All Nate Walker had wanted from the evening was a beer or two and some quiet anonymity in which to clear his brain. The night's work had been grueling, the band exorbitantly demanding, as if the pyrotechnic oohs and aahs could make up for their lack of true talent.

But he'd noticed the dark beauty the moment she came in, her hair wild and tangled, eyes haunted. She'd walked right past him without even a flicker of notice, taking a stool at the opposite end of the long, polished concrete bar from where he sat. He'd silently watched as she'd ordered a shot she never drank, and then as she danced with a never-ending series of partners she didn't seem to notice, let alone speak to.

She was somewhere else altogether.

Too bad the guys seemed to view her as right here, right now—and fair game, to boot. His beer had gone warm and untouched as he watched them dance with her, one after another. The more they'd drunk, the closer they danced, and the brighter the predatory gleam in their eyes.

He'd started to curse himself for being here in the first place. He could've stayed in his hotel room, ordered up a meal. Steered clear of trouble until his plane took off for Las Vegas tomorrow. He didn't want to get involved in some dark-eyed beauty's private pain, and yet something drew him to her.

God knew, he'd always been a sucker for troubled women, frail old ladies and little kids who couldn't find their parents. Not to mention homeless mutts. But he'd had his fill of the savior role. It always seemed to backfire.

And yet...

If bad luck hadn't brought him to this spot, on this night, what would've happened to this woman? His chest clenched. For all he knew, he could be the single twist of fate that stood between her and some heinous crime.

It's that kind of thinking that gets you in trouble.

Total melodrama. He smirked to himself. He should write screenplays.

She looked strong enough. Lean and mean—in a sexy, feminine way—but beneath that tough veneer lurked a sweet vulnerability she couldn't quite keep under wraps. It tugged on his heart, and he felt pretty sure that the pack of predators caught on to it, too. His insight, however, brought a wave of concern for her. Protectiveness. The insights of the guys in the bar seemed to be guiding them down a whole different, much more self-serving path.

The waitress stepped into his line of sight.

He tried not to frown. The woman was only doing her job, after all.

"Beer's warm," she told him, pulling his attention from the woman on the dance floor. "Bring you a fresh one?"

"No. That's okay." *Just go.*

"You still want the warm one, then?" she said, leaning her hip toward him in that provocative way that said, (a) she wanted him, or (b) she wanted a big tip.

He threw a ten on her tray, trying not to seem impatient or rude. "No thanks."

She shrugged, set the warm, full beer bottle on her tray, and moved out of his way...just as one of the guys moved in on the woman on the dance floor and tried to slip his hands up the front of her T-shirt.

She smacked his hands away, and swung around into the arms of another guy, who pulled her in toward him and slid his palms down to cup her very shapely rear.

Damn it.

Nate might not want to get involved, but his mother hadn't raised him to stand by and do nothing when a woman was being mistreated. He had sisters, for God's sake. That left him no choice.

With a deep breath of resolution, he stepped off his stool and strode into the fray, glaring away the protests and the men who'd issued them. The woman was already pushing the groper away, so Nate's light tug on her upper arm was enough to spring her loose of the man's clutch.

Placing her behind him, he went nose-to-nose with the man. "Time for you to back off, Romeo," he said, through clenched teeth.

The guy's face reddened with fury. "Screw you. She never said she had a boyfriend."

"You didn't ask."

Standoff.

For a few tense moments, Nate thought he might have to exchange blows with the guy, which he really, *really* didn't want to do. He wasn't a fighter, but he didn't run, either.

Finally, the pissed-off man flapped his hands in a way that said she wasn't worth the fight—which showed how much he knew—then turned on his heel and shouldered his way out of the bar. All the other wolves sank back into the crowded darkness like the cowards they were.

Nate turned toward the woman and studied her face. She really was beautiful, despite her obvious torment. He softened his tone. "You okay?"

She pulled him toward the center of the dance floor and spun around a few times in time to the beat, fanning out her hair. "Just dance. Please."

He started to protest, then decided he'd give her the space she seemed to need for the rest of this song. Maybe she was embarrassed about what had just happened. Who knew? But respecting her wishes was the kindest route.

When the song ended, and another started, she showed no signs of stopping.

Enough.

Nate leaned in. "At least tell me your name."

She opened her eyes, but didn't stop dancing. She seemed to be weighing his question. "Erin," she finally said, in a defeated tone.

"I'm Nate."

She nodded. Kept dancing. "Thank you, Nate. For…that." Her words were almost flippant. Everything about her was incongruous.

He reached out and laid his palm gently on her shoulder. "Erin, are you okay?"

"Don't ask me that." She put her hands over her ears and danced harder, faster. Sweat glistened on her temples.

He reached up to pull her hands down. The alarm bells in his chest had begun to ping. This wasn't just a woman who hadn't been into that night's crop of dance partners. Something was truly weighing on her soul. "Listen, I just want to know if—"

"No!" To his horror, she stopped dead. Her eyes widened and filled with tears until she looked utterly crestfallen. "Stop. You don't understand— Oh, God—"

Without warning, racking sobs seemed to explode from her. She covered her face with her palms and sank in an awkward squat to the dance floor, one knee up, the other bent inward to rest on the worn hardwood. Her shoulders shook with the force of her pain.

Startled, Nate glanced around. This, he hadn't expected. Other dancers started noticing Erin, slowing down to stare and whisper behind their hands. A surge of protectiveness fueled Nate. He squatted and put his arm around her shoulder, leaning in to whisper in her ear.

"Listen. I don't know what's wrong, but I'm going to get you out of here, okay? We'll go outside for some air, get away from all these prying eyes."

All the fight seemed to have seeped out of her, and she acquiesced easily. He helped her to her feet, then sheltered her from the gaping stares as he ushered her from the bar.

Outside, the street was virtually deserted, and the cool black of the October nighttime enveloped them. He led her around the corner of the building to the side, away from the entrance and any on-lookers. People had no shame.

Still sobbing, Erin leaned against the brick exterior and slid to the ground, resting her forehead on her knees. Nate stood awkwardly beside her, letting her cry it—whatever *it* was—out. God knew, she seemed to need it.

When her sobs slowed to hiccups and sniffles, Nate sat on the ground beside her, careful not to touch her. Some primal instinct told him she wouldn't appreciate that sort of consolation.

As her hiccups slowed, then stopped, her whole body seemed to sag. A long period of silence stretched between them. Even with swollen eyes and a red nose, she was lovely. Like a fragile porcelain doll—strong, but at risk of shattering any moment.

"God, I'm…a mess. I'm not usually like this. I'm so sorry," she whispered.

A tender smile lifted one corner of his mouth. "No apology necessary. I didn't mean to make you cry."

She lifted her head, then ran her hands through her hair. "It wasn't you."

What was it? he wondered.

She stared off into the distance, and her chin began to quiver again. Then came the tears, silent this time, but even more forceful for their quietness.

He didn't know what to do.

"Erin…can I give you a ride home?"

Sodium vapor streetlights glistened pinkish-orange in the wet rivulets streaking down her face. She shook her head. "I'm from out of town."

Nate closed his eyes briefly. Of course she was from out of town. That's the way this knight in shining armor stuff usually worked out. He knew that, and yet he kept jumping back into the saddle.

Official verdict: he needed therapy.

"To your hotel, then?"

"I…no. I drove straight through. I mean, I don't have a hotel."

A rock of worry plummeted in his gut. As much as he yearned to bow out gracefully since she didn't seem to want comfort or conversation, he couldn't, in good conscience, let this woman get behind the wheel. Her level of concentration was nil, not to mention the fact that she must be emotionally exhausted. "How far do you have to drive?"

"Too far. But I can do it."

Nate blew out a sigh, turning away to gaze out at the empty street.

"Don't look so worried. It's not your problem. I can take care of myself."

There it was—his easy out. Too bad the bravado in her tone, the intrepid jut of her chin, ensnared him. "Listen, anyone can see you're a strong woman, and I have no doubt you can take care of yourself, and then some, on a regular day. But you're wiped out. You're upset. It's almost 1:00 a.m. You shouldn't drive, and you look smart enough that you probably know that."

She rested her head against the brick wall and closed her eyes. "Everything allegedly looks better in the morning, right?" She shrugged. "I can sleep in my car."

And risk the predators coming back and finding her there, sleeping in a desolate bar parking lot? No freakin' way. Another long pause ensued.

Finally, Nate sighed. "I'm staying at a hotel downtown. Not far from here, actually," he started, regretting this already, wishing he could yank back the eleven words he'd just uttered, but knowing he wouldn't.

She glanced over at him, wary but listening.

That was something, at least.

"Why don't you come and get some sleep there. I'll drive you back here in the morning when you're rested."

Another long pause.

"Why?" she whispered.

Wasn't that obvious? "To pick up your car."

"No. I mean, why are you trying to help?" She searched his face. "You don't even know me."

He laughed, a tired sound. "According to my mom, I'm a born-and-bred rescuer."

"I don't need rescuing."

He ignored that. "Not to mention, I'm a sucker for a crying woman."

"I am *not* a crier," she said, her tone indignant.

"Oh, no." He pierced her with a droll stare. "I can see that."

She glared at him through puffy eyes.

Not wanting to anger her, he winked.

She had the decency to look sheepish as she wiped away her tears. "I mean, I'm not *usually* a crier."

He held her gaze, nodded. "Like I said, you strike me as a self-sufficient woman, but there are days when the strongest of us need a friend. I'm offering my friendship. That's it. No strings."

"There are always strings."

"Wow, you're jaded."

No denial. She eyed him from head to toe. "I don't suppose you're a serial killer or anything, are you? They say serial killers look normal."

"Well, I'm flattered you think I look normal. As for the other, I'm perfectly safe. But I wouldn't expect you to take my word for it." He unhooked his cell phone from his waistband and handed it to her. "Call my mom for a reference, if you need to. Her numbers are in my contacts list under Mom."

Her forehead crinkled with incredulity. "Don't be ridiculous. I can't call your mother in the middle of the night."

"She's an E.R. nurse supervisor and she works graveyards. This is probably her perkiest time of the day."

Erin stared at the cell phone in her hand for several long moments, then flipped it open with her thumb and clicked through his contacts list. He watched as she read the screens for Mom—home, cell, pager and work—then snapped the phone closed and handed it back to him. "Where is area code 702?"

"Las Vegas."

"Are you from there, too?"

"Yes. Born and bred."

"So, why are you here?"

"Business."

She nodded, seeming to ponder this.

Several tense moments passed.

"Do you like animals?" she asked, nailing him with an unflinching stare.

Okay, wow. That came out of nowhere. He cocked his head at her curiously, then opened his phone again. He pressed a few buttons to launch the camera function, then pulled up a photograph of his black cocker spaniel, graying slightly around the muzzle, but still a beauty. "That's my dog. He's nine years old and going strong."

She leaned forward and looked at the picture, her mouth registering the faintest of smiles. "What's his name?"

"Boomer. And—" he clicked through until a photo of a powdery brown, lop-eared rabbit filled the screen "—this is Boomer's pal, Thug. He's just one-year-old."

She gaped at the phone, then faced him, blinking. "You have a bunny named Thug?"

He nodded. "Terrifying, isn't he? He's house-trained. Uses a litter box, and I have to brag that he's quite the neat freak. Not all house-trained rabbits are."

"Huh," she said, wonder in her tone.

Hopeful, he forged ahead. "He and Boomer sleep side by side on Boomer's dog bed. They've done so since Thug was eight weeks old."

"Thug." She paused. "A dog-loving bunny."

"More surprising, really, is the bunny-loving dog."

"Good point." She studied the photo a moment longer, then shook her head and pushed to her feet. "Okay. You win, Nate. Let's go."

Chapter Three

Despite the water bringing out the awful smoke smell again, Erin stood in the stark hotel shower longer than she should have, trying to muster her courage to face the stranger in the other room. It had seemed like a sound decision as they'd driven here, but now, in such close quarters, the second-guessing had begun. Big-time. Her self-consciousness was at an all-time high.

Had she lost her mind?

She'd always been a good judge of character, so it wasn't that she feared Nate anymore. He truly seemed harmless, and she was no idiot. Maybe

Good Samaritans did exist. But nothing mitigated the fact that her decision to take him up on his offer was insanely out of character for her.

Good guy or not, no one in her life knew where the hell she was. No one. She could disappear and wind up on *Cold Case Files* in five years—no leads. They'd show still photos of her with her stupid high school hair, and her family and friends would give tearful, on-screen interviews, pleading for any detail that might crack the case.

That improbability aside, she just didn't head off to hotels or homes—or anywhere—with men, strangers or otherwise. Not since…

The pain stabbed at her again.

Stabbed and stabbed and stabbed.

Oh, God.

How had she managed to avoid dealing with this for so long, only to have it hit her so hard all of a sudden? She took advantage of the shower's loud *whoosh,* leaned her head back, and let her tears come freely, gulping back audible sobs as the water doused her face. She'd cried more in the past few hours than she had in the last decade, and she didn't much like it.

But she had to face facts.

What kind of pathetic life was she living, anyway? Solitary, tormented, getting herself into stupid situations in bars, for God's sake? She threw

herself into work and denial and avoided close relationships like the Unibomber, pretending a
bravado and a "charming snarky humor" she didn't
truly feel. At least not all the time.

This wasn't supposed to be her life.

Bottom line.

She and Kev had been Troublesome Gulch High
School's golden couple. Most likely to marry right
after graduation. Most likely to come to the ten-year
reunion with photos of their two-point-five kids,
and imminent plans to renew their marriage vows.
Solid. Exuberant in their once-in-a-lifetime love
and committed to each other, mind, body and soul.

But, look at her now. Twenty-nine years old, and
she hadn't even kissed, much less made love with,
a single man since Kevin. Couldn't even wrap her
brain around the idea. She wasn't "most likely" to
do jack anymore, except perhaps die alone and
lonely with a fake smile pasted on her face.

Is that what Kevin would've wanted for her?

Was he looking down on her now with pity in
his beautiful green eyes?

She wiped ineffectually at her tears before
turning off the shower. The curtain rings sang
along the metal pole as she pulled the white plastic
aside and groped for a towel. She took her time
smoothing the fluffy terry cloth over the tight, ugly
scar tissue that covered her entire torso, not com-

pletely feeling its roughness, thanks to deadened nerve endings.

As always, she avoided looking into the full-length mirror mounted on the back of the bathroom door. She appreciated her body for what it could do. After all, look at Lexy, who hadn't walked since the accident. Things could be much worse. But still, functional or not, Erin didn't want to glimpse the body she'd never really accepted. At least visually.

It might *be* her, but it didn't *feel* like her.

And yet, the grotesque physical scars from that fire were a mere blip compared to those on her heart.

Wasn't *she* just the total package. Ha.

Before smoothing lotion over her skin, she set out her underwear and the oversized Avalanche T-shirt Nate had thoughtfully picked up for her at the grocery store when he'd stopped for a few toiletries he thought she might need. He'd even bought her a razor—a pink one. She shook her head, one corner of her mouth quivering into a half smile despite her melancholy. Her savior-out-of-nowhere really did seem like a nice guy.

Ugh. What did he think of *her?*

How could she face him?

Her insides bubbled with humiliation.

This whole situation was world-class awkward.

At least, thank goodness, she'd never see him again.

A soft knock on the locked door startled her. She jerked, clutching the towel to her chest before swallowing twice to steady her voice. "Yes?"

"Sorry to bother you. No rush, but a great old movie is available on pay-per-view, *A Guy Named Joe*. Ever heard of it?"

"No."

"Well…it's one of my favorites. World War II flick. If you're interested."

"I…uh…" A movie? This was weirder and weirder. "I'll probably just go to sleep, if that's okay. But I can sleep through anything, so feel free to watch it. Seriously."

"Okay." He paused, but she could tell he was still there. "Are you, um, hungry? I was going to order pizza from room service. They make a pretty good one here."

"No," she said quickly, still frozen in the shower, vulnerable and wanting him to move away from the door so she'd stop feeling so damned… naked. "I'm fine. Thanks."

A pause. "Sure."

She listened, alert, until he was gone. Alone again, she eased out an exhale, dressed quickly, then went through the blow-drying, tooth-brushing, moisturizing routine. She wasn't going for prom queen perfection here. Why would she care what Nate the Savior thought of the way she looked?

She didn't. She was going to bed.

Bed. Ugh.

The land mine zone, as she could see it, stretched between the locked bathroom and the bed. Twenty steps, tops. She wanted to navigate it as quickly and safely as possible, pile herself beneath the covers and slip into oblivion. She wasn't one to take sleeping pills, but if she'd had one, she'd pop it tonight, no questions asked.

Enough stalling. *Now or never.*

She took a deep breath, then eased it out through pursed lips. The lock clicking open sounded like gunfire. She froze again, like a bunny facing a starving rottweiler.

Why was she so edgy? Gee, maybe because she'd humiliated herself in front of a total stranger, and now she had to spend the night in his room?

Nate glanced up with a faint smile as she entered the main room. The phone rested between his shoulder and ear, and he was busy ordering extra this and extra that, thin crust and a side of whatever.

Erin forced her standard fake smile back, then climbed into her bed on the far side. Safety. Thank God she'd made it. She covered herself chin high, chilled to her marrow and shivering, despite the extra-long steamy shower.

Nate hung up. "I ordered an extra large in case you change your mind."

Small talk. Bleh. Oh yeah—that's what strangers did in excruciatingly squirm-worthy situations such as this. "That was nice of you."

He lifted his chin in the direction of the bathroom. "How was the shower?"

"Fine." She forged ahead. "Listen, I didn't thank you for picking all the stuff up for me."

"Yes, you did. You're more than welcome." He stood, glancing toward the bathroom. "Think I'll take a quick one before the pizza gets here. They said it would be thirty minutes, but you know how it goes."

Her mind wasn't on pizza delivery schedules at all at the moment. She twisted her mouth to the side, guilt squeezing her breathless.

Nate lifted an eyebrow. "What's wrong?"

"I didn't realize you wanted to shower. I hope I didn't hog all the hot water."

He grinned. "Not to worry, I grew up with a bath-loving mom and three sisters. I'm used to cold."

Yeah, that didn't assuage anything. She pulled her bottom lip between her teeth. "No, really. I shouldn't have stayed in there so long. It's your room, and—"

"Stop."

They stared at each other.

"Erin, you needed the time. I get that, okay? Besides, these big hotels never run out of hot water."

Feeling slightly better, she relaxed—at least as much as she could when everything was so formal and clumsy and surreal between them.

"Let's make a deal. You stop saying 'thanks' and 'sorry' for the rest of the night. Okay?"

"I'll try."

"Good enough." Nate halted at the end of her bed en route the bathroom. He snapped his fingers, then fished his wallet out of his back pocket. "If, for some strange reason, the pizza arrives while I'm in there, I've got cash for a tip." He lobbed it onto the end of her bed.

Her body went cold as she stared at the worn leather. It seemed too intimate, this wallet so perfectly molded to his backside.

"Now what's wrong?"

She flicked a hand toward it. "I…I can't just dig through your wallet."

He blinked. Poker face. "Sure you can. I just said you could."

She shook her head. "B-but, that's not the point. We just met." She groaned. "This is really uncomfortable. I could be some coldhearted criminal taking advantage of your kindness."

"Are you?"

"No. But that's not the point."

"I can solve this. Answer one question."

She waited.

"Do you like animals?" he asked, playfulness in his gentle eyes.

"You can't use my questions against me."

"Why not? It worked for you." He spread his arms wide. "See?"

She rolled her eyes. "You are way too trusting."

He laughed softly. "Somehow, you just don't strike me as the criminal type."

"I suppose that's comforting." She swallowed thickly, eyeing the wallet as though it were a rattlesnake poised to strike. "Just hurry, okay? Then I won't have to touch it at all, which will make us both feel better. Think, quick shower."

He shrugged. "I'm a guy. How else do we shower except quickly?"

She'd succumbed to a slice of pizza after all—the aroma had gotten to her. Tummy full, she rolled over to leave Nate to his movie, circa 1943, or something like that.

Weird.

She didn't think guys liked old movies, not that she was any expert on guys. And she was probably being grossly stereotypical. Then again, this was a war flick.

Or so he alleged.

Turned out the WWII fighter pilot main character gets killed on a mission, and is forced to come back as another young fighter pilot's guardian angel, only to watch while the guy falls in love with his mourning fiancée.

Yeah. *Not* a war picture.

Partway through, she couldn't contain her curiosity, so she rolled over to watch.

Nate glanced at her. "Is the TV keeping you awake?"

"No. I just…this film seems familiar somehow."

He turned his attention back to the screen. "Richard Dreyfuss and Holly Hunter starred in the remake. *Always.* Late eighties, I think, and a whole lot different. But based on the same story."

A vice gripped her stomach, while her eyes were transfixed on the television. Of course. *Always* was one of the many sad movies about loss of love that she'd studiously avoided. They never failed to rekindle her melancholy to an unbearable burn. What were the odds? Pretty damn good, actually, since *every* sad movie affected her that way.

Ghost? Forget it.

"Seen it?"

She shot a glance at him. "Excuse me?"

"*Always.* Just wondering if you'd seen the remake. Maybe that's why this one's familiar."

"Oh." She dropped her gaze. "Yes." Unfortunately.

"Original version's better."

Great.

She pondered his earlier description of the movie, amused in spite of herself. "Nate, there's something you should know," she said, her tone deliberately grave.

He held up the remote. "Should I pause it?"

"Maybe."

He did. "Okay, what's up?"

She leveled him with a serious gaze. "This may come as a shock, but *A Guy Named Joe* isn't a war flick. Hate to blow your cover."

He did a double take, aiming a thumb toward the still screen. "Sure it is. You saw the uniforms. The planes."

"Doesn't matter. It's a love story. An old-school chick flick. Practically a precursor to *Love Story* itself."

Nate sighed. "Okay. Truth time?"

"Hit me."

"I know it's a love story. But being the only male in my household, it was the closest I ever came to an action flick of any kind." He eyed her from the side. "My sisters—"

"What are their names?" She found herself suddenly curious about this guy. Sisters? A mom? Boomer and Thug? Like, he had a whole life beyond this hellish night, which struck her as so…strange.

"In order, Flannery, Colette and Piper. We're all about a year apart, and I'm second in the lineup, smack between Flannery and Colette."

"Cool names."

"My mom's creative."

"Are they married?"

"Nope. Not even Mom's remarried."

"Where's your dad?" she blurted, before realizing it was a fairly rude question.

He shrugged, as though it didn't matter a bit. "Not really a part of our lives."

"Ever?"

"Well, I don't remember him."

She felt a pang of compassion before another thought struck. "Wait a sec. You're not married, are you?"

He castigated her wordlessly. Those eyes of his could speak volumes.

She held up both palms in surrender. "Just asking. Because if you were my husband, away on business, and you brought some woman back to your hotel room, I wouldn't be happy. To put it mildly. Even if she was a whackjob and you were just being nice."

He bonked his head on the headboard. "So *you're* married. Great. Is some burly guy going to come after me with a sawed-off shotgun?"

She widened her eyes. "Me? No, never. It was just an example."

"That's a relief." He pointed toward the entertainment center. "So, back to why I'm watching a chick flick and calling it a war movie."

"Yes." She inclined her head. "Sorry for the nosy interruption. It just struck me as interesting that you have sisters."

He laughed. "What—you thought I sprang out of nowhere in that bar?"

"Superheroes usually do."

He scoffed. "I'm no superhero. Anyway, it's okay. The interruption, I mean. I like talking about my family, and they're the whole point anyway. The truth is, I was outnumbered growing up when it came to picking movies. And Mom took my sisters' side not because she favored them, but because she didn't want us to watch violence anyway."

"Ah. Well, no shame in that."

"So *you* say. I had to keep some kind of street cred with my buddies," he said. "So I started 're-defining' the movies we watched. *Steel Magnolias?* I've seen it about fifty times. I could probably quote dialogue, a skill that doesn't go over big on the basketball court."

A short laugh burst from Erin, the sound unfamiliar, almost painful on this night. It shocked her so much, she reached up and covered her mouth.

He smiled, the expression etching lines around

his eyes, which were a beautiful shade of turquoise—a great contrast against his black hair and
tanned skin. "So, all my ugly secrets aside, will
you humor me and let me call it a war flick?"

She cleared her throat. "Sure. Go back to your
war flick. I'm going to try to sleep."

"Good night."

She rolled over and settled in. He still hadn't
started the movie. She could almost feel his eyes
boring into her back. "Nate?"

"Yeah?"

"Did I ever thank you for helping me?" she
asked, without turning around.

"I thought we had a deal about that."

"Oh, yeah. Sorry."

"Ah, that was part of the deal, too."

"Right. No more talking."

A pause. "'Night, Erin."

"Good night."

She tried—really tried—to fall asleep. Tried to
buzz the movie dialogue out of her brain. Tried to
forget. It hadn't worked. By the time the credits
rolled, Erin sort of wanted to die. Not literally.
That was one of those oft-used flippant comments
she tried to never think or say, if only out of respect
for her friends who hadn't had the chance. But everything about her trauma, everything she'd hoped

to get in check, had ripped open again, a fresh, un-cleaned wound.

Her back still to Nate, she'd started pretending to sleep about forty-five minutes earlier. The last thing she wanted was a compare-and-contrast conversation about the two versions of this godawful, heartbreaking movie.

The television clicked off, then she heard Nate rustling in his own bed. "Erin?" he asked, softly.

She squeezed her eyes shut and remained still.

Obviously buying her pathetic attempt at fake sleep, Nate doused the bedside lamp. The last thing she heard was his sigh as he punched his pillow and settled in.

The self-lambasting started almost immediately.

She should've told him good-night. Asked him if he still loved his movie after having seen it a million times. She should've gone the give route with this guy, instead of take, take, take.

How hard would it have been to extend a hand of friendship, the way he had?

This wasn't all about her, after all.

She wasn't generally so selfish.

Oh well. It wasn't as if he expected her to act like a normal, sane woman after the crazy evening they'd shared. She might as well leave it alone. After tomorrow, they'd go their separate ways forever. This night of a thousand embarrassments would fade with time until she was nothing but an anecdote he shared with his guy friends during those "what not to do" conversations.

Realistically, in the movie of her life, Nate the Savior was an extra.

Walk on. Walk off. No lines.

Her bloodcurdling scream ripped him from sleep. Nate tore out of his bed and smacked on the lamp, blinking into the glaring light. His glance shot from one side of the room to the other, looking for the intruder, the attacker.

Empty.

Relief flowed through him as he slowly realized the enigmatic woman sharing his hotel room was simply in the throes of a wicked nightmare.

Somehow, not surprising.

He blew out a long breath and ran his fingers through his hair. He yearned to awaken her, but he didn't want her to think he was breaching boundaries, crossing over to her side of the room.

And yet, the nightmare still had her in its talons.

He held back, watching as her scream devolved to panting, then moved into racking sobs and nearly incoherent babble. It sounded like she was saying, "Why me?" or "Why not me?" Or maybe "Whiny?"—not that any of it made sense. Beneath the top sheet—she'd kicked off all the other covers—she curled into a fetal ball, rocking as she cried.

He couldn't take this.

She'd just have to forgive his intrusion.

Sitting carefully on the edge of her bed, he reached out and touched her shoulder. "Erin," he whispered.

Nothing.

He cleared his throat and spoke louder. "Erin."

She sucked in a huge gulp of air as she battled to a sitting position, hair wild, eyes disoriented as she searched the unfamiliar surroundings. "K-kev?"

Kev? He shook his head. "It's me, Nate."

"Oh." She ran a shaky hand through her hair, averting her gaze. "Oh. Shoot."

"You were having a nightmare."

"Yeah, I uh…I have them sometimes." Blotches of color rose to her cheeks. "I didn't mean to disturb you. Again." She leaned forward for the disheveled covers, pulling them up to her chest and tucking them firmly beneath her arms.

"I didn't wake you for an apology." He waited until she looked up at him, her luminous eyes troubled, but so strong. God, something about this woman touched him, right where he lived. "Are you okay?"

The pause seemed interminable.

She pulled her quivering bottom lip in between her teeth. "I don't know. Actually, no."

He lifted his arms and let them drop. "Please talk to me. It's torture watching you go through this when I don't even know what *this* is."

"It's complicated, that's all." She pushed all ten fingers into the front of her hair and held them there for a few moments. "Too complicated for strangers."

Is that what they were? He didn't feel like a stranger anymore. He took a risk, reaching forward to grab her hand.

"Look at it this way. I'm an uninvolved party. Use me as a sounding board. There has to be something I can do." He watched for several long moments while she stared down at the bed coverings.

Her throat tightened with a swallow, once, then again. When she finally spoke, her words managed to sound both stiff and broken. "I don't want to talk about it. It's ancient history, really. But, will you…" She pressed her lips together and shook her head.

"What?" he prompted. "Will I what?"

Her sidelong glance was humiliated and apologetic. "Just lie here with me?"

Surprise riddled through him.

Her complexion blazed red. "I know it seems weird, but…"

"No, it's—" Of all the requests in the world, that

wasn't the one he'd imagined he'd hear. Ever. It actually stunned him silent.

"Please?" she whispered, a wobbly sound.

Don't be an idiot, his brain warned. *Do not get in bed with this woman.* "If you're sure."

"I'm not sure of anything. Except that I don't feel like being alone right now." Fumbling and formal, they moved side by side on the bed, her beneath the covers, him on top. For a few agonizing moments, they remained that way. Staring at the ceiling. Like corpses.

How could this possibly be helping her?

She swallowed. Moistened her lips with a quick flick of her tongue. "It's okay. You can, um, get in."

He turned toward her. "Erin, I don't know—"

"I just need to feel someone close, that's all. I'm not going to do anything to you."

More's the pity. He studied her lovely, if heartbroken, profile for several moments, then moved beneath the covers. The XXL T-shirt he'd bought her covered most of her, but her firm, shapely legs felt smooth and soft against him. Exquisite torture, this good guy stuff. His danger signals wailed louder.

Erin cleared her throat. "May I…ugh, this is absurd…may I put my head on your shoulder?"

"Of course."

She rose up, then stopped, looking down at him through wide eyes. "Oh, God. Never mind.

This was an idiotic idea. I never should've put you in this pos—"

"Shh." He slid his arm beneath her shoulders and urged her head onto his shoulder, smelling the strawberry scent of her hair. "It's okay. Friends, right?"

"Right."

"Just try to get some sleep." He reached over and snapped the lamp off, enclosing them in the safety of darkness once again.

He felt her nod, closed his eyes.

After a moment, she whispered, "Nate?"

He opened one eye. "Mmm-hmm?"

"You're a good guy. Your mom should be proud."

"She is. But thank you for saying so." He smiled into the inky night and snuggled her closer. They might be strangers, and their meeting unconventional, but damned if she didn't feel absolutely perfect in his arms.

Chapter Four

The idea came to her in a burst.

A ridiculous idea, but one she couldn't let go of. She hadn't been able to sleep, the feeling of being cradled by a man so absolutely foreign. But not bad. Not bad at all. She lay there in the darkness pressed against Nate's shoulder, smelling the clean, soapy manliness of his skin, and trying to make sense of the myriad thoughts swirling through her head.

Kevin.

Her life.

The accident.

Nate.

She thought about Brody Austin, and how he'd been able to overcome his emotional wounds from their horrible prom night. Since he'd returned to Troublesome Gulch, Erin had always rationalized that he was much braver than she, able to suck it up and take a leap into the scary unknown. No net. No anything.

Maybe, in reality, having the guts to return had simply been his first step.

One step that had led to another, and another, and another, until he'd fought his way out of the darkness into the joy that epitomized his new life. What was that old saying? The journey of a thousand miles begins with a single step?

She could take that single step.

Right now. Tonight. With Nate.

If she were brave enough.

Her heart pounded just considering the absurd idea percolating inside her addled brain. Since she'd only been with Kevin, she'd obviously never indulged in a one-night stand. But, even in theory, it totally wasn't her thing.

That's what made this idea so…

Still, if she didn't make some sort of an effort soon, she would surely die without ever loving again. Without ever having sex again, and that idea made her sad.

This possible tryst with Nate didn't need to be mind-blowing. Neither of them needed to impress the other. It would be more like ripping off a Band-Aid, at least for her. The quicker, the better. Just get it done.

Surely Nate would be willing. What guy wouldn't want a little no-strings sex? For a brief moment, hope bubbled inside her. Then, *Pop! Pop! Pop!* Gone.

Forget it. She was an idiot.

People didn't *do* this sort of thing. They didn't even contemplate it. Did they?

She adjusted her head on Nate's shoulder, studying his strong profile, admiring the sweep of dark lashes on his cheeks, watching his sculpted chest rise and fall with deep, restful breaths.

Weird, yes, but it wouldn't be horrible. She found him genuinely attractive—a fact that stunned her. She hadn't even looked twice at a guy since Kevin.

Could she do it?

Tentatively, she reached her fingers up and traced his squared jawline which bore a hint of stubble, not at all unattractive. A sudden urge to feel its roughness against the smooth skin of her face and neck overtook her. She'd ignored her own sexuality for so long, and suddenly it reared up, demanding attention.

Now.

Nate stirred. She froze.

For several long moments, she didn't even draw a breath. But he didn't wake up, thank God.

She eased the pent-up breath out through her lips and continued her exploration. Gentle as butterfly wings, she moved her fingers down to his smooth chest, testing her resolve. Could she touch another man? Even for therapeutic reasons? Laying her palm against his warm skin, she smoothed it lightly down his sculpted abs, surprised by the ferocity of the yearning swirling deep within her, in a place she'd believed long dead.

Her hand traced his six-pack. One-two. Three-four. Five-six, and so close to the danger zone. She yearned to touch him there, too—

Quick as a viper, Nate's palm wrapped around her wrist.

She sucked in air.

For a moment, no one spoke.

"What are you doing?" he asked, his voice alert, despite being gravelly with sleep.

"I…" She paused, forced a swallow. What could she say? *I'm trying to figure out if I could stand to make love with you?* Now *that* was a world-class pickup line.

"Erin."

Now or never. *Answer the man.*

It'll be okay, Brody had told her. But it would

never be okay if she kept on doing exactly what she'd been doing for the past decade-plus.

One night.

One hurdle crossed.

That's all she needed.

Nate wanted to help her. He'd said so himself.

"Erin," Nate said again, a bit more adamantly. "I asked you what you're doing."

"I was, ah, touching you."

"Okay. Why?"

She shored up all her courage. "Well, the thing is, I've been thinking. And I want you to make love to me."

Dead.

Freakin'.

Silence.

After what seemed like interminable nothingness, during which all she could hear was the percussion of her pulse, Nate reached over and flicked on the lamp. It was worse, seeing him in the light after just having voiced her insane suggestion.

Apparently, he was equally stunned. His eyes narrowed. "What did you say?"

"I said—" *deep breath…courage* "—I want to make love. With you. Now."

Nate stared at her as though she were insane, then released a sound that was half laugh, half gasp. He ran his fingers through his hair. "Where is this coming from? An hour ago, you called us strangers."

"I know, but—"

"Is this some sort of a game?"

Anger tinged his words, and her throat tightened. She hadn't expected anger. "No. No. It's just—I can explain—"

"Yeah, you'd better explain."

Self-conscious to the max, she moistened her lips. This was, arguably, the most mortifying moment of her life. "Look, we're both adults. I went through something…sort of traumatic today." Her glance slid toward the digital clock. "Yesterday, actually. And I just need to feel alive, Nate."

Another disbelieving stare. "You want to make love with a so-called total stranger to feel alive?"

"No strings," she said, recalling his words. Maybe he thought she was trying to trap him. "I promise." She reached out tentatively and ran her fingers through his hair, relieved to see the expression in his eyes darken with desire.

She could see him fighting it off, and the desire turned to disgust. "No strings." He huffed. "That's what you think I'm worried about?"

"Well, I—"

His body stiffened. "And here I thought we'd started to get to know each other."

"We have," she rushed to say, propping herself

up on one elbow so she could look at him directly. "That's why I thought—"

"That I'd be your perfect candidate?" He whipped back the covers and stood, eyes flashing. "Guess what, Erin? I'm not the kind of guy to go in for an easy lay because it's offered. If that's what you were looking for, I could've left you at the bar."

"I didn't want—" She sat up, tugging at the bottom of her T-shirt. "That's not it. God!" She put her face in her hands. "Never mind," came her muffled words. "It was a stupid proposition. Forget I ever said anything."

She'd never been more embarrassed.

With a sigh, Nate sat tentatively on the edge of her bed. "What is going on with you? Who are you?"

"I'm nobody." She couldn't keep the bereft tone from her words. "I'm a sham."

He reached out and stroked her hair. "Not true."

"No, it is." She tried to focus, to ignore how his touch made her feel. "Want to know something ridiculous?"

He waited.

"I haven't made love with anyone for more than eleven years," she whispered, her voice laced with shame. "I haven't even kissed anyone."

He blinked twice. "By choice?"

She hiked one shoulder. "I guess. No. I don't know."

"Then why? Surely you've had interest. You're a beautiful woman."

"I'm not beautiful. Besides, it's a long story."

He propped himself back on two pillows and crossed his arms. "I've got nothing but time. After your shocking suggestion, I guarantee I'm not going to be able to go back to sleep. So we might as well talk."

She blew out her frustration. Tucked her hair behind her ears. "I was engaged," she said, in a monotone. "My fiancé died. Some people can recover from trauma, others struggle. End of story."

The pause stretched out, riddled with his attempts to absorb all this and her sadness, to find the right words when none existed.

"I'm sorry," he said finally, his tone husky.

She huffed out a humorless laugh. "Me, too."

"Did you love him?"

"With my whole heart and soul."

"Come here." Nate pulled her into his arms and cradled her head against his shoulder, smoothing his palm down her back. "It's not that I wouldn't want to make love to you under normal circumstances. You're sexy. Sweet."

"Celibate."

He ignored that. "But, Erin, despite the fact that

I'm not a one-night-stand guy, I don't even have protection. I don't carry that kind of stuff 'just in case.' That's not the way I live."

She lifted her head to glance up at him. "Which is what makes the whole thing perfect."

He raised his eyebrows, waiting.

"I'm safe, Nate. I can't get pregnant, and I haven't been with anyone in so long, I'm a virtual virgin."

He shook his head at her self-deprecation. "What about me? What do you know about me?"

Her gaze slanted to the side. "I know you don't carry protection 'just in case.' I know you're an exceptional man, a caring man. You took me from a potentially catastrophic situation when there was nothing whatsoever in it for you. I know you'd tell me if I was in any danger at all."

He mulled over that. "True. For the record, I do get tested, and I'm safe. But that's not the point."

"What's the point then?"

"Lovemaking is special, Erin. It's not something you tick off your To-Do List."

Man, he nailed that on the head. What he didn't understand was, sometimes you just had to tackle that damned list. She groaned. "Okay, I *want* to make love with you. Does that help?"

"Not exactly. It might, if you were the least bit convincing."

She shouldered away from him. "Look. I

haven't wanted any man so much as near me for more than a decade, and then you come along and I get all these crazy ideas. It's not like I've been propositioning every guy who comes along."

"Then why me?" he whispered.

There were no words. No reasonable explanation. Instead, she stretched up and kissed his lips softly, which felt strange, foreign, but not horrible. He tasted good, like mint and man. Safe. When he didn't protest, she deepened the kiss, venturing some exploration with her tongue, nibbling at his bottom lip.

He groaned. Obviously tried not to, but it escaped anyway, and he kissed her back. For several long moments, they simply explored each other's mouths. His hands moved up to cup her face gently, and an unexpected storm of desire ripped through her. Wait. This was supposed to be a first step, nothing more.

Yet, it seemed she truly wanted this man.

How could that be?

He wasn't Kevin, but she ached for him. She yearned to feel Nate's weight on top of her, him pushing into her. Her body throbbed. She knew he wasn't comfortable with this, but he just had to—

"Please," she whispered, moist and warm against his lips.

He pulled back, studied her face. "Why can't you get pregnant?"

"An injury," she hedged.

"That's rough."

"I don't care." She leaned in to kiss him again, this time brazenly spreading her palms on his chest.

"Erin," he breathed against her mouth between kisses. "I don't do this kind of thing. For the record."

"Neither do I. For the record. So let's do it together and call it a friendly aberration."

After hesitation, he eased her back on the pillows and started to pull up her T-shirt.

She sucked in a breath, holding it down. "W-wait."

His eyes glittered with scorn. "Let me guess. Second thoughts already?"

"No. No. But, can I…can I leave it on?"

He cocked his head to the side. "Why?"

"It's just been so long."

He studied her, the uncertainty clear in his gaze.

Afraid he'd call it off, she guided his hand down to her bikini underwear instead, urging his fingers inside, though it was excruciatingly difficult to be so brazen.

He caressed her, closing his eyes as he sucked in a breath. "You're so wet."

"I want this, Nate," she said, trying to convince herself as much as she tried to convince him. "I want you. Can't you see? Feel?"

He slipped one finger inside her—an utter surprise. She gasped, bucking instinctively to deepen the connection. The force of her desire floored her.

His breaths coming quicker now, he eased his finger out of her body, then slid her underwear down her legs.

She kicked them off. Shy, but wanting to take this step, she opened her legs for him, watching as he removed the sweatpants he'd worn to bed.

Oh, he clearly wanted her, too.

The sight of him quickened her pulse. The dull throb intensified at her center. She reached for him, wanting to feel his length in her hand. Instead, he pressed his body against hers, holding off some of his weight with his elbows.

"Tell me you're sure about this."

Not at all. "I'm sure."

"Tell me we're not making a mistake."

Who could say? "We're not."

"I am safe, Erin," he reassured. "I'm a good guy. I'd never put you into a bad situation."

She squirmed against him. "If I had any doubt whatsoever, we wouldn't be here like this, trust me. I just…please."

"Please what?"

"I want you inside me," she whispered shyly.

He leaned his forehead against hers, their gazes locked. "It makes no sense, but I want it, too. Even if I don't understand your reasoning. Or mine. I don't know you, but I feel like I've known you forever."

A rubber band of guilt snapped against her skin. His genuineness stung. Obviously, what he felt for her was mere lust. They'd only just met. But his wanting was sincere. Hers was simply that first step toward getting her life back. Wasn't it?

Regardless, tomorrow they'd go their separate ways, each having gotten what they needed, so what did it matter?

She rubbed against his hardness. "Make love to me."

"If you don't stop that, there's no going back."

"I don't want to go back." She reached down between their bodies and wrapped her palm around him, guiding the tip of his penis toward the throb that had intensified to the point that it didn't seem to want to stop. "Now."

"Erin."

"Now."

Gently, but firmly, he pushed into her. Deeply, all the way. For a moment, they stayed locked that way, and he closed his eyes. "God, you feel incredible."

"It's been a long time."

"I'll be gentle."

Some feral part of her quaked. "Don't. Please. I don't want gentle. Not tonight."

She felt his pulse quicken inside her as he stared into her eyes, and then he did her bidding.

Hard. Fast. Deep. Thorough.

Nate proved to be an amazing lover. He caressed her breasts to aching points through the shirt and never complained that she wouldn't fully undress. He awakened her body in ways she hadn't thought possible.

Fear quivered inside her. Why did it feel as though this was turning into more than she'd bargained for?

Pushing away her alarm, Erin gave herself over to the sensations, rising to meet his thrusts, wanting more, more, more. She felt like the first crocus bloom, bursting through the graying snow after an extended, cold winter.

Silent tears crept out the sides of her eyes, rolling down to tickle her ears. She wanted to believe it was because of Kevin, and partly it was. He was no longer her *only,* and that saddened her to the depths of her soul.

But she also knew she was going to creep out of this room the moment Nate succumbed to sleep, leaving no trace. She would never see him again, and somehow, that cracked the only part of her heart that hadn't already been shattered.

She cried out with her explosive climax, wrapping her legs around Nate's waist and reveling in the feeling of his pulsing release inside her.

"Are you okay?" he gasped.

"Yes."

"Did I hurt you?"

"Not at all." She stretched up to kiss him.

"Good." He kissed her back, passionately. "Good." A pause. "Erin. Honey, I—"

"Shh." She laid a finger across his lips. "Let's not ruin it with words. Let it be what it is, okay? Be in the moment."

He settled on top of her, both of them panting, and a part of her wanted to pull him close and keep him there. Inside her. Around her. On top of her. Forever.

She hadn't expected that.

Dear God, she hadn't expected Nate.

Morning's golden glow shone through his eyelids, awakening him. His mind moved to last night, and a slow smile spread his lips. His body felt spent, his mind soothed. He opened his eyes and let them adjust to the brightness of the new day, then he turned over to greet—

But, she wasn't there.

He pulled the covers back and sat up. "Erin?"

No answer.

Standing, he stretched his arms over his head and yawned as he walked toward the bathroom. Empty. Only when he turned back toward the disheveled bed did he notice the note scribbled on a hotel notepad.

Please understand.

He stood frozen, staring at it, pulse pounding in his temples. He should've known. Should've been prepared for this. So why did it hurt so damn much? Crossing to the bed, Nate sat, and picked up the only bit of Erin he had left.

A goodbye.

Chapter Five

Two months later...

"Mystery solved," the doctor said, as she entered her office bearing a file. "You're pregnant."

Erin gaped at her longtime doctor, the incomprehensible announcement ringing in her ears. "But, I can't be. I came in with the flu."

Dr. Kipfer laughed. Rounding the expansive cherrywood desk, she tossed the file down onto her blotter and sat. "Actually, you came in confused. That flu you have? We in the biz refer to it as morning sickness." She winked.

Erin's heart drummed. She shook her head. "No. It's impossible."

The doctor frowned, perplexed. "Do you mean you haven't had sex? False positives can happen."

Erin's skin flamed. "No, well, I...not that. But, I'm not able to get pregnant. Because of the burns."

The doc steepled her hands on her desk and lowered her chin. "Who told you that? The burn treatment center?"

Erin felt more stupid by the moment. "Um, no, actually." She laid a palm on her still-flat tummy that somehow felt different now. "To be honest, I just assumed. You've seen my scarring."

"Scars on the skin don't always translate to organ damage. Clearly, in your case, your organs are fine."

"Oh." Pregnant. Holy hell. She gulped. "How, um...how far along am I?"

As if she didn't know.

She knew the exact night, practically the exact moment she'd conceived. In fact, she'd spent the last two months trying to convince herself that leaving under cover of darkness, without so much as a thank-you, had been the right thing to do. Now she wasn't so sure. Fitful dreams about Nate, a man so kind and selfless, had haunted her nights. Guilt ate away at her days. And the memories. Oh, the memories....

"Eight weeks," Doc said—no surprise. "You've

got a long way to go, and you're considered high risk, so we're going to monitor you very closely."

Erin's heart squeezed for Nate. She didn't even know his last name. Finding him was likely impossible. Probably a blessing in disguise, since she'd assured him she couldn't get pregnant and then bailed like a coward the moment he'd drifted off into dreamland. Whether she carried his child or not, she was probably the last person he'd ever want to see.

Still, *God,* he deserved to know.

That fact weighed on her soul, dampening what should've been an exciting—if scary—moment. The baby was his, too.

She shook off the thoughts. There were so many practicalities to discuss—why focus on what she couldn't control? "What about my skin? I mean, the stretching?" Surely her scar tissue wouldn't accommodate the growth of a fetus. She cringed at the thought.

Dr. Kipfer tilted her head to the side, her blond bob swinging forward to brush along her shoulder. "Well, that's why we have to keep an eye on things. A lot of it will be your responsibility."

Erin's palms grew damp. "Meaning?"

"Your skin will accommodate for some stretching by pulling from your back. The body is amazing that way. But you cannot gain a lot of weight with this baby, Erin," the doctor said, her tone sober. "Twenty pounds, absolute max." She blinked across the desk without an iota of judgment in her expression. "Assuming, of course, you plan to see this pregnancy through to full term."

Erin reeled as though she'd been slapped. She'd had one baby torn from her by an unlucky twist of fate. No way would she ever voluntarily give up another. "Of course. My God, I wouldn't think of—" She couldn't even say it.

Dr. Kipfer held up both palms and smiled. "Just making sure. I don't like to assume. And whatever you'd choose to do, as your doctor, I'd support you."

"Thank you. But, I want this baby." And, she did. She hadn't expected how ferociously. They felt like an inseparable duo already.

"Well, then. I'd say congratulations are in order. You're going to be a mama."

Mama. Her head swirled in wonder. Erin half laughed, half cried. She never imagined this, and part of her keened with the knowledge that it wasn't Kevin's baby. Then again, Nate…

Stop. Be in the moment.

Excitement sprouted a beautiful little bud inside her heart. She wanted to dash out and shop for all the tiny clothes and precious things to furnish a nursery, but she was getting way ahead of herself. Questions, worries and logistical plans filled her brain until she couldn't think straight. The biggest of which was, "What about work?"

"Yes, that." Dr. Kipfer quirked her mouth to the side apologetically. "You'll have to take a medical leave earlier than most pregnant firefighters."

"What does that mean? How much earlier?"

"Get ready to talk to your fire chief. I'll want you off work and resting at home from twenty weeks through delivery. Eighteen weeks, if you can manage it."

"Eighteen weeks!" Dismay gripped Erin. She did, after all, have to support this child on her own. She hoped she had enough sick time banked, or she'd have to request donations from her coworkers. Ick. "That's four and a half months of bed rest."

The doctor held up a finger. "Now, I didn't say bed rest. We can't risk any extra weight gain, so you'll have to continue to exercise. But you're certainly not going to be out there fighting fires or doing any heavy lifting."

"But, that's my job. I have to earn money."

"What about the father?" Dr. Kipfer asked, softly. "Any help from that end?"

Erin merely shook her head.

"You *do* want a healthy birth, right?"

"Of course."

"Then, get used to the idea. Do what you have

to. Friends, family." She gave her a sympathetic smile. "I know you're not one to ask for help, Erin, but now's the time, okay?"

Erin bit her bottom lip, thinking. "Can I do some light-duty work? Administrative assignments?"

"Let's see how things go."

At Erin's disappointed expression, the doctor added, "Look at it this way. For the next seven months, your body absolutely belongs to that baby, and he or she makes every decision about it."

"Wow. I never thought about it like that."

"Sounds extreme, but it's worth it, trust me." The doctor glanced at photographs of her own four children, displayed on the corner of her desk. "And not to worry. After the birth, that new little soul will give everything back. Except, of course, your heart."

Erin laughed nervously. "I think he already has that."

Dr. Kipfer grinned. "Welcome to mommyhood."

After Erin got used to the idea of being pregnant, it took a week to shore up enough courage to tell her parents, a month for her girl-friends to stop squealing every time they saw her, three months before they stopped grilling her about the identity of the father, and five months before her forced "no work" policy drove her to the absolute brink of institutionalization.

She'd done everything Dr. Kipfer asked of her—eating better than she ever had, exercising regularly, taking it easy. She'd kept her weight gain to just nineteen pounds so far, yet she still felt like an unwieldy Winnebago moving through the world. She'd never bumped into so many things in her life.

The fire chief, a father and grandfather himself, flat-out ordered her to stay home once she reached eighteen weeks, even though the pregnancy was proceeding normally and the fetus seemed strong. Now, with two months to go before delivery, she simply had to get out and do something non-baby-related before her brain up and died.

Before she'd had to ease up, she'd taken care of things full force. The nursery was finished, furnished and fine. She'd decluttered and organized her entire house to within an inch of its life. All her flower beds were planted, and there wasn't a speck of dirt or disarray to be found in her garage—a miracle in itself. Not only that, but she'd kept a daily pregnancy diary to give to her child one day.

Three volumes and counting.

It had gotten so bad that Finn, a dog who'd suffered from separation anxiety, mind you, was actually sick of her company. Pack animal or not, the poor dog wanted his space. She could hardly blame the big guy, because she'd been getting on her *own* nerves for months.

As far as the impending labor, Cagney was glee-fully acting as her Lamaze coach, and her birth plan had been written and revised to anal-retentive perfection. Her hospital bag was packed and had taken up permanent residence next to her front door. The phone tree was set up, printed out, dis-persed and tested.

Now, the only thing left was thinking about Nate and wallowing in guilt about everything he was missing. She'd gone so far as to Google "Nate" and "Las Vegas" in the inane hopes of stumbling across him, but the results were too daunting. None of the listings stuck out to her, and no way was she calling hundreds of men to tell them they might be her baby's father.

She'd even sucked up her pride and tried the hotel in Denver where they'd created this new little life together. Unfortunately, privacy policies pre-vented them from giving her any info, and no matter how much she pleaded, they wouldn't budge.

Insanity lurked on the horizon waiting to grab her. Something had to give.

Knowing she was likely in for a lecture, she nevertheless drove to the Fire Department head-quarters, bypassed the department secretary and knocked on the chief's door.

Her throat tightened as she waited.

With a quizzical expression on his face, Chief

John Dresden pulled open the door, then broke into a huge smile. "DeLuca! What are you doing out of your house?" He pulled her into a fatherly bear hug.

"I'm allowed to leave my house, Chief."

He held her at arm's length and studied her. "You look well, you look well. But really, why take any chances?" He ushered her in, actually holding her elbow as she sat in one of his visitors' chairs. She smirked, but didn't comment. The grandpa in him was really coming out, full force.

"To what do I owe this nice surprise?"

"Just wanted to say hi," she lied, in a breezy tone.

"Come on. I know you better than that."

After he'd crossed behind the desk and sat down, she blew out her frustration. "The thing is, Chief, I'm going stark-raving mad sitting around at home. I can't do it anymore. So, I've come to request...okay, beg for...some light-duty work. My doctor says it's okay."

He tilted his chin down. "Now, come on. You only have a few more weeks to go."

She barked out a painful laugh. "That's easy for you to say, but it's eight weeks. Eight, which is technically more than 'a few.' And I've been stuck in my house for fourteen weeks already. That's three and a half months, in case you don't feel like doing the math."

"Well, don't you have things to prepare?"

"All due respect, sir, but are you kidding?" She spread her arms wide. "The nursery was done my first month at home. I won't even go into all the rest of my frighteningly obsessive nesting activities, but let me just say I actually alphabetized my pantry the other day, which is so not me. I'm scaring myself. You have to give me a small assignment. I don't know what I'll do if you say no."

He steepled his fingers, resting them against his lips. "I don't know," he said, finally, stretching his neck side to side. "I don't feel good about the risk."

"There's no risk. Please." She actually clasped her hands together. "Anything. Busywork. Filing. Chief, my dog is even sick of having me around so much."

Chief Dresden chuckled. "Surely you're exaggerating."

"Yeah? Get this. I was tossing his favorite fetch ball yesterday. He literally picked it up, carried it to the section of the gulch that runs behind my house and threw it in."

Dresden's gray eyebrows raised. "He didn't."

"Yes! And then he walked straight past me into the house and lay on the couch, belly-up, for three hours. He totally ignored me, even when I offered treats."

They laughed together.

"Okay, that's pretty bad."

"Tell me about it. I think he'd take *me* to the shelter if he had the chance." Erin cleared her throat, serious for a moment. She stared down at her hands in her rapidly disappearing lap. "Plus, the truth is, I need to get away from my own thoughts."

"Thoughts? About motherhood?" His expression softened. "You'll do fine, Erin. Every new mother is scared, but you'll be a natural."

"It's not so much that. Well, sort of. But, aside from that, lately, I can't stop the obsessive memories." She leveled him with a plaintive stare.

"Ah. I understand."

She knew he truly did. It wasn't just one of those things people say. Chief Dresden had been one of the volunteer firefighters on the scene twelve years earlier. They'd had meager forces and woefully inadequate equipment back then, before they'd become a paid department, but he'd dutifully responded with all the others to the infamous prom night tragedy.

They hadn't spoken of it more than twice in the entire time she'd been on the department, but he knew what Erin, Brody, Cagney and Lexy—not to mention their families and those of the kids who'd died—had gone through. He hadn't lived it, but he'd seen it. That made it easier for her to bring it up.

"So many unpleasant, scary memories, Chief, and with my hormones." She shrugged, twisting her mouth to the side. "I'm not trying to be difficult, but I need a distraction. Badly. I need my work."

He blew out a sigh, sat back in his chair and studied her, rolling ideas around in his head. "In that case, but against my better judgment, there is one thing you can do."

Her heart lifted. In truth, she was stunned. "Thank you. Really? Anything."

"The city has put together a task force to meet with the hotshot pyrotechnics company they've hired for the Fourth of July fireworks show over the lake," he said, disgust underlying his tone. "We need a representative at the meeting who truly understands the gravity of this season's fire danger."

Erin frowned. "I cannot believe they're going to proceed with fireworks. Do they want another Hayman fire situation?" she said, referring to one of the largest wildfires in Colorado history.

"I know, I know. Apparently this company, Walker Pyrotechnics, has an incredible track record for safety. The city manager's office thinks that'll be enough to keep the forest from going up in flames." He waved a hand in dismissal. "If they want to be the fire experts, I can't stop them. I answer to both the city manager and the mayor, as you know. But I want the department's views on the idea crystal clear and on record before it all goes down. I want the people of Troublesome Gulch to know that their fire department is adamantly against the show this year."

Perfect. As passionate as she was about fire prevention, this would be the ideal distraction. She leaned forward. "I'm in. What do I need to do?"

"The big powwow is day after tomorrow." He eyed her baby bulge. "Do you have a Class-A maternity uniform?"

"Yes, I borrowed Ginny Luther's. We're the same size."

He nodded once, then buzzed the secretary. "I'll have Nora get you all the data. Read it over, make some notes about all the various danger areas, every possible issue, DeLuca. Everything."

"You got it."

"And be ready to present a logical argument for canceling the event. Try your best, without alienating the rest of the city, of course."

"That, sir, will be my pleasure."

"Okay. Then, you've got yourself an assignment."

"Thank you. Again. You have no idea how much I appreciate this."

He aimed the pen at her and narrowed his gaze. "None of this is worth getting so worked up about that you stress the baby, understand?"

She laid a palm on her abdomen and smiled. "Not to worry. My baby is adamant about canceling the show, too."

The chief picked up a pen and absentmindedly tapped it on his desktop. "Your buddy, Brody

Austin, from TG Paramedics volunteered for the task force, too, so you'll have backup with your position. And he'll keep an eye on your health."

"Even better." She stood, not wanting to monopolize the busy man's day. "Those pyrotechnic guys don't stand a chance against Brody and me."

Chapter Six

Nate moved about the city conference room with
purpose, reviewing his notes and setting up his
PowerPoint presentation. He wasn't looking
forward to meeting with the City of Troublesome
Gulch Fourth of July Task Force—a mouthful, at
best—but since he had no choice, he'd shown up
early to amp up his A-game.

It wasn't that he had a problem answering
people's safety questions—not at all. Safety had
always been number one for him, hence the overwhelming demand for his business. The issue, unfortunately, was that Troublesome Gulch was in

Colorado, and Colorado reminded him of the elusive and enigmatic Erin.

His jaw clenched.

The way she'd left still stung.

And it shouldn't. That's what made it so crazy.

It had been your classic one-night stand, nothing more. Considering that, he should be relieved there'd been no baggage to lug around afterward. The problem was, he wasn't a one-night-stand kind of guy, and even before their heart-stopping sex, something about Erin had invaded his soul, touched him, entrapped him. Hard as he tried, he couldn't get her out of his mind.

Where was she?

Was she still so sad?

Did she ever think about him?

Pathetic, but he missed her. Thought about her. Gave a damn. After one freakin' night. A blip in his history, really, but there it was. He snorted and shook his head with disdain. He really *had* watched too many romantic movies with his sisters. This was all their fault, and if he didn't rein it in, he'd find himself in the position of having his "man card" revoked permanently.

He exhaled in disgust as he tested his laptop and watched the projection screen, clicking this button and that. Computer in order, he moved on to his notes, aligning them, rereading them—

though he knew the presentation by heart. Busy-work. And he knew it.

His thoughts, of course, kept meandering back to Erin. State of the Union in his life these days. He'd even tried increasing his dating over the past several months to banish her memory, but none of the women he'd met had been half as complex or intriguing as Erin. Plus, it wasn't fair to compare every one of them to her, and that's what he found himself doing.

So he stopped dating, threw himself into his work, and avoided Colorado like a bad investment whenever he could. Since he was the boss, it wasn't difficult. He had a lot of work in the state, but he also had a posse of excellent pyrotechnicians at his disposal, and the power of delegation.

But, this year's fire season along the Rocky Mountain Front Range looked frightening at best. The notion of a fireworks show in the high country struck him as ludicrous, if not outright negligent. Were it his choice, his town, he'd cancel the show altogether. Why risk tragedy? The mayor and city manager didn't want to go that route, though.

So be it.

After he'd turned them down three separate times, the city had increased their offer to an amount he simply couldn't refuse. But he would darn well get all his safety precautions lined up well in advance, because he wasn't going to set the town on fire for the sake of stupid tradition. If that happened, he could guarantee no one would be blaming the city management. All fingers—including theirs—would be aimed directly toward Walker Pyrotechnics.

Therefore, a "task force meeting" called for the owner of Walker to attend, Colorado or not.

Painful or not.

Memories of Erin or not.

Suck it up, Nate.

The door opened, and a stream of people filed in. Nate stepped around the table to greet each of them and introduce himself. There were two men in suits, representing the mayor's office and the city manager's office, a paramedic, a cop and a secretary of some sort who fussed with the refreshments on the side table, then laid out glossy bound reports at each spot around the conference table.

He was caught up in conversation with the city manager, Walt Hennessy, when a breezy voice caught his attention.

"Sorry I'm late."

The back of his neck prickled, and his vision wavered. Rude or not, Nate's attention jerked toward the newcomer, gaping as the secretary assured her that the rest of them had just arrived, and she was just in time.

She being Erin.

His Erin.

His very *pregnant,* excruciatingly beautiful Erin, clad in—of all things—a firefighter's uniform.

This day had officially gone down the crapper.

And it also felt like the best day of his life.

Explain that.

She turned toward him and all the color drained from her face. The two of them stood frozen, staring, and the rest of the room disappeared for Nate. Oblivious, the city manager kept talking, but it became an unintelligible blah-blah-blah in Nate's ear, inconsequential. Annoying.

Erin's hands shook, he noted.

Blood roared through his skull.

The paramedic stepped in and cupped Erin's elbow, asking if she was okay, checking her pulse automatically. Was he her boyfriend? The thought tied Nate's stomach into uncomfortable knots.

"I'm fine," she said, in a testy tone, pulling her wrist away. "Sorry. But you all have to stop fussing over me like I'm some freakin' invalid."

Nate smiled tightly at the city manager. "Excuse me for a moment, sir. I apologize."

"Of course, of course," Walt Hennessy said, in his booming, blustery politician's voice.

Nate crossed the room until he and Erin stood face-to-face, so close he could smell the strawberry scent of her hair. Some insane part of him wondered if he'd simply guessed correctly when he'd bought the shampoo that night so long ago, or if she'd continued using the brand he'd purchased for more sentimental reasons.

Riiiight.

Because a woman who'd leave without so much as a kiss goodbye certainly had a sentimental bent. *Keep fooling yourself, Walker. There goes that man card.*

"Fancy meeting you here, Erin."

He watched her swallow once, then again. She pulled him toward a corner where they had some privacy. "Nate. I...I meant to—I tried to—"

"Wait a minute." The paramedic looked back and forth from the two of them, confusion on his face. "You guys already know each other?"

Erin didn't answer, just continued to gape, eyes glazed, which said everything.

Not wanting to ignore the man, Nate dropped his gaze to her very pregnant belly, let it linger, then leveled the paramedic with a wry stare. "You could say we know each other. Yes."

"Oh. *Oh,*" the paramedic said, drawing the obvious conclusions. He did a few more double takes, absorbing the new info. "Er, why didn't you—?"

Erin turned a pleading glance his way. "Brody, I…I didn't—"

"Wait." This Brody guy smiled at her. "Not now. Not here. It's okay."

"I—I promise I'll explain everything later," Erin said, before casting another sidelong glance at Nate.

The gesture sealed his suspicions.

He was going to be a father.

After quick calculations in his mind, his stomach convulsed. He was going to be a father damned *soon*. End of July.

Shaking himself back into the present, he extended his hand to the paramedic. "Nate Walker. Walker Pyrotechnics."

The medic took his hand. "Brody Austin. Pleasure to meet you." He peered curiously at Erin.

Watching, Nate knew he needed to broach the topic. "Listen," he started, "this is awkward as hell, but if you two are a couple—"

"No!" they said together.

Their vehemence took him aback.

"Brody's my best friend's husband," Erin said, in a reproachful tone, as if he should know that.

As if he'd know *anything*. "Just checking." He didn't want to acknowledge the relief that rushed through him so fast, it left his legs weak. He willed a polite, pleasant tone into his voice. "So, then. This isn't the best time for conversation, as Brody said. Are you free for coffee after the meeting? Decaf for you, obviously."

Her skin paled again. "O-of course."

The Brody guy stepped closer, chest out, chin high. "Erin, if you need Faith and me to come along—"

"No, it's okay," she told him, with a reassuring smile. "It's nothing like…whatever you're thinking. Really. Let's just drop it for now and get this meeting underway. Okay?"

Meeting? What meeting?

The only fireworks for Nate right now were those exploding in his brain. So much for bringing his A-game during this all-important presentation.

Chapter Seven

The meeting passed in a blur of rote presentation mixed with swirling unanswerable questions and pure blinding shock. An irrational part of him resented having been put in that position, even though he logically knew neither he nor Erin would've planned it that way. She didn't know he was Walker Pyrotechnics any more than he'd known she was a Troublesome Gulch firefighter. Still, during the meeting, he hadn't treated her like the bad guy simply because of her choice of profession. It would've been nice if she'd extended him the same courtesy.

In any case, Nate left the city building feeling as though he'd at least conveyed his main bullet points.

Then again, who cared?

An unfamiliar glut of emotions crested and crashed inside him. Joy. Fear. Anger. Excitement.

He was going to be a father. A *father*.

And a damn sight better father than his ever was, too, regardless of the fact that this whole thing was so utterly unexpected. He'd always imagined he'd have a wife long before the father issue arose, but apparently fate had dealt him a different hand. Which was fine.

Still, he felt woefully unprepared. Erin'd had about seven months to get used to the idea while he was left with the cram course.

When the meeting room had cleared, they'd agreed to meet at the Pinecone Diner rather than driving together. Erin wanted to change out of her uniform—or at least that was her excuse. Naturally, he arrived first. He took a table in the rear of the place and sat, back to the wall, waiting. Thinking. Fuming.

Truth be told, the more he went over the whole convoluted situation in his mind, the more wicked-pissed he became. He'd bet more steam rose off him than off his freshly poured mug of coffee, which he gripped with angry hands.

Pregnancy aside, he couldn't get past the fact

that she'd seemed downright hostile during the task force meeting. Why? What had he done to deserve that? First of all, had she been listening to him at all instead of tossing him eye daggers the whole time, she would know that he basically agreed with her stance about the fireworks show, and was doing his best to make it safe. She'd also realize that she hadn't hired him. He couldn't just change things based on her opinion, as much as he'd like to.

Even more aggravating, *she* was the one who'd run out of the hotel room without so much as a courtesy phone number on her quickly scrawled note. Had she not, they might know more about each other at this point. He was blameless in both situations.

Straight up, she should've told him about the baby. Somehow. This was the information age, after all.

At the very least, she shouldn't have lied about her ability to conceive. He'd been honest that night. Open. He'd tried to help her, to comfort her, and— stupid him—he'd truly thought they'd connected on more than a sexual level. How hard would it have been for her to leave a contact phone number instead of skulking out of that hotel room like a criminal? An e-mail address at the very least? Had he given her any red flag indications whatsoever that he harbored stalker tendencies? No way.

Then again, he'd known the game going in. This slap in the face was exactly the kind of treatment a man got when he played savior in a dive bar.

He should've expected it.

His fists clenched. Absurd as it sounded, he just *hadn't* expected the stereotypical ending from the Erin he thought he'd begun to know that night. He'd hoped for better from her. That was the biggest shame in the whole, tangled fiasco.

The bell over the door jingled, and there she stood.

His breath caught.

She was a thousand times more beautiful carrying his child than she'd been that night. Ripe, robust, radiant. Damn it, despite it all, he couldn't hold back his elation at seeing her again, and that weakness irked him. She stopped, scanning the crowd, waving to a few of the people she knew.

In a small town like this, she surely knew everyone. He didn't envy her the task she'd probably faced of explaining how she wound up pregnant when she didn't even have a boyfriend.

But he'd save his sympathy. After how she'd treated him, she didn't deserve it.

When she saw him, her expression registered immediate distress, which he hated. They both knew this was going to suck, but he'd always hoped she would look at him with a very different expression in her eyes if they ever met again.

She raised her hand nervously, and headed his way. It was mid-June, warm for the high country. She wore some sort of billowy white top and jeans. Flip-flops. As she approached, it occurred to him that she wasn't very large for being seven months along. From behind, you wouldn't even know she was pregnant.

A sickening feeling bloomed inside his chest.

Maybe this wasn't his baby after all.

The thought didn't comfort him as one might expect it would.

"Hi," she said, as she slid into the booth. "Have you been waiting long?"

"Only about seven months," he said.

She froze from the ice in his tone, color rising into her cheeks as though windburned. "Nate, God, I—"

"Hey, Erin, honey," said the waitress, sidling up at precisely the worst time ever. "It's good to see you out and about. You look just adorable—you're one of *those* pregnant women, lucky you. Lordy, I was an absolute cow with my kids," she added wistfully, before shaking off the memory. "Anyway, how much longer?"

Erin glanced furtively toward Nate. He could read her dismay at the line of conversation, but what could she do?

Nate sat back, languidly raising an eyebrow,

daring her to answer. Hell, at this point, he wanted to know, too. He tried for a calm demeanor, but beneath the table, his fists clenched.

"Ah, just about eight weeks. Thanks."

His insides shook with relief. Confirmed: his kid. She must just be one of those women who carried small, probably due to her amazing physical condition.

"You have everything all ready?"

She cleared her throat. "Almost."

"Well, we can't wait to meet him or her." The clueless waitress smiled his way before turning back toward Erin. "I already served your friend here. But can I get you something to drink?"

"Just water. Oh, and I guess I'll have a glass of skim milk, too."

"Gotta feed that little one," the waitress sang, as she turned and headed off.

"Should you really do the skim thing?"

She blew out a breath of exasperation. "Yes. I can't gain a lot of weight. Doctor's orders. And please don't start watchdogging my every move. I get enough of that from everyone around here."

Silence descended.

"Nice that the whole world knows everything about you and the pregnancy except the baby's father," he said.

She flinched. "I didn't know your last name,"

she said, her tone low and laced tight with regret. "I looked for you. I swear. On Google and I called the hotel…but all I had was Nate."

"I stay there all the time," he said.

"Yes, and their privacy policies don't include giving out your information to strange women, which I suppose you should be grateful for. It might've made things easier had I known you were a fire setter," she snapped.

He sighed. Again with the hostility. He harnessed flame for entertainment purposes. She was a firefighter. He got the polarity issue. But, her animosity toward his chosen profession was over-the-top and unwarranted, and he was sick of avoiding the real cause. "I'm not a fire setter. I'm a pyrotechnics engineer, and a damned good one. If you'll recall, you didn't want to know anything about me that night or I would've gladly told you. Don't twist this around and act like I hid something from *you*."

She had the decency to look chagrined. "Sorry."

He scowled. "Why did you tell me you couldn't get pregnant in the first place? Why the lie? Just to save you the trip to the donor clinic?"

"No! It wasn't a lie," she said, her tone brittle. She glanced around, lowered it again. "I wasn't trying to rope some unassuming guy into getting me pregnant, okay? No matter what you think.

Please, I realize you don't owe me any favors, but can we agree to keep our voices down?"

She pressed shaky fingers to the middle of her forehead. Long fingers. Short, bare nails.

Sexy.

"This is a small town. Everyone knows everyone, and I don't want us or our baby to be fodder for the Gulch gossip mill."

He inclined his head. "That's reasonable." Frankly, he didn't want strangers here knowing his business, either.

She reached across the table and touched his hand with those warm, sexy fingers, but pulled back almost immediately. "I *honestly* believed I couldn't conceive. It wasn't a lie. This pregnancy was as much a surprise to me as it is to you."

He scoffed.

"It was. And when I found out, the first thing I wanted was to tell you. I've agonized over it for the past five months."

"Really," he said, his tone dubious.

"Yes, and I can only thank God you ended up here now. Belated, but here it is." She spread her arms wide. "You're going to be a father. Okay? I'm sorry you couldn't be here for the morning sickness, the leg cramps and the smothering inquiries from my friends and family, but trust me when I say you really didn't miss much excitement."

"Your perspective."

Her chin quivered. "What else was I supposed to do, Nate? What? Tell me."

He blew out a sigh of resignation. They couldn't change the past, and he had to take her at her word. "Okay, we made a lot of mistakes from the start. Both of us. I guess my bottom line is, you shouldn't have left without saying goodbye. I deserved more."

Misery molded her expression. "I *know*."

"Great. You know. So, what now?" he asked, more roughly than he'd intended.

She bristled. "Now? Nothing." Her tough shell slammed shut around her. "I'm not planning on milking you for financial support, if that's what you're stressing about."

"Financial support?" He could swear his ears burst into flames with the force of his rage. "Is that what you think I'm concerned about?"

She blinked, uncertain and off-kilter from his quick flash of anger. "Well, what else? It was—" she lowered to a whisper "—a one-night stand. I don't expect you to go down on one knee and pledge your life to me."

"Which I have no intention of doing," he hissed, regretting it only slightly when he saw the hurt cloud her expression. "But, regardless of our relationship, or the lack thereof, I intend to be a part of my child's life. I have that right."

Fear rolled off of her like storm clouds over the mountain range, and she rested a protective hand on her belly. "If you try to take my child—"

"Back up one damn minute," He splayed a palm on his chest. "I'm angry right now, yes. I have every right to be. Even you can't deny that."

Standoff.

"Okay, you're right." She sagged. "Sorry."

"Please, try to see past it all. Remember me? Nate? I'm the good guy—your words, not mine. The one you said my mom should be proud of. Does any of that ring a bell?"

She bit the corner of her bottom lip.

"If you honestly think I would take my baby away from his mother, then we connected even less than I imagined. In fact, we didn't connect at all, and considering a child resulted from such a complete disconnect, that's a damned disgrace."

She forced out a breath and pushed all ten fingers into the front of her hair. "No, that's not it. We did connect, Nate."

His heart jumped.

"I—I just don't know what to think. I'm flustered and I'm scared. I never thought I'd see you again. I never thought I'd get pregnant in the first place. And then you're here in Troublesome Gulch. Suddenly."

"Surprise," he said, unable to keep the sarcasm out of his tone.

She ignored it. "No one knows anything about you, not even my closest friends. This is all just so—"

The waitress returned with her beverages, and they both went silent. The woman seemed to sense the seriousness of their conversation, because she didn't indulge in any more chatter. Thank God. When she walked away, Erin finished with, "—so complicated."

Nate leaned forward, winding both hands around his thick, ceramic coffee mug. "What's complicated about it? Introduce me to your friends any way you need to." He flicked his hand to the side. "That part, I don't care about. Next step, you give birth to our child. We share custody. Problem solved." He paused, but she didn't comment. "We're supposedly friends, right? At least, I thought so." He squinted off into the distance. "Then again, there was that note."

"*Enough* with the note already," she said, her tone exasperated. "I've apologized. How many more times can I say I'm sorry?" She ignored the friend part altogether. "Your solution sounds pat and perfect, but the custody arrangement is impossible. I'm not sending my baby off to Las Vegas a couple times a month. Who can afford that?"

"*Our* baby. And no one's suggesting twice monthly interstate flight. Do I look like an idiot to you?"

She lifted her chin, but her bottom lip tremored. "My career is here, and so are my friends and family. I can't start over in Las Vegas. I don't even want to."

"Not a problem, because I own my company and work all over the country." He shrugged. "Where I'm headquartered means nothing to my clients."

She blinked at him. Twice. "What are you saying?"

"I'm saying, I'll move to Troublesome Gulch. Now. Before my child is born."

She gasped.

He held up a hand. "Listen, you can hate me, avoid me, deny you ever begged me to make love to you, even though we both know you did."

Her face bloomed crimson; she cut away her glance.

"Blame the whole fiasco on me if you have to. Whatever gets you through the day. But one thing I can guarantee you, Erin, is that my child will not grow up without a father. That is a nonnegotiable point."

All around them, diner business proceeded as usual while they sat cloaked in weighty, silent distress. The waitresses called orders out to the cooks, diners conversed. Silverware clinked against plates and bowls. Laughter.

"I don't hate you," she said softly. "Not one single bit."

That admission surprised him. He took a moment to school his tone into ambivalence. "Well, there's a bit of good news for once."

"And I'd never blame the whole thing on you. You should give me a little credit, too." She studied him from beneath her long, dark lashes. "But I know I don't deserve your credit, and I'd understand if *you* hated *me*."

He melted a bit, in spite of his ire. "No such luck. You're carrying our baby, remember? I couldn't hate you if I tried."

The tension in her face eased. "I'm…I'm glad. Really. And, for the last time—I hope—" she eyed him pointedly "—I'm sorry for leaving the infamous note. I was wrong. Unfair. But, you witnessed my state of mind more than anyone that night. I didn't know how to handle—" she blew out a breath "—look, I can't change it. You have no idea how many times I've wished I could. But, I'll make it up to you. As a friend. And we *are* friends. Just tell me how. Please."

He sipped his coffee, watching her over the rim. After he'd swallowed, he set the mug back down. "Maybe, as *friends* and for the sake of our baby, we can call a truce, leave the past where it belongs."

"Deal. Thank goodness."

"And…" He toyed with the rim of his coffee mug,

shook his head, unsure. Maybe this was too much to ask at this tenuous juncture in their relationship.

"And?"

Hell, what did he have to lose? "Can you help me find a place to live?"

She worried her fingers together, considering. "That's a reasonable request. But I have one equally reasonable condition."

"Name it."

"You didn't ask to be a father, Nate. I have no expectations of you." She swallowed. Twice. "If there is any chance whatsoever that you're going to disappear in a few years, I'd rather you just did it now. Before the baby gets attached to you. Please," she asked, in a whisper. "I don't want our baby heartbroken."

Emotions from the past swamped him. He leaned in. "Erin, do you remember what I told you about my family that night?"

Bafflement showed on her face. "Um, it was you, your mom and three sisters, your dad wasn't involv—oh."

"Yeah. *Oh.*" He let that sink in. "I do remember my dad, for the record. I remember waiting on the front porch for his promised visits, excited, eager, my Spider-Man duffel bag packed. I remember my mom gently pulling me inside the house as the sun went down, because the bastard never showed.

I remember crying myself to sleep, inconsolable. Those are the memories of my father."

"I'm sorry."

He shrugged. "The point is, I would never put my child in the position my father put me and my sisters into. Never. I may not have asked to be a dad, but strange as it seems, I want this baby."

"I do, too," she said, in a near whisper.

"I want to be a parent to him. Or her. A real parent, not someone to wait for on the porch. End of story."

She cocked her head. "Your word of honor?"

"Absolutely."

After a deep breath, she said, "In that case, I probably know of a place you can buy immediately. If it fits your needs, that is."

He stilled, waiting.

"You met my friend Brody at the meeting?"

"Yes."

"His wife, Faith, is my best friend, and she moved into his house when they married but hasn't sold her condo yet." She shrugged. "It's small— one bedroom—but in a great area downtown, and partially furnished with the stuff that couldn't fit at Brody's. Plus, she really needs to sell. She's pregnant, too. Due in September. And they have a teenage foster son who'll be off to college before they know it."

He nodded once. "Perfect. Sign me up."

Her brows arched. "Really? You haven't even seen the condo."

"Doesn't matter. A place to live, no waiting, help out your friends. It's a win-win."

She gave him an angelic smile that warmed his soul more than it probably should've, considering.

"Faith will be thrilled. It's a nice place, Nate. I promise."

"What matters is that I'll be here."

Erin grew distant, twirled her spoon absentmindedly against the table.

He hated to see her sad. It reminded him of that night. "Why so pensive? Seems like we've made some progress here."

She half shrugged. "I don't know." She bit her bottom lip. "You're really going to uproot your life?"

"What would you do in my place?"

A line of worry bisected her forehead. "But what about your family? Your mom and sisters?" Her eyes widened, and she reached up to cover her mouth. "Oh no. Boomer and Thug."

He frowned. "What about them?"

The ache of remorse weighed down her words. "Pets aren't allowed in Faith's condo building, Nate. They're your family. I know how important they are to you."

True pain lanced through him, but he fought it

off. Somehow, some way, it would all work out. "My child is my family, too."

She thought for a moment, moistening her lips with a nervous flick of her tongue. "Would it be okay if Boomer and Thug stayed at my house? I'm sure Finn would love them, though we'd have to test him with the bunny."

"That's okay with you?"

"It's the least I can do. Plus, who knows? Maybe Faith's condo can be a stepping stone until you find something more suitable. At least it'll get you here now. They'll probably let you move in before the closing."

"It's a solution at least. Thanks. As for Mom and the girls, I have regular work in Las Vegas. The way I travel, I'll see them as much as I do now. More, because I'll stay at their houses when I'm there, and they'll actually feed me. And, of course, they'll want to come here often and see the baby once he or she is born." He hesitated, softened his tone. "Meet you."

She gulped. He could see the whole spiderweb of extended family layering on more complications in her mind. This was why no-strings sex was a big fat myth.

"What are you going to tell them?"

"No clue. I'm still reeling myself."

"I'm so sorry, Nate. You were good to me, and

I never intended to put you in this awkward position with your family. With your *life*. You deserve…the total package. True love, marriage, family." She twisted her mouth to the side. "Instead, you're stuck with me and a baby you never wanted."

Strangely, despite the emotional wood chipper he'd been thrust through today, he wasn't sorry. In a zillion scattered pieces, flailing for emotional purchase, but certainly not sorry. He reached out and covered her hand with his, ventured an encouraging, if winsome, smile. "We've had a bit of a rough start, but everything will be fine. You'll see. We're both adults, and these are modern times. Unmarried parents? Not such a big deal."

"No," she murmured.

"One thing we're both committed to is making sure our baby knows he or she is loved and wanted. Right?"

"Absolutely."

He shrugged, pulled his hand back. "Then we're on the same page. The only page that counts." He paused, searched her eyes. "Be in the moment, right?"

Chapter Eight

Erin's regular Friday lunch date with Faith rolled around a few days after Nate exploded back into her life like a bottle rocket. Everything was in fast-forward mode. He was scheduled to move in to Faith's old condo that weekend, as a renter until they could close the sale. And she wanted to lay out the whole sordid tale for her friends before he was officially a part of their lives. So, she invited Brody, Cagney and Lexy along, with Faith's encouragement.

Once they'd ordered and eaten, she sucked it up and spilled the whole story.

Wasn't easy, either, to say the least.

As she neared the end of the explanation, her paper napkin lay in tatters on her lap, and her friends watched her with concern etched into their sober expressions. "The Millstone apartment fire just really brought it all back for me, I don't know. No other fire has been like that. I think it was Suzette—"

"Who is recovering nicely," Brody said, "as is her beautiful, healthy baby girl."

She bestowed a quick half smile. "I'm glad. But that night, all I knew was she'd lost her husband. I was stupid, out of control." She shrugged. "Nate was there, I was there. Just us in a hotel room, and…I started to think about Brody."

"Yeah—" he puffed his chest out playfully "—I have that effect on women." He winked at her.

Faith punched him in the arm.

Erin forged ahead, ignoring his total guyness. "I mean, I've always claimed that I'd worked through what happened to us on prom night, but it's not true. I've just honed the art of putting up a perfect front."

"Me, too," Cagney said.

"Me, three," Lexy added.

Erin regarded them sadly. "The truth is, my life had been at a standstill since I lost Kev. And the baby. The first baby. Brody had returned to the Gulch and done such a good job of working through his issues."

He curled Faith against his side. "Thanks to my lovely pregnant wife and the best in-laws a man could have."

She leaned up and kissed him on the chin.

Erin and the others smiled. "You two. Anyway, in my desperate and probably not-so-rational analysis of the situation, I concluded that Brody had gotten on with his life because he'd taken one difficult step—moving back to the Gulch, no matter how terrifying."

He leaned his head side to side. "Pretty much true."

"See? So, I decided to take *my* one difficult and terrifying step. With Nate." Heat suffused her whole body, and she rested a hand on her belly. She didn't even want to know how red-faced she was. "I guess I don't have to tell you what that step entailed."

"No, we get it," Faith said.

"And who knew," she tossed off, her tone wry. "All that crap they pounded into our brains during high school health class was dead-on. You truly can get pregnant from just once."

"Aw, honey. No one blames you," Lexy said. Her hair was red this month, an ultramodern cut, always the little siren. "None of us have any room to judge. You're a grown woman. Besides, I've seen Nate Walker at the city building. That man is fine, fine, fine."

Erin cleared her throat, feeling itchy inside her clothing. "That was part of it, sure. He was the first guy since Kev to actually make me think…along those lines." She choked back a wave of embarrassment. "But the night didn't start that way, honestly. I was a mess, and he was only trying to help. He's such a nice, genuine guy."

"No one's implying he seduced you or took advantage of you in your time of weakness, if that's what this is all about," Cagney said.

Erin nodded. "It is. Part of it. I'd been so scared for so long. But, I could never have done that with anyone who wasn't…"

Nate, she thought, with a lightning bolt of shock.

She couldn't have made love with any other man.

That sudden insight shook her to her core.

"I'd say he's more than just nice," Cagney interjected, her sandy blond hair in its neat, workday French braid, though strands of it had wisped their way out to frame her delicate features. She'd taken a lunch break in order to join them, still wearing her TG Police uniform. "I mean, he's uprooting to a whole new state just to be an involved father." She shook her head in amazement. "Not a lot of guys would go that far."

"I approve," Faith said, raising a hand.

Brody nodded. "Stand-up man, that Nate."

"You are my closest friends," Erin said. She

looked at each of them in turn. "I really wanted to tell you this, excruciating as it was, well, first, because of the blame issue. I didn't want you to feel like you had to take sides."

"We don't," Faith said. "Truly."

"Good." Erin readjusted in her chair. "But I also wanted to have this talk because I hope…" She pulled her bottom lip in between her teeth, feeling an unexpected surge of protectiveness toward Nate.

"Hope what, Er?" Cagney urged.

"I guess…that each of you will find a way to welcome Nate into the fold, too. I mean—" she held up her palms "—he and I are not a couple. Despite the baby. After the way I left things, trust me, that could never happen."

"Never say never," Lexy sang, studying her manicure.

Erin couldn't even address that notion. "But, after all he's sacrificing, I want him to have friends here, and you're the best people I know. You have to believe none of this was his fault."

"It wasn't yours, either. You were in a bad place, and you did what you had to do. But you have great instincts," Cagney said. "If you welcome him, we'll welcome him."

A chorus of agreements went around the table.

"That said," Cagney added, placing her palms on the tabletop, "I, unfortunately, have to get back to the old day-in, day-out grind." She pulled a face. "But, if you want him to take over as your birth coach, all you need to do is tell me. I'll understand."

Erin slashed her hands through the air. "No way. You are my birth coach. Period."

"Well…okay," her quietly stoic friend said, unsure. "I'm absolutely here for you. But, if I may ask, what does Nate think about that?"

Erin shrugged.

"Erin?" Cagney pressed.

"It, uh, hasn't come up."

Lexy lowered her chin. "You're due in less than eight weeks. He's the father. It *needs* to come up."

"I know, I know. And when it does, I'll deal with it. Promise. No more running. But I need Cagney with me in the delivery room. And, before I confront anything about the actual birth, I need to get past the fact that he's moving here. Tomorrow. Oh, my God." She waved a hand in front of her face, breathing rapidly.

Lexy maneuvered her wheelchair closer to Erin and leaned forward to hug her. "We love you, you big dork. We're just trying to help. Stop depriving your fetus of oxygen."

"I'm trying."

"No one cares that your pregnancy is the result of a one-night stand. The baby has seemed to make you happier, and I, for one, just want you to be happy." The tiny little firebrand glanced around at the table of friends. "I want you all to be happy, since any unhappiness you might feel, as we know, is my fault."

"No, it isn't, Lex. Let it go, already," Cagney said, scraping back her chair to stand. "We make our own joy, we make our own sorrow."

Lexy brushed her off. She'd always blamed herself for the radical changes in their lives, discounting the fact that her change—at least physically—was the most extreme by far.

Cagney leaned down to kiss Erin on the cheek. "I've really got to go. It's all good, girlfriend. Nate's a good guy. Your baby's healthy. Your friends love you and so does your family. So, don't worry. It'll all work out somehow." She winked at the others and left the restaurant.

The remaining friends moved their chairs in closer.

"Speaking of tomorrow, Jason and I still plan on helping Nate move in, whenever he rolls into town," Brody said. "Any idea when?"

"None. Sorry."

"Does he have my numbers?"

"Yes."

"I'll help, too," Faith said.

"Like hell you will," her husband said, giving her a dark glare. He aimed a similar one at Erin.

"If I catch either of you lifting or moving anything, I'll have Cagney handcuff you inside her car for the duration."

"Well, we want to *be* there," Faith said. "We're pregnant, not helpless, for God's sake. This isn't 1812. We can at least provide refreshments."

"Fine. You can be there." He pointed at Erin. "Keep my wife a minimum of ten feet away from the coffeemaker. She still can't manage to brew a pot of joe that isn't pure, choking poison."

"Deal."

Faith scrunched her nose at Erin. "Traitor."

Erin shrugged in apology. "Your coffee sucks, Pip. We can't lie, because we love you."

Lexy laughed.

Brody raised his brows at Faith. "And you, keep Erin from working. We all know how she is. If she so much as unpacks one pillowcase, I will rat her out to Dr. Kipfer and the fire chief, with not an iota of guilt."

"Geez, you play dirty, Austin," Erin said, amused by his overprotectiveness. She had to admit, it felt good to be cared for. Sometimes. She sipped her lemonade, a huge burden lifted from her shoulders.

"Damn right I do." He grinned, then turned to Lexy. "And your task, little one, is to keep the city running smoothly tomorrow while the *finest* of TG's finest are busy, okay?"

She rolled her big, green eyes. "Duh, Brody. Don't I always?"

"That, you do."

"I may not have made it to my coronation ceremony on prom night, but never forget, I will always be the queen of Troublesome Gulch." She laughed. "Wow, I'm a legend in my own mind."

The moving in went smoothly enough, though the day ran painfully long. It seemed as if Nate hadn't brought much. Erin didn't know if that was because he lived simply due to all his traveling, or because the whole situation really was temporary to him, despite what he'd claimed. Worry set her on edge regardless.

That, and raging hormones.

She hated the freakin' things.

PMS had nothin' on pregnancy.

When they'd finished situating all of Nate's stuff, Jason, Brody's and Faith's foster son, sat on the floor playing with Boomer and Thug, and Brody and Nate engaged in some mind-numbing, irrelevant sports prattle, getting along fine, no worries whatsoever—damned irritating males. Erin and Faith hovered on the outskirts tentatively. Like…okay, guys, what next? Frankly, going home seemed like a grand idea.

Erin's jaw clenched. She desperately yearned

for some alone time and a much-needed nap. Plus, she could tell by her friend's pinched expression that Faith's back hurt, an issue she'd suffered from since her first trimester.

Faith wouldn't readily admit to her pain, though. She was too nice for her own good. One palm pressed to her lower back, she smiled stiffly at the guys. "So, we're done. That wasn't too awful," she lied, in a pathetic attempt at hint dropping.

Erin snorted, not caring if she sounded unladylike.

Brody glanced at Faith. "How about we all head over to our house for dinner, babe? Nate's pantry isn't stocked yet, and a home-cooked meal sure would be a great welcome tonight."

Inside, Erin groaned. Brody and his big mouth. Friend or not, she so wanted to smack the guy. God knows, he probably wasn't offering to whip up a welcome meal, and she darn well wasn't going to stand by and watch Faith slaving away. "Actually, we might as well have dinner at my house," she said, throwing a subtle stink-eye Brody's way.

"You don't have to cook for me." Nate smiled at her. "Thanks, but restaurant food is a staple in my life. Besides, I'm sure both you and Faith are tired."

She appreciated his perceptiveness about their exhaustion, as Brody didn't seem to have clue number one. However, she still felt unduly peeved that Nate had considered, even for a moment, the notion that she might stand before a hot stove on his behalf. Or anyone's, for that matter.

Nearly eight months pregnant in *summer*—hello!

"Oh, trust me, I'm not cooking. We can order out. But we do need to get Boomer and Thug settled. I wouldn't mind having everyone there in case Finn suddenly decides Thug looks like dinner instead of a new furry pal."

Jason's head whipped up, one hand protectively stroking Thug's back. "Dude, that's cold. Ain't no way you should let Finn eat this rabbit. He rocks, 'specially his name."

"Well, I wouldn't *let* him—"

"Don't call Erin 'dude,' Jase," Faith interrupted, sounding as though she were balanced, tiptoe, on her last nerve. "It's disrespectful. I've told you that a million times."

Jason had always hated disappointing Faith. He ducked his reddened face. "My bad. Ms. DeLuca."

"Ugh," Erin said, rolling her eyes. "You can't call me *that,* either. It makes me feel ancient. And *fat.*"

"Uh, fat?" Jason cast a confused, pleading glance toward Brody.

"Don't worry, buddy." He sent the teenager a reassuring wink. "Pregnant women are known to be virtually incomprehensible."

"Shut up!" Erin and Faith said, in stereo.

"My God, Brody!" Faith's eyes flashed. She

planted her fists on her hips. "*That's* what you want to teach him about women? That we're irrational because we're carrying *your* children?"

Awkwardness descended as a WWE match between Venus and Mars unexpectedly ensued. It might be two against three, but the men were hormonally outclassed, in a pro ball versus Little League sort of way.

"Ah…I'm sorry?" Brody ventured.

"Is that a statement or a question?" Faith asked.

"I have a better idea," Nate interjected, in as light a tone as it seemed he could manage while venturing into the danger zone. He smoothed his palms together a couple times. "Boomer and Thug are fine here tonight. They've always been quiet. No one will know the difference. Why don't you ladies take the evening off. Relax in a testosterone-free environment."

"Sounds like bliss," Erin said.

"More like nirvana," said Faith, with a sigh.

"Or heaven," said Erin.

"Then, it's settled. Brody, Jason and I will head off for some food and get out of your way." He glanced toward Brody, who eagerly nodded.

"Don't forget, I'm supposed to spend the night with Gramps," Jason said, referring to old Mr. Norwood, who used to own Brody and Faith's A-frame and had become an integral part of their little patchwork family. "He scored the newest Xbox game, so I have to kick his butt at it a few times before he works on his skills. Dude has way too much time to practice. It's not fair."

"Perfect," Brody said, grabbing the escape rope from the hormone hell pit he'd unwittingly fallen into. He tried to match his tone to Nate's, but sounded a bit too saccharine, as though carefully addressing homicidal maniacs. It didn't help his case.

"Babe, we'll drive you and Erin home, drop Jase at Herman's and then Nate and I will make ourselves scarce. Sound good?"

"Whatever," Faith snapped.

"Don't bother. I can drive Faith home," Erin said, holding up one palm as Brody opened his mouth to comment. "And if either one of you even starts to say that I shouldn't be driving, I can't be held responsible for my actions. You'd better just get out while you can."

Eyes round, Jason shot to his feet and backed away from the women. Brody clamped a hand on his shoulder. "Son, a wise man simply listens to a pregnant woman and does what she says—"

"Preferably without *comment*," Faith added, pointedly. She ground her fist into her back. "God, I need a heating pad. And a margarita, but ha ha, joke's on me, right?"

Concern furrowed Brody's forehead. "Does your back hurt, babe?"

"Of course her back hurts. She's carrying twenty-five extra pounds up-front, for God's sake," Erin barked, pointing toward the front door. "Stop asking idiotic questions, Austin. Go!"

All three men scurried off.

"We'll lock up if that's okay, Nate," Faith called after them. "Erin can give you the spare set of keys tomorrow or whenever."

He held up both hands in acquiescence, saying nothing. Smart man. When the guys closed the door behind them, as quietly as possible, Faith and Erin exhaled simultaneous sighs of relief and ex-asperation. Then, unexpectedly, they looked at each other and burst out laughing. Hard.

"I hate men," Faith said, when the hysteria had subsided. She wiped tears from her eyes.

"I hear you. Such an annoying breed of human."

"And clueless? Geez."

"Completely."

"I never realized just *how* clueless until I got pregnant. 'Babe, why don't we all have dinner over at our house,'" Faith said, mimicking her husband's voice. She bugged her eyes at Erin. "What was *that?*"

"That was Brody being Brody. You'd usually melt at how sweet he was being."

"Sweet, schmeet. I wonder if I have a cheese-cake in the freezer?"

Erin smoothed a palm over her belly. "Ready to go? I'm exhausted. The baby's been kicking the crap out of me all day, and I'm *so* over it. I'm hoping a bath will zen him out."

Faith palmed the extra set of keys from the coffee table. "More than ready. I want a cup of tea, a heating pad and silence. And, so help me God, there'd better not be one single sock or pair of boxer briefs on my damn floor, or those guys are in for it."

That sent them into hysterics again, until they were both crossing their legs and holding their bellies. Once they'd pulled themselves together, they staggered side by side toward the door. Erin hugged Faith around the shoulders. "It's so comforting to go through this insanity with someone who really gets it."

"I know." Faith chuckled, then blew out a sigh. "Although even *I* don't get it sometimes. I've got to snap out of it. That whole exchange with Brody felt like an out-of-body experience."

"Yeah, I kept waiting for your head to spin around," Erin said, in a wry tone.

Faith grimaced. "I suppose we were a little hard on them, you know?"

"Eh, screw it." Erin flicked her fingers to the

side. "They're probably going to devour big plates of greasy Mexican food—"

"And *my* margarita," Faith said.

"Like they possess such good taste. Please. They'll drink beers."

"True."

"And then they'll shoot a few games of pool as if they have no cares in the world. All while we sit at home, cranky and contemplating our swollen ankles and aching backs."

"Good point. Jerks." She hesitated, then sighed again, ever the romantic. "Still, I'm madly in love with Brody, and despite his forays into the supremely annoying, he's so good to me."

Erin thought of Nate. "I know what you mean."

Faith did a double take.

"What?" Erin asked.

A smug smile overtook Faith's face.

"What?"

"I didn't say a word."

Erin started shaking her head before she even uttered a sound. "Oh, no. Don't go there. I *so* did not mean that I felt the same way about Nate. Don't even think you're reading between my lines."

"Uh-huh."

"You and Brody are *married*," Erin enunciated, as they opened the front door. "Nate and I don't even know each other."

"Whatever you say." Faith paused, still looking smug. "But, you must admit, he *is* really sweet. Sure seems like a guy worth getting to know."

"Whatever you say," Erin echoed, with sarcasm in her tone, although she secretly agreed. But, she'd never cop to it, no matter how much she wished they could just start over. After the way she'd treated him, no chance she would set herself up for more heartbreak.

She glanced back at Boomer and Thug, nestled together on the dog bed. Boomer thumped his tail against the floor and Thug twitched his long whiskers, which made her smile. They were male, true enough, but at least they were neutered.

"Have fun in your new temporary house, fuzzy guys. See you tomorrow."

Chapter Nine

They'd consumed mass quantities of excellent
Mexican food and had each ordered a second beer
delivered to the pool table they'd laid their quarters
on earlier. It felt good to be out of the female cross-
hairs, enjoying uncomplicated male companion-
ship for a while.

Nate would always love Vegas, because it was
home. But he had to admit, he'd felt really
welcomed since his move to Troublesome Gulch.
So far, the small town atmosphere suited him.

He knew he had Erin to thank for that.

Not that he had a clue how to thank her.

Brody aimed his pool cue. "Eight ball, side pocket." He leaned down for the shot, knocked it in cleanly.

"Good game." Nate offered a hand, which Brody shook.

"Another?"

Nate shrugged. "Why not? First night in a new place is always uncomfortable, and I'm thinking you'd be wise to avoid going home for a while yet."

Brody whistled through his teeth as he racked the balls. "This pregnancy thing. Man, it's rough. My Faith was a perky, cheery little angel before it all hit. Now, some days, all Jason and I can do is walk lightly and dodge the direct shots."

Nate laughed. "I'm just grateful to finally be a part of it, mood swings and all."

"Oh, I am, too. But, it's nice to have another guy to commiserate with." Brody chalked his cue, then lifted his chin. "Go ahead and break."

Nate lined up his shot.

Brody sniffed. "You know Erin would've told you sooner had she been able."

Nate raised an eyebrow. "You think?"

"I've known the girl since high school, basically, although I've only gotten to know her really well in the past year. She's solid."

Nate broke hard, sinking two stripes. He moved around the table looking for a new angle, but his mind was on the lines of communication about Erin that Brody had opened up. Nate had so many questions. He called his shot, missed, then stepped back toward the row of bar stools to give Brody room for his turn. After a long pull on his Corona, Nate braved it. "Can I ask you a question about her?"

Brody, circling and scrutinizing the table, didn't even glance up. "About Erin? Sure."

"Why was she so hostile toward me during the task force meeting? Couldn't she tell I was more on her side than on the city manager's?"

"It wasn't you." Brody leaned down, lined up and knocked in a solid so crisply, he left the cue ball spinning in place at the mouth of the pocket. "I just don't know that she can be objective about that stuff, buddy. Ever since she was burned so badly in our prom night accident, she's pretty against recreational fire of any kind. It's understandable."

Shock riddled through Nate. His fingers tingled. "Erin was burned? Where?"

Brody froze, dismay moving over his expression. "Damn it. I assumed you knew. You two had... I mean, she's...." He pantomimed a big round belly.

Nate put it together. "Her abdomen is burned?" He clenched his fists, lambasting himself silently. That explained the long period of celibacy, the unwillingness to remove her shirt when they made love. It could even explain her belief that she wouldn't be able to conceive in the first place.

It explained *a lot.*

God, he wished he could gather her into his arms right then, apologize, reassure her that everything would be okay. Not that she'd want his comfort. Brody still hadn't answered.

"Is that it?" he pressed. "Her abdomen?"

He could see Brody silently chastising himself for the breach of trust, but it was too late now. "She was in that burn treatment center for months, I guess. I've never seen the scars, of course, but Faith says they're extensive. You, uh, you didn't notice them yourself?"

"Well—"

"Never mind." Brody held up a hand. "I don't need intimate details. You have to know, I didn't intend to spill any secrets Erin didn't want spilled. I'm feeling a bit guilty."

Nate sank onto a bar stool. "I'm feeling stunned myself. She didn't say anything. To answer your question, no, I didn't see any scars."

Brody studied him quizzically.

"Long story for another night and many more beers. I mean, she said she had an injury, which is why she thought she couldn't conceive, but—" He shrugged.

Brody leaned on his pool cue, seeming to contemplate the situation. Finally, he nodded his head once, mouth in a grim line. "Listen. This isn't my story to tell—"

"Of course. I understand. Shouldn't have asked."

"Wait. Thing is, I suffered through years of turmoil until Faith forced me to face my demons. If I can help force Erin face hers, no matter how pissed off she might be that I told you, it's worth it."

"Yeah?"

"As long as you have true feelings for her."

"Are you kidding? She's having my baby."

"Changes a lot, doesn't it?"

"Sure. But, the truth? I'd have feelings for her even if she weren't pregnant. She got under my skin like no other woman has in a long time." Nate made a regretful face. "That's between you and me. Erin doesn't exactly know how I feel."

"Exactly?"

"Okay, at all. The way it went down—" He shook off the thought. Nate drilled his new friend with a stare. "How about a deal. Man-to-man. I keep your secrets if you keep mine? For as long as it's necessary."

Brody hung up his cue. "Let's grab a booth."

An hour, the entire tale of the tragedy, and two additional beers each later, Nate sat back and shook his head, squeezing the bridge of his nose between thumb and finger. "I can't believe everything the four of you survived. No wonder your friendship is so strong."

Brody nodded. "A crisis like that, man, it changes everything. Not just your life. Your whole life *perspective*. I can't even explain it." He hiked his chin. "If I didn't have Faith to help me through the rough times, I'd still be floundering. I miss her sister, Mick, every single day. She was my best friend."

"You still feel responsible?"

Brody hiked one shoulder. "I probably always will. But it's lessened some. The guilt. I can get through a day, an hour. I feel like my life has purpose again, like Mick would approve of me and Faith, and that's something."

"What about Erin?"

"I don't know. It's hard to get a read on her, as you well know."

Nate snorted, took a sip of beer.

"She and Kevin were—" he shook his head, then twisted two fingers tightly together "—you know. *That* couple. The ones everyone knew would make it. I can't lie to you, man. Losing him and their baby ripped out a big part of her heart and soul. She's different now."

A combination of sympathy and envy assailed Nate, twisting his gut into a tight knot. He'd never be Kevin, didn't even think he could halfway fill the man's shoes in Erin's eyes. Still, if only he could find a way to help mend her broken parts, he'd move the earth to do so. He wanted her to be happy.

He wanted to be the one to make her happy.

The story made her incomprehensible actions that night and the morning after fall neatly into place. If only he'd known. All the anger he'd felt after the task force meeting, the cutting words he'd used against her at the diner—she hadn't deserved them. If only he could take them all back…

He blew out a breath. "We made a lot of mistakes, Erin and I."

"Everyone makes mistakes. But, this baby— your baby," Brody said, "it's made a huge difference. As rough as the pregnancy's been for Erin emotionally and on her job, it's brought her out of a really dark place. You have to believe that."

Nate swallowed back a lump in his throat. "I don't know what to do next."

"Persist. Be there. Help her even when she tells you to go to hell, which she will. Frequently."

Nate smiled sadly.

"Call her bluffs, 'cause she's an expert at them." He took a big swallow, finishing his beer. "Erin's tough as they come on the outside, which makes her damned good at her career. But inside? She's just like the rest of us, Nate. Vulnerable. Looking for that forever safe place."

"What are the odds she'll let herself find that place with someone other than Kevin?"

Brody aimed the neck of his beer bottle across the table and sucked in one side of his cheek. "That part, my friend, is up to you."

Nate huffed. "In other words, I'm dead in the water."

"Don't be so sure."

"How do you figure?"

"Simple. Erin's always been a hot commodity in these parts." He flipped a hand. "I mean, look at her."

"Yeah." Nate's body reacted almost immediately. No doubts. The physical attraction? Alive and well.

"But, the point is, despite mad interest, she never dated anyone. Not a single guy. Until you." Brody let that sink in.

Nate glanced away. "We didn't exactly *date*."

"Maybe you should, then."

He squinted. "Ask her on a date?"

"Why not?"

As if it would be that easy. Wasn't that like backtracking? *First I'll get you pregnant, then we'll go out for coffee.* There had to be something more. Something that would prove to her how much he respected her. He'd brainstorm the whole problem later. He rolled Brody's idea around in his head. "A date, huh?"

Brody laid his arm along the back of the padded

booth. "I probably don't need to remind you, but she's carrying your kid. So, yes, ask her on a freakin' date. What have you got to lose?"

"Everything. That's the problem."

Brody curled the edges of his mouth down. "Listen, I'm no expert on women, but I do know Erin pretty well. I'd say, if you want to be, you're still afloat. Just keep paddling, brother. Keep paddling."

The next day, Erin felt the overwhelming urge to check on Nate, see how he was settling in. Now that he lived in her airspace, she couldn't stop thinking about him. She had way too much free time on her hands.

She sat in her kitchen, on edge, and listened to one, two, three rings before Nate's voice mail kicked in. She sighed, both disappointed and relieved by the reprieve. She waited through his greeting—where was he? As if she had any business wondering—but after the beep, her heart began to pound. Oh yeah, she had to talk.

Coherently.

Straightening her spine, she cleared her throat. "Um, hi, Nate. It's Erin. Sorry to bother you." *Think, Erin. Think.* "I just, uh, thought we might set up a time to get Boomer and Thug acquainted with my big lug of a dog, and—"

"Hey, you," she heard, after some scrambling. "I couldn't make it to the phone in time."

She smirked, knowing a lie when she heard one. "Right, because your place is so huge. Screening calls, are we?"

He chuckled. "Guilty as charged. I'm working on a new project idea. Figured I could return any business calls after my brainstorm ended."

"Don't let me keep you then."

"No. No. It's business calls I'm avoiding." His voice dropped to a silky tone. "You, I want to talk to."

She smiled, surprisingly pleased by his words.

"Is it okay to ask how you're feeling?" he ventured.

Erin cringed. "Listen, about yesterday. I can't explain it, but sometimes that irritability just demands center stage. I'm not usually prone to such mood swings. It's the whole pregnancy thing."

"No harm, no foul. Truly, you can feel however you want to."

She exhaled, releasing her pent-up worry that he'd decided she was an evil whackjob to be avoided at all costs. "Thank you. He was kicking me all day yesterday, which hurts. It really wears on you."

Silence.

Her throat squeezed.

They still didn't know each other well enough to read silences. "What's wrong?"

"A boy? We're having a boy?"

"Oh, that." She laughed softly. "I don't know. Haven't checked, and I kind of like the idea of being surprised. It's just easier than saying he or she all the time."

"Gotcha."

"I'd tell you, Nate. If I knew."

"I appreciate that." He hesitated. "So, which do you want? Boy or girl?"

"I want whoever this little soul is. I just want a healthy baby. Sounds so cliché." She smiled. "How about you?"

"Same. Although, I won't lie. I've been surrounded by so many females all my life, a boy would be cool."

She nodded. "I can understand that. Especially after what Faith and I put you through yesterday."

"Shoot, woman, that was small potatoes. When I was a clueless teenage boy, all my sisters had their periods at the same time. One week a month, I was the family whipping post, verbal and physical."

She laughed. "I can't believe we're talking about this. How can I ever look them in the eyes?"

"Consider the positive side—I'm not afraid to buy *any* product at the grocery store, if you know what I mean."

"Bonus."

"So, about the beasts—"

Back to business. "Yes. I'd planned to invite you three over now. But, you're busy, and I've already taken up enough of your time."

"Actually, it's not that. I'm going to talk to the condo association about their obsolete 'no animals' rule. I own the place—or will, as soon as we close. As I see it, I should be able to keep my pets as long as they aren't unruly. Every condo owner should."

"Brave move. I wish you the best of luck, but if it doesn't work out, my offer is open-ended."

"Thank you. I'd be lonely without them here, though."

"I know what you mean." She glanced over toward Finn, snoozing tummy-up in a sunbeam.

"If it all works out, what do you think about me hiring Jason to care for them when I travel? The kid obviously liked them, and he's going to need money for college."

Her heart expanded. "Oh, Nate, that's a great idea. Faith will really appreciate you putting your trust in him, and it will do so much for his self-confidence."

"Good. Good. I'll call them later."

They fell into a small silence, and she could hear him shuffling paper on the other end.

"Well, you sound busy. I'll let you get back to work." Strange. She didn't want to hang up.

"Erin, wait. Does Troublesome Gulch have a decent-sized fairgrounds?" he asked.

She blinked, surprised by the out-of-the-ether question, but glad to still be talking to him. "Sure. The county fairgrounds are here. Why?"

"I'll explain later. Can you show the place to me?"

"When?"

"No time like the present. There's a free lunch in it for you if you say yes," he teased.

"Make it free ice cream, and you're on."

"Are you sure? I'm not watchdogging you," he assured, "but you told me you weren't supposed to gain much weight."

"I know." She groaned. "But I've been watching my diet so closely, I feel like one of those skeletal Hollywood starlets, and it's making me cranky. I've held steady at nineteen pounds gained for so long now, I'm starting to feel safe. What are the odds I'll blimp out in the last few weeks?"

"Slim to none, no pun intended. You're far too disciplined for that."

"I'm glad you agree. I'd never do anything to compromise this baby, but I think every pregnant woman deserves at least one serving of ice cream in a nine-month period. Don't you?"

"Absolutely. Ice cream it is." He paused. "Can I pick you up?"

For a split second, she started to suggest separate cars. But they were past that, weren't they? Didn't she want to be? She extended the small olive branch, hoping they'd sail over the hump on their way to true friendship. "Got a pen? I'll give you directions."

The fairgrounds were absolutely perfect. A vast flat area flanked by a half circle of flatiron peaks. He itched to get home and draw up his plan, but despite the short time frame, he wouldn't give up these stolen moments with Erin for the world.

They sat atop a picnic table in a small park they had all to themselves near the center of town, a block or so from the ice-cream parlor. Dappled sunlight shone down on them. A light breeze swirled Erin's dark hair.

She groaned in pleasure at her first bite of ice cream, letting her eyes flutter shut. "Mmm." She swallowed. "I'd kill for this stuff. I really would."

"Should I move a prudent distance away?"

She shook her head, taking another bite through a chuckle. "You indulged my urge, so you're safe."

"Thank goodness." He grinned, sipping from his milk shake. "So, tell me about your family. I've told you all about mine."

"Well, let's see." She thought through another bite. "Mom and Dad have been married forever. They lived here until they both retired two years ago, and now they live in Crested Butte."

"Do you miss them?"

"Of course. But they visit all the time. And I go there. It's not far. They have their dream property, at last. My mom's a potter. She was the art teacher at our high school since I was a kid—the teacher everyone adored. Cagney especially."

"She's an artist?"

"Was. Her dad's kind of a jerk, and strongly opposed an art career, but it's a whole, 'nother long story." She grimaced. "Anyway, Mom finally has her own workshop, with different-sized kilns, all sorts of shelves and drying racks and, most of all, space."

"Cool. Good for her."

Erin nodded. "She's in heaven. Dad was the high school phys ed teacher. Now he works ski patrol part-time. He tried the 'retired old guy' thing, but first of all, he's not that old. Secondly, he drove Mom nuts."

"We men have a knack for that," Nate said, ruefully.

"Yep. I think he grew a little stir-crazy himself." She shrugged. "Anyway, he loves it, and it keeps him in shape and healthy."

"Brothers and sisters?"

"Only child. I always wanted a sister."

He nodded, listening to the birds and studying his and Erin's feet side by side on the picnic bench.

He tried to keep his tone light. "How do they feel about the pregnancy?"

"I knew that part was coming." She eyed him. "They were shocked at first, of course. Since I'm…single. But they couldn't be more excited now. I mean, I'm twenty-nine years old, and they weren't sure I could ever conceive, either, so they'd pretty much given up on the grandparent plan." She shook her head. "This kid is going to be so spoiled, Nate. I have to apologize for them in advance."

"Don't worry, he'll be getting it from both sides. My sisters and Mom?" He rolled his eyes. "Pure insanity."

They shared a smile.

He held her gaze. "Do your parents know about me?"

She paused a beat. "Not…exactly."

He pressed his lips together, nodded. Her words left him beyond disappointed, even though, deep down, he'd been expecting them. His family knew the whole story. Then again, he'd had to explain why he was up and moving to Colorado, seemingly on a whim. They'd rolled with it, as he'd known they would, and were all chomping at the bit to come for a visit and meet Erin. But he begged them to hold off until he got his bearings, figured out what this strange relationship between him and Erin was all about.

"I'm going to tell them," she rushed to add. "It's just, well, they can be old-fashioned. I'm trying to figure out how to explain that we're not a couple and make them realize that it's really okay."

Was it? he wondered, peering over at her. She was so achingly beautiful in the sunshine, humming in ecstasy over her single scoop of ice cream. Simple pleasures. She took his breath away every time he saw her. "Anything I can do to help?"

She quirked her mouth apologetically. "Bear with me? I'm not keeping your identity from them because I'm ashamed of you or anything. If we were together, it would be a whole different story."

If only they were. "No worries. I get the parent thing. But you'll tell them before—"

"Yes. Definitely."

He didn't point out that she'd begun finishing his sentences, but it cheered him. Maybe they did have a chance after all. The challenge was proving he was worth risking her already-broken heart.

She scraped the last vestiges of ice cream from her dish with the pink, plastic spoon and ate it, whimpering when she peered into the empty cup.

"If you weren't here, I'd lick this cup like a shameless dog." She stilled. "Oh."

"What's up?"

"I think the baby liked it as much as I did. Feel."

She reached for his hand without an iota of hesitation, then laid it flat against the side of her belly. Beneath his palm came the press of a tiny foot, once, then again. Harder.

"Ouch," she said, frowning down at her belly with a playful shake of her head. "Little bully."

Unexpectedly, tears of awe rose to his eyes. "He's really a little person in there."

She smiled. Then, noticing how choked up Nate had become, she touched his face. "Amazing, isn't it? And kind of freaky, if you want the whole truth. Hard to explain, but I sort of feel like one of those Russian nesting dolls, where you pop one open, and a smaller version's inside."

He could only hope their baby was a smaller version of Erin. Talk about a gorgeous kid. He clenched his jaws, fighting back the flashes of emotion bursting inside him. "Thank you. For sharing that."

"You don't have to thank me. He's your baby, too."

Their gazes locked.

He had so much he wanted to say to her, but he didn't know how to start, or if his words would even be welcomed. He opened his mouth. Nothing emerged.

"Shh." She laid a finger along his lips. "You don't have to say anything."

"God, Erin," he said, his tone husky. "The truth

is, I would freeze this moment if I could, and I'm not ashamed to admit it."

He impulsively pulled her into his arms, burying his face into the soft heat of her neck. She stiffened initially, then let herself relax against him, smoothing her hands up and down his back. He felt the pulse in her neck against his lips and kissed it.

She allowed it. Even seemed to nuzzle closer.

"Ah, Nate." She sighed.

"I know."

This was one moment he didn't mind being in.

Chapter Ten

She'd never imagined a simple scoop of ice cream could become an emotional bridge between two people. But, following their afternoon in the park, her connection with Nate shifted in a million subtle ways. They began talking on the phone, then hanging out together, as though doing so went without saying. Little by little, the omnipresent awkwardness between them dissipated.

They watched her favorite reality TV show side by side on his couch or hers in the evenings, after which she'd read and he'd work. He and Boomer joined her and Finn on her daily morning walks. And, their conversation grew easier every day.

More importantly, their silences transformed from clumsy to comfortable and compatible— something she hadn't expected to happen so soon, if at all. She didn't know what it all meant, exactly, just that it felt good.

The first time she read a whole chapter of a book without commenting, and without feeling self-conscious about lying there in silence on his couch while he worked, she knew they'd reached a different level. But, a different level of *what?* That was the question. All for the baby? Platonic? Platonic with options? Romantic? Try as she might, she couldn't get a read.

There'd been no further physical intimacy. Not even another kiss on the neck, although she relived that delicious first one as she closed her eyes to sleep each night. And yet, despite their obvious physical distance, she still felt closer to him than ever.

She'd even gone with him to shop for nursery furniture for his condo. Of course, that trip ended abruptly when she'd succumbed to an emotional meltdown at the thought of being away from the baby overnight.

The pregnancy hormones hit, and BOOM— from normal to sobbing and shaking in a matter of seconds, just as they were about to choose between the natural wood or sweet little painted crib. But, reminiscent of the bar scene that fateful night, Nate had whisked her out of the furniture store immediately, comforted her until she'd recovered her composure, and they hadn't brought up shared custody issues since.

Time for that later, she supposed.

All these snippets combined added up to no more than a dip of her toe into the water of their new, strange compromise, but so far she hadn't felt the urge to pull back.

For her, that was huge.

As amazing as it seemed, in a couple short weeks, Nate had begun to feel like a fixture in her life. Dinner without him now struck her as odd. They didn't plan it, they just did it. Her house, his house, a restaurant. Didn't matter. Finn refused to walk now until his new beloved buddy, Boomer, showed up.

Life felt somehow fuller with Nate around.

Still, there was so much they didn't know about each other, which amounted to a huge concrete wall between them, at least in her mind. And she had no idea how to breach it.

Her friends, wisely, stayed out of their blossoming whatever-it-was…*relationship,* she supposed, was as good a word as any. Even matchmaker Faith had, surprisingly, kept her trap shut, which was surely due to Brody's thumbscrew influence. Erin appreciated the space.

But when Cagney invited the whole crew to her loft for her monthly, much anticipated dinner party, Erin and Nate sent a positive RSVP—as a couple. Or a duo. Or, like, they were going to show up in the same car together. Whatever.

The point is, it didn't feel weird.

Which, in and of itself, was weird.

Nevertheless, when the evening of the dinner party arrived, nerves bounced around inside Erin's tummy like a bevy of racquetballs with minds of their own. It was the first time all her friends, as a group, would observe her and Nate in this new "format," and she hoped that didn't spell disaster with a capital *D*. Things were still fragile between the two of them, despite the progress they'd made. She needed time to work it all out in her own mind before she spoke about it aloud with anyone. Really, what would she say?

She'd borrowed the least maternity-looking sundress in the pack from her coworker, Ginny Luther's, excellent pregnancy closet, appreciating the way the V-neck halter highlighted her enhanced cleavage. The deep turquoise perfectly matched Nate's eyes, which she hadn't planned. It also matched the beaded sandals and drawstring handbag, which she had.

Hair done, makeup on, she twirled a bit in front of the mirror, surprised that she felt sexy and filled with anticipation. She hadn't felt sexy in…well, forever about covered it. And she hadn't anticipated a date—if you could call this a date—since high school.

Probably because she hadn't had one since.

Pathetic.

She was leaning toward the mirror slipping simple hoop earrings in when the doorbell rang.

Her heart revved.

Finn barked, launched himself from the window seat in her bedroom, and clickity-clacked toward the entryway.

"It's unlocked," she called out, knowing Nate would hear her through the open windows.

She heard the ancient door hinges creak, then the murmured sounds of Nate talking to Finn as she gave herself a final once-over.

Oh, God. It felt like a date.

Self-consciousness hit her like a rogue wave, knocking her flat, but hell, it would have to do.

She took in a deep, cleansing breath.

She could do this.

She *wanted* to do this.

Grabbing her handbag off the end of the bed before she lost her nerve, she snicked off the ceiling fan and headed out. She found Nate by the front door, bent forward giving Finn an excellent scratch behind the ears. Finn looked love-struck, the big sap.

She couldn't help but smile. "Hey."

Nate glanced up and froze. His eyes widened. "Whoa." He straightened slowly, taking in her appearance with an appreciative gleam in his eyes.

Thrilled by his response but determined to keep it casual, she said, "I take that to mean I don't look like a big, turquoise balloon float from the Macy's Parade?"

"Far from it. You look amazing."

"Amazing's probably a stretch, but you're a generous man. Thank you." She reached into the jar of dog treats on the hallway console table and pulled out a biscuit, handing it to Finn, patting him on the head.

As the dog crunched away, she assessed Nate. "You look pretty darn amazing yourself," she said, in as light a tone as she could manage considering how dizzy she'd become in his presence.

Amazing? Understatement.

He wore khaki pants and a loose, black, short-sleeved shirt that made his eye color stand out even more than usual. Casual, masculine, yum-yum-yummy. His hair had been trimmed, but his face bore an attractive amount of groomed stubble that begged to be touched. He looked like a movie star—no lie.

And he was her *date.*

Impulsively, she leaned forward and kissed him on the cheek, inhaling the citrus scent of his skin as she did so. Just a friendly greeting, she told herself. As she pulled away, he grabbed her elbow to stop her. Their gazes met, held. His darkened, then dropped to her lightly glossed lips. Pure primal craving bound them together.

Her throat cinched, and all the key parts of her body reacted.

Moving closer, he kissed her gently. Once, then again, letting his mouth linger against hers. "Thank you."

She swallowed, the sensual stimulation of his stubble and warm breath against her mouth leaving her nerves humming. "You're welcome. Ready?"

"You bet I am," he said, cryptically, leaving her to wonder exactly what question he'd been answering.

Once they were seat belted in and on the road, the tsunami of heightened sexual awareness between them retreated, thank goodness, but the emotional destruction remained in her brain. She needed to regroup. She didn't want to walk into the party surrounded by a cloud of pheromones, after all. Her friends would be watching them closely enough as it was.

Focus on the present.

"Do you know the way?" Well, it sounded

casual enough. Yay, her. She surreptitiously admired his hand, draped over the top of the steering wheel. She knew what those skilled hands felt like on her body, inside her—

Stop it, Erin.

He tipped his head to the side, seemingly unaware of her turmoil. "I looked it up on computer mapping, but it appeared to be a warehouse." He shrugged. "I probably had the address wrong."

Erin smiled. "Nope, that's the place."

He flashed her a quizzical glance. "Cagney lives in a warehouse?"

"A warehouse *loft*," she corrected. "Her single act of rebellion against her father in the past twelve years, which rocks. She doesn't rebel much anymore, unfortunately, but back in the day, she was the queen of it. Man, was her dad pissed when she bought that old building," she added, savoring the memory.

"I can appreciate rebellion, but why would she want to live in a warehouse in the first place?"

"Wait until you see it," Erin said. "She's the renovation queen. The ground level is still unfinished, but she lives on the second and third floors. It's probably the most amazing residence in the entire Gulch. Plus, Cagney always wanted to live in a huge loft. Of course," she added ruefully, "that was when she still planned on being a working artist and using half the loft as her studio."

Nate flicked on his blinker, then merged onto the Gulch's main drag. "What happened with that?"

"Long story. But the bottom line is, her dad fought so hard against it that she eventually lost her will."

"Her dad sounds like a piece of work."

"Totally. And he's the chief of police."

He flashed her another quick glance before refocusing on the road. "She works for the guy?"

"Yep." Erin shook her head. "It's a damn shame, too. Cagney's a great cop. Must be in her blood. But I don't think she's happy. My mom still waxes poetic about little Casey's unbelievable talent and what a crime it is to waste it. But, she had utterly no support from home."

Nate sucked one side of his cheek in, sympathetic but still exuding optimism. "Well, she's got her own home now, and it's never too late. She's only twenty-nine. Maybe she'll go back to it."

Erin hadn't mentioned the heartbreak. The betrayal. The loss that led up to Cagney's total abandonment of her life's passion. So much loss in Erin's little circle of friends. Her heart squeezed for Cagney. For all of them, and she sighed. "I don't know, Nate. Sometimes, for some things, it is too late."

Before he could comment further, she pointed up toward the huge building they approached. "There it is. We can just park anywhere."

Festive lights shone through the floor-to-ceiling windows, and Erin found herself excited about another celebratory night of good food and laughter with her friends. And with Nate.

In fact, she realized as they parked and got out, it wouldn't feel complete without him.

Just as she'd suspected, everything had changed.

Dinner had been spectacular, not to mention low in both fat and carbs in deference to Erin's weight gain directive. Not that you could tell from the incredible flavors. She loved Cagney's quiet consideration of her.

Erin and Nate hadn't been able to avoid slipping into their newfound comfort with each other. She even caught herself finishing a few of his sentences, and vice versa. She found each of them watching the other as he or she spoke to the group. The way couples do. And throughout the evening, she sensed her friends, one by one, noticing, sizing things up.

After Nate's copious compliments on the loft while they enjoyed coffee and dessert, Cagney had offered to give him the full tour and regale him with the tale of her solo, two-year-long renovations. Erin knew Cagney loved to talk about all she'd done—it was as artsy as she'd allowed herself to be since prom night. Though he'd seen it all before, Brody tagged along. He and Nate had really hit it off. Maybe because they were the only two guys in the mix.

Meanwhile, she, Lexy and Faith cleared the table, chattering about this and that as they did so. Shoes, TV, work gossip—all the normal stuff.

Erin set the last large stack of stoneware next to the sink and turned around, coming face-to-face with a determined-looking Faith and a highly intrigued Lexy. She lifted her brows. "What's up, Pip? Lex?" As if she didn't know.

"Yeah, I think that's our line," Faith said, crossing her arms over her distended belly.

"I don't know what you're talking about."

"Sure you don't, doll face." Lexy grinned. "Seems like you and Mr. Hottie are getting along better."

"Well, that's not exactly true. We've always gotten along fine. I mean, except for when he popped into town unexpectedly and found this." She framed her belly with her hands. "But you can't blame him for that."

"You know what we mean," Faith said.

Erin toyed with the idea of blowing off their probing questions, but after a wonderful evening ensconced in the circle of her pals, she suddenly craved the sounding board of her best girlfriends. God knew, she wasn't figuring this thing out so well on her own.

She leaned back against the counter. "Yeah,

well." She sighed, crossing her arms as best she could with this gigantic belly to contend with. "We've been spending a lot of time together lately. For the baby's sake," she added.

"What about for Mommy's sake?" Faith pushed.

"It's not that easy." Erin bit the corner of her lip, glancing around to make sure Cagney and the guys were nowhere near. "He doesn't know anything about the burns. Kevin. My other baby." She sighed. "Kind of limits true intimacy when I can't even talk about my biggest life events, you know?"

"So, talk about them. What's the issue?"

Lexy glanced at Faith, a chastising look on her face. "Faith, come on. We all have to do scary things in our own time. Your own husband should've taught you that."

Faith blew out a breath. "I know. He did, and I do understand your hesitation, no matter how impatient I seem." She beseeched Erin. "But, if you could see how that man looks at you, Erin, how the two of you together look to the rest of us." She hugged herself. "Nate is exactly what you need to help you heal. You may not see it, but he's been so good for you already."

"I do see it," Erin admitted. "But there's Kevin…" Her words choked off, and she reached a hand up to cover her mouth.

Lexy reached out and held Erin's other hand. Faith stepped forward and cupped the sides of

Erin's face. "Sweetie, we all know Kevin was The One, and you two had an amazing ride, while it lasted." A pause. "But…he's gone. He's been gone for a long, long time. He's in Heaven with Mick and Randy and…whatever that guy's name was, Cagney's date." She cringed. "God, that's awful. He's irrevocably part of us, and yet I have this mental block about him that's so unfair. We should know the poor kid's name."

"Tad. Tad Rivers," Lexy said.

"Tad, right." Faith refocused on Erin. "Kevin's with them now. Not with us."

Tears rose to Erin's eyes. "I still love him, though. Just because he's…" She couldn't say it. "That love hasn't gone away."

"You always will love him, and you should. No one thinks you should stop loving Kevin."

"That would be like asking me to stop loving Mick," Faith said.

"But it *is* possible to love again," Lexy said softly. "A real here-and-now love, with the relationship, the family, the dogs, the whole nine. Shoot, you and Nate are ninety percent there. You even have a bunny."

Erin sniffed, glancing down at Lexy. "Yeah? And when are you going to take your own advice, chickie?"

Lexy lifted her chin. "Someday," she said,

breezily. "But, we're talking about you, so stop trying to change the subject. You're the one giving birth in a few weeks."

Erin thought for a moment, then shuddered. "I can't imagine how to even begin that conversation with Nate. It's all just too painful and unmanageable." Erin pointed toward the sitting area anchored in the center of the wide-open space with a deep red area rug. "Can we please sit? My legs are aching."

The two women ushered her to the love seat, where Erin moved the coffee table back so Lexy could maneuver her chair closer. She pulled up directly in front of Erin, then patted her lap. "Put your feet up here. I may no longer be the dancing queen, but I give a killer foot rub."

"Me next?" Faith asked, wistfully.

"Of course."

No arguments from Erin. She slipped out of the beaded sandals and lifted her feet to rest on Lexy's lap, groaning in pleasure when the magic fingers took over.

"So," Lexy said, once they were settled. "How about I ask some simple yes or no questions?"

Erin acquiesced with a nod.

"Do you have feelings for him?"

She sucked in a breath, held it, then blew it out. "Yes."

"Does he have feelings for you?"

"That, I don't know." She pulled her mouth to the side. "We've been spending a lot of time together, sure, but we don't discuss relationship stuff. At all. And we don't—" She rolled her hand.

"Oh, he has feelings for you," Faith said, sounding one hundred percent sure.

Erin cut her a sharp glance, her chest squeezing. "How do you know? Did Brody say something?" They *had* been hanging out quite a bit.

"He hasn't said a word. You know how guys are." Disappointment drained through Erin.

"I can just tell," Faith continued.

"You're such a matchmaker," Lexy teased.

"Lex, they're having a baby together. I want her to be madly in love, like I am. It's the way it should be."

Lexy held up a hand. "Oh, I'm not disagreeing. Anyone can see he's into you, Erin."

"So? What should I do? And don't say throw my body at him." She splayed her hands on her distended middle. "At this point, that is *not* an option."

"How about taking an even bigger risk?" Lexy asked.

"Bigger than getting naked when I look like a beached whale? A burned beached whale at that?" She arched her brows. "This ought to be rich."

"Open up to him about your past." Lexy paused,

searching her face. "Take the chance and tell him about Kev, the baby, your scars."

"God." Erin covered her face with both hands, feeling sick to her stomach. "I'm so scared. What if—?"

"What if what?" Faith spread her arms wide, leaning closer for emphasis. "Isn't it better to know before you fall even further in love with him?"

"I never said I was in love with him," Erin muttered, as her whole body heated.

Her friends gave her indulgent smiles.

"No matter what happens, you'll always have your friends," Faith said. "So you'll be no worse off if he freaks out and leaves town."

Surprisingly, Erin found this to be cold comfort. How wrong Faith was. She couldn't imagine losing Nate now, no matter how little of him she had at this point, no matter how superficial. No. It was easier to keep her secrets, live in comfortable denial, and keep him close by for as long as it lasted. The risk? Too scary. She couldn't talk to Nate about her past. Not yet. She'd come up with another way to bring them closer…somehow.

She smiled tightly, easing her feet to the floor while hoping to put this conversation to rest, at least for now. "I'll try. You guys are the best. Thank you."

"We love you. We want to know what's up," Lexy said.

Guilt stabbed Erin. "I know I've been…distant. I'm just trying to figure things out. But I'll keep you in the loop from here on out. Promise." She pointed toward Lexy's lap. "Your turn, Faith. Be prepared for the foot massage of a lifetime."

Erin had been uncharacteristically pensive the whole ride home. He didn't know why. He decided to try for some easy conversation, lighten things up.

"You were right. Cagney's loft is amazing."

She stirred, as though out of deep thoughts. "Isn't it? As much as I adore my cute, 1900s farmhouse, I envy her that place. It's so hip. Such a showplace."

Her words and the enthusiasm behind them didn't match up. He reached over and laid his palm lightly on her thigh. "I had a great evening. Thanks for taking me."

"You're always welcome."

"Did you? Have a good time?"

"Yes. Great," she said, way too monotone for the Erin he'd come to know.

A pause. "Everything okay, honey?"

She leaned her head back. "I'm just tired. Long night."

He nodded. Another lag in the conversation. "I really love your friends."

She rolled her head to the side and flashed him a sad smile. "The feeling is mutual. Believe me."

That warmed his heart. But he wished Erin loved him even half as much as her friends did. He patted her thigh and put his hand back on the steering wheel. "Let me get you home so you can relax, put your feet up. Get some rest."

"Nate?"

"Mmm?"

"Have you ever been in love?" Her voice wavered on the question.

He tipped his head side to side, eyes firmly on the road. "More like infatuation. Not that I'm knocking infatuation, mind you. But I've never asked anyone to marry me. Never been consumed with wanting to be with one woman above all others." *Until now.*

She nodded. He couldn't read the gesture. Part of him wanted to lob the question back at her, but he already knew the answer, and he didn't see the point in pushing. She'd tell him when she told him. Period.

"I've been busy building my career," he explained. "You know how that goes."

"Sure. I understand."

"Here we are," he said, pulling into her driveway. The gravel crunched beneath his tires. "Home sweet home."

He cut the engine, and for a long stretch, they just sat there. Finally, he cleared his throat. "Let me walk you in."

"Okay."

They got out of the car and headed toward the house in silence. Erin fumbled with the key, her hands shaky.

He laid his hand on hers. "Let me."

She handed the key over without argument and stepped back. He opened the door, then stood aside so she could enter before him. Finn rose from his dog bed for the requisite ear scratches and love, before returning to his favorite spot. Three spins in a circle, and he was out cold again, with a big doggy sigh.

He set her key ring on the console and dipped his chin, studying her. "Sure you're okay? I don't mean to keep nagging you, but it seems like you aren't feeling well. Or maybe like something's weighing on your mind."

"I feel fine, really. For a huge preggo, that is."

"Well, okay." He paused, hoping for more. "I guess I should go then."

"Wait." She flicked her tongue over her lips nervously. "Do you remember that night? At the hotel?"

"All too well."

"Not that part. I mean, when I asked you to hold me?"

He nodded.

Looking as though she were garnering her courage, she stepped forward and wrapped her arms around him, resting her face against his chest. "I need that again," she whispered.

He gladly embraced her. "What's going on?"

"I'm not sure. I just don't want you to leave."

"Aw, Erin—"

"Please?" She tipped her face up and rained small kisses on his lips. "I don't want to be here alone, no offense to Finn."

He didn't want to leave, either. Ever. Still, he had to be sure she was saying what he hoped she was saying. "I could call Cagney for you. Or Lexy."

"No." She paused, her rapid pulse visible in the side of her neck. "What I meant was, I don't want to be here alone without you. If you need to go get Boomer and Thug and bring them—"

"They're fine."

"Then—?"

"What are we doing?" he whispered, smoothing the backs of his fingers down her silky soft cheek.

"I don't know. I don't know yet. I just want you to hold me. I want to fall asleep in your arms. If that's okay with you."

"Sweet girl, it's more than okay."

He swore he could feel the tension drain out of her. "Good. Thank you."

"When are you going to stop thanking me?"

"When I stop feeling indebted. And guilty."

He threaded his fingers into the sides of her

hair, then leaned in and kissed her. Gently at first, deeper when he felt her response, the vibrations of her moan against his face. After several long minutes of sensual exploration, he pulled back. "You're driving the bus on this crazy trip, Erin. If you need me, say the word."

"Okay, I need you," she said, in a bereft whisper. "But, God, if you only knew. I don't deserve you."

"That," he said, guiding her toward her bedroom, "is where we'll have to agree to disagree. Now, let's get you ready for bed. You need your rest."

She stiffened. "Wait. I can do it."

"Erin," he said lightly, "I wasn't suggesting that I tear your clothes off. I'm well aware that's not what this is about."

She exhaled. "Okay. Sorry. I'm just a little on edge." She paused at the bedroom door, clasping the jamb with one hand. "I'll be a minute."

"Take your time." He held her chin with two gentle fingers, leaning in to nip at her luscious lips. "I'm not going anywhere."

"Swear?" she whispered.

"I am absolutely here for you. And that's a promise."

Chapter Eleven

She and Nate fell into the habit of spending their nights together at her house or his. They held each other as they drifted off, kissed some. Nothing more than that and, unfortunately, no in-depth conversations.

Her wall, it seemed, remained.

She was no closer to knocking it down.

A week prior to the dreaded Fourth of July fireworks show—something she and Nate never discussed—Chief Dresden called to inform Erin about an emergency meeting of the task force that had been called for that day. She had two hours to get ready. Granted, she and Nate avoided the whole fireworks issue by tacit agreement, but it still seemed odd he hadn't mentioned it before he'd left that morning. She supposed it could've been a surprise to him, too. In any case, her curiosity was piqued.

She showered quickly, dressed in her borrowed Class-A maternity uniform, then headed to the city building. After entering the conference room, she slid into the seat next to Brody, jostling her shoulder against his as a hello.

He smiled at her. "Hey, you."

"What's with the emergency task force meeting?" she whispered.

"Your guess is as good as mine. I just got word a couple hours ago."

"Same here."

He lifted his chin toward the man who stood at the front of the room, readying his equipment as they awaited the arrival of everyone else. "Nate didn't mention anything?"

"Nope." She shook her head in feigned annoyance, then leaned in to rasp, "I'm having a kid with the guy, and I don't even get insider info. How jacked up is that?"

"Having a *baby* with him doesn't merit insider info." He held up a finger. "Now, having hot, sweaty *jungle sex* with him? Whole different story."

"Do not make me kill you."

"Kidding! Only kidding." Brody smirked. "I don't know why we're here. Maybe the city manager got a brain and realized risking a wildfire was the quickest, surest way to lose his seat during the next election."

Erin huffed. "Yeah, sure. And maybe I'm pregnant with a litter of puppies."

"Cool, can I have the runt? Hope would dig a playmate," he said, referring to the puppy he'd bought for Faith when he proposed.

She pierced him with a withering stare. "How does your wife even tolerate you, Austin?"

He waggled his eyebrows. "Mad skills. What more can I say?"

"Nothing." She held up a hand and pretended disgust. "News flash—you shouldn't mention sex to a ready-to-pop pregnant woman, and you've done it twice now in a matter of two minutes. For that matter, you should *never* mention it to your wife's best friend."

"You started it. Besides, how do you know I was referring to sex, Assumption Queen?"

"Duh. You're a guy, aren't you?"

"Good point." He grinned shamelessly.

Their banter ceased as the mayor and city manager walked in, greeted Nate, nodded to the rest of them and took their seats. They looked as expectant as everyone else on the committee.

Now her curiosity really kicked up a notch. If *they* hadn't called the meeting…

"Thanks for taking time out of your busy days, everyone," Nate began. "You're probably wondering what this is all about, so let's get to it." He glanced at the secretary. "Polly?"

Nate had known about the meeting, Erin marveled. And he hadn't said word one. She didn't know how to feel about that.

Polly doused the lights. The projection screen eased its way down from the ceiling. As it descended, Nate continued.

"At my request, my researchers conducted an in-depth analysis of the fire danger this year, and we've concluded that a live fireworks show would pose too great a risk to the dry forest, not to mention the town proper." He paused. "Folks, bottom line is, it's simply not worth it."

Hushed exclamations of surprise rose from the darkness. Stunned but thrilled, Erin glanced around at the shadows of the other people in the room.

A silvery light hit the screen, casting Nate in a magical glow. "Before all the questions I'm sure you have, I'd like to assure you that Walker Pyrotechnics has no intentions of abandoning Troublesome Gulch. As most of you know, I live here now." He smiled. "I have a vested interest in the community."

"Yeah, but what are we supposed to do?" Walt Hennessy asked, blustery as usual. "July Fourth is a week away. There's no time to hire another pyrotechnics company this late in the game."

"That's what I'm here to show you. Another option. All I ask is that you keep open minds." Nate pointed a remote at his laptop. "In addition to traditional pyrotechnic events, Walker provides numerous alternative technologies, two of which could far surpass the excitement of a standard fireworks display. Not to mention, they'll be a lot safer."

The screen came to life, showing a mountain as the background for a spectacular light show.

A collective gasp rose from the group.

Erin recognized that range. It surrounded the fairgrounds. She couldn't believe it. The project he'd been working on so diligently had been for them. A rush of emotion swirled in her chest as she looked from the screen to Nate. Happiness, gratitude, other feelings she didn't dare name. He might not understand her vehement disapproval of the fireworks show, but he cared. Enough to find a way around them this year, and that touched her in ways she couldn't even voice.

A lump rose in her throat.

"This technology is called VisionPlex, a high-resolution projection system capable of shooting images onto 3-D surfaces, such as the mountains cupping the county fairgrounds."

"How does it work?" asked Commander Bresil, the representative from the police department.

"It's a process that involves simultaneous imaging from numerous high-tech projectors working in conjunction with one another. The options for the images are as endless as our imaginations. You want safe fireworks? You've got them. This technology has been used on the Academy Awards and Emmy shows, among others."

"Wow," said Commander Bresil, clearly impressed.

"We tested it on the fairgrounds last week, as you can see. We used images of traditional fireworks bursts, but that's just one option." He paused, letting the screen speak for itself. "Let me assure you, it's even more sensational live. To enhance it, we'd also use FogScreen technology along the sides, to frame out the show."

"Which is?" Brody asked.

"FogScreen is a device that produces a wall onto which more images can be projected. A wall," he added with a smile, "of misted water. Much safer in light of this fire season, I'm sure you'll agree. FogScreen technology is the innovation of the decade in the special effects world."

"What's the catch?" Walt Hennessey asked.

"No catch. But here's the best part." Nate rocked slightly on his feet, a smug smile on his face. "We'd be the first city in the nation to use these technologies in an outdoor alternative Fourth of July event. Little old Troublesome Gulch— imagine that? Environmentally conscious. Cutting edge, not to mention spectacular. The total package, if I do say so myself."

"We stand to make history," said Mayor Ron Blackman, with wonder in his voice.

"Bingo," said Nate, pointing toward him.

Erin could do nothing more than sit back and watch. Her heart felt full to bursting for the thought Nate had put into this idea. He spoke so passionately, captivating the whole room. Well, except for, perhaps, Hennessey, but that was to be expected.

Watching Nate, so sexy in his element, she sighed.

Brody jostled her with his shoulder and whispered, "Stop looking like a lovesick sophomore."

"Oh, shut up." She scrunched her nose at him.

"What about the sound? The flash-bang? The oohs and aahs?" Hennessey asked, his tone almost plaintive.

Erin accidentally scoffed, but covered it just as fast with a fake cough into her hand. The city manager had always been known as a whiny control freak. Even he couldn't deny this was the best choice for Troublesome Gulch, but he'd darn well try.

Now, if it had been his idea in the *first* place…

Ah, gotta love politics.

"Sound's included," Nate assured the man. "Music, laser, special effects—all tailored to what we, as a committee, decide. Polly?"

The secretary flipped the lights back on.

Nate spread his arms. "As always, it's your choice. I know we'd have to work quickly, but I have a lot of jumping-off points. Walker Pyrotechnics simply can't stand behind a fireworks show with the liability so high, though. My two cents?"

He paused.

The entire group held their breath.

"Why risk everything during one of the worst fire danger seasons we've seen in years when you have the opportunity to put Troublesome Gulch in the news with something this unique?"

"What about cost differences?" Brody asked, playing devil's advocate. Erin knew he was one hundred percent behind the light show.

"Technically, the VisionPlex and FogScreen alternative would almost triple the cost, but I don't plan to charge the city an extra cent. Consider it my gift to my new hometown. A hometown I do not want to see go up in flames."

More murmured excitement.

"Not only that, but the Pinecone and a couple of other local restaurants I contacted have agreed to provide boxed picnic meals, gratis. A community-wide effort for safety. What more can you ask for?"

He crossed his arms over his chest and looked to each one of them, his eyes gleaming when they met Erin's. "So. Do we mitigate the fire danger and give the city something really special this year?"

"I vote, yes," said Mayor Blackman quickly, shrugging when Walt threw him an incredulous glare.

"Absolutely," said Brody, the same time as Erin. They laughed.

"Copycat," she whispered.

One after another, everyone eagerly agreed to the alternative show, until the whole room sat staring at Walt Hennessey, who couldn't hold back his pout. "Well, if you all think it's a decent alternative…"

"Not decent. It's a fantastic alternative. Ground-breaking," Erin emphasized. She could see the others nodding in her peripheral vision but kept her focus on the recalcitrant city manager. "Let's give the Gulch a legacy beyond the infamous prom night tragedy, Walt, which is just about all we're known for anymore. It's about time, don't you think?"

Hennessey seemed to roll this around in his head, most likely calculating how the change would reflect on his position personally. Finally, he threw up his hands. "Okay, Walker. Looks like I'm outvoted. You're on." He released a peevish sigh. "I'll arrange a press conference to let the citizens know."

"Excellent. If you'd like, I can have my people write up some media releases, Walt, since we're intimately acquainted with the technology."

"Fine." Walt pouted. "I'd like to read everything before it goes out, though."

"Of course," Nate said. "I wouldn't think of handling it any other way." He smiled at the group. "I'm glad we could settle this so quickly, and I applaud your progressiveness. We'll need to meet tomorrow to iron out some of the details. But, I promise, you won't regret this."

The task force members dwindled away one by one until only Brody, Erin and Nate remained. Nate was at the front of the large room. Erin fussed around and took her time at the other end, although she only had to pick up her purse and her information folder and leave. It had to be pretty obvious she was stalling.

"Want me to walk you out, Er?" Brody the Clueless said.

She shot a glance toward Nate and lowered her tone to be sure Nate couldn't hear them. "If you don't mind, I want to have a word with Nate first."

Brody half sat on the edge of the table, casually crossing his feet. "Okay, I can wait."

"No," she said, a bit too quickly. She felt the heat rush into her complexion. "I mean, you don't have to."

His face spread into a slow leer, and he waggled his brows. "Well, hot damn, DeLuca," Brody said under his breath. "Want me to lock the conference room doors behind me?"

She lifted her chin. "Oh, be quiet. I said *talk*."

"I know what you *said*." Brody leaned in. "Just in case you wondered, I approve completely."

"Gosh, I can rest easy now," she said, in a droll tone. "Thanks."

"Seriously, give him a chance, Erin," Brody said, as he pushed away from the table. "I remember you telling me you wanted to take the scary steps, to find your way out of the darkness, like I did."

She angled her gaze away, crossed her arms tightly and rested them on her baby bulge. "Yeah? So?"

"It's not easy, sweetheart." He chucked her under the chin gently. "Believe me, I know. But it's worth it. And Nate's a damn good guy. I befriended him initially because you asked us to. But, after getting to know him, he and I would've been friends anyway."

She bestowed a sincere smile. "I'm glad."

He spread his arms. "Look what he pulled off today. No more fire danger worry. He's top-notch."

"I know. I'm just not sure I'm ready for more steps. He might not even be interested." The thought made her feel ill.

"How will you ever know if you don't try?" Brody cocked one eyebrow to punctuate his rhetorical question, then squeezed her shoulder and headed out.

The door closed behind him, and Nate looked up from where he'd been packing up his equipment. "Still here?"

She hesitated at the back of the room. "Is that okay?"

He grinned. "Of course."

How will you know if you don't try?

Brody's question rang in her ears, thumped in her heart. The damn man had a point. Shoring up her resolve, Erin strode toward Nate as confidently as a lumbering Winnebago in an ugly uniform could. She stopped directly in front of him. He looked up, questions in his gorgeous turquoise eyes.

"Can I help you?" he asked, playfully.

"You already did." With that, she took his face in both of her hands and kissed him. Deeply.

Wow.

She couldn't be less interested in sex at this

point in her pregnancy, but damn if that kiss didn't set a deep, primal throb in motion in spite of her. When she pulled away, his eyes were dark with desire, too.

"What was that for?"

"To thank you."

"You're welcome." He set his remote pointer aside and pulled her against him. "Thank me anytime. For anything."

"Nate, honestly. I've been having nightmares about that damned fireworks display, but no one in city management was going to listen to me." She expelled a breath, searching for words. "What you did, coming up with an alternative, and an amazing one at that—" she shook her head in wonder "—you have no idea what that means to me."

For a few moments, he seemed to battle with his next comment. "Actually, I do."

Confusion drew her forehead into a small frown. "What do you mean?"

"I did the whole thing for you. Because of you." He grasped her upper arms and leaned back, studying her. "Before I explain, how are the hormones raging today?"

She shrugged out of his grasp and whomped him on the chest, laughing as she did so. "Shut up and tell me."

"Okay. It's about time anyway." His shoulders

raised with a deep breath, then dropped. "I know everything, Erin. About your prom night, what happened."

Her eyes widened. A million different feelings tumbled through her in a split second, leaving her breathless. "How?" she managed to choke out.

"It accidentally slipped out in conversation."

"Brody," she said, shaking her head.

He pressed his lips together. "Please don't blame him. He would never violate your confidence. He just assumed I knew since we'd... been intimate."

"Oh. Of course." She stared at the floor. "How long have you known?"

"Awhile." He paused, lowered his tone. "I wish you'd told me."

She pushed out a frustrated sound. "How do you tell someone that? How?"

He pulled her against him, wrapping her in a hug, smoothing his palms down her back. "I understand your fear. But, had I known—" a sigh "—some of the things I said in anger when I first found out about the baby—"

"It's okay." She rested her cheek against his chest, melting into the embrace, inhaling his now-familiar scent. "I deserved them."

"No, you didn't. I'm sorry."

"I'm sorry I haven't said anything. I've never

been in this position before, and I honestly didn't know how."

"It's okay."

"That night…I don't know what I would've done if you'd been, I don't know, disgusted."

"Ah, Erin." He kissed the top of her head, reached up to stroke her hair. "I wish you could get inside my head so you could see yourself through my eyes. You grabbed my attention the moment you walked into the bar that night. Everyone else melted away. If you had any clue how beautiful you are."

"I'm not, though. You haven't seen—"

"I don't care." He pulled back and hunkered down slightly, holding her upper arms in his hands and forcing her to look at him directly. "Not one bit. You make my breath catch every time you walk in a room, do you know that?"

"Man, you're easy."

"No. Don't try to joke your way out of this. You're…you're special, scars or no scars." He shrugged. "Hell, do you think I'm physically perfect?"

"Uh, yes," she said, with sarcasm in her tone.

"You do?" he said, sounding both pleasantly surprised and distracted by her answer. "Sweet."

She shouldered away from him, but he pulled her back into an embrace, laughing. He held her there in his arms, rocking slowly. The tone sobered. "Listen to me. This is hard, but it all has to be said sometime, so…here goes. I know I'm not…Kevin."

"Oh, God." She sucked a breath, buried her face against his chest.

"It's okay," he rushed to say. "It really is. I'm not trying to replace him."

"You don't have to say this," she pleaded.

"Yes. I do."

Ashamed, she held on tightly, wadding the back of his shirt in her hands.

"I can accept not being the love of your life, Erin. I'm secure enough in who I am for that, okay?"

"But—"

He laid a hand on the back of her head. "Please let me finish."

She felt ill, but didn't continue to protest.

"We're having a baby. And we've become friends easily. Closer than friends. Even you have to admit that."

"Yes," she whispered.

"I just want a chance. I know I said I didn't care if you and I had any kind of relationship that day at the Pinecone. I didn't mean it. That was *my* lie." He paused. "You crushed me when you left that hotel room."

She looked up at him, chin quivering. "God, Nate—"

"Shh. I'm not asking for another apology, and I'm not going to bring up that damned note for the rest of our lives, okay?"

She nodded.

"I just want you to know…it wasn't a no-strings, one-night-stand kind of deal for me. For one thing, I'm not that guy. That aside, every moment with you felt different from the beginning. More intense."

She swallowed, with difficulty. "For me, too. Hence the note. I panicked. I ran."

He pressed his lips together, looking sad.

"I'm so scared, Nate," she whispered, pressing her cheek against his chest again.

"Of course you are. I am, too. We'd be idiots if we weren't. We're going to be parents, and we're just now becoming a part of each other's lives. That's damned terrifying."

She couldn't comment.

He lifted her chin with one finger, urging her to meet his gaze. "I really do get it. I'm not asking you to pledge your life to me. It's way too soon for that, for both of us. I'm just asking for a chance. A new start. That's all I want."

"How? After all we've already been through?"

He kissed her gently, nipping at her lips. "How about something simple. I ask you for a date and you say yes?"

She laughed wryly, glancing down at her belly. "That's definitely doing things backward. I'm carrying your child, and we spend virtually every night together."

His lips twitched. "Yeah, I thought of that, too. But who says we have to do things like the rest of the world? Conformity is overrated."

He kissed her again, and she leaned into it, breathing him in, leaving her lips against his after the kiss.

Finally, he pulled away. "We're special. Don't you feel it, too?"

"Yes, but—" She bit her bottom lip and blinked, warring with herself, with all her mixed-up feelings. She peered up at him, wary. "I honestly don't know if I can let you see my scars. I don't even look at them if I can avoid it."

"Honey, there is no rush. I'm talking sweet, old-fashioned courtship, not hot sex."

She smirked. "Bummer."

"Well now—" he held up a hand "—that can be renegotiated at any time. Believe me."

"I was kidding. I'm an elephant, if you hadn't noticed."

He cupped her face in his hands. "All I've noticed is that you're my beautiful Erin. And we're having a baby."

"I'm not beautiful, though. That's what I keep

trying to tell you." Distress pooled tears in her eyes. He just didn't get it. "I'm scarred. Extensively. I've had a million surgeries, it seems. Skin grafts. Plastic surgery." She raised her shoulders, then let them drop in defeat. "There's nothing more they can do, and it's not pretty."

"Erin DeLuca. Every part of you that makes you the woman you are is beautiful to me. I couldn't care less about the scars."

She wanted to believe it, but…

"That's just because you haven't seen them."

"Not true. Once you know me better, you'll believe that. The point is, I don't have to see them. Until you're ready."

"What if I'm never ready?"

A look she couldn't quite name moved across his face. "We'll work through it."

A thick pause ensued.

"There's more, yes?" he urged.

She nodded. Gulped.

"Might as well lay it all out on the table."

Fear clutched at her. "Please understand—ugh, I shouldn't even ask that of you."

"It's okay. Whatever it is."

She trembled, knowing that once she said it, she couldn't take it back. But she had to say it. Do or die. "I feel…disloyal."

He tucked his chin. "To Kevin?"

She nodded again, hating that she had to voice this part of it at all. Nate deserved so much better.

"Because I want to take you out on a date?"

"No." She met his gaze directly. "Because I really, really want you to take me out on a date. And I want to keep sleeping in your arms like I have been. And whenever you touch me, all I want is more." She held up a hand. "Post-pregnancy, of course."

His lips twitched with amusement. "Of course."

"Is that wrong?" she finished, in a wavery whisper. "I swore I'd never feel a thing for any other man again. I feel like such a liar."

"Aw, honey." He pulled her back into an embrace. "It's difficult to be the survivor. But we can't control our feelings. Maybe…just maybe… Kevin would want to see you happy."

"But it breaks my heart that you'd feel like second place in any way. I want *you* to be happy, too."

"Then say yes. Being with you makes me happy. It's enough for now. Truly."

"Even when I stand here, pregnant with your baby, and tell you I feel disloyal to a boy I loved who's been…gone for almost twelve years?"

"Yes."

She took in a deep breath. "Well, then, go ahead."

"Go ahead?" he asked.

"You haven't actually asked me out yet."

"Oh. That. Thanks for the reminder." He readjusted his stance, preparing. "Erin DeLuca, would you please be my July Fourth date?"

She eased away enough to meet his gaze. "July Fourth? Don't you have to work?"

"I called in my VisionPlex and FogScreen experts." He smiled. "This next week I'll be working hellish, exhausting hours pulling the whole gig together, don't get me wrong. But on the day of the show? All I have to do is sit back and bask in a job well done. With you. If you agree, that is."

She angled her head to the side, her expression growing serious again. "No promises, okay? And we have to take things slowly. I'm skittish, Nate, and I'm…not whole. In so many ways."

"Whatever you need. I mean that."

"In that case, I'd love to be your date." She smiled cautiously up at him.

"Excellent." He kissed her forehead as though this kind of affection were second nature to him now, then went back to packing up his equipment. For a few moments, they enjoyed a comfortable silence. "You know, Brody thought you might want to kill him for accidentally spilling your secrets."

"Months ago? Probably." She twirled a lock of hair in her fingers. "But if he hadn't told you, I don't know that I ever could've."

"Really?"

"Yeah. The night of the Millstone fire, after it

had all hit me but before I met you, Brody assured me things would get better. I couldn't see how, and I asked him for help. So, it's on me." She hiked one shoulder. "I owe him."

"He'll be relieved to hear that."

"Nate, I have to tell you one more thing." She cut her gaze away, unsure if she could go on. She wasn't quite as brave as Brody yet.

"Tell me."

Could she? Yes. She had to. He deserved some consideration, too. She lowered her chin, regarding him through her lashes. "I've told you before, but it bears repeating. I didn't intend to get pregnant. You know that. You believe me, right?"

He nodded.

Her heart pounded so hard, the baby started to squirm in protest. "But, since it happened, you also have to know…really know, right here—" she pressed her palm to his chest, right over his heartbeat "—that I'm so glad the baby is yours. I am. I couldn't ask for a better father for my child. For a better man, period."

He searched her face for a long time, then reached over and tucked her hair behind her ear, running the backs of his fingers along her jawline before letting the caress drop away. "You know what? We're going to be okay, honey. No matter what happens between us."

"Are you sure?" she whispered.

"Sure enough for both of us. For all three of us," he amended, laying his palm on her belly. "That's plenty for now, yeah?"

She smiled, grateful. "Yeah."

Chapter Twelve

The alternative fireworks show was, naturally, a massive hit. Walt Hennessey took credit for the whole thing, but Nate had seen enough of his kind to anticipate that would happen. He didn't care. As long as the show made Erin happy, the rest didn't matter.

In addition to the whole town and residents from nearby towns, representatives from Denver's major media outlets had shown up. The positive press they'd receive for thinking environmentally about the fire danger would definitely give Troublesome Gulch a bigger pin on the Colorado map.

The fact that Nate had had a hand in making that happen swelled his heart with pride.

He sat on a blanket with Erin cradled against his chest. Brody and Faith had joined them, as had Lexy. Mr. Norwood accompanied Jason and a couple of his friends, and they sat just a few yards away.

Cagney was on duty—she always seemed to be on duty—but she stopped by to say hello, which they all enjoyed.

They'd indulged in fried chicken and biscuits from the Pinecone—grilled, skinless chicken skewers for Erin with fresh fruit—and now they simply basked in the aftermath, enjoying the music.

"You're a miracle worker, Nate," Faith said. She eyed Erin sitting comfortably in his arms. Pointedly. "And not just because that was, bar none, the coolest Fourth of July celebration the Gulch has ever seen, if you know what I'm saying, and I think you do."

"Let it go, Faith," Erin said softly.

Faith held up her hands. "I'm not pushing, Erin, except…it almost makes me cry to see you looking so happy. It's all I ever wanted for you. That's all." She mimed pulling a zipper over her lips.

To his great pleasure, Erin didn't protest. If anything, she snuggled closer. To him that said she was happy enough to not hide their burgeoning relationship from her friends. But he didn't want to read too much into anything at this point. He just wanted to enjoy every moment.

"I agree with Faith," Lexy said. "And, on that positive note, I have to go. I promised to cover part of the graveyard shift in dispatch."

"You work too damn much," Brody chastised.

She simply shrugged. "My work gives my life purpose. I love it. You know that."

"Wait, Lex, we'll walk you to the parking lot." Faith ran her palm against Brody's face. "We should go, too. I'm exhausted, and I have to work in the morning."

Brody immediately got to his feet and offered a hand to his wife. "What my babies want, my babies get."

Faith winked at Erin. "He's so trained, girl."

Everyone laughed.

After a round of goodbyes with the new friends he'd already come to treasure, Nate found himself blissfully alone with Erin. He slid his arms around her and laid his palms gently on her belly. Putting his lips close to her ear, he whispered, "I swear, I could hold you like this forever."

She squirmed languidly against him. "Man, I wish I weren't pregnant right now."

His body stirred. He nipped gently at her earlobe.

"Stop with the ear thing. You're driving me crazy."

"You know," he said, in a slow growl, "pregnant women *can*—"

"Not this pregnant woman. Sorry."

He chuckled softly. "Can't blame a guy for trying." He snuggled her in closer. "I won't lie, Erin. I want to make love to you so badly, it's painful."

"I want it, too. Just not yet. It'll be a while now."

He groaned. "I need a cold shower."

"Typical man, one-track mind," she said, in a teasing tone. She eased her way out of his embrace, despite his protestations, and started to gather up the trash from their picnic dinner. "We should probably go, too."

"Wait. I have something to tell you," Nate said.

Her hands stilled. After a moment, she glanced up.

"Don't look so scared. It's nothing awful. Well," he added ruefully, "nothing *too* awful."

"What?"

"I'm afraid the Walkers are descending. I held them at bay as long as I could."

Her eyes widened. "Your family?"

"Every last bossy, estrogen-packed one of them, and they will come bearing baby gifts. Be fore-warned. You might want to rent a storage unit."

"Oh, God, I'm scared." She laid a hand at her throat, then laughed. "Then again, I can't wait. When?"

"Day after tomorrow. So, I've been meaning to

ask you, which hotel in town is best? My place is way too small for the four of them."

"Nate, they're family!"

"I know, but you've seen the condo. They won't be comfortable packed in like sardines."

She sat back on her knees, biting the corner of her lip. "What if they stay at my place? I have a guest room that'll sleep two, and my living room couch folds out. That'll sleep the other two." She shrugged. "It's not private, but it's better than a hotel. And if it's too awkward, two of them can take my bedroom and I'll stay at your place with you."

"Now, that sounds like a plan."

"Oh, you."

After a moment, he reached out and took her hand. "You'd really put my family up in your house?"

"Of course, silly," she said, softly. "They're sort of my family, too. Connected by the little one, of course."

It hit him right then, like a Louisville Slugger to the skull. He loved this woman.

Loved her. With every fiber of his being. Not because they'd created a baby together, either. He'd fallen headfirst in love with Erin DeLuca, simply because of who she was.

Gulping back the knowledge, he went for stern. "You will not play hostess. If you so much as lift a finger—"

"I won't. I'm way too exhausted these days." She rubbed her tummy. "I honestly wonder if I'm going to make it all the way to my due date."

"Not to worry. They'll wait on you hand and foot—I'll make sure of that."

She laughed. "And I'll gladly let them. Call them. Tonight. Now, if you have your cell phone." She nearly bounced with excitement. "Tell them they're welcome to stay with me, if they'd like. And I can't wait to meet them."

He whistled low through his teeth. "You don't know what you're in for, honey." He unclipped the cell phone from his waistband. "But, okay, you asked for it."

All the Walker siblings were on the tall side and had Nate's dark hair and turquoise eyes, except for Colette, a petite and surprisingly natural ash blonde with a heart-shaped face and bright green catlike eyes. All of them were stunning beauties, at least in Erin's estimation.

Their arrival had been a flurry of chatter and laughter, bear hugs and belly touches. Everyone talked over each other, and no one lost track of any conversation threads. Erin felt a little awed and overwhelmed by all of it, but not necessarily in a negative way. She wasn't used to big families, but she found herself so grateful that her little son or daughter would have aunts. And someday, maybe uncles and cousins, too.

After the initial onslaught, Flannery, Piper, Colette and Nate went to unload the SUV. Erin and Nate's mother, "call me LeAnn," sat in the Adirondack chairs sipping lemonade, with Finn snoring at their feet.

Despite her heartfelt desire to relax, tension hummed inside Erin, pulling her shoulders taut. She wanted them to like her, to approve. But there were things she needed to say, and she was determined not to lose her nerve.

"You have a lovely place, sweetheart," LeAnn said, in a casual tone, taking it all in. "It's no wonder my Nate didn't hesitate to move here."

This was it. Her chance. She cleared her throat. "Ms. Walker—"

"Ah—" the older woman held up a hand "—LeAnn, remember?"

"Right. Sorry." She smiled tightly. "Anyway…I just wanted to say…well, it's difficult."

"What's on your mind?"

Erin exhaled. "I honestly didn't mean to get your son tied up in this mess. I hope you know that. I even offered him an easy out."

LeAnn barked a laugh, then reached over and covered Erin's hand with her own. "I don't mean to laugh, but my Nate would never take an easy out."

"I've learned that since." Erin smiled. "Still, please, accept my most sincere apologies. I don't want you to think badly of me."

LeAnn turned and studied her. "Sweet child, let me tell you something. Any mother would want to see her child married and blissful before starting a family, that I won't lie about. But Nate has never done anything the easy or expected way." She shook her head. "I don't know the details of how this whole thing came about, and I don't need to. You're both grown adults. Just know that Nate has been happier since he moved to Troublesome Gulch than I've seen him in years, and mind you, he's a generally happy kid. That's saying something."

Erin nodded, amused to hear Nate referred to as a kid.

LeAnn leaned closer. "Listen here. You're the mother of my first grandchild. Do you know what that means?"

Erin swallowed, then shook her head jerkily.

"You're family, from here on out. Period. No inquisitions, no judgments, no nothing. It's the way we Walkers operate."

Erin breathed a sigh of relief. "I'm so…well, glad seems such an inadequate word." She shrugged. "I know Nate and I aren't your traditional parents, but we're both going to love this baby, and I'm so grateful he will have you and the girls as his family."

LeAnn quirked an eyebrow. "I don't want any more apology talk, hear? Family is family, no matter how it comes about. The girls and I are thrilled about the baby. And Nate?" She lifted her eyes heavenward. "Over the moon."

"He's an incredible guy."

"Yes, he is. And I take full credit."

"You should. I told him his mother should be proud of him that—" she gulped "—that first night we met."

LeAnn eyed Erin sidelong. "To hear you talk about my son, I just have to be nosy. Is it simply that you don't want the married life, sweetie? Not that it's any of my business, but believe me, I'd understand."

"It's not that." Erin sighed. "It's complicated."

"Well, there's time. Things have a way of working themselves out the way they should."

"Thank you, LeAnn. For being so...nonjudgmental. And for raising such an amazing man. I couldn't ask for a better man to be the father of my baby."

"You're absolutely right." LeAnn nailed her with an unwavering look, her tone light but pointed. "Keep that in mind when you're facing all these so-called complications, sweetheart. Okay?"

Erin dropped her gaze.

"Now, enough of my not-so-subtle hints that I'd like to see you and Nate together in a more permanent way." LeAnn laughed out loud. "To the nitty-gritty, and I'm sure Nate warned you I'd ask. I'm a registered nurse and a four-time mom myself—not the least bit squeamish. So? How's the pregnancy been so far? As Grandma-to-be, I want all the gory details."

The Walker women took time to rest and unpack, while Erin and Nate left to pick up food.

"How's it going so far?" Nate asked warily.

"Your family is amazing. I love them already." The deep yearning to be a part of them shocked Erin to her core. She hadn't wanted to be a part of a family this fervently since Kevin's.

Again with the guilt.

Nate smiled, turning into the pizza place. "That, they are. If it helps any, they love you, too. And this after only knowing you for a couple hours. But I could've predicted that."

Erin demurred. "It's only because I'm carrying their grandchild-slash-niece or nephew. Otherwise I'd just be one woman in a long line of them, I'm sure."

"I'm not going to waste time being offended by that last comment." Nate huffed. "When are you going to give yourself a little credit?"

She crinkled her nose. "I'm not sure I deserve it."

Their pizzas were probably ready and waiting,

but Nate killed the ignition and angled to face her. "You and Brody." He shook his head sadly. "Don't tell me you blame yourself for the prom night accident, too?"

"No, not really. But…there's Kevin. Sorry. Plus, I feel like I roped you into this makeshift family thing, and you're just too nice to say so. It's not a good feeling."

A beat passed.

"How am I going to get through to you?"

"What do you mean?"

"I wouldn't want to be having a child with any other woman, Erin. I don't want any other woman in my life. Can't you see what you've come to mean to me?"

She studied him quizzically, then reached out to hold his hand.

"I could fall in love with you in a split second," he said, in a silky-rough tone. "Lord knows, I'm half-crazy in love with you already."

Her chest warmed, but she brushed him off. He didn't know what he was saying. "Don't be silly."

"I'm not. I'm holding back in deference to you—period. But I think you're the most amazing, beautiful, complicated, intriguing woman I've ever come across, and I want to go on record right this minute saying, I'm ready and waiting whenever you're ready."

"And waiting?"

He pulled her toward him. "Honey, you won't have to wait for a second. All you have to do is say the word."

"Nate," she said, on an exhale.

"It's true."

Her throat squeezed. "Kiss me. I need you to kiss me."

He hesitated for only a second before maneuvering closer to her. Cradling her face in his hands, he kissed her gently, butterfly kisses.

"Kiss me like you mean it, Nate." She lowered her tone to a purr. "I know you can. I know I'm gross and huge and pregnant, but kiss me like you want me."

His gaze deepened, and he released a half laugh, half groan. "You're neither gross nor huge, although I'll concede, you *are* pregnant. And, just FYI, I *do* want you." He threaded his fingers into the back of her hair and did as she asked, exploring her mouth with his own, trailing kisses down her neck and across her collarbone.

"Why does this feel so good?"

"Because it's right," he said, nibbling at her bottom lip. "Because it's time you stopped fighting me so hard."

She kissed him this time, throwing every bit of her pent-up sexual tension into the kiss. When they broke apart, they both breathed heavily. "I'm not fighting you, Nate. I'm scared."

"I know, babe."

She rested her head on his shoulder. "You're so good to me."

"Then let me be."

A protest lit on her lips. She bit it back. "We should get the pizzas."

"I don't want to leave you."

She sighed. "I don't want you to leave me."

He pulled her closer. "Screw it. We can let my family starve. I don't mind."

She laughed, the intense moment broken. "Oh, be quiet. They're my guests. Our guests. I won't let them starve in my own house."

He released a put-upon sigh. "Fine, fine. Pizzas it is." He pulled away, but kept hold of her hand. "Know this. I want you, Erin. You and our baby. I'm not going to lie about it anymore."

She searched his eyes for several long moments, then squeezed his hand. "I'm working on it, Nate, but I'm not quite ready. And I don't know what to do to get ready. You deserve better than always having to wait."

"I don't want better. Better doesn't exist. I want you. Besides—" he pulled away before she could protest "—I'm more than willing to bide my time. You, sweet one, are more than worth the wait."

Chapter Thirteen

For two days straight, Erin and Nate focused solely on his family. They showed them around town, introduced them to their friends. Mostly, though, they spent time at her house just talking and laughing, getting to know each other. None of them let Erin do a single task in her supposed capacity of hostess.

Piper, Erin quickly learned, was an avid—okay, obsessed—knitter. No matter where they went, the woman always had her needles clickity-clacking. She'd finished a veritable motherlode of absolutely darling booties and caps and sweaters for the baby already, in every color of the rainbow, and she showed no signs of letting up.

But she was running low on yarn.

Catastrophe for a knitting addict like her.

The third day, Erin woke up exhausted, her back aching and her head pounding. She didn't want to spoil the Walkers' visit, so she begged off a planned road trip into Denver, assuring them she just needed to catch up on sleep and she'd be good as new when they returned that evening. She equipped Nate with the addresses of and directions to three great knitting shops in the metro area—The Recycled Lamb, Showers of Flowers and Simplicity—then shuffled the whole family out the door, demanding they have enough fun to share with her later.

Not thirty minutes after they'd left, she'd fallen into a fitful, restless sleep.

A few hours into her nap, she became half-aware of a sense that someone was standing in her room, right at the end of her bed. Finn hadn't roused to attack an intruder—a good sign. She felt so groggy, she didn't have the sense to feel afraid.

Still, she opened her eyes to see who was there, more out of curiosity than anything.

She sucked a breath.

"K-Kevin?" Her heart hammered in her chest.

No. Couldn't be.

Kevin was dead.

He'd been gone for more than ten years.

A hallucination.

She squeezed her eyes closed, then opened them again, slowly.

He still stood there. Incongruous in the bedroom of her adult home, but on the other hand, so normal. Close, but distant. He wore his Troublesome Gulch letter jacket and looked just as he always had. Sweet, alive, loving.

Young.

It had to be a dream or a hallucination.

She'd aged. He hadn't.

He looked just as he had before he'd died.

Still, she wanted him there.

Terrified he'd disappear without warning, she eased into a sitting position slowly. "Kevin?" she whispered.

Why wasn't he talking?

"Say something," she demanded, urgency seizing her in a way it never had before. Tears filled her eyes and spilled over. "Please say something to me."

Nothing. But he reached out a hand.

She edged to the end of the bed and sat back on her knees, sobbing full force. She reached toward his hand, but felt…nothing. "Oh, God. Kev, why are you here now? When you're not *really* here? Why?"

"Let me go," she heard him whisper.

She reeled back as though she'd been punched. Had she imagined those words?

"Let me go," she heard again.

"How?" She wadded fistfuls of the quilt in her hands. "Tell me how, Kevin, and I will. I know I need to. It's been so long, and I haven't really been living, but you don't get it. You were the love of my life."

"I get it."

She gulped several times. "I have so much I want to say to you. So much I never got to say. I feel angry and sad and cheated."

"Say it."

"But you're not real!" she yelled in frustration, then felt an immediate stab of remorse. "I mean, you're real in here." She touched her chest, just over her heart. "I will always love you. But you're not real on this earth anymore. I can't be with you."

He didn't move, didn't speak, just smiled.

Everything about him seemed serene.

In contrast, she sobbed harder, and the baby kicked, pulling her into her current reality. She laid her palm against her belly, then blinked up at the spectre of the young man she'd thought she would spend the rest of her life with. Surely he couldn't miss the huge bulge.

"I'm having a baby, Kev." She swallowed

thickly. This felt so weird. "With a great guy. Nate. You'd like him, I think."

He smiled. Nodded. "I like him."

"God, Kev, I can't believe I'm saying this to you, but I think I'm in love with him. No—" She held out a hand, knowing she couldn't lie anymore. Not to herself, and definitely not to Kevin. "I am in love with him."

He nodded.

"I'm so sorry," she whispered, her words wavering. "I never meant to betray you."

"There's no betrayal."

"Do you hate me?" she pleaded, through ever-increasing sobs.

"I love you," he said, simply.

The pain lanced through her. "I love you, too. I always will. But I love Nate, too. And I don't know what to do. C-can you understand that?"

"Yes. So, let me go. Be happy. Please…"

She jammed shaky fingers into her hair, frustrated for the unfairness of it all. "But I was supposed to have your baby, Kevin."

"No. You weren't."

Her eyes bugged. What? How could he say that?

"D-don't you remember our baby?"

"Of course I do. You don't understand. There's a grand plan." He paused. "I'm with her. Our baby. She was for *me*. Not you."

"Oh, God," Erin keened, clutching at the front of her T-shirt.

"She's beautiful. Happy, too. Don't worry about us." He smiled, gesturing toward her belly. "You're supposed to have *this* baby. With Nate. Please, Er-bear, let us go. It's time."

He started to fade, and panic set in.

"Wait!" she yelled, scrambling to her knees. "What if I can't, Kev? I—I don't know how—"

"You know," he said, with quiet confidence. "It's inside you. Stop hiding." He faded further.

"Kevin!" she sobbed. "Kevin, please, wait!"

But he didn't.

The last vision she had was of him blowing her a kiss that she actually felt like small wings against her cheek.

A baby girl. She'd lost a baby girl. Bereft, she couldn't even revel in a sense of peace that the little angel was with her daddy in heaven, loved and cared for.

She fell onto her side, curled protectively around the baby in her womb and wept. She wept until she didn't have a drop of moisture left in her body, it seemed, then fell into a deadweight, dreamless sleep.

When she jolted awake, late-afternoon sunshine slanted through her windows. Strangely rejuvenated, she glanced around the room—just as it had been when she'd fallen asleep that morning.

Had the whole thing been a dream?

It had to have been.

The fetus she'd lost was too small to discern gender—they'd told her that at the hospital. A girl? How could anyone know?

But, it had felt so real.

And everything she'd said to Kevin felt real, too, she realized, a sort of zen calm settling over her. She loved Nate. She wanted to be whole for him, to be with him, and finally, she had an idea of what she needed to do to gain some closure.

Time to stop hiding, and this would be step one.

After showering quickly, she dressed, fed Finn, and scribbled a note for Nate.

Running errands, back soon. Don't worry.

She hesitated, then added, *Love, Erin.*

The thirty-mile drive to nearby White Peaks didn't take her too long. Kevin's parents had moved there after the prom night accident that stole their only son. They couldn't face living in Troublesome Gulch without him, and she could hardly blame them.

She arrived at their cedar-sided bungalow right about 7:00 p.m., glad they'd be done with dinner. God knew, she wouldn't be able to swallow a single bite if they offered her a meal.

Anxiety rose and fell within her, like a runaway cart on a roller coaster. She hadn't spoken to Kevin's parents since last Christmas. Sadly, after years of family-like contact, it had come to that…a phone call each Christmas, probably to avoid pain on both sides. And yet, she realized she really wanted them to know about her baby. More than that, to *know* her baby. Like her, Kevin had been an only child. Their dreams of being grandparents had died on prom night, along with their son.

None of it was fair.

Heart in her throat, she pressed the doorbell and stepped back, listening to the chimes. Through the door, she could hear the television. When footsteps approached, she resisted the insane urge to bolt, forget the whole ridiculous idea. Since when had she been afraid of Kevin's parents?

The door swung open, and there stood Kevin's lovely mom, PJ, an expectant smile on her face. Her expression brightened even more.

"My goodness, Erin!" She started to step forward for a hug, then her gaze dropped to Erin's belly. Tremulous fingers raised to her lips, tears rose to her eyes, and she whispered, "Oh, honey."

"I wanted you to know," Erin blurted, her words watery and shaky. "I should've come much sooner. Please forgive me."

"Come here." The two women dissolved into tears, hugging and rocking each other on the front porch.

"I loved Kevin," Erin said, her words muffled against his mother's shoulder. "I hope you know that."

"Of course you did, honey." She pulled back, laying her palms on Erin's belly. "But you have to move on. We all do. I've worried for so long that you never would, but look at you now."

"Yeah. Big and fat."

"Beautiful." PJ laughed through her tears. "He'd be so happy for you, honey. He would. I'm happier for you than I can even say. When are you due?"

"About three weeks."

PJ put her arm around Erin's shoulders and ushered her in. "I can't tell you how pleased I am that you came. Better late than never, they say. Marcus!" she called out. "Erin's here!"

"Our Erin?" he said, and she could hear the excitement, the welcome, in his tone, and it warmed her. She recognized the sound of the newspaper being set aside, and of the footrest of his favorite green recliner clicking down. Familiar things.

The house smelled of lemon furniture polish and pine, as their houses always had, even though this one was relatively new. Some things carried though a life, like a safety line to normalcy.

"Yes," PJ called to her husband, "and with a big surprise."

Marcus Jennings, looking so much the way Erin had always imagined Kevin would in their later days, rounded the corner and stopped dead, taking in the sight. His eyes grew suspiciously bright, and his chin quivered. He opened his arms wide. "Erin DeLuca. You make an absolutely beautiful mama, like we always knew you would. Come here, little one."

Feeling like a teenager again, she cried in Marcus's arms, but the tears cleansed her soul this time rather than weighing on it. "I'm having a baby," she said, unnecessarily.

Everyone laughed.

"Come." He cradled her against him as though she were a precious thing. "Sit down and tell us all about it. This is a happy day. A happy day, indeed."

With the ice broken, their conversation came as easily as it always had prior to the tragedy. She didn't go into all the embarrassing details, but she did tell them about Nate and his family, about the baby and her pregnancy.

Finally, she worked up the urge to admit the dream she'd had about Kevin, and what he'd said about the baby granddaughter they'd lost. Of course, no one had known she and Kevin were expecting on prom night, but they all found out in the aftermath. By then, it was the least of anyone's worries.

PJ tucked her feet beneath her on the couch as she listened to the story of Erin's "Kevin dream." "I'm not surprised. Kevin comes to me on a pretty regular basis. Whenever I need him."

Erin gaped, unable to speak for a moment. "Why hasn't he come to me before?"

PJ smiled, looking so much like Kevin—at peace and serene. "You weren't ready. Now you are. You're prepared to heal and move on. Thank the Lord."

Erin pondered this, nodding. It really had been a gift, seeing Kevin that way.

"I knew about the baby girl, too."

Erin peered curiously at PJ. "How?"

"Kevin told me. He calls her Phoenix."

A melancholy overtook Erin, but she shook it off. This wasn't a time to dwell in the past. She looked up at the two people she'd considered a second family since high school. "I wanted to tell you both about the baby…and about Nate. I love him so much."

"You didn't have to wait so long," Marcus chided.

She nodded, biting her lip. "I didn't know how much I needed to tell you until Kevin came to my room. Before that, I'd been floundering. Confused. I couldn't figure out what I needed."

"He's watched over you this whole time, honey. Every step, and he'll continue to do so," PJ said. "But it's about time you lived your life. Please believe Kevin would've wanted that for you—love, life, family. Take advantage of the chance he lost."

"I will."

"You're going to be such a good mom."

She grimaced. "I'm glad you think so. It's terrifying."

PJ laughed. "You'll get the hang of it. We all do. That's just part of it."

"Will you bring the baby by?" Marcus asked, in a far-off, wistful tone, his fists in a knot on his lap.

"That's the thing." She looked from one to the other, then leaned forward and took their hands into hers. "Why I came, really." She paused.

"What is it, sweetheart?" PJ asked.

Erin garnered her courage. "I want you to be a part of this baby's life. A big part. I know you won't be his or her real grandparents, but I consider you my family and always will."

"The feeling's mutual."

"The way I figure it, a child can't have too many great adults in his life, you know?" She watched them nod, preparing for her next words. "So, please, will you be my baby's godparents? Will you take an active role in his or her life? If it's not too much to ask, that is," she added shyly. "Mom and Dad live farther away now, and Nate's family is from Las Vegas. Nate travels extensively for his business, and I'm eventually going back to those.

twenty-four hour shifts, too. He or she will need a loving place to stay."

PJ had begun crying silently.

"As far as I'm concerned, he can have Grandma and Grandpa DeLuca, Grandma Walker and Nana and Papa Jennings."

PJ sniffed. "Oh, Erin. We'd love nothing more. Such a gift in all our lives, this child. And you. Thank you, sweetheart. Thank you."

Marcus swallowed convulsively, reining in his emotions. "Is Nate okay with our involvement?"

She squeezed their hands one final time and released them, smiling. "I haven't discussed it with him, but I know him well enough to say yes. Definitely. He's an amazing, selfless man. You'll love him."

"If he loves you, I can't see how we wouldn't." Marcus looked at his wife, grinning. "Time to go baby shopping, Mother. We've got some work to do, turning that spare room into a nice nursery and playroom for our godchild."

"Yes." PJ gulped back tears and gratitude, her hands clasped at her chest. "And I can't wait. Three weeks, goodness, it seems a lifetime now."

Erin navigated the quickly darkening roads with extra care, despite her urgency to get home. A lightness of being had overtaken her; she hadn't felt this free since high school. She could hardly wait to tell Nate everything. That she loved him—heart, mind, body and soul. She wanted to tell him about Kevin coming to her in a dream, about visiting Kevin's parents, about breaking through her own self-imprisonment and finally—*finally*—being ready to move forward.

With him. The man she adored.

Her back throbbed even more from all the time spent in the car, but she was flying so high on emotion, she didn't even care.

Thoughts of the new life that awaited her raced through her brain as the miles rolled beneath her tires. The closer she got, the more excited she became.

Just on the outskirts of Troublesome Gulch proper, a sudden, blinding pain shot through her abdomen, and she jerked the wheel. By the time she'd identified it as a labor pain, everything moved in slow motion, and she realized it was too late to regain control of the careening car. As a seasoned engineer, she knew this.

Still, she had to try.

She gripped the wheel as the car screeched toward the empty oncoming lines and the mountain that flanked them. She couldn't hit that. Overcorrecting, she turned the car, tires squealing to the other side where it dipped off the edge of the road into a ditch.

She held her breath and prayed though the jolting and crunching, the sounds of breaking glass around her, until finally the vehicle came to rest on its side.

Eerie silence filled the car.

She'd struck her head hard on the driver's side window, and it took her several moments to shake off confusion, to get her bearings. A second blinding labor pain helped the process along. She reached up to touch the side of her head and pulled away bloody fingers. So, what now?

She fought back panic, knowing she could handle herself in an emergency like this. She did it for a living, for God's sake.

First step, get help.

Glancing around, she caught sight of her purse splayed on the splintered passenger side window currently pressed against the gouged earth. She flailed for it, but it was just out of reach.

Fear set in, icy and raw. She struggled to squelch it. No matter what, she was not going to give birth to her baby in a crashed car with no one around. Scared or not, she absolutely *had* to keep her wits about her.

Carefully loosening her seat belt without actually unlatching it, since she didn't want to fall, she managed enough slack to hook the strap of her purse with her fingertips, wrenching her shoulder in the process. Cringing against the new pain, she pulled the purse toward her, then dug inside for her cell phone. Relieved to have a signal, she pressed in 9-1-1 with shaky, bloody fingers.

"Troublesome Gulch 9-1-1, what is your emergency?"

"Lex?" she said, through gritted teeth and the onslaught of another contraction.

"Erin?"

Consumed in the pain, she couldn't speak.

"Erin! What's wrong?"

The agony eased, and she sucked a breath. "I, uh, had a little accident."

"What do you mean?" her normally calm, cool and in-charge friend asked, clearly alarmed.

"I mean my car's in a ditch on it's side, and I'm in it. Dangling from my seat belt. I hit my head."

"Is the baby okay? What are you doing out driving, for God's sake? You could've called any one of us."

"I had something I needed to do. Alone. But now I need help." Her voice shook. "Please tell me Brody is working a rig tonight."

"He is. And so is your crew at Station Eight."

"Thank God. Can you send them? All of them?" She provided her exact location.

"Stay on the phone with me, understand?"

Another contraction hit, and Erin couldn't speak. They seemed to be hitting closer together than they should at this point.

"Erin? Erin?"

"I'm here. Hurry," she said, her voice choking.

"Everyone's going code three."

"Wait. One other thing, Lex."

"Yeah?"

"I'm in labor."

"Oh, God. Are you bleeding?"

It was the first time Erin had ever heard Lexy lose her cool in an emergency. She peered down. "Just from my head. It's okay. The baby's okay, I think. He or she just wants out. Soon. Please, please hurry."

"You know we will." She covered her mic and said something to her partner. "Dane has already dispatched, and they know who their patient is."

"Tell them to drive carefully."

"Hang in there, doll face, okay? I am right here with you and I'm going nowhere."

"Mmm-hmm." She sucked a breath and held it through another fierce contraction. When it ended, she said, "Lex? I'm scared. The contractions are too close together."

"I'm right here, hon. It's going to be fine."

"Can you call my parents?"

"Dane's on it."

"Tell them—"

"I know what to tell them. I have the phone tree."

"Cagney's my coach."

"I know, sweetie. Stop worrying. Let us worry. You just try to relax so your baby can, too. Remember your breathing, okay?"

"Okay." She gulped back her rising panic. "Can you also call Kevin's parents?"

A pause. "Really?"

"It's a long story for later, but yes."

"Done." Erin could hear Lexy's fingers typing lightning fast. "How painful are the contractions?"

"They suck." Erin tried to laugh. "Lex, can you do one more thing for me?"

"Anything."

"Can you call Nate? He should be at my house, but use his cell phone, just in case."

Lexy blew out a long breath. "I was hoping you'd say that. Of course."

"Tell him—" she gulped "—tell him I love him."

Lexy's tone softened. "You can do that when you see him. Okay? You're going to be just fine."

"Yes."

"Did you lose consciousness when you hit your head?"

"No. At least, I don't think so. But I'm bleeding."

"Right. Listen, you know how head wounds bleed. You're going to be perfect, Erin," Lexy assured her, all her normal confidence regained. "And, hey, you're going to be a mom."

"Yeah, wow, huh?" Erin focused on her breathing, listening as the sirens moved closer. "I always wanted to be a mom," she said, sniffling a bit.

"Funny how things work out, isn't it? Stick with me, sweetheart. The cavalry's almost there."

Chapter Fourteen

Nate burst through the doors of High Country Medical Center's Emergency Department, still unable to feel his extremities. His lips were numb, his brain buzzed. Fear nearly blinded him. His mom and sisters flanked him as he whipped a glance this way and that. He knew she'd come in by ambulance. "Mom?"

"Stay right here."

Flannery, Colette and Piper surrounded him while their mother strode purposefully to the desk and calmly explained their situation to the charge nurse. Thank God for Mom.

Nate had always heard that certain phone calls could cut ten years off a person's life in an instant, but he hadn't believed it until now. If he lost Erin—

"Damn it, I never should've left her today." He clenched his fists. "She's been saying for a week that she didn't feel like she'd make it to her due date."

"She's going to be okay, Nate," Flannery said.

"I can't lose her, Flan." He searched his older sister's face, gulping back his surging emotions. "Or the baby. I love them so much."

"We love them, too," Piper said. "*Nothing* bad is going to happen. I just know."

His sisters wrapped him in a hug.

His mom returned, all efficiency, no stress. "Labor and Delivery. Fifth floor. Come on."

He grasped his mother's arm. "Did they say how she was doing?"

"Of course not. We're going to find out."

The five of them rushed to the bank of elevators, and Colette pushed the button. They stared up at the display as all six elevators took their sweet time descending to the lobby floor—Murphy's Law.

"Come on, come on," Nate snapped, feeling as if he might explode.

His mother faced him, grasping both of his biceps to give him a little shake. "Nathaniel Walker, take a deep breath and pull yourself together this minute. The woman you love is about to give birth to your child. My grandchild. You need to be strong for her, understand?"

"I am." *Deep breath.* "I will."

Ding!

They all whipped toward the doors until they saw the ones with the indicator light glowing over them. In a pack, they pushed their way into the empty car before the doors had completely opened.

Again, Colette pushed the button for the fifth floor. Repeatedly. After an eternity, the doors eased shut, and the car began to ascend. When the doors opened onto floor five, Nate saw Brody and Faith pacing in front of the nurses' station. Nate couldn't read his friends' faces. Brody turned to the nurse. "Here. This is the baby's father."

"How is she?" Nate demanded.

Brody clasped a palm on his shoulder. "She's fine. Good. She has a slight concussion and a few stitches in her head, but labor's going well. That's what matters at this point. Not the head."

Nate sagged with relief. "I want to see her."

"Of course," Faith said, taking his hand. "Come on. She's in room twelve."

She ushered him forward a few steps, then he whipped back. "Mom?"

"Go, son. Your sisters and I will be in the waiting room whenever you need us."

He nodded.

At the door he hesitated. "Listen," he told Faith, expelling a breath. "I'm sure you know Cagney's her birth coach."

"Yes. But I know she wants to see you. She's been asking for you constantly." She tried to pull him in.

He held her arm. "Wait. I haven't seen her burn scars, and I'm not sure she wants me to during the birthing. I promised her I'd wait until she's ready. Can you go in first? Tell her I'm here and just… make sure?"

Faith smiled. "Of course, sweetie."

He flicked his hands to hurry Faith along.

She'd only been in the room for a moment before she emerged with a smile on her face. "Come on in, Daddy."

His eyes widened. "Already?"

"No, no. You haven't missed anything."

He nodded. Digging down deep for some inner calm, he entered the room. Erin was on the bed, all covered up. The side of her head was swollen and bruised, a bandage covering what was surely the stitches. His heart clenched. "Honey."

She glanced over, tears rushing to her eyes. "Come here." She held out her arms. "I'm so sorry. I didn't mean to scare you. I'm okay, really."

He reached her bedside in two long strides, bending down to cup the uninjured side of her face and kiss her deeply. "I'm so glad you're not—You really *are* okay, right?"

She nodded. "They gave me Tylenol for the head. Oh, and an epidural. Let me say, I've never been so happy to see such a frighteningly long needle in my life."

He gritted his teeth, warring between the need to be there for her completely and the need to apologize. "I should've been there with you."

"You didn't know. How could you? *I* didn't even know."

Cagney hovered uncertainly on the other side of the bed. "Hey, listen." She aimed a thumb over her shoulder. "I can leave if you'd like, Erin. Now that Nate's here."

"No." Erin held tightly to Nate's hand, but reached out for her friend's, too. She beseeched Nate. "I want you to stay, Nate, like I told Faith. I have so much to tell you—"

"Later."

"Yes. Anyway, I hadn't planned it this way, but I guess this will be the great unveiling of my hideous scars—"

"I don't care about your scars."

"I know." She gulped. "But I do. I'm scared out of my mind." She flashed a grateful smile at Cagney. "So, on that note, is it okay if Cagney stays for the birth, too? For moral support?"

With his elbows resting on the side bars of the gurney, Nate smiled tenderly. "You can have absolutely anyone you want here, love. Of course it's okay if Cagney stays. She's your birth coach. I'm just the hapless father."

They all laughed.

"I'm just going to dash out and update the crowd, okay?" Cagney said, clearly psyched that she would still be able to witness the birth.

"Hurry back," Erin said.

Once they were alone, Erin took both of Nate's hands into her own. "I didn't expect this to happen so soon. My parents are on the way, but it'll be a while. I told them all about you," she rushed to add. "I'm sorry it wasn't until now. I thought I had more time."

"It's okay."

"Also, this is harder to explain, but Kevin's parents are on the way."

He peered down at her curiously.

"It's part of the long story for later, and I hope my instincts were correct. I asked them to be the baby's godparents."

"Oh, honey."

"Please understand. They lost their only son, Nate, and any chance of being grandparents. I just thought—"

"Baby, stop. It's perfect."

"Really?"

He squeezed her hand. "And truly. You're the most giving person I've ever met. I expect they were thrilled?"

"Beyond," she whispered. "I told them you'd support the decision. I told them—listen, this is one part of the long story that I can't wait to tell you. I don't want to."

He opened his mouth to speak.

"Wait. Let me get this out before another contraction hits. They're not excruciating now, but I can still feel them."

He inclined his head.

"Nate Walker, I'm in love with you. Completely. Totally. I love you more than anything."

"Erin," he whispered, in wonder.

"It took a weird dream and a long-overdue visit to make me realize how much, but I'm sure. And before this all gets ugly, I have something I want to ask you."

"Anything."

She searched his eyes. "Will you marry me?"

He barked out a shocked laugh, but warmth ran all through him. "Hey, isn't that supposed to be my line?"

"I didn't mean to steal your thunder. I just can't go through this whole birth thing not knowing. Besides, who says we have to do things like the rest of the world? Conformity is overrated." She smiled. "A really smart guy told me that once."

His heart expanded more than he ever thought possible. "Are you sure?"

"I've never been more sure of anything in my life. It's not like we've done anything the normal way from the very beginning, so why start now?" She held up a hand, pausing through a contraction, then expelled a breath once it had eased. "But, the bottom line is, I haven't truly lived for twelve years, Nate. Then you came into my life and filled up all the empty spaces in my heart. Kevin will always have a place there—"

"As he should."

"Yes," she whispered in a fervent tone, "but I love *you*. I see it now, so clearly. You're the man I'm supposed to be with, and our baby is the one fate intended me to deliver and raise." She shook her head. "I don't want to do it without you."

"Aw, Erin—"

"Look, I'm sorry I didn't think to get you a ring for the proposal. I was too busy crashing my car, getting a concussion and going into preterm labor. I hope that's not a deal breaker."

He chuckled. "That's where I draw the line."

She inhaled. "You're saying no?"

"Of course not. But I will get *you* the ring."

Her eyes widened. "Does that mean—?"

"Yes. One hundred percent. Because I can't imagine spending my life without you, either." He leaned down and kissed her tenderly on the lips. "I love you, Erin DeLuca. And I'd love to be your husband more than anything in this world."

Tears filled her eyes and rolled down into her ears. "Yay, me. I'm going to be a mommy and score the man of my dreams. I rule."

Cagney returned, glancing from Nate to Erin, then back. "What's going on?"

Nate gave her a wry smile. "Erin proposed to me."

"And he said yes!"

Reserved, stoic Cagney started sniffling. "I'm so, so happy for both of you. It's absolutely perfect." She rounded the bed and wrapped Nate in a bear hug, then leaned down and kissed Erin on the cheek. "You done good, kid."

"It's not over yet." She grimaced. "There's still this delivery thing to contend with."

As if on cue, the nurse whisked in. "Let's give you another check, honey. See how close you are."

Fear paled Erin's complexion. "Nate?"

He leaned closer to her face. "I'm going to look right here, into your beautiful eyes. Okay? There's no need for you to feel like a specimen on a table. When you're ready for me to look, you tell me."

"Okay."

The nurse did her thing, then pulled off her

gloves, dropping them into a nearby trash bin. "Miss Erin, it's time for you to have this baby."

"Really?" Erin's voice shook with nerves.

"Really." She raised her brows at Nate. "Time for you to get gowned and gloved, Daddy, if you're planning to stick around."

"He is," Erin insisted.

"Okay," Nate said, nervous, too, but more excited than anything. He started to follow the nurse.

"Wait." Erin grabbed his hand.

He turned to her.

She blinked twice, the trepidation clear in her eyes. "I want you to see them first. The scars."

He cocked his head. "Honey, look, there's plenty of time for that later. You don't have to do this now."

"Yes, I do. Because I want you to see our baby come into this world, and you won't be able to if you aren't allowed to look at my body. Please."

"They're not as bad as you think, Er," Cagney said, in her kind, reassuring tone.

Erin smiled at her friend. "Will you pull the blanket down, Cag?"

Cagney did so, then moved discreetly to the other side of the birthing room to give them privacy.

Erin squeezed her eyes shut. "Okay. Just do it."

With careful, gentle fingers, Nate raised the hospital gown. Erin's burn-scarred flesh ran from just beneath her full breasts all the way down to her pelvis. Extensive, sure, but all he saw was beauty.

He saw strength.

He saw a survivor.

He smoothed his palms gently over her body, then leaned down and kissed her, just over the baby.

"Well?" she choked out, eyes still clamped shut.

"Do you want to know what I see?"

She bit the corner of her bottom lip, hesitating. Then eased her eyes open and nodded.

He lowered the gown over her again. "I see a body so beautiful, so capable, that it carried our baby from conception until now. I see the woman I love. I see the pain of your past, sweet girl, but mostly I see our future." He paused. "These scars?" He shrugged. "They're nothing." He flicked his hand to the side. "The point is, look—we accidentally made a baby together, and the sky didn't fall. I've seen your scars, and the sky didn't fall. Best of all, we fell in love with each other, and now, Erin, the sky can never fall on us again."

"Nate," she gulped out.

"Enough of that." He clapped his hands together once, smoothing them palm to palm. "What do you say I get suited up so we can meet our baby?"

"Yes." She nodded happily. "Yes."

* * *

It took an hour and a half of pushing before their healthy baby boy emerged, red and squinty-eyed and squalling, into the world. All of them cried, including Cagney, the nurse and Dr. Kipfer, as Nate cut the cord.

Cagney left shortly thereafter to inform the crowd.

The little guy weighed in at just over six pounds, healthy, with all ten fingers and all ten toes, just like they'd prayed for. After he'd been cleaned up and swaddled in a soft, white receiving blanket, Dr. Kipfer handed him over to Nate with a wide smile. "Why don't you introduce him to his mother?"

Erin watched as Nate stared down at the wrinkly little bald-headed human he held. "What do you think?"

"I think he's the most beautiful thing I've ever seen. Next to his mother, that is."

"Bring him here."

He carried him over and placed him gently on her chest. Her heart squeezed.

"Say hello to your son."

"Oh, my God." Erin studied him in wonder. "He's perfect, Nate."

Nate lowered the side bars and perched next to her, cradling her shoulders as they admired their child. He had her nose and chin, Nate's gorgeous eyes. And as a pleasant and quite amusing surprise, he had Colette's ash blond hair, though not much of it.

"I have a great idea," Nate said.

She peered up at him. "What's that?"

"Let's name him Kevin Jennings DeLuca Walker."

Wide-eyed, Erin studied Nate's face, scarcely believing the immensity of her love for this man. It took her several moments before she could speak. "You're the most selfless person I know, Nate Walker. But I have a better idea."

"Lay it on me."

"He looks like a Nathaniel Kevin Deluca Walker to me. If that's okay with you." She peered into her son's squinchy little elfin face. "Frankly, I think it sounds just perfect."

Nate's voice came out husky, "Little Nate Junior, huh?"

"Is it okay?"

"Are you kidding?"

They laughed, and then Nate took hold of her chin. "I will love you, Erin DeLuca, and all of our children until the day I die. That's a promise."

"And I will never make you feel like second place again," she whispered. "Because, you're not. You're the man I was meant to spend my life with. It just took me a while to catch on. Deal?"

He kissed her nose. "Deal."

"Now that we've settled all that, how about we introduce the little man here to his friends and family before he knows what hit him?" She rolled her eyes. "If we don't open the floodgates soon they may riot, and we'll never hear the end of it."

A few minutes later, the room filled. Her parents, his mom and sisters—all of whom seemed to be getting on like old friends. Marcus and PJ Jennings, overcome with emotion for having been included. Brody, Faith, Jason—even Mr. Norwood. Cagney, of course, and Lexy, who'd just gotten off duty.

Family.

With Nate by her side and her healthy baby being passed from one person who loved him to another, Erin finally felt whole again.

She closed her eyes, at peace.

Just…being in the moment.

* * * * *

The Texas Bodyguard's Proposal
by
Karen Rose Smith

The door to the library at the McCord family mansion suddenly opened and an absolutely stunning woman with long, wavy, honey-blond hair rushed in—Gabriella McCord. Her face and figure had been on every fashion magazine cover in the free world…and in a few tabloids.

Rafael Balthazar's breath hitched, though he'd never admit it. He did not want to protect a socialite model who'd grown up with every luxury at her fingertips! But as security consultant for McCord Jewelers he had no choice, not when Blake McCord had asked him for this favor.

In a peacock-blue, figure-fitting dress, matching high heels and swingy gold earrings, Gabriella could take any man's breath away. Just not his. He didn't go for divas.

"I'm sorry I'm late," she began with a smile that added punch to her beauty.

Their gazes locked and, for a few moments, Rafe actually felt a shift in his universe.

No way.

"My…plane was delayed," she explained, her gaze still on his. "I just checked in and rushed over—" She stopped when she realized he wasn't smiling or crossing the room to greet her.

If she expected him to fall at her feet, she was going to be disappointed. "Miss McCord, I'm your bodyguard. My duties will begin tonight when you return to the Sky Towers. Blake assures me a driver will chauffeur you back to the hotel after his mother's birthday dinner. I'll meet you there and we'll go over your itinerary for the upcoming week."

Gabriella's small, well-defined chin came up and her back straightened. "It's so good to meet *you,* too, Mr. Balthazar. I just want you to know I don't feel I *need* a bodyguard. This is Blake's idea, not mine."

Nope, Rafe wasn't moving toward her. He had to establish an impenetrable boundary now. In a low, controlled voice, he responded, "You don't need a bodyguard? I understand there was a scene at the airport when you arrived." Blake had filled him in on *that* disaster. Rafe hadn't been available sooner. He'd been handling a security problem in Houston and had just returned in time to meet Gabriella before Eleanor McCord's birthday dinner.

Gabriella's cheeks flushed a bit. "Paparazzi somehow found out when I was arriving. I managed to slip away."

"More than paparazzi found out. There was a crowd waiting for you and it blocked the limo from leaving. Two things you'll learn while I'm guarding you. One, you have to be honest with me. Two, you must not put yourself at risk unnecessarily. Understood?"

Gabriella's golden-brown eyes sparkled with defiance. "Understood? I understand that you were once a Secret

Service agent, and a very good one. That's super. I commend your service. But I will *not* let you dictate where I go and what I do. Do *you* understand?"

He had to admit she was one beautiful, feisty package. Something he had to ignore...yet manage. "My job is to keep you safe."

"So you'll just have to do your job. As spokeswoman for McCord Jewelers, I'm going to do whatever Blake has planned for me and that will probably involve crowds. I also have a few engagements of my own and I can never predict what will happen."

"Like a stalker accosting you?" Rafe knew that had happened last year.

Gabriella's face drained of color, then she recovered her composure and gave him a new smile. "I haven't had any stalkers recently, so no worry there. And you only have to cover me for a few weeks. I'll be returning to Italy for a short time at the end of August. When I return to the States, Blake will have screened someone else and you can go back to your job concentrating on the security of the stores."

"In the meantime, we have to work together."

"No, Mr. Balthazar. You just have to make sure fans don't tear me apart."

Unbidden, an image took form in front of Rafe's eyes, a photo of Gabriella that had appeared in a tabloid last month. The paparazzi had snapped a picture of her dancing in a London club. It was a money shot because the clasp on her designer dress had malfunctioned. Just as the top of the dress had fallen—

Had the episode been an accident? Or had the whole situation been planned for publicity's sake?

This time Gabriella's face rapidly gained color, and he knew she was recalling the same image. Abruptly she turned away from him.

"Miss McCord…"

"We'll talk later," she murmured. "I don't want to keep my aunt waiting on her birthday."

And Gabriella McCord was gone.

"That went well," Rafe muttered and raked his hand through his short-cropped, black hair.

Gabriella McCord would be even more trouble than he'd expected, but he could deal with her. He'd protected the president of the United States. He wouldn't let one pretty model throw him off his game.

Not now. Not ever.

© Harlequin Books SA 2009